"I am Jalav,

war leader of the clan of the Hosta, foremost among the clans of the Midanna," I informed the captive. "You have been chosen to serve my warriors the while, and shall be released upon the end of that service. Should you continue in so insolent a manner, however, I shall order the leather applied to you quite differently. I am amused to see a male act the part of a warrior, yet have I little patience now to tolerate it. Be warned."

"Warned?" he roared in true fury, struggling against his bonds and my warriors. "By the slaying foot of Sigurr the Terrible, am I to be warned by a black-haired female child who stands in naught save a wisp of cloth about her hips? No! I am the true warrior here, and shall take my leather to the back of any strutting female I lay hands upon! Scatter quickly, girl children, for now I come to punish!"

SHARON GREEN writes: "I've been reading science fiction since the age of twelve, began writing even before then, but never got serious about writing science fiction until five years ago. I read a speech of Robert Heinlein's that said, "Don't talk about it, do it!" So I did. Once turned on, it hasn't stopped yet. In my youth, I studied archery, fencing and horseback riding; taught archery at summer camp, rode in the drill team, and fenced at college. In the present I've studied belly dancing for two years and karate for one, and will probably go for further advancement in karate this spring. I sell steel for a living, and sometimes say to myself, "Bar steel by day, edged steel by night."

The Crystals of Mida

Sharon Green

DAW Books, Inc.
DONALD A. WOLLHEIM, PUBLISHER
1633 Broadway, New York, NY 10019

DEDICATION

For Joyce and John Pacholek,
for holding high so long
the shield of Mida.

FIRST PRINTING, JUNE 1982

1 2 3 4 5 6 7 8 9

DAW TRADEMARK REGISTERED
U.S. PAT. OFF. MARCA
REGISTRADA. HECHO EN U.S.A.

PRINTED IN U.S.A.

CONTENTS

1.

The tower of the Crystal —and a captive is taken

I stood in the center of the cold stone room and gazed down upon the bodies of my warriors. The three of them lay upon the rounded cobbles, grotesque in death as they had not been in life. The clan colors worn by all Midanna, about their hips and thighs, had been torn away and scattered about the room, leaving my warriors completely bared to their attackers. Life signs, worn on leather strips about their necks, had been left on two, but the third no longer wore hers. Perhaps its leather had been severed when the blade of the dagger was brought to her breasts, possibly in an effort to have her cry out in pain. I had known that warrior well in life. She would not have cried out.

Three strong warriors, dead, though not in battle. Their attackers had come with stealth, overwhelming them with surprise and numbers. The Keeper's Attendants, who had also been in the Tower, had been quickly put to the sword, yet my warriors had been kept the while, to be used for the sport of those who had come to steal the Crystal of Mida. My proud warriors had had their wrists bound tightly with leather behind them, had been thrust to the bare, smooth cobbles of the Tower floor, had had their clan colors ripped from their bodies, had been forced to stare up at the raftered heights of the highest Tower room as their bodies were taken and used by the scum of city thieves. And when their shame had at last given the thieves satisfaction, their throats had been cut

7

where they lay, their wrists still bound, their clan colors no longer upon them. To take a warrior's clan colors, to cut her throat as though she were an animal to be slaughtered, stealing from her forever the honor of dying in battle—these things were the most unforgivable. Should any of the thieves be taken alive when the Crystal of Mida was recovered, they would pay for their crime many times over, seeing the light of as many hands of feyd as possible before being allowed to die. Only in such a way might the souls of my warriors find rest.

I looked next at the Keeper's Attendant where she lay upon the sleeping leather, her long, graying hair crushed beneath her, her breathing loud and harsh in the silence. She had taken the sword of the thieves as had the others, yet clung to life till they had gone, and still longer yet, awaiting the relieving warriors' arrival. Her clan colors, worn long to the ankles as befitted one of her station, were damp with the red of her blood, yet she was able to relate the coming of the thieves, guessing that they came from the city of Ranistard, far to the north. One had mentioned the city, she thought, and she would have the war leader know. Now I knew.

Slowly, I walked to her where she lay upon the sleeping leather, gazing through the window at the brightening of the fey. Well she knew that she would not see the coming of dark again, and wished to remember the feeling of life upon her body to carry with her to the Realm of Mida, where she would be made young and strong again, where she would again know the pleasures to be had with males of worth and valor equal to hers. Yet would she never again be warrior as she had been in her youth, for she had given up the glory of death in battle to Attend the Keeper of the Crystal of Mida. Now the Crystal had been stolen, and her life as well, and what had been done could not be undone.

"Remad," I said quietly, and she turned to look at me.

"I hear, Jalav," she whispered weakly. "How may I serve the war leader?"

"Already have you served truly and well," I said, stroking my life sign. Hers lay upon her slowly rising breast, a near mate to mine. We shared the sign of the hadat, that fierce, furred, long-toothed, sharp-clawed messenger of death sent by Mida to smite her enemies, though our symbols of that sign were not identical. Each warrior must, upon reaching her womanhood, carve her life sign from the wood of the tree that has been marked as her own at her birth. Should her tree die before she reaches her womanhood, she is taken to the dwellings of those who follow males, and left to be made a slave-woman to them, for should a warrior enter battle without her life sign upon her breast, her soul would surely be lost.

"Remad," I said, "I would have you look upon one who was captured a short while ago. Are you able to know if he is one of those who took the Crystal of Mida?"

"I shall know," she whispered. "Long did I gaze upon the faces of each of them as they fouled our warriors with their touch," she rasped. "I shall know."

"Bring him," I ordered, and two warriors ran to do my bidding. The fury I felt at what had been done in the Tower of the Crystal was a terrible thing, and my sword would drink well before my vengeance was fulfilled. I thirsted for blood to pay for blood.

I turned at the sound of struggle and beheld the captive, he who had been taken just as word had reached us of the theft. Six of my warriors surrounded him with spears at his throat, and still he attempted to resist them. Lofty, indeed, was his height, a full head greater even than mine, and his wide, muscled body was encased in the garb of one from the cities, a brown cloth which covered all but his arms from neck to mid-thigh, as though his body would be shown to his shame. He wore neither clan colors nor life sign, for those of the cities have no souls to be lost, and also his feet were encased in leather, to keep him from the touch of the sweet ground of Mida. His red-gold hair was of a decent length, bound by leather at the back of his neck as though he were prepared for battle. His arms were bound, each wrist to the opposite elbow behind his back, leather stretched between his ankles, leather pulled tight across the cords of his throat, yet still did he struggle. Should he be proven innocent of the crime in the Tower, it would be wise to detain him, so that my warriors might be allowed to take his seed for themselves. Not many of the males who travel our land are found fit to mate with a warrior.

The captive fought to free himself as he was drawn forward by the warriors. He shouted to the air the oaths of city males, mistaking my warriors for their pale sisters of the cities, swearing to do upon them things which would never be borne by them. Forward did they draw him with difficulty, till his eyes fell upon my dead warriors, and then his struggles ceased as though he had been touched by the hand of Mida.

"The deed was not mine!" said he harshly to Remad. "To take the lives of mere girls in such a manner. . . ."

"Silence!" I commanded, and struck him full across the face as he knelt before Remad. In fury, he attempted to rise, yet was held in place by my warriors, and I turned to Remad. "Is he one of those who came, Remad?" I asked. "Study his features well and then speak."

"It was not he," she whispered, gazing up at the captive. "Had he been among them, war leader, I would have remembered."

"Look again and be sure," I said to Remad. "The journey north may be shortened, should we find one to speak to us."

"He was not among them, Jalav," Remad whispered as I pressed the point of my dagger to the throat of the captive. Surely he saw in my eyes my need to spill blood, and therefore he remained silent.

"So be it," said I, resheathing my dagger. "The journey to Ranistard must be taken without sight. We shall have the words of the Keeper this darkness, and begin with the light that follows."

"Ranistard?" said the captive, with a frown of displeasure. "No man of Ranistard would perform so senseless a deed. Ranistard was badly touched by the hand of Sigurr with a fever of death, and few are the females now left to tend to the men. Had men of Ranistard been here, the wenches would have been carried off with them."

"Something of greater value was carried off in their stead," said I to the captive, then to my warriors. "Take him to the gandod and have him secured between two of them. We return shortly to the camp."

"Hold!" shouted the captive, standing his full height even against the weight of my warriors. "I have been proven innocent, and demand to be released at once! Order the leather removed from me, girl!"

Once again I gazed upon the captive with approval. His spirit would do well for the warriors of my clan, his large body strong enough to serve many of them. I calmly returned his heated glare.

"I am Jalav, war leader of the clan of the Hosta, foremost among the clans of the Midanna," I informed him. "You have been chosen to serve my warriors the while, and shall be released upon the end of that service. Should you continue in so insolent a manner, however, I shall order the leather applied to you quite differently. I am amused to see a male act the part of warrior, yet have I little patience now to tolerate it. Be warned, sthuvad."

"Warned?" he roared in true fury, struggling against his bonds and my warriors. "By the slaying foot of Sigurr the Terrible, am I to be warned by a black-haired female child who stands with only a wisp of cloth about her hips? No! *I* am the true warrior here, and shall take my leather to the back of any strutting female I lay hands upon! Scatter quickly, girl children, for now I come to punish!"

He attempted to part the leather which held him captive, and at the same time he threw himself toward my warriors with a pale city battle cry. My warriors laughed in delight at this entertainment, all but one stepping to him quickly to urge him on with a caress, and then dart easily out of his blundering path. The caresses enraged him still more and, still bound, he turned this way and that, not knowing which of my warriors to pursue. His chest rose and fell with his anger, and a magnificent sight indeed was he. I, too, felt the attraction of him, and resolved to have him in my sleeping leather before the journey north.

Red-haired Larid stood herself before the male, laughing lightly and stretching her arms out toward him to lure him to her. With a deep growl, the captive took her lure and began striding toward her in fury, forgetful of the leather stretched between his ankles. Binat, from behind him, did grinningly place the butt of her spear before the leather thong, holding the leather in place and tripping the captive. Down he did go to the cobbles quite heavily, unable to break his fall with his still bound arms, and my warriors were upon him immediately. He was turned to his back while still dazed from the fall, and Larid applied her knowing hands to his body, bringing immediate response from him, then did she quickly take possession of him. Her face showed great appreciation as his eyes blinked open and he regarded her blurrily, then realization came to him of his possession. He shouted wordlessly and fought to free himself, yet did Larid retain her place with laughter and pleasure. Two of the other of my warriors knelt, one upon each of his shoulders to hold him down, and Larid was able to drain him well before she stood again.

I beheld another of my warriors preparing to take the place of Larid, and therefore stepped forward and spoke. "The sthuvad may be had again later at our camp," I informed them. "Take him now to the gandod and secure him well. I shall join you shortly."

My warriors were disappointed at my words, yet am I war leader and to be obeyed. The sthuvad was pulled to his feet, where he stood, filled with cold fury, to gaze upon me.

"This insult shall long be remembered, girl," said he to me. "In time you shall know the anger of the warrior Telion of Ranistard, and shall fall to your knees before him! Your body shall be mine as mine was hers, and you shall pay many times over for the shame given me! For this you have my word!"

"My fear of the word of the male of the cities is great," said I, smiling at the laughter of my warriors. "You will forgive me for having you taken to the gandod lest I succumb to so great a fear."

I nodded, and my warriors forced the captive from the Tower room. My eyes fell again upon my dead warriors, and the cold of the room entered me once more. Remad, I saw, lay upon her sleeping leather, a small smile upon her lips, memory strong in her eyes. She, too, had taken captives in her youth, and the memory of them had returned to her in the last of her life.

"Other Attendants have been sent for," I said to Remad, "and will see you safely to the Keeper's Tower. The Keeper shall speak the words to bring you to Mida's Realm, and we shall meet again in Mida's gaze when I, too, am called. Fare you well, Remad."

"I would ask a favor of the war leader," she whispered. "My service to the Crystal of Mida is done, even should it be returned upon the instant. I wish to greet Mida with sword in hand, as the warrior I was in my youth. Will the war leader honor me in such a way?"

"The honor is mine, Remad," said I, smiling at her pale, thin face. "My warriors shall prepare you."

Two warriors raised Remad to her feet. Her pain was truly great, yet not a sound escaped her lips as she was held erect and handed a sword. She faced me then in true warrior fashion as I drew my own blade.

"I salute you, Jalav," she whispered roughly. "Strike quickly lest I go before the thrust!"

I did as she bid, plunging my sword deep within her breast, and she slid to the cobbles quickly, already in the arms of Mida. My warriors and I raised our swords to the memory of a true warrior.

"Have the life signs removed for the Keeper," said I to my warriors, "and the bodies brought to the forest for the children of the wild. I return now to camp."

They nodded in obedience to my word and I left the Tower room. I would be very pleased to find those who had taken the Crystal of Mida, and would remember to send one to Mida's chains in the name of Remad. Too many were the warriors who had been stolen from me that fey.

Outside, I found the captive secured between my gando and that of Larid, and he looked up at me uncomprehendingly. My gando stood quietly, having been reminded of its place, and, mounted, I pulled against the long thong of leather about its neck that led to the neck of the captive. It was secure, as was the thong from the gando of Larid, therefore did I direct our departure.

My warriors, eight hands plus two in number, all sat upon gandod of their own. The Midanna use naught save gandod to carry them into battle, for the gando is superior to the soft kand of the city people. The gando is no larger than the kan, yet its scales protect from sword thrust as the hide of the kan does not, and its many sharp teeth, urged on by its unreasoning temper, make its worth in battle far greater than that of the passive kan. The red kan of the captive was held by one of my warriors, drawn along by the leather of the lead reins against its will, fear of the silvery gandod turning its eyes round and wild.

"Why must I walk as a peasant would?" demanded the capitve as we left the stones of the Tower clearing for the dirt of the road. "My kan is at hand, and I may be tied to the saddle should you fear my escape."

"You do not care to walk?" asked I, glancing at Larid, who grinned.

"No, pretty black-haired girl, I do not," said the captive, speaking to me as though I were a child. "I have little regard for the need to walk, therefore shall you order those others to. . . ."

"He does not care to walk, Jalav," Larid said with much glee. "May we not assist him in the matter?"

"Indeed, Larid," said I with a laugh. "Let us assist him."

Larid and I struck our mounts, sending them into faster motion. The captive was made to move faster and even yet faster, the thong between his ankles forcing him to take small, rapid steps. The sight caused laughter among all of my warriors.

Shortly did we leave the road for the forest, for we were not far distant from the current camp. It is Mida's fortune that we had not been on the hunt nor in the midst of battle when her Crystal had been taken, else would it have been long before the loss could be reclaimed.

The captive breathed heavily as he ran, looking as though he would have enjoyed much warrior blood upon his hands. He spoke no word, to conserve the breath within him, yet did I feel his pace might be increased. I therefore took a leather strip, flicked it sharply across his shoulders, and called, "Run for the war leader Jalav, sthuvad, run as quickly as you may! Should your movement please me, I will have you brought to my sleeping leather! Run nicely for Jalav!"

I touched him many times with the leather, light touches which caused very little pain, yet which boiled the fury high in him. My warriors laughed, seeing the leather applied so gently to his back and legs, and even higher did he rage at the laughter, though all save running was beyond him. The leather strips were tight to the straining of the cords in his throat, and he had to run to keep from being dragged.

Shortly we came to the outskirts of the camp, the black and green of our clan tents showing clearly through the trees. The sentries that we passed gazed upon the captive with delight, for it had been long since one deemed worthy had been taken. Despite the loss of the Crystal, there would be merrymaking in the tents of the Hosta. We drew rein before the largest tent, that of the war leader, mine. The captive pounded to a halt, much of the fight taken out of him, a tall, heaving, quieter male, fit for the use of warriors. I left him and my gando to be seen to by others, and entered my tent.

"Mida's blessing, Jalav," said Fideran, placing himself swiftly upon his knees. "I am pleased to see that you have returned so quickly. Is all to be well now?"

"All shall be well, Fideran," I assured him, gazing upon his fair and lovely face. Fideran had been taken as sthuvad, yet had refused release when it had been offered him, choosing instead to remain in my tent, and serve my needs upon his knees. Though he disliked being given to those of my warriors who desired him, he heeded my word upon such occasions rather than go his way back to his own people. He had long since professed love for me, a feeling which I, as a warrior, understood naught of. I kept him for my pleasure alone, yet was I faced with a dilemma. Fond as I was of him, it was impossible to take him to the north with me. I would have to leave him with another, one whose arms would soothe his loneliness and pain. That would be a kindness to be smiled upon by Mida.

"Brew a pot of daru, Fideran," I said as I removed my swordbelt, "and see that it is kept fresh against the visit of the Keeper. She shall arrive soon to speak with me of grave matters, and shall likely feel the need for daru."

"At once, Jalav," said he, asking naught of the reason for the Keeper's visit. Well he knew that the matter was one for warriors, and not to be discussed with him.

I settled to the leather of the floor of my tent, and thoughtfully began filling my pipe. It would be to the greater honor of the Hosta should we alone retrieve the Crystal, yet would it be wiser for all Midanna to prepare for the necessity of war. The clans of the Midanna rarely rode as one, yet the retrieval of the Crystal should unite us all. We would ride against the northmen in the rightness of our quest, and bring their dwellings down upon them, should the Crystal not be yielded up. The Crystal was ours to guard with our lives, not a bauble to be handed to the first male a warrior would see smile.

"By Sigurr's claws, have a care!" snarled the captive, he being brought within my tent to be tied to the ground post by the leather about his neck. Playfully had a warrior poked at him with the point of her spear, merely to keep him moving without harming him, yet had she misjudged her aim and come perilously close to an integral part of him. Were such an integral part to be damaged, he would be fit only for the pleasure of my warriors, for offspring would then be impossible; however, despite the near catastrophe, I could not help but smile.

"Smirk as you will, girl," he said to me, his chest still rising with the shortness of breath, "yet shall I see the time when I may smirk at the sight of you. That is what I shall live for."

"A worthy life purpose for a city *warrior*," I laughed, amused by his distress. Fideran, too, had spoken in such a manner when first made captive, yet had not gone his way when given the opportunity. Males are strange creatures indeed, far beyond the understanding of warriors, beyond reason even for Mida.

The captive scowled, then sat upon the black leather of the floor, normal color slowly returning to his face. His scowl deepened when his eyes fell upon Fideran, who sat beside my sleeping leather as he waited for the daru to brew itself to the proper point. Fideran scowled as well, disliking the manner in which the captive's eyes swept the brief clan covering—without clan colors—which he was permitted to wear. There had not been a captive since Fideran had been taken, and Fideran did not seem to care for the clan's newest acquisition.

"This tent is stark indeed," said the captive. "Have you no frills to liven your life, girl?"

"I do not take the meaning of 'frills,'" I said, regarding him with some curiosity. He seemed to know less of warriors than had Fideran, who had known little indeed.

"Frills," repeated the captive impatiently. "Such as light-colored silks to brighten this dismal dark leather, sparkling jewels to hang about your throat in place of that bit of wood, tempting scents to make you pleasing to a man and to cover the stink of that burning bit of kan held in your hand. Those are frills."

"For what reason would I desire such?" asked I in amusement. "Other colored silks would betoken other clans, all of which are less than the Hosta. Sparkling stones are to be given to males, to comfort their upset when they are taken, and should be of little use in battle. My life sign guards my soul, so that it may not slip away to naught should the edge of the enemy reach me. As for scents, males must please *me*, not I them, and strong would be the laughter of all should the war leader of the Hosta appear for battle bedecked with *scents*. The thought is truly amusing."

"For a wench to know naught of frills is saddening," said the captive in a lowered voice. "Yet more disturbing still is the thought that she wishes to know naught of them. Your life is a cruel one, girl, touched heavily by the twisted hand of Sigurr. That should not be."

"All is as Mida wishes it," I informed him gently. "Do not despair in your lack of understanding, for one without a soul is unable to understand the workings of Mida. You may accept my assurance that all is as it should be."

"Without a soul?" he echoed blankly, and then became angry once again. "You believe I have no soul and therefore pity *me*? By Sigurr's rotting teeth, I shall not be pitied by a half-naked savage of a *girl*! Remove these bindings at once!"

Again he struggled against the leather which bound him, and I smiled as I accepted the small pot of daru which Fideran carried to me. The leather of the Hosta of the Midanna is not so poor that it may easily be parted, as the captive was beginning to know. Soon there would be other things for him to know.

His blazing eyes returned to me once more, and his teeth clenched tightly at the sight of the steaming pot of daru which I had brought to my lips. The hearty aroma of daru filled the tent, and made one anxious for the taste of it.

"Am I to be starved and tortured as well as bound?" the captive demanded. "I have had neither food nor drink since I was set upon by those females of yours!"

"A drink shall soon be brought you," I assured him. "We have no desire to see you suffer from lack of sustenance."

"They'd best be quick about it," muttered the captive, somewhat mollified, for he did not see the quiet smile of Fideran. Fideran knew what drink was to be brought, yet he spoke not a word in warning to his fellow male, but stood straight with arms folded firmly across his chest. He had not stood so since he had been taken.

I had sipped only twice at the pot of daru, when Larid and another warrior entered with a pot. No steam arose from this pot which they brought, and the captive looked upon it with interest.

"Fetch it here, girl," directed the male easily. "The dust of that run lies heavy within my throat."

Larid smiled and approached him with the pot, holding it carefully so that its contents did not spill. The captive sniffed cautiously, found its odor inoffensive, then he sipped at it with Larid's aid. The sip pleased him considerably, and he drained the pot with a great deal of gusto. Larid and my other warrior exchanged satisfied glances, then they looked toward me. I nodded with a smile, and my two warriors left with purpose.

"Unusually refreshing," the captive observed, smacking his lips over the lingering taste. "I wager the taverns of the cities would pay much in coin to receive shipments of that. How is it called?"

"It is called, 'a man's downfall,'" Fideran laughed before

I was able to reply. "I believe you will find it *too* refreshing before long."

"Of what does your pet male babble?" asked the captive of me, his broad face creased in a frown. "Have his wits gone away with his manhood?"

"When you are unbound, we shall speak of manhood!" said Fideran, approaching the captive to stand above him. "I have not forgotten the use of a sword!"

"Fideran," I said gently to my male, "he has no understanding as yet. In time shall his words be withdrawn."

"Perhaps," Fideran replied rather tightly, much disturbed beneath his unsmiling face. I did not wish to see him disturbed, yet was unable to fathom his distress. Males, as I have said, are beyond a warrior's understanding.

My daru was nearly gone when the captive began to move uncomfortably by the ground post. Fideran had returned to his place beside my sleeping leather, yet his eyes had not left the form of the captive. My eyes, too, studied the captive closely, and the captive reddened beneath the double examination.

"At what do you two goggle?" he demanded quite heatedly, attempting to hold himself still at the post. His attempts were in vain, of course, as the appearance of his garment spoke eloquently of his condition.

"We gaze upon a man who has been refreshed," Fideran replied, glancing at the evidence of this statement. "Know that you shall remain refreshed for many hind to come, and shall not require freshening again until the dark."

"You speak without meaning!" snarled the captive, looking away from a grimly pleased Fideran. "I require naught from savages and slaves!"

"You require naught?" asked Fideran softly. "Look you upon Jalav. You have no need of the softness of her breasts, the comfort of her belly, the heat of her thighs? You have no wish to feel her midnight hair upon your face, her lips upon your body, her hands at your loins? You wish none of the fire burning in her large, dark eyes? You. . . ."

The captive snarled again, but this time as a child of the wild as he looked upon me. Had he been unbound, he would have been upon me, the lust born of the drug in his drink firing his blood to the point of madness. He roared and fought his bonds, fought to free himself yet not to escape, but to reach me, and I smiled in satisfaction.

"He responds quickly and well," said I to Fideran, who came to kneel behind me. "We shall have much use from him. Larid!" Larid and a hand of other warriors entered at my summons, gazing eagerly upon the struggling captive. "You may now remove him to the use tent," said I, "yet have a care that he is not damaged through overuse. He is larger than many, though he is still only male."

"We hear, Jalav," Larid murmured, unable to remove her eyes from the captive. The captive, though, continued to strain toward me, his wildness increasing when Fideran's hands circled my waist to rest at last upon my breasts. Happily I moved at the touch, and the captive was beside himself, causing my warriors to use their spears to remove him from my tent. When they had gone, I turned to a Fideran who also seemed to have partaken of the drug. He held me to him fiercely, his lips hot upon my throat, and nearly did he forget himself to such an extent that he began to press me flat to the leather of the floor. I regretted the need to put my dagger to his throat, yet there was no help for it. A war leader may not receive from a male, but must take whatever he offers. Fideran withdrew reluctantly, then placed himself so that I might use him. I did so with much pleasure, yet was his response not as it normally was. His need was strong, yet he seemed to receive little of the satisfaction he craved.

When the heat had gone from both of us, Fideran sat himself facing toward the rear wall of my tent in silence. He seemed to be studying my shield and spear, which had come to me when I won the place of war leader. A long, clean oval was the shield of the Hosta war leader, and many a war leader had carried it proudly, never having shamed it in battle through retreat. A war leader stood to the last, never showing her enemy her back, choosing, instead, the glory of death. Many times had the spear and shield been retrieved from a battleground, but never had they been shamed.

"You must not use him," Fideran spoke suddenly, surprising me. He had not turned, but sat in his colorless clan covering, his back rounded at the shoulders.

"Of what do you speak?" I asked, intent upon adjusting the leg bands which held my dagger.

"You must not use the new male!" said he, turning to me with blazing eyes. "Think you I remain here in this tent, clothingless and without pride, serving you as a slave, merely to share you with another? He shall not have you!"

"No," said I, rising to my feet. "He shall not have me. I shall have him. Has his presence disturbed you so deeply that you have forgotten?"

"The point is the same," he insisted, rising also, so that our eyes were level. "It matters not who does the having, only that another shall possess what is mine! You may not use him!"

"*May* not?" said I very quietly. "Indeed Fideran forgets himself. I belong only to the Hosta of the Midanna, never to a male. You may take your earlier possessions and return to your people."

I began to turn away, yet Fideran fell to his knees, throwing his arms about my legs and pressing his face to my body. "No!" he cried, the depth of his voice muffled against me. "Do not sent me away, Jalav! The stranger desires you, and I have seen his like before! Should he come to know the bliss of your arms, he shall not release you again! I love you, Jalav, and wish to live only for you! Do not send me away!"

I sighed deeply at his pain, and stroked his hair with a gentle hand. His dark hair was not of a length with the captive's red-gold glory, yet it was of a pleasing length, as he had allowed it to go unshorn in the time he had been with me.

"Fideran, hear my words," said I. "Your happiness is a sometime thing among the Midanna, and it would be wise of you to return to your people. I am pleased that you find love for me within you, yet saddened too, that I cannot return your love. Never will it be possible for me to do so."

"Allow me to remain!" he begged, pressing himself yet closer to me. "Perhaps one fey I may be able to give you a child as I have done with others. Then, Jalav, then shall you feel love for me!"

"Perhaps you are correct," I murmured, stroking his hair again, understanding that he knew not why he had not given me a child. A war leader must chew the leaves of the dabla bush, so that she is ever prepared to lead her warriors to battle. A war leader with life in her may not perform such a function, therefore the dabla bush insured against such a happening. It was said that the bush could be countered, yet I had never known it to be done. Perhaps the Keeper would have had such knowledge, but I, as war leader, did not.

"See to the daru, Fideran," I said, "and should the Keeper arrive before my return, see to her comfort as well."

He released me slowly and reluctantly then, moving back

to seat himself upon the leather of my tent floor, his head hung in misery. He nodded in silence, obedient to my word once more, and I left him and withdrew from my tent.

The fey was bright, warm with Mida's light, drowsy beneath the leaves of the trees. The black and green home tents of the Hosta were a brave sight to a daughter of Mida. On the hunt and in battle, warriors fetched naught save their weapons and sleeping leather, for it is foolish to tell your quarry or enemy where you take your rest. Only upon our own lands might the home tents be used, and then only with sentries alert all about us. A warrior joys in the sight of her home tent, yet must she sleep lightly when she is within it. Much of the joy would be removed, should she awaken to find the point of her enemy's sword at her throat.

I thought to see many of my warriors about, yet the camp seemed oddly deserted. For a moment I felt puzzled, then heard the laughter from the tent set in the middle of the camp, the tent which lacked our Hosta clan colors. I knew then where my warriors were, and smiled at their interest. The captive was an attractive one, more attractive than any save, possibly, Fideran, yet Fideran had been with us a considerable time, and the captive was new to all. I walked toward the tent in the center of the camp, hoping that my warriors remembered my words. Despite his robust appearance, a male is often a frail thing, and may easily be overused to the point of worthlessness. The Harra, another clan of the Midanna, held their captives as slaves, often resorting to raids upon small villages to replenish their supply. I had seen the slaves of the Harra, cringing in their fear of being touched and used, and I regretted then that the Herra were sisters to the Hosta, rather than blood enemies.

I stepped just within the entrance of the tent, standing quietly and watching my warriors as they, spread out and crouching down in place, watched the captive. He had been placed upon his back and staked to the ground, the leather about his throat preventing extreme movement of his head. A warrior had just finished with him, yet even as she stood, in possession of his priceless seed, his readiness for another was evident. The lust was still upon him, as it would be for many a hin yet, but a spark in his eyes showed his fury at being used so, his rage at his inability to control his body's demands. Even as another warrior took her place upon him, even as his hands grasped futilely for her, I knew the captive would not be one to remain with us when his service was done.

Kilin crouched to the left of the captive, laughing with the others as he first attempted to deny the warrior who had him, then acceded to his need and attempted to use her. Neither attempt was successful, yet Kilin urged him on to greater effort with amusement, enjoying the spectacle of the brash city male being taught his place. I made my way to her, and she rose and grinned.

"Soon it shall be my turn, Jalav," she said. "My spear cast was poor, yet was enough to gain me a time before he is too far drained. I shall enjoy using him."

"That is his purpose, Kilin," I said, amused at her delight. "I would speak with you briefly before you partake of your enjoyment."

"I hear, Jalav," she acknowledged, and began to follow me from the tent. Before leaving, I chanced to glance at the captive and found, to my surprise, that he gazed not upon the warrior who had him, but upon me. His long, red-gold hair had become disarranged, and it hung about his strained, sweat-soaked face, yet still did he gaze upon me with heat. I smiled and left the tent, knowing that when next I saw him, his heat would be considerably diminished.

Kilin and I walked several paces before I spoke to her. Mida's light danced brightly upon the silver ring of a blooded warrior which gleamed from her right ear, showing her as one who had met the enemy in battle and had survived. I, too, wore such a ring, as did all blooded warriors, yet was mine matched by another in my left ear, proclaiming to all that here stood a war leader. In such a manner did war leaders find one another in battle, searching for the second ring and a suitable match within which to test one's blade. Too, there might be no more than one second ring for each clan, so the ring passed from one bested war leader to new war leader, it being taken from the body, no matter whether she had fallen in battle or during a challenge. A long moment did Kilin and I walk in silence, before I was able to find the words.

"Kilin," I said, "I would ask a deed of you. All know that I ride with the new light to seek the Crystal of Mida and those who came to steal and slay. The warriors of the Hosta ride with me, yet there are those who must stay with the Keeper. You are one of those whose time with the Keeper has long since been appointed."

"Do you wish me to ride with you, Jalav?" she asked, excitement rising in her voice, happiness appearing on her face. "I have already attempted to give my place to one who rides, yet none would agree. At the word of the war leader, however. . . ."

"No, Kilin," I said, shaking my head and placing my hand upon her shoulder. "All must bear burdens in these times, and yours is to remain behind. I would have your sword with mine in the north, yet this may not be."

"I hear, Jalav," she sighed, resigned once again to her fate. "I would ask what deed I may perform for you."

"I have given much thought to Fideran," I said, gazing upon a tree which stood before us. "He has served us all well, and I would not see him hurt. I believe he would attempt to follow me north, and this I shall not allow. I would have you and the others remaining behind hold him once again as captive, using him gently with naught of the drug, till there is no hope of his following successfully. You may then allow him to remain with you, or you may release him to go his way. I have seen in the past that you used him gently; please care for him for me."

"I shall be pleased to do so, Jalav," said she, a tender smile upon her face. Her hair was brown, as were her eyes, a soft brown that showed gentle feeling for much about her. She was a valiant warrior, fearless in the face of the enemy, yet was gentle too, when gentleness was required.

"I have not told him, Kilin," I said, "nor shall I do so. Come to my tent when darkness has fallen, after the meal, and fetch him away with leather."

"I had thought raiding was not permitted to the Hosta of the Midanna," she laughed, greatly amused at the thought. "I now see I am to begin my raiding in the tent of the war leader. Is this the manner in which all Midanna begin?"

"It is the manner in which they cease," said I, laughing too. "Should one come without my permission, she would have little need of that for which she raids. You may return now to the use tent, for I would not see you passed over. With the return of the balance of our warriors at darkness shall come a greater demand for the captive."

"Perhaps they will have seen to their needs in Islat," suggested Kilin. "The trading is often tended to in less time than return is expected."

"It would be well for the captive to hope so," I chuckled,

taking a leaf from the tree upon which to chew. "So many more warriors demanding his service would not be pleasant for him, and it may already be seen that he does not care for the service which he performs for us."

"It would be well should Mida send to us one who does not require the drug," she sighed, also taking a leaf upon which to chew. "It is said that once there were males of a strength to see to the needs of Mida herself. I have come to disbelieve such tales; however, I find myself hoping I am wrong."

"How would it be possible for such males to exist?" I asked with reason. "They dwell within their cities, never knowing the true world of Mida, refusing to their slave-women the glory of battle for fear that they will be left unattended. They are able to do naught for themselves, but must ever be sending others to do for them. Is such a life to produce true males?"

"Indeed not," said she with a further sigh. "We are all blessed in that our forebears left the city males to their ruin, and chose to follow Mida, else we, too, would be slave-women without hope."

"Yet we are not slave-women," I said. "Therefore we must guard our freedom so that it is not lost to us. Go you now quickly, lest your time with the captive be given to another. I believe he, too, would do well with your gentleness."

"He shall have little gentleness." she laughed, throwing away the leaf as she began to move toward the use tent. "The sight of him stirs my desires, Jalav, and I would feel him beneath my hands and in my possession. He .is the finest sthuvad I have ever seen."

She lifted a hand in farewell, then moved quickly toward the use tent, in the gait a warrior uses on the hunt, when the quarry is ahead and must be run down. She disappeared within as laughter came again from the tent, and I chewed my leaf, considering returning there myself. I had not cared for the look the captive had given me, nor did I care for the manner in which he had addressed me, yet I had allowed him to go unpunished so that he would be fit for the use of my warriors. Should he be foolish enough to so address me again, he would not again go unpunished.

I had nearly decided to add my laughter to that of my warriors, when I beheld the arrival of the Keeper. Her procession moved slowly into the camp, with all the dignity required by the person of the Keeper. Fully ten hands of warriors accompanied her, clad not only in the colors of the Hosta, but of the Harra, and the Helda, and the Hitta as well. Warriors of each of the ten clans of our sisterhood rode there, guarding our Keeper as would the ten clans of enemy Midanna guard their own. The Keeper herself sat upon the Seat of office, a seat covered above for the Keeper's comfort, yet open upon all sides to the sight of Mida. Her arms rested easily upon the arms of the Seat, her feet flat upon the Seat's wide platform, which platform was borne along by the strength of four gandod. The platform swayed to the pace of the gandod, yet the Keeper did not seem to mind in the least. A tall, strong woman was our Keeper, pleased with the place Mida had given her, vital yet, in spite of her age. I smiled and walked forward then to greet her, pleased as always to see Rilas the Keeper.

Rilas took note of my approach, and smiled a greeting as her gandod were stopped so that she might descend to the ground. She wore a clan covering to the ankles, one which only the Keeper might possess. All colors of our clans appeared upon her covering, against the black of all Midanna, the green, the red, the blue, the yellow, white and brown, orange and violet, gold and rose. She was the Keeper of our clans of Midanna, and she who did wait most avidly till the Crystal of Mida would speak to us.

"Mida's blessings, Jalav," said she as she was assisted from her Seat. "I am ever pleased to visit the Hosta, yet would I wish for other circumstances. You prepare to ride in search of the Crystal?"

"Aye, Rilas," I said, gazing upon her proud form. Her hair reached nearly as long as her covering, yet no longer was it the gold of her youth. She, too, had been a warrior, for how else may a Keeper show that the love of Mida is with her? Had she refrained from taking part in battle, none would have known that her survival was Mida's demand for further service from a well-loved daughter.

"We shall ride with the new light, Rilas," I continued. "Part of this fey must I spend with Mida, and we may speak of what aid you may give me, at darkness. By the new light, all shall be seen to."

"I am well enough pleased," she said. She looked upon the use tent, and her brows rose. "Have you this soon brought one of them low, Jalav?" she asked.

"No, Rilas." I smiled, looking, too, toward the use tent. "A captive was taken, yet has his innocence been confirmed by the Attendant Remad before she joined Mida. He is merely a sthuvad, and even now amuses my warriors. Should any of them find herself with child from him, I shall send her back to the tents by your Tower. The new lives shall not be wasted."

"Good." Rilas smiled, then grew serious. "Jalav, I visited the Tower of the Crystal before coming here," she said with compassion. "I would be with you when you speak with Mida, and also relate the merits of those who have gone. You need not be alone to speak of her who bore you."

"Your presence will be welcome," I said to her, remembering the look of my warrior, the look of her who had borne me. Her breasts had had a dagger taken to them, perhaps in an effort to make her cry out. I well knew that she had not cried out.

I sent a warrior to my tent for my sword and a pot of daru for Rilas, then she and I entered the woods away from the camp. When the distance was sufficient, I unsheathed my sword and stood straight, Rilas also straight by my side.

"Hear me, Mida," I called softly to the sky, my arms and sword held high. "I would speak with you of those who wish to enter your Realm from the Hosta of the Midanna. They are brave warriors all, and the fault was not theirs that final battle was denied them. I, Jalav, war leader of your Hosta, shall seek out those who took their honor, and avenge the glory. I ask now that they be allowed to enter your Realm, and not be forced to wander the gray place forever."

I resheathed my sword and drew my dagger, then I set the edge of it to the side of my left arm. A line of blood appeared, and I drew two fingers through the blood and held them toward the skies.

"My blood has been spilled, Mida!" I cried. "She who bore me was foully used and senselessly tortured, then robbed of her place in your Realm! Well do I know that those of the cities have been forsaken by you, yet would I ask your aid in my vengeance! Smile upon me, Mida, so that the blood of my enemies may be spilled with mine! Your warrior asks no more of you than your blessing in her quest!"

I withdrew my blood from the eye of Mida, then crouched down where I stood, to bring back memory of her who bore me The use of sword and dagger, spear and bow, had I learned from that kindest of warriors, and her pride at my winning the place of war leader had increased my joy in the deed tenfold. Very young had she been when she bore me, only just into her womanhood when the captive had been taken, and still did she have the appearance of a girl upon her death. Always had she stood in battle upon my left, a sword to be counted on and trusted. Now she was no more.

I crouched in memory for many hind, Rilas beside me, her hand upon my shoulder, her voice raised softly to Mida. She recounted the lives of my warriors who were, then crouched beside me in memory. A Keeper feels the loss of each of the Midanna, having often been present when they first wailed with the pain of new life. Rilas had been Keeper for many Kalod, and knew each of us well.

The darkness was nearly upon us when Rilas and I returned to my tent. The candles had been lit by Fideran, and he had prepared meat for the Keeper and myself. The Keeper smiled at his efforts, amused that a male saw so carefully to my needs. Other captives had, from time to time, chosen to remain with Midanna who would have released them, yet Rilas told me that Fideran seemed the most zealous. He did not wish to return to his city, and for this he could not be faulted.

The Keeper and I drew our daggers in order to take the meat from the fire, and Fideran cried out and grasped my left arm.

"Jalav, you have been hurt!" he said, holding my arm gently with much pain in his eyes. "I shall fetch cloth immediately to wash and bind it!"

"No, Fideran," I said, taking my arm from his grasp. "It must be left till the new light comes, and then it may be washed. It is our way."

"I—see," he said heavily, knowing it as a matter for warriors alone. The ways of the Midanna disturbed Fideran, for he could not accept them, nor could he change them. He withdrew from the fire and sat by my sleeping leather, his head down. I was pleased that soon Fideran would have another to tend, and my doings would no longer disturb him.

The Keeper and I were about to seat ourselves for our meal, when another joined our presence. The captive, having been removed from the use tent, would be returned to the ground post for a time so that he might regather his strength for further effort. He was no longer enraged. Instead, he leaned heavily upon the supporting arms of my warriors, his arms once again bound behind his back, his step painful and slow. His red-gold hair was completely unbound, hanging limply with the sweat that had soaked his entire body, the color bright against a face that had gone pale with the passing hind. No sound did he make as he was lowered to his side upon the leather beside the post, yet was the pain in him easily sensed. The thong upon his neck was attached to the post, and my warriors then withdrew.

"A fine specimen," Rilas observed as she tasted the meat upon her blade. "It is fortunate that he was uninvolved in the matter of the theft, else he could not have been used so. A pity the Hosta may not use him longer."

"If ever I regain my freedom," said the captive in a low, exhausted voice, "the Hosta shall be no more. I will see justice done for what has been done to me."

"Perhaps I may give him to the Harra," I mused. "Their warriors number greater than ours, and I am told their needs, too, are greater."

"Jalav, do not torment him," Rilas scolded, yet she also found the need to mask a smile as the captive paled further still. "The Hosta have ever released their captives when the service was done," said she. "Are you to change your ways on the eve of riding to battle?"

"There is little reason to cling to but one manner of behavior," I said, tasting the meat Fideran had prepared. As always, it was too well done, but I said nothing. "The Harra require many captives to replace those who are used too far and are thereby rendered useless," I added. "Think you, Rilas, he would not joy in giving service to warriors till he is no longer able?"

"You, girl!" the captive snarled, struggling to lift his head so that he might glare at me further. "You shall pay the most! You shall one fey feel my leather upon your back, and know the meaning of being well used! This do I swear by all I hold sacred!"

I placed the meat upon the leather of my tent floor, rose to my feet, then stood above the captive. He gazed up at the full height of me, and surely saw my anger.

"I am Jalav, war leader of the Hosta of the Midanna," I said coldly. "Should it be the will of Mida, sthuvad, my life shall end in the coming battle, yet am I still war leader of the Hosta. You have given me insult for the final time."

I then called my warriors and ordered the captive beaten. As they removed him from my home tent, he fought them as best he could, yet he was much spent from his hind of service. He made no outcry as he was removed, nor did I expect one. Had he been fortunate enough to be of the Midanna, he would truly have made a warrior.

Rilas spoke no word, as was only proper, for the Keeper may not interfere in matters of a war leader; however, Fideran was much disturbed by the course of events. He rose to his feet at my call to my warriors, and stood as though he would keep the captive from his due, making no sound as the sthuvad was removed. His soft eyes gazed upon me in upset, then lowered in misery. Again he folded to the floor by my sleeping leather, and I returned to Rilas and my meat.

Rilas and I fed in silence, savoring the bounty of Mida as do all Midanna. I thought deeply upon the matter of the Crystal, yet spoke no word of it, as it is not proper to discuss battle as one partakes of the bounty of Mida. All things must be kept in their proper place, and one does not taint one's provender with the blood of one's enemies. The captive was returned silently to his place by the post, his mouth and eyes grim, his back well striped by the leather of punishment. Rilas and I continued to feed, taking no notice of his arrival. Fideran did silently turn his face to the back of the tent.

With the meat consumed, Rilas and I filled our pipes from my sack as Fideran brought to us pots of daru. The daru was properly brewed, and I smiled somewhat as I realized that soon I would find the need to brew daru myself. Fideran, who had returned to the fire and knelt before it with his back to us, saw naught of my smile, nor did he see the silent entrance of Kilin and two other warriors. I nodded to Kilin, and she and the others stole up behind Fideran, seizing him quickly, throwing him to the leather of my floor, and binding him fast with thongs. Fideran cried out, in surprise as well as distress, yet the deed was done, and he could not resist the leather.

"Jalav, what is to be done with me?" he cried, as Kilin and the others urged him to his feet and from the tent. "I do not wish to be taken from you!"

"Mida's blessings, Fideran," I said, gazing upon his frightened, retreating form. "Perhaps, one fey, we shall meet again in the sight of Mida."

His pleading grew fainter as distance increased, and I put him from my mind and addressed Rilas.

"All clans of our sisterhood must prepare themselves for battle, Rilas," I said. "Should the numbers of the Hosta prove too few when the thieves are discovered, all must ride. I shall appoint couriers to carry the word."

"And I shall visit the clans to instruct them." Rilas nodded, taking the pipe.I held out to her. "You ride directly to Ranistard?"

"Aye," I said, lighting her pipe and my own with a flame fetched from the fire. "It lies to the north, and shall not be difficult to find. I shall decide then what is to be done there."

"You and your warriors have never seen nor visited the cities to the north," Rilas mused. "Once, in my youth, I was honored to aid in the death of one such city. The walls were scaled in stealth, Jalav, so that the gates might be opened from within. Weighted lengths of knotted leather were cast to the pointed metal set atop the walls, warriors climbed the knotted leather, then they removed the weight, held the leather about the point, and descended the doubled leather to the ground. The leather was then removed from the metal, leaving no trace, one end simply being pulled, the other released. The wretches of the city were lax in their watchfulness, and so paid the final price of laxity. The walls of remaining cities have ever since been guarded carefully, war leader. This must be considered by you in your thinking."

"Indeed, it is a thing to consider," I said, my sight within rather than without. "The walls of Ranistard, stout or not, must fall before my warriors at some time. Yet, should the fall be too long in coming, those holding what is ours may well seek to destroy it. I must not allow such a thing to occur."

"Perhaps it would be wise to learn of a city's ways before reaching Ranistard," suggested Rilas. "An error made elsewhere would not have the effect of one made in Ranistard."

"An excellent thought," I said.

"I have heard tell of the city of Bellinard, more distant from here, perhaps, than from Ranistard. It might well prove profitable to enter Ballinard first, to see what might be seen. Yes, I shall think closely upon this."

I reclined upon the leather of my tent floor, considering the possibility of entering Bellinard. We would have to see the city first to decide how to enter it, there was much to think about. I saw, without true sight, the entrance of two of my warriors bearing hot meat for the captive. The meat was cut small and fed to him by both warriors as they gazed upon him with pleasure. The captive accepted the meat from their hands with little gratitude, and had his need not been so great, well might he have refused it. His jaws worked as he chewed the meat placed in his mouth, yet his eyes fastened themselves not to my warriors, but to me. I paid little heed to his unvoiced fury, and thought about the matter of Bellinard.

As the captive continued to feed, another warrior entered the tent and presented herself to me. She had been one of the warriors in the tower of the Crystal, and she held in her hand the life signs of my warriors who had been, and those of Rilas's Attendants.

"I bring the life signs as you directed, Jalav," she said, handing them to the Keeper with a sign of respect. "Yet were we unable to find the third of our warriors' life signs. It was to be discovered neither in the Tower nor in the stones below the Tower. Do you wish us to seek further?"

I shook my head, dismissing her, knowing full well the whereabouts of the life sign of her who had borne me. It lay with the Crystal of Mida, marking those who were destined to feel the edge of my blade, the heat of my rage. Mida would guide me to the life sign of her daughter, and there I would avenge the theft of glory. Rilas, knowing in some manner the turn of my thoughts, sat silently with her pipe, the life signs given her wrapped carefully about her free hand.

A disturbance by the captive caught my attention. The captive had consumed the meat brought for him, yet refused the drink which followed the meat. My warrior stood before him with the pot in her hands, and he looked at her with contempt.

"Do you take me for a fool, girl?" he demanded of her. "Sooner would I die of thirst than drink again in this camp! Take that from me, and do not return with it!"

"I see no reason for reluctance," the warrior answered. "There is naught in the pot save fresh spring water."

"And I am to believe that!" The captive laughed, shaking his great head at her. "I would indeed receive my due, were I to be so foolish. Be gone, girl child, and allow me my rest."

The warrior, indifferent, left with the pot, the second warrior accompanying her. The captive watched them gone, then gazed silently upon me with amusement, as though to say that he had bested us. I drank my daru, and smoked my pipe, and did not disabuse him.

The effects of the drug reachèd him sooner the second time, as is the way with the drug. His amusement left him slowly as he attempetd to deny the beginnings of what he felt, and I smiled as I watched the onset of his willingless movement, and laughed when full realization at last claimed him.

"The pot contained naught save fresh spring water," I informed him as he again fought the leather which bound him. "The drug was in the meat given you, cooked in to enhance the taste of it. Did you not find it enjoyable?"

"No!" he cried, throwing himself about in his despair. "You cannot force me to endure such treatment again! I am a warrior! A warrior!"

"You are merely a sthuvad," I informed him from where I lay upon the leather of my tent floor. "A sthuvad is for the enjoyment of warriors, not a warrior himself. Is it that you were borne by a warrior and given to those of the cities to raise, that you speak of yourself as a warrior?"

"I am only of the cities," he said, his eyes darting about, seeking escape. "I knew naught of your pack of female vipers before I was taken, yet I shall never forget what was done to me. Never!"

"We have found," Rilas observed calmly, "that those who are taken and thereafter released seldom speak of their capture to others. I have often wondered why this is, yet I feel that in such a manner are the Midanna given further service. Few would travel within our reach should word of our practices be spread about. You, too, I believe, will say naught."

The captive sent her a hate-filled look, proving the truth of her words, then fell back to the leather of the floor, writhing in his need. Laird and a hand of others appeared, laughing lightly, to once again remove him to the use tent. The meal had been taken by my warriors, and now they would seek entertainment.

The Keeper and I sat for some hind, discussing the why of the taking of the Crystal. Had the thing been done by enemy Midanna, the reason would easily be seen, yet for city males to wish to take it was beyond understanding. The Crystals had been given to the Midanna to guard, given by the heralds of Mida many and many kalod earlier, against the fey Mida would once again wish to use them, and city males would have no interest in them. None knew the proper use of the Crystals, yet was it thought that Mida would in some manner speak through them, informing her warriors of her wishes. The Hosta saw to one Crystal, and the enemy Silla saw to the other, though no word had come that the Crystal guarded by the Silla had been taken or attempted. I saw the need to send warriors to the Silla, to learn of the condition of the Crystal they guarded. I spoke of this to Rilas, and she agreed, insisting that the deed be done by Attendants. Knowing how keenly she and her Attendants felt the loss, I thought it best to accede to her wishes. The Attendants would be sent, and should they learn of something to aid me in my search, I would be quickly informed.

Rilas then retired to her tent. I found Fideran's absence left a loneliness behind, so I went out into the darkness beyond my tent. The darkness was well lit by the presence of the Entry to Mida's Realm, and the glowing, rounded gap in the darkness that ever changed its place made pale the tiny rends to all sides of it. To the despair of all Midanna, the Entry was not always in the skies, yet Mida knew of the needs of her daughters, and at such times allowed a memory of the glory of her Realm to shine through the tiny rends. My eyes gazed upon the Entry to Mida's Realm, and I knew a sadness that all could not hope to be allowed through to the everlasting days of battle and happiness that were the rewards of the Midanna. I then heard the laughter of my warriors who had found interest in the use tent. I recalled the look of the captive, then smiled and also recalled my earlier resolve. My steps led quietly to the use tent, and I went in.

The use tent was warm with the bodies of my warriors, crouching within, and much did they laugh and compare the captive with others taken before him. A fire had been made for the brewing of daru, and many of my warriors sat upon the leather to one side of the captive, sipping from the pots of daru and calling instructions to the captive or the warrior who possessed him. The instructions were entirely in jest, yet the captive felt the barb of them deeply enough to attempt escape once again. His attempts caused further laughter, so alike were males and their ways—a simple jest often returned life to the most enfeebled of them.

I moved through the press of my warriors till I stood above the captive. He had been used hard, and had he not been of the strength he was, he might not have survived. His wrists and ankles bled from his struggles, his face had lost its color, his covering was stained and twisted about upon him. Only his eyes remained the same, filled with an endless store of fury and hate. I stood beside him quietly, my eyes examining his form with pleasure as my warrior continued to make use of him. His own eyes came to me, and did not leave me again.

My warrior finished with him and arose, and still I remained standing at his side. No warrior stirred in the tent, for though they knew that use of him was at an end, still they wondered if the war leader would honor him. I felt the leather of the tent floor beneath my feet, saw the rise and fall of the captive's chest, smelled the sweat that covered his body and caused his red-gold mane to lie about him in greasy strands. My eyes moved to his and I smiled at the desire I saw ablaze there, a desire even greater than the fury that had gripped him so many times that fey. The sthuvad found pleasure in the sight of Jalav, war leader of the Hosta of the Midanna, and his desire blazed forth, above the urging of the drug, for all to see. I stood a moment longer, holding his eyes, then spoke to my warriors without turning.

"Secure him through the darkness," said I, "and see that he is well guarded. I would not care to have him stolen from us when he has rendered such faithful service."

The laughter of my warriors, and the sounds of their rising from their places, covered the snarl of the sthuvad as he again writhed in rage. So sure had he been that he would be honored, that his desires would be seen to, that I would use him as my warriors had. Yet I was war leader, and did as I wished. I turned from the captive and strode from the use tent, returning immediately to my own tent. The sight of the shield and spear of the war leader warmed me as always, and I regretted having given Fideran to another. I extinguished the candles, then sought my sleeping leather, my dagger fast in my hand as was proper.

2.

Islat—and a
city is spoken of

The arrival of the new light saw my warriors and myself already mounted in preparation for departure. More than twenty hands in number were we, a force large enough to press an advantageous attack, yet small enough to disguise its presence should it become necessary. My warriors were anxious to be gone, and I was too. Rilas, who had come to bid us farewell, stood beside my gando.

"The fey will be a warm, fair one," she observed, examining the bright streaks in the slowly lightening sky. "Mida smiles upon your efforts, Jalav."

"That remains to be seen," said I, regarding my warriors in their places. Their clan colors about their hips showed them proudly as Hosta, their life signs tied firmly about their necks showed them eager for battle. Their hair, like mine, was bound with war leather, for we rode to recover the Crystal wherever it might be found. "A fey black with the clouds of rain may be fairest of all, Rilas," I said, "should victory in battle show Mida's pleasure."

"True, Jalav." Rilas smiled, placing her hand upon the binding scale of my gando. "It is when the warriors of Mida ride out in such a manner that I wish I, too, were yet a warrior. The sight stirs my blood, war leader, and brings memories of long ago. Much glory do I wish you, Jalav, and ask Mida's blessings for you and your quest."

"We shall return with the Crystal should it be Mida's will."

I smiled, then placed my hand briefly upon hers. "See to that of which we have spoken, and perhaps we may one fey speak again."

She nodded then, and stepped back with a smile, her hand raised in farewell. I looked again at my warriors, felt the proud weight of my shield upon my left arm, the smooth, slim shaft of my spear in my right hand, then nodded too, and struck my gando with my spear. I led my warriors from the camp and we rode forth upon our gandod, perhaps to victory, perhaps to the glory of death in battle, none knew and none cared. It is the privilege of a warrior of the Midanna to ride forth when there is need and desire.

I had considered Bellinard, and therefore led my warriors to the road to Islat. It would be well to seek quiet entrance to Bellinard if possible, therefore we should stop in Islat to exchange gandod for Kand. The gando, while excellent for battle, is feared for its temper and intractability, and never may one be found within the walls of the cities. If we wanted to ride between the gates of Bellinard, it would best be done upon the backs of kand, and kand might be had in Islat. The road to Islat was a short one, a mere four hind in the traveling.

Islat was a village much larger than the Hosta camp, and had found a safety for itself in trade with the Hosta. Little did my warriors require that they were unable to obtain for themselves, yet were there articles such as clan silks and woven goods, candles, arrowheads, and well-made knives, that those of Islat might offer. In turn, we of the Hosta provided pelts of the children of the wild, those that village males and city males feared to seek themselves. The woods and forests looked harshly upon those who had insufficient knowledge of them, and too often had the Hosta found the remains of those who had tried for the pelts and had failed. The Hosta had let it be known that Islat lay beneath our protection, and only once had it been necessary to avenge a raid. A small, independent band of Harra had taken males from Islat, yet there had been little difficulty in tracking them. All six Harra had been taken, the two males released from the leather which bound them, and the Harra, bound themselves, were given over to the remaining males of Islat. The time had been before I had become a warrior, therefore the fate of the six Harra was unknown to me, though it was known well enough to others that Islat had never again been touched in raid.

The new light was high and bright when first we reached the beginning of Islat. The village spread about upon the bank of the Dennin river, which ran east and west through the land of the Hosta. Crossing the Dennin was necessary and fairly easy. All crossings were known to the Midanna, and I, myself, had crossed it while still a warrior. I would cross it now as war leader, and touch its wetness to my forehead as reminder that we rode to battle where wetness of another sort would be expected. Some thought that the wetness of the Dennin would guard against the free running of blood from a wound, and it would be foolish to overlook the possibility.

The males of Islat emerged from their low dwellings to stand in surprise beside their staring slave-women as we rode through the village to the Headman's dwelling. Even had the Hosta not traded there the fey previous, the sight of the shields and spears we carried was sufficient to inform them that a thing not often seen was beginning. The slave-women were ordered within their dwellings with the little ones, and the males accompanied us toward the center of their village, wary and distrustful, and keeping their distance from my warriors and our gandod. I smiled at their actions as I rode, reflecting that the distance they kept would hardly have seen to their safety had it been their village against which we rode. The farthest of them was still well within reach of our spears.

Maranu, Headman of Islat, stood before the entrance to his dwelling, awaiting us. Although he did not retreat before the snapping snouts of our dancing gandod, he seemed tense. He wished to know why we rode in such numbers to his village, for never had he seen such a thing. Strangely, he had been Headman for many kalod, and remained Headman in spite of his graying hair. Perhaps his still-strong figure allowed for this, perhaps the vigor he retained did. Or perhaps he was most aided in that the males of Islat had no battles to face—the youth of the warriors of the Hosta stood protection for them and their village. I reined in my gando, and gazed down upon him.

"We of Islat make you welcome, war leader," said he in a tone which neither took nor gave. "May we do a service for you and your warriors?"

"Indeed, Maranu." I smiled to ease his tension. "The Hosta ride to battle, yet we need to trade for a small number of kand."

"Always are we honored to trade with the Hosta," Maranu replied with a smile of his own. The other males about him seemed relieved to learn that we came for naught save trade. "Would Jalav care to step down and accept the poor warmth of my home?" Maranu offered.

I wanted to get on with our journey, but it would be discourteous to refuse the offer. "Maranu is most kind," I said, giving to Larid, who rode beside me, my shield and spear. "I shall be pleased to share the warmth of his home."

I slid from my gando, then walked to where Maranu waited. His dark eyes were on a level with mine, and it pleased me that they did not avoid my gaze. Many of the males who stood about looked nervously down as my gaze brushed them, remembering, perhaps, the sport my warriors may have had with them at some time.

Maranu stepped aside, motioning with his arm that I was to precede him to his dwelling. Never would I allow one who was not of the Hosta to remain behind me, yet it was necessary to do such a thing in Islat. Their customs were not like those of the Midanna, and for the sake of peace, I must follow them. Therefore I preceeded Maranu into his dwelling.

The dwelling was of rude wooden logs rather than leather, and was divided within to form more than a single room. One entered a room given over to strange odors and stale air, a large fire, and the clutter of many objects, all of which were used in the partaking of food and drink. Many pots of various sizes were ranged about the room, yet none stood upon the small, legless platform which was positioned beneath the wide window in the left wall. I went to the platform as I knew was expected of me, and sat easily upon the dirt floor beside it. Maranu, directly behind me, took his place upon the floor on the other side of the platform, then turned to his slave-woman.

"Bring daru for our guest and myself, Yereh," he said to the woman. "There is trading which must be discussed between us."

The woman turned obediently to the large pot of daru which stood to one side of the room. She wore a garment which covered all of her. Maranu himself wore no more than a brief cloth about his loins, a comfort of dress which village men did not permit to their slave-women. They jealously guarded the sight of their women's bodies, thinking, perhaps, that to gaze upon them would cause such bodies to fade from view. The fact that the bodies of the Midanna did not fade from view was a lesson doubtless lost upon them.

Two pots of daru were brought by the woman, and were placed upon the platform between Maranu and myself. The daru had not been brewed to warmth as was the custom of the Midanna, for those of the village disliked the added potency brewing produced, and therefore drank it as it was in its fermenting pot. Though unbrewed daru was little more than flavored water, males liked it. Long since had the Hosta taken to adding the sthuvad drug to it for captured males, and never had a sthuvad disliked its taste to the point of rejecting it.

I sipped courteously from my pot of daru, then looked about to see that Maranu's slave-woman still stood before the platform, her eyes upon me, a determined expression upon her aging face. Her hands twisted briefly together before her, then one hand went to where her life sign should rest, and the other to her hair which was braided and tied in obedience to the will of males.

"Maranu, not again," she whispered, her eyes hard upon me. "The trading was to be done for the time, and this one is war leader! Please, Maranu, not again!"

"Yereh, Jalav is our guest," Maranu scolded gently. "The trading will be brief, as the Hosta ride to war."

Yereh's eyes closed briefly, as though from the pain of memory. She stepped to Maranu and knelt beside him, then circled him with her arms as her head rested upon his chest.

"Maranu, she is war leader," Yereh wept as Maranu held her close to him. "Have you not been shamed enough? Must you endure this thing as well?"

"My lovely Yereh," Maranu crooned, stroking her hair to give her comfort, "my shame has always been yours to endure. Do not agonize, Yereh. All shall soon be done with, and again my arms will hold you alone. Leave us now, that the trading may be seen to properly."

Yereh clung to him a moment longer, then hurried to the curtain which led to the next room.

"Forgive her, Jalav," Maranu said. "She has never accustomed herself to the needs of trading. What number of kand do you require?"

"But one hand shall suffice," said I, sipping again from the pot of daru. "She knew me as war leader, yet never have I seen her before. How is it that she knew I lead the Hosta in battle?"

"She must have seen your shield before you entered," Maranu replied. "We have the kand, and ask only five lenga pelts in return."

I replaced the pot of daru and smiled. "A hand of lenga pelts would fetch us more than two hands of kand," I informed him. "I offer one lenga pelt, and six freshly killed nilnod."

"We have meat aplenty." He shrugged. "Four lenga pelts."

"Two pelts," I countered, "and we shall keep the nilnod to feed us upon our journey. What shame did your slave-woman speak of?"

"She is not a slave!" he returned angrily. Then his gaze dropped to the platform, and he said with difficulty, "Three pelts and the thing is done. The kand are prime stock, well worth the pelts."

Again I felt my lack of understanding of males. It had almost seemed that had Maranu had a weapon, he would have been foolish enough to draw it. His anger was without reason, and I wished to know why.

"Maranu," said I, "it was not my intention to offer insult. I merely asked of the shame spoken of."

He glared at me again, and finished his daru quickly, with determination.

"Very well!" he said abruptly. "I shall speak of the shame, yet must you remember that it was not I who first asked of it! Always am I shamed when I must trade with the Hosta, for my manhood is forced from me along with my goods! The warriors of the Hosta demand my body and those of my men each time they come, and should we refuse, our women and children may stand victim for us! Yet are we men, war leader, and do not care to be used by women!"

I considered his words, confused. For what reason would the males of Islat dislike being used by Hosta? Nearly all of them had slave-women, therefore the act was not unknown to them.

"The Hosta are ugly to the men of Islat?" I asked. "The males of Islat feel repelled by them?"

"No, no!" He laughed, as though surprised. "The Hosta are far from ugly, and the men of Islat feel great desire when gazing upon them. Yet it is not a matter of desire. It is more—" He paused, searching for the proper words, then smiled and shook his head. "You are very young, war leader," he said quite gently. "Perhaps a greater age shall bring you understanding of men and their ways. Three lenga pelts and the thing is done."

"Two lenga pelts," I said, feeling no younger than he. I, too, led my people, and no war leader is known to have grown gray in her position as had Maranu. "You may recover the difference when the kand are returned to you in trade."

"The kand are to be returned?" he said. "Then they are not for battle." He paused briefly to consider this, and then nodded. "Very well," he agreed. "Two lenga pelts against the return of the kand in trade."

The trade was agreed to and done, sealed as we spat upon the backs of our right hands, and pressed our fists together, binding the trade as our spittle mingled. Maranu's fist was larger than mine and more squarely made, seemingly shaped for the weapons it so rarely grasped. Should age be the only thing to bring understanding, I would undoubtedly be long beside Mida before I understood.

Maranu withdrew his fist from mine, then rose to his feet. "Our trading is done, and naught is left save the last requirement," said he with a strange look about him. "There would be little shame to the matter, Jalav—were you not war leader. Come to the mat with me, war leader, and I shall soon be ready for you."

He turned about and strode to a wide, woven mat that lay before the fire, while I remained seated. He seemed to feel no shame at the thought of my touch, yet I was able, in a small way, to see his difficulty. A warrior of the Midanna might take from or receive from a male as she wished, yet a war leader was forbidden to receive from him. A war leader must only take from a male, and Maranu, for some reason, did not wish to be taken from. His woman had known at once that he would be taken, and her distress had been clear to any with eyes. Though I lacked understanding of their feelings, I was not without feeling of my own. Maranu was no passing sthuvad, and little point was there in observing the customs of the village merely to give insult to its Headman in his own dwelling. Therefore I rose easily and stepped forward.

"I thank Maranu for his offer," I said, "yet must I, with regret, refuse it. My warriors and I have a distance to travel, and the journey were best begun quickly. Perhaps, should

Mida continue to smile upon her warrior, another time may
see the thing done."

Maranu, standing beside the mat, paused in removing the
cloth from about his loins, raised his eyes from a frown, then
slowly replaced the cloth. He gazed upon me with such pain,
that I believed I had insulted him. I was about to repair the
error, when he spoke.

"Jalav," said he, coming to place his hands upon my shoulders, "indeed are you the highest among the Hosta. Yet you
are so young—!" Deep was his sigh, and deeply felt. "Should
your Mida not smile upon you, I shall feel the loss most
keenly. Would that you were my daughter that I might see
you safely beside a man of my choice!"

I stepped back stiffly. "Maranu had best remember that I
am guest within his dwelling!" I replied, stung that he would
speak so to me. "It would be the act of a boorish host to
force his guest to the necessity of spilling blood!"

Maranu seemed startled a moment, then he laughed with
hearty good cheer. "I beg your pardon, war leader," he said
with a wide grin. "It was not my intention to insult you. I
surely know of no man with whom you might be paired. I
shall personally see to the selection of the kand, and offer the
comfort of my dwelling for your use."

He stepped back with a small bow, and I watched him depart, sure that he had made sport of me in some way. His
words betrayed naught save apology, yet his manner. . . .

"War leader." I turned at the softly spoken words, and beheld Yereh beside the entrance to the other room. Her dark
eyes held gratitude, and she smiled most gently. "War leader,
I would offer my thanks for your not having stabbed at the
pride of my man," she said. "The gesture was small, yet required a great warrior in the doing. I ask Mida's blessings for
you, and shall speak to the skies of your wisdom."

"You have the sound to you of the Midanna," I observed,
studying her, "but surely this cannot be."

She reddened somewhat, and lowered her head. "I was of
the Midanna," she whispered, her hand going to where her
life sign would lie. "I was of the Harra, but was taken by the
Hosta for raiding, and given as captive to this village." She
seemed pained. "I have been here many kalod, yet have I
never forgotten the ways of the Midanna."

"Why do you remain?" I asked, surprised to learn she had
once been a warrior. She seemed no different from the other

slave-women of the village, although I then realized that she had known me by the presence of the second silver ring of the war leader.

"At first, I remained because Maranu held my life sign." She smiled, somehow amused by so terrible a fate. "Though he beat me when I disobeyed him, I could not return to the Harra without my life sign. I planned for long and long, searching for an opportunity to recover it, and then, at last, I did. Then I discovered, upon its recovery, that Maranu held my heart, war leader, and with my life sign upon my breast, I found that I could not leave him. He beat me soundly when he discovered that I had taken my life sign from him, but he has never beaten me since. My life is his, till the day that Mida calls."

"It is difficult to see how Mida might allow such a thing," I said, shocked that a warrior would fail to return to her clan when she was able. "Perhaps Mida was offended by you in some way."

"Perhaps." She nodded. "And yet there is another possibility. Perhaps Mida found herself particularly pleased with me. It is the first thing I shall ask when Mida's throne is before me."

"You are wise in your choice of First Question," I said, pleased that it was Mida's lot, and not mine, to answer her. The strange odors and stale air of the dwelling disturbed me, so I went out to return to my warriors. The village males still stood about, some inspecting my warriors, some avoiding their eyes. My warriors waited at ease, many inspecting the village males in turn, some regarding the passage of the light with impatience. I, too, felt impatience, so led my warriors to the enclosure that contained the village's kand. Maranu and two other males had chosen the hand of required kand, and had made a string of them with a long length of leather. The kand were frightened when one of my warriors rode close upon her gando to take the end of the leather, yet were easy to manage. The warrior led them to the rear of our host, and so as far as possible from the gandod they feared, and two lenga pelts were thrown to the feet of Maranu. The two males with him quickly and carefully lifted the pelts from the dirt, brushing at the long, magnificent fur, both of the color of golden light. Village males seem more than fond of lenga pelts, and do not understand why the Hosta do not use such pelts themselves. Yet when one has fought the lenga in the

forests, it is truly a slap to Mida herself to debase so glorious
a fighter when the battle is done. The lenga is the life sign of
many of the Midanna, as the hadat is mine, and its pelt is
only used for things the Midanna must have. The living evidence of a life sign should not be casually slighted.

Maranu examined the pelts, then turned to me with a
smile. "A matched pair," said he in approval. "The two are
indeed the worth of three. Even should the kand not be
returned in trade, Jalav, I shall consider the matter equitably
seen to."

"I am pleased you are satisfied," I said. "May Mida guard
you and your people till our return."

I raised my hand in farewell, as did Maranu, then led my
warriors past the kan enclosure toward the river. The crossing I wanted to use was not far distant. The two males who
had stood beside Maranu had seemed surprised and a bit
uncertain at my words to the Headman. The Hosta, though
often riding to battle, did not commit their entire number
to a venture, nor did they leave Islat unprotected. Now,
should it become necessary, the males of Islat must fight to
protect themselves till the Hosta returned. Perhaps the males
did not care overmuch for such an eventuality.

Islat was long out of sight when we paused for the
crossing. My warriors and I would cross in four sets, the first
set being the most dangerous position. Should an enemy be
waiting on the far side, those of the first set might be downed
with arrows before they were able to reach the bank and
draw blade. Some small help might be had from the bows of
the warriors who had yet to cross, therefore were bows strung
and arrows nocked as I rode with the first set toward the
water.

The river was warm yet refreshing after our ride, and our
gandod entered it eagerly, pleased to be allowed its wetness.
We swam the distance across, our shields held before us, our
spears above the water level, our eyes moving constantly to
catch the first sign of movement from the opposite shore.
From the middle of the river I dabbed the wetness on my
forehead, and each of my warriors did the same. Then the
far bank was reached and the next set began the swim as the
warriors about me watched carefully that we might not be
taken by surprise. The kand, in the care of two warriors
rather than one, crossed in the third set, and soon stood

shivering in our midst. The fourth set came and joined us, and we paused to feed before continuing on.

Nilnod do taste as good raw as when cooked, and sufficient had been slain so that we and the gandod might feed to our fill. Midanna rarely cook meat when on the move, for a fire, like a tent, announces one's presence to enemy and quarry alike. The kand ate only the grass beneath their feet, and that nervously and with poor appetite. Kand are delicate beasts, and I was afraid they might die before we reached Bellinard, therefore I directed a hand of my warriors to ride ahead with them, leaving their gandod, so that the odor and presence of gandod might be spared the beasts. My warriors didn't like this but obeyed, and our journey north continued with purpose.

The land through which we traveled was unfamiliar. The feyd were as warm as those to which we were accustomed, yet the dark was colder. Through forests empty of all life save that of the children of the wild we rode, and saw no dwellings even far from our lane of passage. A strange peace was upon us, strange in that though we rode to battle, our minds were free and without care, there in the vast forests, beneath the skies of Mida. My warriors laughed much among themselves, joking lightly with each other as we went farther and farther. Although few might return to the home tents of the Hosta, we were happy.

At dark upon the eleventh fey, we halted as always to take our final meal, and then to seek our sleeping leather. The kills of the fey were being divided when the abrupt return of the hand of relieving warriors for the kand surprised me. No longer had they the meat they had taken with them, and their haste seemed an omen of ill tidings.

"War leader!" gasped the first of them breathlessly as she slid from her gando before me. "Our warriors have been taken captive—by males!"

All within hearing muttered angrily, and I demanded of her, "How many?"

"Four hands was I able to count," she panted, her life sign rising and falling with each breath she took. "They fell upon our warriors from the trees, nearly before our eyes. There was no hope for battle with the others already taken, therefore we returned here."

"A wise decision," I commended her, my hand upon her shoulder. "Should these males be those in possession of the

Crystal of Mida, we would not care to have any of them escape us. Two sets will be ample to see to them." I turned to another warrior. "Sets one and four shall accompany me, sets two and three remain here. Inform the others."

Unhappily, she nodded, then turned away to pass on my word. She was not of set one or four, therefore would be left behind. Not many reckid was it before the sets were formed, and I led my warriors on foot toward where our sisters had been taken, the five relieving warriors showing the way. Quickly and silently we moved between the trees, flowing with the light from the Entry to Mida's Realm, making no greater disturbance than the light itself. Carefully we watched for posted sentries; however, the males had not seen fit to provide such. As we sighted them within a clearing, about the forms of our warriors, I smiled, realizing that they would soon regret their foolishness.

Indeed four hands in number were the males, big and well-made, yet covered as were all city males in garments that reached to the middle of their thighs. My warriors grinned at the sight of them, for never had we taken males in such numbers. These males would provide much sport if they had not stolen the Crystal. They stood between two fires, in a tight circle about our warriors, who had been stripped of their weapons and bound, and as we neared, we heard their laughter.

"A fine catch," one of them laughed, walking forward to a pale-haired warrior, releasing the war leather which held her hair at the base of her neck. She struggled against the leather which kept her wrists behind her, and again the male laughed. "Do not tire yourself so, little lovely," he chided gently. "There will be other things to take what strength you have. I will ask yet again, and this time expect an answer: what do you and these others do here in these woods all alone? From whence do you come and for what purpose?"

My pale-haired warrior held his eyes, yet she spoke not a word in answer. Indeed, I would have been surprised if she had. The high, excited chirp of a lellin told me that the males were surrounded, therefore I stepped farther into the clearing.

"You are mistaken," I said quite clearly, causing the males to whirl toward me in surprise. "They are not alone."

The males reached for the swords they wore, but my warriors stepped from the trees, bows bent and arrows hard upon targets a warrior might not easily miss. The males looked about themselves and saw their deaths clearly in many places. I stood beyond the fires they had lit, my arms folded beneath my life sign, prepared to order them feathered should they refuse to yield. They then looked to the male who had been questioning my warrior. He nodded his head sourly, and all of the males threw down their weapons. Two hands of my warriors put down their bows, went quickly to the males, then took the lengths of leather we had fetched with us for the purpose, and bound them well. My five warriors who had been captured were released, and they joined in examining the prisoners.

"You had an excellent reason for remaining silent," the male who had questioned the light-haired warrior said to her, a rueful expression upon his broad, dark face. "Might I now know the reason for so many lovely girls abroad in these woods?"

My warrior smiled and looked toward me, and the captive looked upon me also. He was dark complexioned yet had light eyes, with dark brows beneath unruly, dark hair. He and the others had shorn their hair to well above their shoulders, showing that they felt shame in its appearance. City males truly have no souls.

"We travel to see Bellinard," I said, smiling at the discomfort the male appeared to be experiencing. "Is it yet far distant?"

"Merely a three-fey ride to the northwest," he said, his eyes beginning to blaze as they inspected me. "We are hunters from there, my lovely, and I would assure you that these woods are not safe. My men and I have been well punished for our laxity in guarding ourselves; now must we be released so that we may see to the safety of all of you. I would not have the beasts rend your bodies while we lie here helpless."

I laughed lightly at his words. He sought to make Hosta fear the forests, thinking us, no doubt, sisters to the slave-women of his city. I raised my eyes from him to note the return of the warriors I had sent to seek the mounts of the males. The leader of them informed me that the Crystal of Mida was not among the goods the males carried, and I was not surprised. The thieves of the Crystal would know well the appearance of Hosta clan colors, and would have little need to question the presence of Hosta in their vicinity. These males were innocent of the theft, and therefore free for the taking.

"Enough of this foolishness, girl!" the male leader snapped. "I know not from whence you come, nor do I care! You have had your amusement at our expense, now you shall release us and return our weapons! At once!"

In the mutter of agreement from the others, his gaze was sharp and strong upon me, his anger doing much to counter his desire for me. The flickering light of the fires illuminated him but partially, but I was able to see his strength. I removed my swordbelt and crouched, then placed my hand upon his covering.

"Is your body truly so ugly that it must be hidden?" I asked softly, stroking my hand down his side to his bare thigh. "Surely your comfort would be greater if this were removed?"

His consternation consumed him so, he did not seem to hear the gentle laughter of my warriors. His eyes widened at the caress, and he moved beneath my hand, then smiled hungrily, and his voice turned husky.

"I had not expected this," he said, his chest rising higher with his breathing. "Free me quickly, girl, and I shall remove the covering the moment we have reached the darkness beyond the fires. You shall be well seen to in the darkness, this I swear!"

"I much prefer the light," I said, "and I should be pleased to remove the covering from you as you are."

He blinked at the dagger in my hand, then rolled about in protest as I brought it to his covering. "No!" he shouted, attempting to free himself from the leather which bound him. "There is no need for this! I have not refused you!"

"Nor shall you," I murmured, applying my dagger to the side of his covering. Easily it split open from neck to waist to thigh, and a sigh of appreciation escaped from my warriors as the covering was moved aside. Amid the silence of the other males, the captive moved in fury, his hard, broad body before us, in no manner ugly. I replaced my dagger in its leg bands, then placed both hands upon him.

"Perhaps you feel a chill in the air of darkness," I murmured, my hands and eyes exploring him with pleasure. "I shall not allow you to remain cold long."

I brought my lips to his firm, flat belly, pressing them there, then moving them about. The male moaned with his arousal, nor was it he alone who moaned. The eyes of the other males were upon us, some raised up as best they might to see better. The smell of a male in need was strong, and the captive, his skin coarse with hair, writhed beneath my hands.

"No," he protested weakly, his head moving back and forth, attempting to deny his need. "Release me and I shall see to you. I swear it!"

"You find no interest in me as you are?" I asked, and then placed my knees across and to either side of him. Slowly I leaned down, sliding a short way onto his thighs, the tips of my breasts brushing his hair-covered chest. "Shall I then choose another of your males to give me pleasure? Which of them should it be?"

"Me!" cried one of the males in a choked voice, moving hard in the leather which bound him. "Come to me, girl! I shall not disappoint you!"

I gazed down upon the captive beneath my hands and thighs, then leaned farther down so that my hair fell across my left shoulder and brushed him. "I see there is one who would be pleased to have me use him," I murmured, exciting myself further in the feel of my breasts against his chest. "I shall go to him, then, and allow you your chill solitude."

I moved against him slowly, then made as if to rise from him. His breath came harder and harder still, his head tossed about, his light eyes blazed with the agony of his need, and surely, had he been free, he would have pulled me to him with fingers like stone.

"No!" he choked out abruptly, his body attempting to rise after me. "Do not go to another!"

"You wish me to remain?" I said, reaching behind my neck as I sat upon him, so that I might free my hair from the war leather holding it close. "You must then ask me nicely."

Deep in his throat he growled in fury, yet his skin burned beneath my own. He held my eyes as his teeth clenched, and his shoulder muscles tightened in desperate attempt to free himself, but he had been bound expertly. I waited a scant moment, then shrugged and again made as if to leave him.

"No!" he gasped yet again, fear of being left unseen to turning him wilder still. "I—wish you to remain with me."

"So that I might use you?" I prompted softly, leaning to him slightly, my hands gentle upon his ribs.

A sound, nearly a sob of desperation, escaped his lips, and his eyes closed to curtain his pain. "So that—you might—use me," he whispered, the words choking him terribly. Part sigh, part moan came from others of the males, and I smiled and moved to the captive's thighs, taking possession of him to feed my own high excitement. Quite hard did he move, attempting to use *me*, yet this I would not allow. He had asked that I use him, and this I did and well. More than once was he drained, and the amusement and encouragement of my warriors sounded out above his grunts of release. When my satisfaction was complete, I rose to my feet and reclaimed my swordbelt, then spoke to Larid, who stood near to me.

"Use the others as far as they will go," I directed as she grinned, "then force upon them the sthuvad drug so that none of our warriors might be excluded. We have three feyd yet before we shall reach Bellinard. Let us put the darkness to use."

My warriors laughed happily at my words, then they turned to the males. Cries of protest came from the males as their coverings were removed, and soon all were busily engaged at the hands of hungry warriors. The pale-haired warrior who had been questioned stood above the captive I had used, staring down upon him with a faint smile evident upon her slender face. The captive looked upset. He would not, I knew, ask to be used again, yet a warrior need not be asked. A Warrior took what she wished, finding no need to be asked.

A strong watch had been posted about the clearing, and I took those warriors who would not soon use the males, and returned to our camp. Word of males to be had spread quickly to those warriors who had been left behind, and there was much bustling and preparation. I gave orders that all kand, ours and those of the prisoners, were also to be brought to the camp when the males were, then cut for myself a good slice of nilno. A taste of daru would have been pleasant, yet was daru ever left behind when the Hosta moved to battle. I made do with water from the skins, smiled at the excitement of my warriors, then took to my sleeping leather. The strong male smell of the captive was still upon me, and I savored it till sleep claimed me.

3.

Bellinard—and encounters
with city ways

The new light brought the tears of Mida to us early, although the sky was clear when we halted for our first meal. The Hosta do not eat upon first arising, for it is not wise to stay overlong at a campsite. Far better to pass one meal each fey, than to pass the balance of one's life. Belly down were the male captives tied across their kand, and little sound came from them. Briefly had I awakened in the darkness when they had been brought to our camp, and then again when the sthuvad drug had been forced upon them. The new light had shown them surly and well used, their coverings hanging as cut, from their bound arms. They snarled when prodded toward their kand, yet the feel of leather striking their backs silenced their snarls. We rode through the dripping forests, my warriors, at least, pleased with the feel of Mida's tears upon their bodies, until we came to the edge. Before us lay gently swelling hills, brightening as the skies touched them with new gold. There, at the edge of the woods, we halted to take our meal, the males being removed from their kand so that they, too, might be fed. They were placed upon the still damp ground, surrounded by warriors, but I had to approach them when they made a disturbance upon being offered food.

Fayan stood in charge of them, an excellent warrior nearly of a size with me. She had heavy golden hair and dark eyes, keen battle delight, and a well-made figure, but little patience had she for males. She frowned at their refusal, then gestured me to her.

"What may be done with these, Jalav?" she asked in annoyance. "If they continue to refuse to feed, they will be of little use even with the sthuvad drug!"

"We do not refuse!" protested the leader of the males in anger. "We are not animals that we may be given uncooked meat! You have seen fit to bind us helplessly; now you may also feed us properly!"

"We give you only what we, ourselves, feed upon," I informed him, taking a strip of the meat from a warrior who held it. I approached the male and crouched near him, took a bite of the meat to chew, then proffered the meat for him to taste of. He frowned at the bloody meat.

"What manner of women are you?" he demanded. "You wear almost no clothing, you treat hunters with contempt, you bear weapons like men, have no fear of the forests, and eat raw and bloody meat! Never before have I seen your like!"

"We are warriors of the Hosta of the Midanna," I informed him, then I tasted of the meat again. "You have never heard tell of the Midanna?"

"But the Midanna are the stuff of fools' tales!" he scoffed, glancing for support at the other males bound near him, who nodded. "They are unreal save in the minds of frightened old men! Many kalod ago, a city to the east fell of its own neglect, and it was then said that it had been taken by Midanna. What foolishness! A city cannot be taken by mere women. . . ."

His discourse broke off at sight of my smile, then he paled somewhat as he glanced about at my warriors. The other males stirred and muttered, yet no distinct words came from them. Their leader returned his gaze to me and looked worried.

"Not Bellinard!" he rasped, his anger in part desperation. "You cannot be thinking of taking Bellinard!"

"We merely mean to visit Bellinard," I assured him, then stood straight once more. "I am pleased to learn that Midanna will not be known there. We shall in that event, have little difficulty in entering its gates." His anger was for himself, then, realizing how much he had told me. It is truly said that one word is but the first of many. "We shall not build fires merely to feed males," I continued. "You may feed as we do, or go hungry. How would you have it?"

In silence he measured me with his eyes, then he smiled very slightly and leaned at ease in his bonds. "If wenches may eat uncooked meat," he said lazily, "hunters may do no less. We have done so before this, and shall undoubtedly do so again. That other, I believe, called you Jalav. Bring the meat to me, Jalav, that I may satisfy my hunger."

His smile lengthened and became grin. I, too, grinned at the jest, for he spoke of a hunger other than of the belly; indeed I, too, had the desire, but unfortunately had not the time.

"Those charged with your care shall see to you, hunter," I said, returning the meat to the warrior from whom I had taken it. "Should you prove to be less troublesome the balance of this fey, I shall perhaps have you brought to me when camp is made."

A flash of anger appeared in his eyes as I turned away, and that pleased me. City males must be taught that we were not slave-women. Fayan grinned and nodded to me, saying without words that the male would be brought to my sleeping leather after dark. I left the area of the captives to take my own meal, sitting upon the grass so that I might watch my warriors at play. Some few of them cast spears at trees, each trying to outthrow the others. A knot of eight tilted at each other from gando-back, coming as close as possible without drawing blood. Should blood be drawn, points would be lost by that warrior clumsy enough to miss her mark. Some warriors played at daggers, others loosened their swordarms, and some lay upon the grass, watching others expend energy. The string of kand were kept well away from our gandod, and seemed a shade less nervous than before. The warriors seeing to them also seemed less annoyed with them, as though a fondness of sorts had grown. Truthfully, should one discount the needs of battle, kand have greater attraction than gandod. Their gentle grace allows a warrior to think when upon them, rather than be ever alert for a turn of temper. Had the needs of Midanna not been with us, the kan would have been a superior mount.

When the meal was done, we continued on our way. Many eyes-ahead did I send off, to be sure that none noted our passage across those clear, open hills. There were dwellings, though few in number, and we had to avoid them. Those in the dwellings tended land and kept herds of small animals. I, myself, saw one of these from a distance, and saw also the male and his slave-woman who dwelt within. It seemed strange that they had left their city for the openness, for all know that the city-bred feel discomfort beneath the naked skies of Mida. I thought briefly about it, then went my way once more, wondering at the age at which understanding may come. It is surely a very great age, one which I had little hope of seeing.

Mida smiled upon her warriors, for a good-sized stand of trees was reached at dusk. We spread among the trees to make our camp. After having seen to my gando, I walked about to inspect guard posts. Despite the presence of males, all was as it should have been, therefore I took my meal in solitude before returning to my sleeping leather. The smell of the forest was pleasant in the darkness, yet the chill air reminded me that we trod foreign ground. Beyond the Dennin river the air was sweet and warm, fit for the lungs of warriors of the Midanna.

"You were long in returning," a voice spoke from near to my sleeping leather. His arms were yet bound behind him, though his ankles had been freed, and a length of leather circled his broad neck, then ran to a tree. He leaned his back against the tree, his mind and body entirely free of the sthuvad drug. I smiled, realizing that Fayan had been impressed with his ability, for had she thought the drug necessary to my pleasure, he would have had it.

"Indeed the duties of a war leader are demanding," I said, removing my sword and seating myself upon my sleeping leather, then reaching for my pipe and sack. "The position is a great responsibility, yet one which I accept gladly. Not all may so serve Mida."

He watched in silence as I struck a spark from my firemaker and lit my pipe. When the pipe had been puffed to life, and the firemaker replaced with the sack, he observed softly, "You are exceedingly strange women. Have you really no fear of the darkness, Jalav? Do you never wish for the safety of a home, and a man to guard it and you?"

My laughter was gentle, not intending to give insult. "Why must males always ask the same of us?" I inquired, seeing his shadowy face before the tree. "Can you conceive only of slave-women, unable to live without a male to serve? The Midanna serve only Mida, glorying in her service till we are called to her side. Such are our ways, and such they will ever be."

"I had thought the Midanna a myth," he said, sliding with difficulty away from the tree and closer to my sleeping leather. "From what I have seen, the stories told are pale and feeble in comparison with the reality. The girls who saw to our feeding and other needs spoke highly of Jalav, who is war leader. They obey Jalav without question. Tell them to unbind my men, Jalav, and to cease feeding them that brew of Sigurr's devising. I shall stand hostage for their continued presence and lack of disturbance."

He sat close beside me, almost to the end of the leather about his neck, and as I puffed upon my pipe, his lips gently touched my shoulder. I felt his warm breath, too, upon my shoulder, and I smiled into the darkness.

"The warriors of the Hosta obey me without question," I said, "for I shall never be so foolish as to endanger them. Our camp has no need of males who are free to bedevil us."

"They shall not interfere with your purpose," he murmured in my ear, then kissed my neck. "I would have my arms about you, Jalav, and draw you to my lap and warmth. Order my men released, so that we may touch without thought of other things. Quickly, war leader, I cannot long contain my desire."

"Mida teaches patience to her hunters, hunter," I said, puffing the last of my pipe. "Your desire need not be long contained, and I shall give little thought to your males. My attention shall be solely for you."

"You will not have them released?" he asked, and a coldness had entered his tone as he moved farther from me. "My word on the matter means nothing to you?"

"Here, only the word of the war leader prevails." I shrugged, and then emptied my pipe upon the ground. When the ashes were well doused, the pipe was returned to its place with the sack and fire-maker.

The male sat straight in his bonds, in angry silence. When I turned from replacing my pipe, he said, "It would be pleasant, Jalav, to see *you* bound before *me*. Perhaps it may sometime come to pass."

I heard his cold words, and nodded my head. "All things are possible, should they be Mida's will," I said, then stretched out flat upon my sleeping leather. "I find that I am

weary, and have little stomach for warming the cold from a
stone. You may sleep unmolested."

I turned upon my side on my leather, presenting my back
to him, angered that his much-spoken-of desire had been for
the release of his males, rather than for me. Males must ever
be devious, wanting one thing as they ask for another. Even
Fideran, who had been so anxious to please me, had at first
attempted to involve himself in matters which only Hosta
might concern themselves with, and had used his presence in
my sleeping leather to indulge his curiosity until I told him
that another question from him would result in his being
beaten. I do not care to be questioned, nor do I care to be
used.

The male sat where he had been silently, but the darkness
was filled with sound and not from the children of the wild.
My warriors had divided the other males among them, and I
heard the small noises of their pleasure. My blood burned
from the touches of the male behind me, and the sounds did
not cool the burning. However, I would ache rather than
touch the male in return. I was war leader, not to be manipu-
lated by males.

In but a few reckid, I heard from behind me, "Jalav, do
you sleep?" I made as if I had not heard the soft words, and
did not stir. Then, slightly louder, came, "Jalav, I had not
thought I was brought here to sleep unmolested. Do you not
know that captives must be much used by their captors? It is
tradition." Again I did not stir, though a smile came unbidden to my lips. I heard a sound, as though a body slid upon
the dirt, then the male cursed softly. "This Sigurr's strand
about my neck will not let me reach you!" he said angrily.
Then his lower body and legs touched me, for although his
head must stay at the end of the leather, he was able to move
the rest of him. "Jalav," he murmured, rubbing his coarse leg
along my smoother skin, "should I be left unmolested, I shall
inform everyone at large that the Midanna do not know the
ways of holding captives. Do you wish the Midanna laughed
at through your lack of doing?"

The feel of his skin upon me was more than I could bear.
Abruptly, I sat, removed my dagger from its leg bands,
buried its point in the dirt far out of the male's possible
reach, and then turned back to him. The touch of my belly
upon his filled him with fire, and his lips reached up for mine
as his legs thrashed wildly about. I took him and used him,

crushing my breasts to his chest, grasping his flesh with demanding fingers. Well used was he by this Midanna, and his own pleasure was no small thing. He panted and gasped, urging me on, yet there was no need for urging. Once, deep in his pleasure, he cried out, "By Sigurr's fetid breath, I must have my arms free about her! I *shall* have my arms about her!" Then he struggled to free himself, to no avail. When my every need had been satisfied, I returned to my sleeping leather and grasped my dagger in preparation for sleep. The male said nothing, but his leg was near mine as the clouds of sleep covered me.

At last we stood within sight of Bellinard, our host behind the swell of a hill, seeing yet unseen. The massive gates of Bellinard stood opened, and many were those who streamed within its walls. Most came on foot, carrying small bundles; some upon kand, as well as perched atop strange, wheeled contrivances which were drawn by kand. There were many kinds of wheeled things, some roofed over, some not, and all were allowed within the gates of Bellinard. Those gates remained opened throughout the presence of Mida's light, but were closed fast when darkness descended. We had watched Bellinard a full fey, and now were prepared to enter.

I went to where our kand were held, along with the captives. We had come upon some caves when yet a number of hind from Bellinard, and there would the balance of my warriors remain with the captives till I and the others returned. My gando danced uneasily, having disliked the sight of Bellinard, and I was glad that I had no need of taking it within those walls. I, too, had disliked my first view of a city, and had no wish to add to any difficulties which might arise.

As I passed the captives, I saw that the eyes of the leader of the males were upon me. He looked angry, for I had not again had him brought to my sleeping leather, leaving him instead for the use of my warriors. I had used another of the males who had thereafter been puffed up with importance, almost battling his leader, but my warriors did not wish to see them damage themselves. They had been parted and separated. I did not concern myself with such small matters, and did not heed the leader's request that he be allowed to speak with me. I simply used the second, and left the first for my warriors.

Now, as I passed him, he struggled to his feet and called,

"Jalav, you must take me with you to Bellinard! You do not know the ways of a city, and must be advised! Jalav, heed my words!"

My warriors shoved him back to the ground, for I had no wish to hear him. I did not trust him. He had but to send a superior force against us, hoping to surprise us before we might end his captured band. He would not succeed, yet he would try. I would be fool indeed were I to allow him his freedom.

Beside the kand waited those warriors who would accompany me. Red-haired, blue-eyed Larid, an excellent warrior and often my second, was amused by the male's outburst. She grinned in his direction, as did brown-haired, brown-eyed Binat, who also found amusement with males. Fayan, however, frowned at his actions, thinking, no doubt, that a taste of the punishment leather would do well for him. Annoyance filled her large, brown eyes and it was well for the males that she rode with me.

The last of our party was Comir, a warrior barely into her womanhood, but avid to join us. Her soft brown hair was like Kilin's. She had been with me at the Crystal's Tower, and had seen what had been done to my warriors. Her need for vengeance was like mine, for one of the warriors who had been slain was close sister to her, as the same warrior had borne them both. Angrily had she demanded the right to ride with me, and I had seen her need and had allowed it. She stood now holding the leads of the kand, smiling slightly toward the males.

As I slid from the back of my gando, black-haired Gimin approached and stopped before me. Gimin had hopes of becoming war leader in her turn, although she had not as yet seen fit to challenge me. If a thing is to be done, it should not be left too long undone, and sooner would I have her challenge than leave her desires to fester within her. I had named her leader in my absence, thinking a taste of leadership would sway her one way or the other. When I returned, I would know how sound my thinking had been.

"It is time to depart, Gimin," I said, handing her the lead of my gando. "We shall see what we may see, and return as soon as possible. Should a hand of feyd pass without our return, you are then to continue on to Ranistard and enter it as I have described. Allow no warrior to follow us to Ballinard, for you shall need every sword when you reach Ranistard. The Crystal must be recovered."

"I hear, Jalav," she said, her gray eyes searching my face. "You think to give me your place without my having to do battle for it, yet this may not be. A war leader who has not earned her position has little to find pride in. Upon your return, the matter will be settled between us."

"As you say, Gimin," I smiled, and placed my hand upon her shoulder. "When I return, the matter will be determined. May Mida guard you in this strange land."

"And you, Jalav," she said, smiling in return and also placing her hand upon my shoulder. "Be alert, war leader, for it is impossible to challenge one who sits beside Mida."

"Should there be a way, Gimin," I laughed, "I don't doubt that you will find it. Take the others to the caves as soon as we have gone."

She nodded her agreement, then watched as I joined the others at the kand. I jumped upon the back of the kan I had chosen, and my four warriors, too, were mounted quickly. We raised our hands in farewell, and my warriors who remained drew their blades to salute us. We rode off then, urging the kand to a decent speed, and thought no more about our sisters.

As we carried neither spear nor shield, the kand had little difficulty bearing us toward the gates of Bellinard. The kan I had chosen was a light gray in color, sleekly muscled beneath its soft hide, prideful of its long mane and tail. It, being male, was larger than the other kand, and the farther it went from the presence of gandod, the more it attempted to pull from my hand. As its head went forward for the third time, I wound my free hand in its mane, then hauled back sharply as my knees jabbed tightly in its sides. A sound of surprised pain came from the beast, and thereafter it made no further attempts to set a pace of its own. When one has ridden gandod, kand pose no insurmountable difficulties.

In less than a hin, we were nearly to the gates of Bellinard. With the strengthening of the light, more and more city folk had joined the throng at the gates, till they stretched well away from their destination. We slowed our kand as we passed them, and each of those we passed looked upon us strangely. There were many males, and many slave-women as well, and some attempted to speak, yet all, in the end, kept silent. Larid and Binat examined many of the males, grins

wide upon their faces, although few seriously attracted them.
The males were small for the most part, work-wearied and
lacking in vigor, and a warrior may find little pleasure from
such a male. Their slave-women seemed soured by their lot in
life, and not a smile showed upon any of their faces. Truthfully, it is not difficult to understand such a souring. Even
slave-women should be allowed a male possessing vigor.

As we rode up to the wide-standing gates, we saw the reason for the delay, which had not been apparent from a distance. Armed males stood at the gates, searching the
belongings of those who would enter. To the right, a male
afoot and his slave-woman waited as their bundle was gone
through, and to the left was a large, covered, wheeled conveyance searched by three of the armed males. I guided my
kan to the space between these two sets, and as I made to
enter the gates, one of the armed males quickly moved to
take hold of the guiding leather of my kan and stopped it.

"Hold!" he cried, his broad face creased with a wide smile
as he inspected me. "Bellinard may not be entered even by
one as tempting as you, girl, save she be given permission by
gate guards. Perhaps you seek to smuggle items past us, eh?"

"How would she smuggle, Dominar?" laughed another,
coming toward the first. "She and her kan are almost equally
bare!"

The other armed males joined in the laughter, and all approached my warriors and me. These males wore the same
short covering of all city males, topped with a contrivance of
leather and metal, designed, I fancied, to protect from arrow
and sword thrust. The metal was reinforced at those points
where a warrior's sword would be most likely to concentrate.
The leather and metal rose high to guard the males' throats
as well, leaving their heads entirely bare. What sense was
there, I wondered, in guarding throat and body, when the
head is left completely unprotected?

"Do not scold the girl for her manner of dress," laughed
the one called Dominar. "Should the decision be left to me, I
would see all females dressed so. And perhaps she smuggles
beneath that strip of cloth at her hips. I feel it my duty to investigate the place personally."

Amid guffaws from the others, the male left the head of
my kan and approached me more closely, his hand outstretched to touch my clan covering. I waited till he was well
within range, then quickly raised my leg and kicked him in

his unprotected face. The blow sent him flying backward, his arms swinging wildly in a vain attempt to remain upright. He sprawled in the dirt upon his back, the breath knocked from his body, and the remaining armed males laughed as though they would burst. I found little amusement in such foolishness, and could not understand the glee of the others.

"We wish to enter the city of Bellinard," I announced above the raucous laughter. "Must we do battle first?"

Another of the armed males, controlling, somewhat, his mirth, approached me and stopped with his fists upon his hips, a clear distance from the swing of my leg. He, too, inspected me briefly, then turned to my warriors.

"Do any of you carry anything to be declared to the High Seat of Bellinard, so that the High Seat may subtract his rightful proportion?" he asked. I had not the faintest idea what he meant; I only knew we carried nothing of concern to any in Bellinard.

"We have nothing of interest to you," I answered "and would now be on our way."

"That, pretty child, is a lie." He laughed. "But not a lie for which you might be detained. You have much we would find interesting, but you may, in spite of that, enter. Perhaps we shall meet again when I am no longer on duty."

His gaze was hot, and he was not unattractive, but I had important matters to attend to. I therefore took no note of him and kicked my kan into motion, guiding it past the male who was only now regaining his feet. My warriors and I rode past them all, farther into the city of Bellinard.

I had much difficulty at first in comprehending what I saw. Never before had I been in the midst of so many hurrying males and slave-women. The ways of Bellinard were broader than the road to Islat, but were clogged with bodies both human and animal, all seemingly going in every direction. I stared with dismay upon the confused motion, and my warriors, too, seemed struck by the masses, as we gazed about in disbelief.

I soon felt a terrible sense of imprisonment and wanted to turn back to the land of the Hosta. The dwellings to either side of the ways were not as lofty as trees of the forest, but they stood one close upon another, to hover massively and threateningly above our heads. Strips of cloth hung from some of the windows in these dwellings, and many of them were open in the lower part of their fronts, with broad steps

leading to their interiors. Males and slave-women came and
went from these dwellings, for what purpose only Mida
would know. I swallowed down the fear a war leader should
never feel, and slowly led my warriors to the flow of the
throng.

We rode along, going we knew not where, no pleasure in
our hearts. The noise which surrounded us was deafening,
and even the sound of my kan's hooves upon the stones of
the way was inaudible. Lengths of wood had been placed
above the entrances of many of the dwellings, and strange
slashes appeared upon them. Some also possessed drawings,
somewhat like the carving of a life sign, yet even the
drawings made little sense to me. For what conceivable purpose would one mark her dwelling with the drawing of a
male beside a kan, or a slave-woman holding a tall, thin pot
filled with liquid, or even a heavy, horned beast beside a
small, feathered one? In the midst of these things I felt weakened, and was sickened by the numerous smells that assaulted
me, so mingled that I could not tell one from the other. A
glance at my warriors showed that they, too, were pale with
the attack upon their senses. Much, indeed, would I have
given for a single breath of pure, forest air, or even for the
scent I had disliked in the dwelling of Maranu. There was no
hope for that, though, and we merely rode on, miserable in
our duty.

Those about us stared at us without recognition. We were
unknown to the city folk of Bellinard, and I had some difficulty deciding whether that was just as well. Granted, we
were not called upon to bloody our swords and thereby bring
unwelcome attention, but it was necessary to kick and cuff
many males from us, as though they thought us something we
were not. Many, too, were the slave-women who looked as if
they thought us responsible for their state of slavehood. I understood almost nothing of what I saw, heard and smelled,
nor was I anxious to extend my investigations to touch and
taste. A city is a vile place; I would have been much happier
to have learned nothing of it.

The crowds seemed to be going in all directions but were
in reality moving only in one major direction. This I discovered when we were at last carried toward a wide, open space,
surrounded by small, tentlike dwellings in many colors, where
grass and a tree or two might be seen. My heart leapt, and I
urged my kan toward the place, brushing past male and fe-

male alike in my haste. My warriors came behind me, and we were able to leave the crush of bodies as soon as we passed the line of small tents. I rode to a thin, scraggly tree, then dismounted to draw a breath of almost fresh air. My warriors also dismounted, and we stood and looked at one another.

"Jalav, I shall not fail you," said Fayan weakly, a much wilted look to her. "I ask but a moment before we must reenter that Mida-forsaken city."

The others nodded their agreement, only I saw what they did not see. "We have not left the city," I said. "Look you there, beyond that unbelievable dwelling in the distance, past these open fields. Is that not the wall of the city, proving that we are yet within?"

They turned to where I had pointed, and the slump of their shoulders confirmed my statement. We had not, as they had thought, left the city, but were still well within its bounds.

"Is that truly a dwelling?" asked Larid, raising her hand to shade her eyes as she peered into the distance. "Never had I thought so large a thing might be!"

"How may one know?" I asked in turn, also studying the vast structure. It contained many windows, a wide, easily seen entrance above loftily piled steps, and it appeared that armed males stood before the entrance. I could conceive of no rationale for so large a dwelling, yet how may a warrior know the thinking of those of the cities?

We tied our kand to the tree, then sat upon the grass in an attempt to restore ourselves. Many were the city folk who entered the open area, some moving toward one or another of the differently colored tents, some adding their own tents to the ring already begun. Those who moved about the tents often emerged from them with items in their hands, pelts, and cloth, and food, and tall, thin, strangely made pots. One slave-woman emerged with a male, both laughing gaily. They paused to examine her bright armlet, then the woman took the male's arm and walked off with him. Had the woman won an honor of sorts, that the male looked so proudly upon her?

Those who did not pause at the tents made their way to areas bounded by leather strung between wooden posts. Many stood before each of these areas, and therefore it was difficult to make out what went on beyond the leather. Males were in the areas, yet the backs of other males and their slave-women hid what was done there. Curiosity moved me to my feet again, and I summoned my warriors.

"Comir, you are to remain here with the kand," I said, "Binat shall remain with you, while Larid and Fayan accompany me. We should not be long."

Fayan and Larid rose to their feet with smiles as Comir and Binat nodded unhappily. "We hear, Jalav," said Comir, her green eyes clear, "yet next it shall be my place and Binat's to accompany you."

"Perhaps," I said and smiled at her. "All shall be known in Mida's time."

Larid, Fayan, and I left them then, and made our way toward the closest of the areas surrounded by onlookers. Soon our path was crossed by a small male, thin and poorly muscled. His short cropped hair seemed never to have been washed nor combed, and badly soiled and stained was his covering. He rocked upon his feet, as though attempting to stand in the midst of an earth tremor, and gazed upon each of my warriors and myself with large, rounded eyes. He then drew himself up to his full height, then bowed low before us.

"Ladies," said he in a slurred and shaky voice, "I would offer my personal welcome to Bellinard's fair, and ask that you show me the location of your pavilion. I shall patronize it most gladly, foregoing even the taste of another brew for such delights as yourselves." Again he peered at us, expelled air noisily, then pointed with an unsteady finger. "I trust that those blades are not worn in the presence of customers? They would be somewhat constricting, I fear."

Larid, Fayan and I exchanged glances, but the male's words meant nothing to any of us. Larid grinned.

"He is taken with daru sickness," she said. "His words have no meaning for us. It is not worth considering."

Fayan and I agreed with this, and she brushed the male from our path as we continued on. The male sputtered and screeched behind us, but we paid him no notice.

We reached the throng about the area we intended to see, and made our way forward to the leather boundary. Those who stood before us we moved to the side, and many turned angrily, intending, perhaps, to protest, yet their protests were quickly swallowed at sight of us, for few even wore daggers, not to speak of swords. These city males were poor indeed, yet their slave-women clung to them, as though we intended such women harm. Where is the warrior, I wonder, who would have the stomach to harm so low a creature as a slave-woman?

The open space of the area, we saw at last, contained males of a different sort. Large and well-made, some even had hair of a decent length. They wore the coverings of all city males, although they held spears within their grasp, and stood about in groups of two and three, relaxed and speaking with each other, and gazing toward those who stood at a place marked in the grass by a wide length of bright cloth. Those at the cloth aimed their spears for a target board in easy distance from the cloth, and all did indeed reach the board, yet some of the casts were so poor, that had the board been a living enemy, surely it would have remained a living enemy. My warriors laughed at these attempts, and I, too, smiled at the clumsiness; none of the males within the area shared our amusement. One turned at the sound of our laughter, frowned toward us, and then approached. He was as large as the others, with shorn hair of a reddish tinge, and he carried his spear.

"What do you girls do here, laughing at warriors and hunters?" he demanded quite angrily, glaring from one to the other of us. "Have you never been taught proper behavior? You have obviously not been taught manner of dress."

"What else is one to do in the presence of lack of ability?" I asked rather mildly, wondering at his anger. "Is the one lacking ability to be encouraged falsely, and thereby sent to a quick and useless death? One may cast badly at a board in safety, but not at the hadat, lenga, or falth."

"You speak as though you have some knowledge of such," the male mused as he leaned upon the shaft of his spear, all anger gone out of him. "Are your men hunters that you know these things so well?"

"*We* are the hunters!" returned Fayan with heat. "Males are only good for the sleeping leather!"

"Indeed," murmured the male, looking upon Fayan with annoyance. "Perhaps, then, you three—hunters—would care to enter our competition? The prize for first throw is a well-filled purse—and first throw is thus far mine."

My warriors looked toward me, and the male regarded me as well. That they played at spear casting was clear, yet I didn't know the meaning of a "well-filled purse." I considered the matter briefly and then I shrugged.

"There is no reason for refusal," I said, at which Larid and

Fayan grinned, "but we have not brought our spears with us."

"Spears will be provided," the male answered in satisfaction, then he stepped to one side. "Enter the field now, and I shall see to the arrangements."

Fayan, Larid and I stepped over the strung leather, and followed the male to the line of cloth. Those others standing about with spears followed as well, and soon we were before three males, of greater age than the others. All short-haired were these males, and they looked at my warriors and me with distaste.

"What foolishness is this, Nidisar?" one of the males demanded. "For what reason do you bring pavilion-shes to our field?"

"They are not pavilion-shes, Arbitrator," the male addressed as Nidisar replied with a laugh. "These are mighty hunters you see before you, and they think little of our ability. I have therefore invited their participation in our competition, and they have graciously agreed to grant us an exhibition of their skill."

"Many here are in need of such exhibition," Fayan commented, looking about her. "To see the thing done properly precedes one's doing it so oneself."

The male who had been called Arbitrator had been about to speak in further anger, but he halted upon hearing Fayan's words. He gazed at Fayan thoughtfully as the other males muttered behind and about us, then he nodded his head.

"Very well," he said. "The competition is open to all hunters and warriors. They shall be allowed their throws. Nidisar, accompany them to the line."

He called Nidisar, who was well pleased, waved a hand toward the cloth and then walked there. My warriors and I followed, stopping, as did he, just before the cloth. Many stood about us with spears, and all those many smiled as well. A short distance before us was the target board, to which Nidisar pointed.

"See you there, upon the target," said he, indicating the board which was much marked by the points of spears. "Do you see the stroke of black at the center of the ring? The stroke indicates my throw, which none have as yet equaled or bettered. You must throw toward that stroke, and attempt to approach it."

We glanced at the stroke and nodded, and then were

handed spears. The length of the spear, just short of three paces, was like those of the Midanna, yet the shaft was slightly thinner. It gave the spear a pleasant lightness as I weighed it in my hand, feeling for its balance, and Larid and Fayan too were pleased.

"Should the line be crossed in your throw, you will be disqualified," said Nidisar, indicating the cloth. "Which of you will throw first?"

"Laird shall cast first," I said, "and then Fayan. My turn will be last."

"As you wish." Nidisar grinned, then stepped farther to the side. "It will at least be pleasant watching each of you throw. You may proceed.

Under his eyes and those of the other males, Larid stepped back from the cloth. She smiled slightly as she glanced again at the board, brought her arm back, ran three small, quick steps, then threw. Straight to the board the spear flew, but she had misjudged her aim. It struck, not upon the stroke, but just above it and a shade to the left. A babble of noise broke from the watching males, and Larid reddened with shame for so poor a cast. Nidisar stared at the spear where it hung quivering in the board, none of the amusement he must have felt showing upon his face, and Fayan tightened her grip upon the spear she held.

"The turn is now mine," said Fayan stiffly, also stepping back from the cloth. "One must remember the lesser weight of the shaft."

She, too, ran briefly toward the cloth and threw, yet her cast, too, was off the mark, though by very little. Her spear stood out from the board a scant two fingers from the stroke. Again the watching males commented noisily, and Nidisar turned from the board to look at Larid and Fayan with unwarranted disbelief. My warriors already felt shame for their casts, and didn't need to be further shamed.

Slowly I walked from the line with my own spear, calling upon Mida to guide my arm. All was silence about me, from the watching throng as well as from the males close by. Clearly I saw the stroke, felt its place within my mind, ran three short steps, then threw. The spear flew straight and true, and the stroke could be seen cleanly divided in twain. My warriors smiled with pleasure and raised their voices in appreciation—unheard above the roar that came from the throats of those about us. Nidisar laughed as though there were cause for amusement, and the Arbitrator approached me with a smile.

"Truly may you shes claim the name of hunter," said he, in plain approval. "You, girl," said he to me. "How are you called?"

"I am Jalav," I said, refraining from naming my clan of the Midanna. These males had no need of such knowledge.

"Well, then, young Jalav," he said, "it is my pleasure to inform you that your throw has equaled that of Nidisar. When each competitor has completed his throw, you and Nidisar and any other who also equals you, shall throw again for the purse. I ask you now to stand aside so that the throws may be completed."

His arm gestured toward where Nidisar stood. Nidisar grinned as we approached him, and he bowed with exaggerated deference.

"My apologies, hunters," said Nidisar with amusement. "I had thought that you spoke with as little truth as you threw, yet I have been proven wrong. Do you dwell distant from Bellinard?"

"Distant indeed," said I, turning to watch the throws of those at the cloth. "We have never before entered the gates of Bellinard."

"Then you must allow me to show you my city," he said. "I shall be adequately funded to do so when I have won the purse."

I turned my head to study him, and it was as I had expected. He spoke with complete assurance, as though first throw were his alone. I was annoyed that he took what would be my throw as his own.

Not many more were there to throw, yet those who did gave to Larid and Fayan a lessening of shame. No closer than a male's hand did any come to our marks, and most fared poorer still. I had thought about returning to Binat and Comir. However by remaining we attracted less attention than would have come to us through refusal. Once, I turned to look at those who stood beyond the stretched leather, and was surprised at their number. Had I known what a simple throw would bring, I would not have entered the match.

At last, there were none left to try their arms, and Nidisar and I were called again to the cloth. A new board had been placed where the old had stood, and the Arbitrator came and stood before us, his arms folded across his chest.

"The final throws are yours," he said, looking to Nidisar and myself. "You are each to throw at your own stroke, and the purse shall go to that one coming closest to the mark. You may begin."

Nidisar gestured toward the board. "You may throw first," said he, a grin large upon his very male face. "I shall merely enjoy the sight as I await my turn."

He gazed upon me in amusement as he leaned upon his spear. Fayan, who stood to one side with Larid, was angered by his appraisal of me, and angered, too, by the light laughter of those males who stood close enough to have heard Nidisar's words. I was annoyed as well, yet did I put my annoyance from me, for I saw the reasoning behind Nidisar's actions. He sought to brew anger within me, so that my arm would throw far of the mark, but I was not to be gulled in such a manner. I took the spear which had been handed me, walked from the cloth, turned, ran, and threw. A great cheer arose then, for my spear had reached the stroke precisely.

I turned again to Nidisar. "The throw is now yours," I said, showing as much amusement as had he. "The stroke is there before you, and may, as you have seen, be easily reached. I suggest you stand a bit more to your right."

Nidisar frowned at my words, then moved to his right. He did so in anger, amid the laughter of the males, all believing that he obeyed my word, while in truth, moving so had been unavoidable. Fayan and Larid laughed as well, which angered him further, yet had he control of his anger. He stalked from the cloth, turned, ran, and cast, and his spear, too, hung aquiver from the center of the stroke.

The watchers roared, their feet stamping out their approval, their voices raised high in acclaim. Nidisar turned from the board to grin at me, no trace of anger remaining.

"In truth, the stroke is indeed easily reached," said he above the clamor. "Shall we cease attempts to befuddle one another, and merely give our attention to the target?"

I smiled at his attempt at reconciliation, and then nodded. "It would, perhaps, be best," I said. "It would not do for either of us to take the place of the stroke."

He then laughed at my words, nodding, too, in amused agreement. Friendly play sometimes turns to blood feud, and Bellinard was not the place for that. I had not come there with intentions of spilling blood.

The spears were returned to us by other males, and again,

in turn, did we cast. We each cast three times further, the board being removed to a greater distance each time, yet each time was the stroke struck squarely. The watchers had grown silent again, and a communal sigh arose each time the mark was reached. When Nidisar had, for the fourth time, matched my throw, the male Arbitrator stepped before us and held his hands up, signaling a halt to the play.

"I see that this might conceivably be continued through the darkness without other result," he said, and he took a small sack of leather from another of the older males who had done no more than watch others throw. "We, the arbitrators of this competition, have therefore decided that the purse is to be divided between Nidisar and Jalav, share and share alike. You are both mighty wielders of the spear, and we salute you!"

The watching masses cheered at this final word, and Nidisar turned to me. "I am minded to accept the decision," said he, speaking so that none other would hear. "We are well matched, Jalav, and further contest would in truth be futile. How say you?"

"It is but play," I said with a shrug, wishing an end to the matter. "There is little need for continuation."

"Well spoken." He nodded, and grinned at me. "I shall tell them." He turned again to the three elder males. "Jalav and I have agreed to abide by the decision without recourse to higher review," he said. "She and I shall share first throw."

The three elder males smiled to the accompaniment of further cheering, then the Arbitrator brought the small leather sack to me. "The coins are of an even amount," he said, weighing the sack in his palm. "Do you wish them divided here?"

I did not understand his words, and was about to ask his meaning, when Nidisar stepped closer and took the sack. "Jalav and I shall see to the division," he said, grinning. "I have promised to show her and the others our city, and shall begin with the fair. I bid you a good day, Arbitrator."

Nidisar then took my arm and hurried me to where Larid and Fayan waited. When we reached my warriors, I found Larid pleased by the outcome, but not so Fayan. She scowled about her, then faced Nidisar.

"You males always cease before a thing is clearly done," she said, folding her arms below her life sign. "Had you continued, Jalav would have surely prevailed."

Nidisar looked annoyed. "'You would do well to recall, girl," he said, "that it was Jalav's throw, and not your own, which equaled mine. See to your tone when you speak to me, else I shall take great pleasure in teaching you that I am a male who need not cease even when a thing *is* done!"

Fayan growled low and put hand to sword, but that was no place to avenge injured pride. "Fayan!" I said sharply. "He is unarmed, and only a male! Would you take his words as those from a warrior?"

"I do not care for his manner," Fayan said coldly, but took her hand from her sword. "Let us return to the others, Jalav, and see what we may see as quickly as possible. I would be gone from this place as soon as may be."

"We shall indeed see what there is," I said. "Nidisar here has said that he will show us about his city. Thus may we know where we go."

Fayan did not argue with my decision. She stayed well away from Nidisar as we made our way toward Binat and Comir, and Larid was well amused by the heated glances exchanged between warrior and male. I, too, felt amused, although I hoped that Fayan's sword would remain sheathed. I had come to be slightly fond of the male, and did not wish to see him slain.

Binat and Comir listened with interest as Larid related the happenings. After having inspected these other warriors of mine, Nidisar turned to our kand and gestured me closer.

"This is truly a fine beast," he said, stroking the kan's side. "Do your people breed these in your homeland?"

"We merely traded for these," I informed him, seeing that the light had already passed its highest point. "The time passes swiftly, and we have seen little. I would have you show us the city now."

"Ah, but first you must see the fair," said he, giving to the kan a final, appreciative slap. "And first at the fair must we see a pavilion which provides food. The competition has left a void in me, which this purse may help to fill."

He patted the sack of leather which he had hung from his belt, and still his meaning escaped me. Perhaps the sack contained that which might be traded for food and drink. A great desire had I to ask of it, yet I thought that might be unwise, and therefore I merely shrugged.

"I, too, would enjoy a meal," I said. "I shall fetch the others."

I gathered my warriors, and we, leading our kand, followed Nidisar across the sickly, yellowish grass to the ring of brightly colored tents. Males and their slave-women continued to move about in and around them in great numbers, and some of these males paused to speak words of praise to Nidisar and myself. Nidisar accepted all praise as though it were due him, and led the way, after many halts, to a tent striped in many shades of red. The front of the tent was open and in its interior we could see long platforms of the sort Maranu had had, yet these platforms stood upon legs rather than upon the ground, and beside them, one to each side, stood another shorter, narrower platform upon which certain of the males and slave-women sat. To the right stood truly large pots, stirred by slave-women, and through a small opening in the tent beyond the pots, we could see a large fire, over which roasted an entire nilno. The nilno was tended by a young male, and a short, older male of rounded proportions stood near to the pots in the tent, speaking with other males, and accepting from them something he placed in a large, leather sack at his waist. I did not know what the stirred pots contained, but did not like the odor, and a glance at my warriors showed that they, too, disliked the aroma and the appearance of the tent.

"You may tie your kand there," said Nidisar, indicating a log which lay before the tent. Then he led the way directly into the tent and toward the pots. The rounded male turned from others, and gave to Nidisar a wide smile.

"May I serve you, master?" said he with a sweep of his arm. "Sednet soup, perhaps, or a steaming bowl of lellin stew?"

"One of each, proprietor," responded Nidisar jovially, "and a flagon of renth as well, to wet my throat." Then Nidisar turned to me with a grin. "And what would you have, Jalav? If you wish, you may also feed those others lightly from your share of the purse."

"I shall have no more than a bit of yonder nilno," I said, knowing my nose wrinkled from the odors arising from the pots. "My warriors, too, will have the nilno."

The rounded male of the pots frowned as he inspected me, and drew himself the straighter. "The nilno has not yet been completely roasted," he said in stiff anger. "Should the female so dislike my other offerings, master, she and her trollops may simply go hungry!"

"What means 'trollops'?" I demanded, disliking his tone, his manner, and his "offerings." My hand did not touch my sword, yet was it not far away.

"Females!" Nidisar interposed hastily, a hand upon my arm. "It merely means females, Jalav! As the nilno is not yet done, allow me to recommend the lellin stew. Its manner of preparation here is quite tasty."

"I shall have none of it," I said, my eyes hard upon the rounded male. "You may cut for us a hand of portions of the nilno, male, else *we* shall cut whatever pleases us."

Abruptly, Fayan stood beside me, her dagger in her hand. The short, rounded male paled.

"I—I ask your pardon," said this frightened male. "I would gladly serve the ladies nilno, but it has been upon the fire for less than a hin! It won't be fit to eat for some time!"

"Bring the portions," I directed, annoyed. "We have little time to be wasted here."

The male then scurried quickly toward the opening beyond which lay the nilno. One of the slave-women, fear upon her face, gave to Nidisar two wooden pots of whatever the larger pots contained. Nidisar accepted the pots with a pleasant smile, then stepped the closer to me.

"You must not treat people so, Jalav," he hissed. "It is scandalous for a woman to act so, and we do not wish to have the Guard called down upon us! Curb your temper, girl, else you shall be shown only the dungeons of the High Seat!"

"A warrior may not be spoken to in such a manner," I said, also annoyed. "Yonder cringing male had best learn manners, as it seems it is not his wish to don sword."

Nidisar made a sound of vexation, as the rounded male returned with a small square of wood which was piled high with nilno. This square of wood he nervously handed to me, then turned to Nidisar. Nidisar put his fingers in the small sack at his waist, bringing forth a flat, five-sided, silverish piece of metal. This the rounded male took without comment, placing it within his own sack, and returning to Nidisar several other pieces of metal, also the same shape, yet of a reddish tint. Nidisar put these in the sack in place of the one he had given to the rounded male, and I knew I had been mistaken in my original suppositions. The sack did not contain something to be traded for items one wished, for who would take metal of that sort for items of worth? And not a word of bargaining had been spoken between them. No, the exchange of metal had other meaning that I did not understand.

"Let us sit and eat," said Nidisar, taking up once more the pot he had placed upon the platform. "I believe that board in the farther corner would serve us best."

With a movement of his head he indicated the place, and led us there. Again I followed, bearing the nilno. Nidisar approached a platform which stood close to the cloth side of the tent, and placed upon the platform the pots he had been given. The platform stood well away from others which were in use, and seemed to please Nidisar. He perched himself upon the shorter and narrower of the platforms, then began feeding with a' smooth bit of wood which was widened and carved a bit at one end.

I disliked the look of the platforms and did not care to attempt their use, therefore I took my nilno, still bloody and nearly raw, and passed the rest to my warriors. Then they followed me to crouch down by the tent side, the cloth at our backs. Nidisar paused in his feeding, his eyes wide and disbelieving, shook his head, as though unclear upon some matter, then returned to his provender.

When the nilno was gone, Binat fetched a water skin which had been tied to her kan, and we all drank from it, while Nidisar stood and drank from his pot till it was emptied. Then he approached us with good humor well restored.

"An excellent meal," said he in satisfaction, patting his hard, flat middle. "A shame you did not see fit to partake of it. How much of the nilno was edible?"

"All of it," I said in surprise. "Did you think otherwise?"

His grin disappeared, and again he stared in disbelief. "But the nilno was raw!" he insisted with a small headshake. "I, myself, saw that! What manner of women are you, that you may eat nilno raw?"

"Hungry women," I said with a smile of amusement. Males must ever have their provender well cooked, else it seems not natural to them. "We would now see what there is to be seen of your city."

Nidisar frowned. "Your manner is that of one used to command, Jalav," he said, and then he folded his arms across his chest. "I do not care to be commanded by a wench, not even though she be one who throws a spear with a man's skill, and eats her nilno as it stands. Should you wish me to guide you, girl, you may ask my aid politely."

Again Nidisar seemed angered, yet could I see naught which would anger him. Was I not a war leader? "I had not thought my words impolite." I shrugged, bothered that his aid would not be forthcoming, yet not overly so. "That Nidisar finds them so is unfortunate. We shall see the city ourselves."

I turned from him then, and led my warriors to our kand. We began walking toward the gap between the tents, which was not far distant.

"Hold!" called a voice, and I turned to see Nidisar hurrying to reach us. He had stood within the tent as we had left. "Jalav, I have changed my mind," he said as he reached me. "In truth, your words were not as impolite as I had at first thought, and I now recall that the offer to guide you was originally mine." Then he grinned at me. "Also, I believe I would miss the way you shrug. I have never seen a shrug quite as attractive as yours."

"He is pure sthuvad," said Fayan in disgust. "I believe he would service all of the Hosta just as he is."

"What is the meaning of 'sthuvad'?" demanded Nidisar angrily. "Should it be what I believe, there shall be a female among you who is made to regret her words!"

"It merely means male," said I, showing to Fayan my annoyance.

"I somehow feel the word has other meaning," Nidisar said. "Yet I shall accept your meaning for the time. Come. There is one other thing I would stop for at the fair, then we may explore the city."

Nidisar once more led off, and took us past the point where folk entered from the city. We passed many tents, some open, some closed, and finally came to one which was gold and white. Although others of the tents reeked of spoiled vegetables and meat, the dye of cloth, oils and spices, and metal covered in some manner, the gold and white tent gave forth no such odor. Closed it was all about itself, and few entered it.

"I shall be but a moment," Nidisar informed me, then disappeared within. When Nidisar again appeared, upon his left arm he wore a golden wristlet set with bright stones, and he seemed quite pleased with the acquisition. He rubbed the wristlet against his covering, then held it for me to see.

"I have long wished for one such as this," said he, deep pleasure in his tone. "Is it not worth whatever price might be asked?"

"It is quite attractive," said I, wondering at the use of such a thing. Thin was the metal, too thin to turn even the blade of a dagger, and its high shine would betray a warrior's position in all save full darkness. Perhaps, I thought, it might be used to blind an enemy, so that one's swordpoint might reach them more easily.

"I have also gotten something for you," he said, and reached within his covering to withdraw a small, thin comb, seemingly of the same metal from which his wristlet was made. "It will look well against that deep-black mane of yours."

I looked more closely at the comb, and then smiled. "Nidisar had best keep the comb for his own mane," I said. "The comb I use each new light is thrice the thickness of that, made of good, strong wood, and still occasionally breaks. One like that would break upon first use."

"No, no, Jalav," he laughed, "you misunderstand. This comb is not to be used, it is to be worn. Have you never worn a comb in your hair?"

"Never," I said, noting the passage of the light. "Have you now completed whatever you must do? Time moves away before us."

"Can nothing distract you from your purpose?" Nidisar asked, annoyed and dismayed. "I would have you see the proper use of a comb such as this, and it will take but a moment. Come with me."

He then gave to Larid the lead of my kan, and took my arm to propel me toward the large, garish tent that stood to the left of the gold and white one. A number of males had entered that tent, but few had left it, and its interior could not be seen for it had not been opened to sight. I was not sure that I wished to enter it, yet Nidisar urged me within before I was able to voice my doubts, and then I could only stare about me.

The area we stood in measured perhaps ten paces by ten, and was lit softly by many colored small boxes which were open at their tops, so that the heat of the candle flames within might escape. The walls of the tent were hung with orange and pink silk, and soft lenga pelts, shamefully dyed orange and pink lined the floor from wall to wall. Large, tightly stuffed squares of cloth, of a black that stood out sharply against the orange and pink, lay here and there upon the pelts, for what purpose, I knew not. A small, round, black platform stood in the center of the floor, and above that, hanging from the roof, was a strip of silk with rounded bits of metal upon it. Nidisar strode to the hanging bit of silk and shook it, whereupon was produced a number of tiny, tinkling sounds.

We waited but a moment, and then appeared from behind the silk, a slave-woman whose like I had not before seen. She had not my height, yet was tall and slenderly built, and she moved as though she slid on oil, so effortless did it seem. Her body was covered with silks like those of the tent walls, but all of her could be easily seen through them. Beneath the silks, where Midanna displayed their clan colors, this woman wore small, golden-linked chains, arranged, so it seemed, in a manner which would allow a male who used her to guide her movements as he pleased. Should she attempt to deny such a male, the position of the chains would give her much discomfort, if not true pain. She wore nothing upon her feet, and her dark hair was piled high about her head, held here and there with small bits of metal. This slave-woman was fair of face, and she smiled upon seeing Nidisar, and moved slowly toward him. As she approached, a strange odor came with her, an odor at once sweet and heavy, the like of which I had never before encountered. The odor was not at all like that of the eating tent, yet it, too, offended my senses.

"My dear Nidisar," said she, stopping before the male and placing her hand lightly upon his arm. "Have you returned to us so soon? It is ever our pleasure to serve you."

"I have come for another purpose entirely, Melai," laughed Nidisar, his hand moving behind her in a familiar way. "I merely wish you to show Jalav the proper use of a hair comb such as those you wear. Your pavilion was near, else I would not have disturbed you."

"It is no disturbance." The slave-woman studied me closely, and a puzzled look came to her eyes. "Though young, she is quite a woman, Nidisar," the slave-woman said in apparent approval. "I congratulate you on your fortune, yet I fail to understand the reason for the weapons she wears. Surely she has no intentions of attempting their use?"

"Jalav is quite well-versed in the use of weapons," Nidisar made answer, more in annoyance, I thought, than in approval. "I would now see her learn the use of other adornments. Therefore have I purchased this comb for her."

He again produced the comb, which the woman Melai

took from his hands. "It is indeed lovely," said she, moving her fingers upon it. "You, too, are fortunate, Jalav. Come closer, child, and remove the leather from your hair."

I studied her as she had studied me, and knew a moment of curiosity. "Do you have—'frills'?" I asked, gesturing toward her tent and her silks. "And do you wear—'scents'?"

At first she seemed rather startled by the questions, then laughed gently. "Indeed. I have both frills and scents. Why do you ask?"

"I merely confirm the foolishness of males." I laughed, resting my hand upon my sword hilt. "I shall not remove the leather from my hair, nor do I wish to waste further time with useless frills. Do you come now, Nidisar, or do we continue without your guidance?"

Nidisar appeared angered; however, when the slave-woman shrugged and returned his comb, he replaced it within his covering without comment. I turned then and led the way from the tent, amused that Nidisar would be so foolish as to think me sister to slave-women.

We returned to my warriors, who gazed longingly upon those at play with bow and shaft, and then left the area of tents, once more returning to the city ways. Nidisar chose ways which were narrow and badly kept, the dwellings to either side seeming about to crumble in upon us. He spoke, as we walked, of the street of cobblers, and the street of coopers, and the street of smiths, and many more such, equally meaningless, yet he seemed to know his way. We trod upon thrown refuse, skirted ugly, evil-smelling puddles, threw aside males who were badly taken with daru sickness, and still we continued to follow, for we were to learn the ways of a city.

Much time had sped when at least we came upon a broader, cleaner way. No refuse was there upon it, and males who rode or walked upon it showed no signs of sickness. Many of the males wore the leather and metal coverings of those who had been at the gates, and all gazed upon my warriors and myself with curiosity. Presently it was possible to see the unbelievably large dwelling which we had seen from the open space.

"The Palace of the High Seat," said Nidisar, gesturing toward the immense dwelling. "A formidable sight, is it not?"

"Is that a gate I see to its right?" I asked.

"It is indeed a gate." Nidisar came to me where I had stopped in the way beside my kan. "You have now seen all of my city, save the street of hunters, wherein I dwell. That I have left for last, as it is best. Come there now, Jalav, and I shall procure for you your first taste of renth—the memory of which you shall surely take back with you to your own land."

He stood very near to me, there in the broad way, and his eyes told what he felt. He was not unattractive, and I would not have refused him my sleeping leather, yet was there that second gate to consider.

"I would move a bit closer," said I, looking into his eyes. "To see more of yon dwelling. Your street may be seen at another time."

Angry, but controlled, he nodded curtly. "Very well!" he said, his voice tight. "The Palace first!"

Again he led off, anger quickening his pace, yet was I not of a mind to match him.

At last we stood before the entrance to the immense dwelling. Two hands of leather and metal clad males stood before it, atop the pile of steps, for the entrance itself stood opened. The dwelling was of a smooth, pinkish stone, which contained many windows, from side to side and up and down. Through the opened entrance, one could see many-colored cloth upon the floor, many people hurrying to and fro upon the cloth, and little else. No desire did I feel to enter such a place, and turned instead to regard the gate which lay to the right of the dwelling.

The second gate was nearly of a size with the first, but was less used. It did not stand open as had the other gate, but allowed only the entrance or departure of mounted leather-and-metal clad males. These males, I had noted, unlike those at the first gate, all wore head coverings of leather and metal. Those who stood before the dwellings, those who stood by the gate, those who rode from the city, all wore head coverings, yet those who had been at the other gate had not. I knew not the true reason for such a thing; perhaps those at the first gate scorned the males and slave-women there, not caring to provide full protection. Males who looked down upon protection in the face of those they considered harmless were fools indeed. One may consider the hadat harmless till the very moment of its attack. Perhaps the Hosta would be fortunate enough to encounter fools of that sort in Ranistard.

I looked again at the gate and turned to my warriors. "It would be best if we left this city now," I said. "Darkness will soon be with us, and I do not wish the gates closed while I remain within them."

"Nor I," agreed Fayan fervently, and the others also concurred. We made to mount our kand, but Nidisar's hand was suddenly upon my arm. Had I expected him to be filled with anger, I should have been mistaken, for his face showed a good deal of amusement.

"Alas, Jalav." He grinned. "This gate is solely for the use of members of the Guard, and you would not be allowed through it. The other gate, I fear, is much too distant for you to reach before the fall of full darkness. You must remain within the city till the new light, therefore you now have the time to visit the street of hunters. Would you care to have me guide you?"

Fayan made a sound of disgust. "The sthuvad lies!" she snapped. "He seeks to prison us here for his own purposes! Do not heed him, Jalav!"

"I shall learn the truth of the matter," I said as Nidisar scowled upon Fayan. "Larid, Binat. Ride to yon gate and say we would ride through, then return here with their answer."

"We hear, Jalav," replied Larid, then she and Binat guided their mounts toward the gate. Nidisar stood silently with folded arms, watching, as my warriors spoke briefly with those at the gate, then turned and rode back to us.

"It is as he claimed," said Binat in annoyance, drawing rein before me. "We may not use this gate, nor do we have time enough to reach the other."

"The males would not allow us through the gate," added Larid, tossing her red hair, "yet were they eager to offer accommodations till the new light. May we not loosen our blades, Jalav, and test the ability of these males who think themselves so well protected from us?"

"Aye, Jalav!" Fayan urged, coming to place her hand upon my shoulder. "Let us try these males with swords! Less than two hands of them stand before the gate!"

"Have you lost your wits?" demanded Nidisar of Larid and Fayan, his amusement gone, and a strange sort of anger filling him. "These are Guardsmen you speak of trying! Do you wish to see your lifeblood spilled before the gates?"

"Perhaps it might be done," I murmured, taking no note of Nidisar, who was, after all, merely male. I looked to where the other males stood, gauging the distance between them and those at the gate, estimating the time it would take for them to reach the gate, should they come to the aid of their fellow males. The main difficulties, as I saw them, were two. I knew not how long it would be before the protection of the males might be broached, and the gate we wanted to use did not stand open. Even should we best the males soon enough that their brothers had not time to aid them, we would still have to open the gates, which could occupy us much too long.

"Jalav, do not be foolish!" Nidisar growled, his hand hard upon my arm. "I had thought you wiser than these others, despite your tender age! Can you not see the guardhouses, to either side of the gate? Within sit more Guardsmen, fully prepared to aid those at the gate if necessary. But consider—you wear not even clothing, not to speak of armor! I demand you come away from here at once!"

It was true, with other males so close at hand, our numbers would prove far too few for other than a gesture, though had not the Crystal of Mida yet to be recovered, the gesture would have been worthwhile, to be told and retold over the kalod in the tents of the Hosta. Regretfully, I turned from the gate.

"It is Mida's will that we await the new light," I informed my warriors. "Our swords will be needed elsewhere at another time."

They then glanced upon one another with disappointment and were reminded that Ranistard, and not Bellinard, was the goal of our blades. They nodded in obedience to my word, and again Nidisar was pleased.

"You do well to heed me, Jalav," he said, his hand now soft upon my arm. "Come, I shall show you to the street of hunters."

"May we not pass the darkness in the place of the tents, Jalav?" asked Fayan, the innocence of her expression matched by the softness of her tone. She would not argue with Nidisar in disobedience to my will, yet she was determined to see him receive no pleasure from our presence.

Somewhat fond was I of Nidisar, but Fayan was my warrior.

"It is a thing to consider." I nodded most soberly, inwardly amused at Nidisar's wrath. He gazed upon Fayan with great anger, and she returned his gaze quite calmly, knowing I would not interfere should Nidisar be so foolish as to attack her.

"The fairgrounds may not be used past the time the

torches are extinguished!" Nidisar snapped. "Should you attempt it, the Guard would be called! I go now to the street of hunters! You may follow or not as you wish!"

He then strode angrily away, his back straight and his head high, easily the picture of an offended male. My warriors and I laughed at his actions, so childlike are males in their need. He strove to show that he had no desire for us, yet had we ridden away, his misery would have been great. Nidisar led us from way to way, at last pausing before a dwelling which bore above it the picture of a male with bow in hand, being given a tall, narrow pot by a slave-woman. Nidisar stood before the entrance to this dwelling, and we stopped nearby and dismounted.

"You may tie your kand at the post," he said, gesturing toward a raised post standing beside the steps which led to the entrance. "The renth here is of excellent quality, and served well, too. I believe you might find a good deal of interest here."

His face showed renewed amusement, nor was he impatient as we tied our kand and slowly trod the steps before the entrance. Darkness had already come to the city ways, yet were torches lit upon the dwellings so that one might see one's step. Within the dwelling Nidisar had entered were torches also, illuminating a room perhaps twenty-five paces by twenty. A heavy cloth of many shades of brown and green covered the wood of the floor, and six to eight hands of males lay about on it, also leaning upon large, stuffed squares, the like of which I had seen in the tent of the slave-woman of frills and scents. The walls of the dwelling bore no silks, being properly covered, instead, with many weapons, and the males upon the cloth had, each beside him, a low, round platform bearing either a square of wood, a round, wooden pot, or a tall, oddly shaped pot. Some of the platforms bore more than one of these things, yet all bore the tall, oddly shaped pot. Many of the males called greeting to Nidisar, and raised hands to him in welcome. They looked, too, with interest upon my warriors and me.

"Nidisar!" called one, who lay with a hand of others to the left of the room. "Is that not she who matched your throws at spears in the competition? Bring her and the others to us! We shall be pleased to assist you in entertaining them!"

"An excellent thought!" Nidisar laughed, then made his way toward the males. "I have promised them a taste of renth before they leave with the new light, for never have they tasted renth."

These words the other males greeted with loud laughter. Larid, Binat, and Comir examined them with interest, for most of the males were acceptable by Hosta standards, and Fayan, too, seemed to find them passable.

"Perhaps some time might be profitably passed here," Fayan murmured, a small smile upon her lips. "I merely regret that we have not had the opportunity to hunt, for hunger has returned to me."

"To me, as well," I agreed with a nod. "But we must wait till we are no longer within this city. Not all places have the nilno which was to be found earlier beside that tent. Those of the cities are Mida-forsaken indeed, to feed so poorly."

We approached Nidisar where he stood. He turned to us with a large grin, and gestured toward the seated males. "These are brother hunters," he said, "all anxious to make your acquaintance. Brothers, allow me to present Jalav, Larid, Binat, Comir, and Fayan, also wishing to be known at large as hunters."

"They may join *my* hunting parties whenever they wish," said one, a large male with hair nearly as red as Larid's. "I wager their presence would turn the darkness of the woods a good deal warmer than is usual."

The other males laughed again in agreement, and my warriors and I smiled in remembrance of the warmth brought to the woods by the hunters the Hosta still held. Perhaps they, too, were brothers to these who sat before us.

"Let us take our ease before the renth is brought," said Nidisar, seating himself upon the brown and green cloth. Of much assistance had Nidisar been to us that fey, and within his chosen dwelling would it be rude to give insult. Therefore I reluctantly seated myself, cross-legged, beside him, and my warriors, too, took their places. The cloth was warm and almost smooth to sit upon, though there was something of a scratchiness to it which caused annoyance. Much do I prefer the feel of leather beneath me.

As Nidisar rubbed his hands together in pleasant anticipation, a slight sound caused me to turn my head to the right, and I saw, approaching us, a slave-woman. Comely was she to a large degree, wearing only a short, thin draping of sheer cloth about her. The sound which had taken my attention came from a band of leather about her right ankle, to

which rounded bits of metal were attached, and the tiny, tinkling sound would perhaps have been louder had not the
males been making their noises. As the woman neared, I saw
that she wore about her throat a narrow band of metal,
which must have been hidden behind by her brown hair,
which was loose and reached midway down her back. She
hurried to us with small, light steps and, though she seemed
startled when she looked upon my warriors and myself, she
stopped before Nidisar and fell to her knees without hesitation.

"The house welcomes you, master," she said, her head low.
"What may this one be privileged to bring you?"

"My companions and I, six in all, wish renth," responded
Nidisar, his eyes upon the slave-woman, a small sly smile
upon his face. "But before you fetch it, I would have you tell
my companions the name of this house."

Nidisar had motioned to me, and the slave-woman turned
somewhat in my direction. "The house is called, 'The Hunter
and Slave Girl,' Mistress," said the woman, her eyes still lowered. Nidisar's eyes, however, were fixed upon me, and his
smile had become one of anticipation. I glanced about, and
saw that the eyes of the other males, too, were upon me, yet
could I fathom no reason for that.

"Why do you thus look upon me?" I asked of Nidisar, my
left hand comfortably upon my sword hilt. "Did you think I
would know the name?"

"Does the name cause you to feel naught, girl?" Nidisar
demanded with a snort of amusement. "Do you not realize
that all females within these walls be slave?"

"I do not take your meaning," I said. "Are not all city females slaves? Wherein lies the difference?"

"I believe he thinks us sisters to one such as she!" Fayan
exclaimed, then threw her head back and laughed heartily.
My other warriors laughed as well, and I, too, was amused,
for the confusion upon the faces of Nidisar and the other
males was comical indeed. At last I understood that I was to
feel much upset, caused by the presence of a female who had
been named slave. It was clear that these males knew nothing
of the ways of Midanna.

The slave-woman had not raised her eyes, yet there was a
light red color to her cheeks, as though mention of her state
gave her discomfort. Had I not known that those of the cities
had no souls, I would have told her that it needed but the

opened throat of he who owned her to make her free. However, I spoke not such words, for one without a soul lacks also the stomach with which to accept them.

"You may now fetch the renth," said Nidisar to the slave-woman, a bit of annoyance in his tone. The slave-woman rose quickly to her feet and sped away, and Nidisar moved more closely to me. "I would have the truth, Jalav," said he, taking my hand between both of his so that he might toy with it. "How can you think yourself different from that slave? Are you not both female?"

"Certainly," I agreed, pleased at the feel of his shoulder against mine. "We are both female, and all males are male, but is there no difference between males as well? Some are scrawny and small, all life and heart gone out of them, and some are tall and strong, fit for a warrior to look upon. Why, then, would you think me the same as that slave? Do you believe she would cast a spear as well as I have done?"

"No." He smiled, and touched my cheek. "Yet would I be pleased to see you and those others clad as the slave was, kneeling at my feet. In that, I can see no difference between females, save that some would make more pleasing slaves than others."

"Little pleasure would you receive from Jalav as slave." I laughed, amused by his innocence. "You would live in fear of closing your eyes in sleep, lest Jalav find her way free and to your sleeping form. Think you your life would not then be forfeit?"

He sighed. "In truth, I know it would be," he murmured, "yet perhaps, for a certain female, a man might feel the price a not unreasonable one. It is something to be thought upon."

His words, too, were something to be thought upon, yet was I unable to find meaning within them, for quickly was the renth brought. Three slave-women, clad as was the first, carried to each of us a small, round platform, upon each of which was placed by a fourth slave, a tall, oddly shaped pot. I took the odd pot from the platform beside me, and tasted of the contents within, finding it a near match to unbrewed daru. Thinner was it than daru, and sweeter, yet it was not unwelcome after so long a time with nothing to drink but water.

When I lowered the pot, again I found Nidisar's eyes upon me. "What think you of the renth?" asked he with a smile.

"It is adequate," I allowed, and finished what there was in

the pot. "It would sit best, however, beside a portion of nilno. A pity there is none to be had."

"Of course there is nilno." He laughed and emptied his own pot. "I should have thought to offer it sooner. I shall have some as well, and we may have our flagons refilled while we await it."

He again called the slave to him, ordered the pots refilled, then requested six portions of nilno. The slave hurried off to see to the nilno, and we had again drained our pots by her return.

When we had finished with the good-sized portions of nilno, much renth had also been finished. The males with whom we sat had moved themselves about, so that some of them were beside and about each of my warriors. My warriors were pleased to have full stomachs and a pot of near-daru, and laughed lightly with the males, thinking, I was sure, about which of them they would take. The large, red-haired hunter who had spoken earlier sat beside Fayan, his eyes hungrily taking her in. She, too, seemed pleased with his form, and I felt he would not find her dagger at his throat, should he put his hands upon her. Nidisar still sat beside me, matching me pot for pot of the renth, yet he was quieter than he had been, and his eyes strayed often from me to rest upon Fayan. He, however, would have had little chance with her, for she disliked him, and had not looked upon him even once.

Who first spoke of it, I knew not, yet suddenly, amid much laughter, were my warriors and I challenged to a game of throwing daggers. Comir stepped up first, although she was very young and not well used to the taste of daru and the like. She peered unsteadily at the board upon the wall, brought her arm back slowly for the throw, and dropped the dagger behind her without knowing it. We all of us roared with laughter as she scratched her head and searched about her for where the dagger might have flown. Solicitously a hunter retrieved the dagger for her, and she took it with a smile, then fell forward against him, taken herself by the renth. The hunter laughed and lifted her in his arms, then carried her away from the rest of us. No move did I make to stop him, for the lesson would be a useful one for Comir. When she awakened with the new light, her head ringing with the remains of renth, her body having been used by a male without her consent, she would thereafter take heed of what she drank, and would not soon again place herself in so foolish and vulnerable a position.

Binat was next, and her throw was straight and true to the center of the board. The hunter who took her place had had a bit too much of the renth, which caused his dagger to strike the wall rather than the board, and again all laughed.

I awaited my turn, expecting Fayan to throw next, yet when I looked about, she was nowhere to be seen. The tall, red-haired hunter with whom she had been now stood beside Binat, and I surmised with a shrug that she had found another who interested her more. I threw my dagger the short distance to the center of the board, then was unexpectedly touched upon the shoulder. I turned and saw standing there the male who had been at the gate upon our arrival and who had spoken of seeking me later.

"An excellent throw," he said, a smile upon his lips. Dark of hair and eye was he, strong of face, and unashamed of the hair he wore bound in leather.

"At such a distance, how might one miss?" I asked, returning his smile. "Also, the board does not attempt to evade the throw."

"Quite true." He laughed, and his hand moved to caress my back. "Might I offer you a flagon of renth? I am Pileth, Captain of the Guard of the High Seat."

"I am Jalav," I said, "and I would be pleased to accept renth."

Pileth grinned and walked with me to where my small, round platform sat. Six other males of the Guard had he brought with him, and these males placed themselves at a distance from our position. It was then that I noted the absence of Nidisar, and felt much relieved. This Pileth held considerable attraction for me, and had Nidisar remained, I would have had the difficulty of the hunter's bewailing his rejection.

A pot was brought Pileth, and he and I shared renth with few words. Once, when a slave-woman came to renew the renth, a male not far distant from us put his hand upon the slave-woman, causing her to gasp and spill the renth upon my arm. Pileth became angered, and the slave-woman fell to the floor in terrible fear and trembling, as though the fault had been hers. Annoyed by the interruption, I rose to my feet and carried my pot of renth to the male who had touched the slave-woman, and emptied the pot upon his head. He rose up sputtering, in great anger, but the sight of my own anger and

my hand upon sword hilt stayed his words and actions. He
returned silently to his place upon the cloth, and I returned
to Pileth, who laughed softly where he lay. The slave-woman
quickly replaced my spilled renth with a small smile, then
took herself off, and Pileth insisted upon removing the renth
from my arm with his tongue. The action heated my blood
above the level it had already attained, yet when I reached
for him, he stayed my hand and rose to his feet, urging me
up with him.

Pileth led me toward a wide doorway to the rear of the
room. The doorway was one that had seen much use since
my arrival, it being the one from whence the slave-women
came, and also the one through which many of the males had
passed, only to return at a later time, seeming much satisfied.
Pileth led me in and I saw that we were preceded by a male
who had a slave-woman in tow by the hair. The slave-woman
whimpered, yet made no attempt to escape the grasp of the
male, and then had little chance of doing so. The male thrust
her through one of the many small doorways inside, and then
pulled the door shut behind him. Most of the small doorways
were also closed, but some few still stood open. Pileth chose
the first of these that he reached, and drew me past him to
the narrow space beyond, then pulled shut the door and slid a
bar into place. Barely two paces wide by three long was the
space, and it had naught save a lenga pelt upon the floor, and
a single candle within a box upon the far wall. As Pileth began removing his leather and metal covering and swordbelt,
I, too, removed my swordbelt and put it aside. Quickly, then,
were the male's hands upon me, giving me pleasure as
Fideran had so often done. It is truly said that a warrior loses
half the pleasure to be had when she must use a male who is
bound. As we took ourselves down to the caress of the lenga
pelt, I heard the sob of a woman not far off. The sob had not
been one of pleasure, and as Pileth's lips sought me, I surmised that the slave-woman had now been taught the foolishness of not at least attempting escape. Therefore, I thought
only of the pleasure of Pileth.

4.

*The Palace of the High Seat
—and its dungeons*

I stretched lazily upon the lenga pelt, then rose to my feet and retrieved my sword. Pileth had already gone. He was angry, which I truly regretted. Magnificent had he been in use, although he much resented the presence of my dagger, which had assured that the war leader Jalav would not receive from a male. He, too, had had pleasure, of this I was certain, yet did the maleness of him resent the position in which he had had his pleasure. He had dressed and quickly left, speaking no words, and this had caused me to sigh with regret. Why must males be as foolish as they are? From their actions, one would think they thought themselves of the Midanna.

I retraced my steps through the narrow area, seeing more of the small doors standing opened, then pushed through to the large room once again. The same number of males seemed present, and Larid and Binat sat laughing with the hunters, he who had been pursuing Larid now all smiles with his arm about her. Pileth sat with the males he had brought, his back stiffly toward me, a pot of renth tight in his hand.

"More renth!" called he who sat by Larid, a large grin upon his face as his arm tightened about her. "Renth for me, and renth for everyone! I now have the price to bathe in renth!"

All laughed at his gleeful words. However, as I approached the hunters and my warriors, Pileth and his males rose from the cloth and as cold as the depths surrounding the Entry to Mida's Realm were his eyes.

"I would know from whence came your sudden riches," Pileth said to the hunter, pointedly not noticing my presence. "I feel the High Seat shall find interest in such information."

"Do not fear, Guardsman," laughed the hunter, swallowing at his renth and spilling a good deal of it upon his covering. "There is more than enough to allow me to bathe in renth, and still leave the High Seat's proportion untouched. Look you here."

The hunter removed his arm from about Larid, and then opened his hand. I smiled when I saw two of the bright stones that are given to males by Midanna, to ease the male's insult at being used. Greatly pleased must Larid have been with the male, for never had she given more than one stone in the past. I, too, carried a number of the stones in a small pocket on the underside of my clan covering, and I regretted not having thought to give one or two to Pileth.

"More than enough indeed," nodded Pileth coldly, staring at the stones in the hunter's hand. "Yet, I have still not heard from whence they came."

"They were given me by this lovely child," laughed the hunter, replacing his arm about Larid. "I have often said that my performance is fit to be paid for by famales. This one has merely proven the point."

All about laughed at this comment, all, that is, save Pileth and his males. His eyes were still as cold as they had been, yet something unnameable gleamed from within.

"No mention was made of this when first you entered the gate," said Pileth, and a great silence fell all about us at his words. "I, myself, was present, and clearly do I recall that no mention was made."

"I had not known that you would earn nor desire such a stone," I answered, "Gladly will I give you two of the same, for surely your use has entitled you to them."

Pileth's lips tightened to a straight, thin line, and the hunter beside Larid rose quickly to his feet in the silence, his face considerably paler than it had been.

"Captain, I had no knowledge of this!" he cried, his fist tight about the stones. "And surely do I believe that these females knew not what they did! In the name of the blessed High Seat, allow them to declare the jewels now!"

A murmur of agreement arose from the other hunters who

still sat upon the cloth, although I did not understand what disturbed them. Pileth smiled coldly.

"As Captain of the Guard of the High Seat," said he in a flat voice, "I arrest you for smuggling, for attempting to evade the payment of the just proportion to the High Seat, and for attempting to bribe an officer of the High Seat. Guardsmen! Gather the others of these she-gandod!"

I still had no understanding of his words, but his actions required no explanation. As his hand moved toward my sword, abruptly he found it already unsheathed and pointed toward him. He jumped back quickly with an oath, losing no time bearing his own blade, and then began to advance upon me again.

Now was there much shouting about us in the room, and Pileth's males had also drawn their blades. Larid and Binat were quickly upon their feet with blade in hand, and two of Pileth's males moved to engage each of them. The final two, moving before Pileth, remained to try the ability of the war leader, and forward they came with confidence, sure of the protection they had with their leather and metal covering. I joyfully sounded the battle cry of the Hosta and charged, my sword slashing at them as they moved, forcing them to defend themselves, and retreat. The male on my left reacted foolishly to a low thrust, and the point of my blade rose quickly and entered his left eye, ending his sight and his life as well. As quickly as thought, I slashed to the right, causing that male to scream as his head was shortened, yet quickly did the scream end as his body fell, and none save Pileth still stood before me.

Pileth glanced at his fallen males, his face pale with the realization that now I came toward him. I was Jalav, war leader of the Hosta of the Midanna, and in battle there can be no forgiveness nor quarter. Well I knew that my eyes shone with battle joy, my body alive and readied, my hand firm upon the hilt of my sword. Pileth, his eyes clearly upon me, raised his sword and stood his ground, and that pleased me mightily, as a warrior dislikes the slaughter of the helpless and fearful. Again I stepped toward Pileth, but one farther step from him—and was struck from behind upon the head, a blow hard enough to make my senses blur. I felt that I sank to my knees, unable to stop myself, my hands before me upon the brown and green cloth. Well I knew that Pileth would now be free to take my life, and I called a greeting to

Mida even as I attempted to rise once again to my feet. I would die erect as a war leader should, yet was this glory denied me. Again a blow came from behind, and the chill of darkness claimed me.

Not long could I have been wrapped in darkness. My eyes opened with some pain, to find that I lay upon the brown and green cloth, my weapons gone, my wrists and ankles tightly bound. Not far from me lay Larid, in a heap, not far beyond her one of Pileth's males, awash in his own blood. Binat still stood and fought; then, even as I watched, another of Pileth's males came up behind her and struck her with the hilt of his sword, much as I had been struck. Binat staggered at the blow, attempting to keep her feet, but her attempt was in vain. The male struck again, and my warrior came to the cloth, just as Larid and I before her.

Pileth's males sheathed their weapons, and in a moment, Larid and Binat were bound as was I. There were but three of them remaining, aside from Pileth himself, and Pileth took two of them to the doorway to the narrow place, where they then disappeared from my sight. All about the far walls of the room stood the hunters, none speaking, all staring, shaken, toward my warriors and me. Among them were two of the slave-women, trembling where they stood, clinging to the males as though something completely untoward had occurred. My head ached with a silent thunder, the cloth beneath my cheek scratched in discomfort, my wrists and ankles slowly grew numb from the leather which bound them, while I attempted to loosen the leather and free myself, for nothing may be accomplished by lying still while one's enemies live. I strained at the leather, hoping unsuccessfully for some slack, and then Pileth and his males returned. One of the males bore Comir upon his shoulder, she still well taken with renth, her wrists and ankles tightly bound. Pileth and the other male brought Fayan between them; she seemed hard used. Gone was the war leather from her heavy gold hair, her wrists bound before her, her clan covering seemingly hastily replaced. Clouded were her eyes, and her lids drooped heavily, and she appeared disoriented.

Pileth held a length of leather which led to Fayan's wrists, and stood with her in the midst of the room while his other male fetched two large, wooden pots of water. Over Larid and Binat were the pots emptied, and soon were my warriors awake again, coughing at the water they had swallowed, shaking their heads to clear their sight. No word was spoken among Pileth and his males, while they knotted a long length of leather to Fayan's throat and freed me about the ankles, pulled me to my feet, and thrust me hard to stand behind her. The leather was brought back to be knotted about my own throat, then were Larid and Binat added to the line behind me. Comir had had two wooden pots of water poured upon her, yet so deep had the renth taken her, that she stirred hardly at all. The males at last ceased spilling water upon her, and one of them raised her to his shoulder again. Pileth looked about the room, noted the bodies of his three dead males, then pulled at the leather which led to Fayan's wrists. In his wake Fayan stumbled, I after her, and so we went out to the darkness of the city.

Our kand, still tied by the dwelling's steps, were bypassed by Pileth and his males. Along the cobbles of the now silent way were we led, from one way to the next, through whatever lay upon the way. The pace was rapid and uneven, our step unsure in the darkness, the torches upon the dwellings doing more to blind than illuminate. We stumbled often, and once my neck was nearly snapped when Larid went down. She regained her feet with difficulty, to the accompaniment of kicks from the males, and again we were led, at a faster pace than earlier. Despite the chill of the darkness, I felt overheated, and began to sweat.

Not an easy march was it to the immense dwelling, yet eventually it lay before us, long squares of light floating in the darkness. They led us not to the entrance we had seen earlier but to the rear of the dwelling, to a door which stood guarded by a hand of males. One of the males opened the door, revealing a narrow space much like that of the dwelling of the hunters, save that the length of the space was twice that of the earlier one, and naught save two doors, one well to the left, one far down on the right, appeared to view. Again, males stood before the door to the right, and it, too, was opened for us. A steep, dimly lit flight of steps lay before us, and by it we descended into the very ground itself.

The descent was long, the stone of the steps worn smooth as though by the passage of many feet. Torches hung in sconces upon the wall, and the stones were damp beneath my feet as we were led forward, and my head swirled again at the reek of the place. I took in the odor of human bodies, and of excretion, and of pain and fear as well. The passage was narrow and ill lit, and seemed to crush me with the weight of the stones and heavy air.

We stumbled forward till stopped by a large, metal door, before which no male stood, yet were there two beyond the door, seen through a narrow opening in it. We were carefully inspected, the door then opened with much noise, and again we were taken forward. I had not thought it possible, yet beyond the door the reek worsened, and strange, low sounds were to be heard, sounds which might once have been human. I pulled at the leather which bound me, attempting to leave that terrible place, yet I was drawn forward by the leather about my throat, deeper through that doorway. I then stood firm, refusing to go farther, and one of the males who had stood within the doorway struck at me with heavy leather, causing my back and right shoulder to burn with pain. I did not cry out, and did not move, yet one of Pileth's males pulled me forward by the neck, deeper into a realm where Mida's eyes have never gone.

No torches were there in that realm of darkness, therefore we were led by one of the males of the door, bearing a torch. Many wide, metal doors opened off the stone to either side of the passage now, and far down we halted by one of these. The male with torch opened the door, stepped aside so that he with Comir might enter, then followed within. We waited in darkness, hearing the sound of metal, and then the males returned. Again the door was closed, a heavy bar slid across it, and we moved on to the next door. Fayan was released from the neck leather and taken within, and when the torch returned, I saw that Pileth's eyes were upon me. He held the leather tied to my throat in his fist, and his broad face showed an expression I was unable to read. He said nothing but seemed to expect words from me. When none were forthcoming, he turned, pulling hard at the leather so that I would follow. At another door, I was released from the leather and thrust toward the doorway.

Inside, by torchlight I could see a windowless room of three paces by three, dirty straw upon the stone of its floor, a trickle of water running near to the corner of the far wall to the left. Buried in the far wall. set firmly in the stone, were heavy metal chains, a hand in number, and to these was I dragged. The males then placed a thick collar of metal about my throat, a collar that allowed my head no downward movement. I attempted to throw the collar off, but could not move it from my throat, and then wide metal cuffs were closed about my ankles. The two males stood as I pulled at the cuffs, and then quickly attached cuffs to my wrists as well, and the sense of confinement nearly drove me insane! Again and again I pulled at the chain which held me, and a snarl like that of the hadat rose up in my throat. Better a thousand times to die quickly and cleanly than to be put in a place such as that!

As I strained at the chain, my eyes fell upon the doorway, and there stood Pileth, the torch in his hand, again staring at me. I snarled the louder and attempted to reach him, and a look of startlement covered his features as he stepped forward.

"I had planned to offer you release, Jalav," he said very softly, his eyes sad. "Had you pledged yourself to me as slave, and begged my lenience, I would have had you chained in my quarters till you were called before the High Seat. Now I see that you are more savage than woman, and will never beg release. I regret not having killed you when I could have. It would have been kinder."

He turned quickly then and left the room, and the door enclosed me in darkness. Not a glint of light was there anywhere, and the heavy metal of the chain increased in weight. I whimpered then, like a hadat in a hunter's trap, and sank to the filthy straw and damp stones. For what reason I had been put in that place I knew not, yet what reasons are required by city males for what they do? I thought of Mida, but dared not call to her, for fear that another would hear in her stead. I knew then that I must not die in that place, for my soul would then be forever lost, though my life sign still hung about my neck. The damp and filth of the floor sickened me, but there was nothing else to stand or sit upon. My flesh crawled and chilled at the contact. However I was war leader of the Hosta of the Midanna, and in the midst of the darkness, I held my head high and awaited the return of the hunter.

5.

The High Seat
—and a price is set

For some time I had been in the darkness, though how long a time I knew not. For a space, there had been nothing and no one, a silence to match the darkness. I watched the darkness, and listened to the silence, and then I slept, my back against the wall, the chains holding me fast. I awoke to a small scraping sound, and then my leg was bitten by something with the smell of animal to it. Quickly I struck at the sound, causing the thing to squeal in pain and fear, and then I struck again and again, till no further sound came from it. With groping hands I found the limp body, broke its neck to be sure it was dead, then fed upon it, using its blood to replace that which flowed from my leg where I had been bitten.

The chains with which I was bound kept me from moving more than a short pace from my original position, yet I was able to reach the water which ran from the walls on my right. It took many handfuls to slake my thirst, and then I brought a bit of the water to my leg, where the unseen animal had bitten me. The bite no longer bled, but it throbbed somewhat with pain, so I pressed the water upon it to draw the pain away. In that realm of eternal darkness, it was no surprise that the pain remained.

A time later, a scream broke the silence. I knew the sound of Comir's voice, and called to her that she was not alone— and reminded her that she was yet a warrior. Her faint reply of obedience barely came to me; then there were no further screams. As warriors we sat within the darkness and silence, awaiting whatever would come.

Six times I lured unseen animals to me so that I might feed, before there came the sound of steps beyond the door. Metal was slid aside, the door opened, and quickly I squeezed my eyes shut against the brilliant glare of a torch. Footsteps neared me, my arms were once again held, and the cuffs of metal were removed from my wrists, only to be replaced with smaller, smoother metal as my arms were forced behind me. Next was the collar about my throat opened, that, too, being replaced by another, smaller collar of the same sort. The cuffs about my ankles were opened, though not replaced, and roughly I was taken from the room to the space beyond the door. I heard the sound of chain and saw a male in leather and metal bring a chain to the collar about my throat. The chain barely touched the collar and was held there, and the weight of the chain added itself to the collar.

The male then moved aside, and I saw, the chain also running to them, Fayan and Comir, facing from me, their arms, too, behind their backs. Presently the chain moved again, and I turned a bit to see Larid added behind me. When she and Binat were secured, the males, one holding the chain before Comir, one to either side of us, a fourth with a torch, moved in the direction we faced, pulling and pushing us with them. He with the torch was left at the large door, and then we retraced our steps to the air above.

The dimness of the uppermost space was not so great that a torch was needed to see the door in the wall to the right, yet was there one in a sconce beside it. The door was opened by him who held the chain, and the brightness within again caused pain to my eyes. We stumbled along a wide, well lit way, whose walls were smooth, pinkish stone, and which was floored by smooth, even squares of stone of a different sort. This way led to an open doorway without a door, and then did we tread a cloth of many colors, and see bright blue silks upon the pinkish stone of the walls. Males we now passed, and slave-women as well, all of whom moved from us with disdain, for surely we brought the stink of the depths with us.

In a matter of a short time, we came to another doorway, this one thrice the height and width of the others seen. No door hung within its dimensions, entrance instead being barred by two hands of males in leather and metal, armed with spears as well as swords. Between these males we were led, to the room beyond, and never had I seen so large a room. Fully forty paces by forty must it have been, its floor so smooth and bright as to seem all of a single piece taken from the skies. Blue silk hung upon its walls in careless folds, more silk than would be needed to clothe every warrior of every clan of the Midanna. Many males stood about in this room, though the greater number of them wore naught of leather and metal. These males looked upon us as we passed, with nearly as many expressions as there were males, and well I knew we made a fine sight—unkempt, filthy of skin as well as of clan colors, unsteady from such long confinement, marked here and there by the unseen animals of the depths. A fine sight indeed were we Hosta of the Midanna. However we walked with heads high, knowing we were warriors.

At the far wall of this very large room stood a high platform, so high that a hand of broad steps were needed to reach its top. Perched atop this platform was a seat not unlike that of the Keeper, Rilas, save that it had no gandod to move it about. Toward this platform we were drawn, toward the male who sat upon the Keeper's seat, a male of gigantic proportions, yet not in height. Pale was his hair, and light were his eyes, but his skin fell in folds about him, much like those of his covering which reached to his toes. He wore bright stones upon his fingers and about his neck, and a slave-woman knelt beside his seat, holding a large square of wood from which he chose portions of meat and ripe fruits. Another slave-woman, to his other side, held a square of wood containing a tall pot, from which, presumably, he drank. The juices of his feeding dripped down the sides of his mouth, yet his covering was unstained, as a blue cloth lay upon his chest to catch the drippings. Before this gross creature, then, were we brought, save that we were not to mount the steps. We stood in a line before him, Fayan and Comir to my right, Larid and Binat to my left, the males who had brought us to either side of the line, and one behind. He upon the seat continued to feed, and looked not once upon us.

More than a quarter of a hin passed so, and then did the gross male cease his feeding. His hands took the cloth from upon his chest, wiped themselves and his mouth, then threw the cloth toward the slave-woman who held the food. His light, narrow eyes came to us, and immediately were we seized by the males who had led us there, and forced to our knees by the chain and collars about our throats.

"They do not bow their heads," said the male upon the platform, in a voice much deeper than one would expect. "Though they kneel to the High Seat, they do not bow their heads. Are these they who would take from the High Seat his rightful proportion?"

"Indeed, Blessed One," came a voice from the left, and Pileth stood there, two steps above the level upon which we knelt. Tall and straight did he stand upon the step, his head held high, his gaze for none save him who sat upon the seat. "They are also those who took the lives of three of your Guardsmen," said Pileth. "I respectfully suggest that they be executed at once."

"Executed?" said he upon the seat, his brows raised high. Then did he laugh and shake his head. "No, no, good Captain, they are not to be executed. The jewels that they carried have been confiscated, and the jewels that they are shall not be cast aside. They shall be sold in the public market, at a price to match that which should have been given the High Seat as his proper due. They reek of the dungeons, yet their beauty may easily be seen. The High Seat shall have their price to add to his coffers."

"Blessed One, hear me," said Pileth, his voice even, though seeming a bit strained. His left hand gripped the hilt of his sword, as though drawing strength from it. "Blessed One, these females are savages, unfit to be slaves in your glorious city! They slew your Guardsmen with swords, showing how great a danger they may be! I think only of the safety of the High Seat when I beg that their lives be ended!"

"How foolish of you, Captain," laughed he upon the seat, gesturing with one ringed hand. "Savages or no, they are only female, and the High Seat fears no female." His eyes filled with laughter, and he inspected my warriors and myself, and then pointed toward me. "You, girl," he said. "I shall ask you. Has the High Seat aught to fear from a slave such as you?"

"No male need fear a slave," said I, in a voice which cracked from long disuse. "Yet Jalav is no slave, and never shall she be. Sleep light, foolish male, for the dagger of Jalav comes swiftly."

A great noise arose from the males about the room, and Pileth seemed pleased by my response. The eyes of him upon the platform, however, were not as pleased as those of Pileth, and all amusement seemed to have vanished from them.

"A savage indeed," said he. "I had thought to take her to serve the needs of the High Seat, yet shall she now be sent with the others. Remove them to the public pens for display—and twenty lashes for her who knows not how to address the High Seat."

We were pulled roughly again to our feet, and quickly removed from the room of him who sat upon the platform. Knots of males stood about and murmured, and perturbation had entered the eyes of many who looked upon us. Pileth, though, had gazed upon me sadly, and then had looked away. Again did we move from way to way, a veritable city within a dwelling, and they who led us continued to say not a word. I had looked upon my warriors as we stood before him of the platform, and each, though weary, had returned my gaze as of old. As quickly as the metal should be removed from us, that quickly would we be free.

At last we came upon a room which was nearly of a size with that which held the platform, yet this room held enclosures of metal, chains upon walls, contrivances of metal and wood, and a large number of males and females. Many of the males and females were within the enclosures, the females with only a metal collar about their throats, the males heavily chained. Those who walked about the room were largely male, yet certain uncollared slave-women were to be seen as well, speaking to the males, or hurrying about various tasks. At the entrance to this odd room we were halted, and waited till approached by a male and a female, each seemingly pleased to note our arrival. Tall and broad was the male, his hair touched with gray as was that of Maranu, and the female stood but a finger less than the height of Fayan, her hair a deep, rich black like mine. Her eyes, of a sharp and piercing blue, examined each of us with care, then looked to the males who had led us there.

"They are to be sold at forty silver pieces each," said he who held the chain, and then he gave the chain to the room's male. "They are to be secured as though they were men, and she of the black hair is to receive twenty lashes."

The female's brows rose at that, and again she inspected me. "So many!" she said in surprise. "For what reason is she to be lashed?"

"She knows not how to address the High Seat," responded

the male. "Have a care with them, Karil, for they be savage and as yet unbroken. Also, they are to be exhibited."

"I see," said the female quietly. "The High Seat is displeased to a great extent. At the fast price of forty silver pieces each, it shall be long that they are exhibited. Inform the High Seat that all shall be seen to."

The male nodded, then he and the two others returned as we had come. The female then gestured toward a far corner of the room which contained only circles and chains upon the wall.

"Secure them there, Bariose," she directed the male who now held the chain. "Rinse the dungeon stink from them, then we shall see to other matters."

"An excellent thought, Karil," said he called Bariose, regarding my warriors and myself with distaste. "They shall be displayed as they are, of course, yet none shall miss that distinctive aroma."

"I certainly shall not," she called Karil agreed, her hands clasped before her. "Nor am I used to such. It is normally your male slaves who arrive so, not my females. We shall have to work together upon this."

"I foresee little difficulty," said Bariose, examining us yet again. "I shall see to their confinement and punishment, you to their positioning and presentation. A simple matter."

The female turned from Bariose, and stepped to me to stare with troubled eyes. "Must it truly be twenty?" she asked, speaking to the male though her gaze was for me. "She is little more than a girl, Bariose, and never have I seen a girl punished so!"

"The High Seat is to be obeyed," the male answered. "It may not be a stroke less than twenty, yet shall I have a care that she is not permanently marked. I would not make her sale more difficult."

"You are a good man, Bariose." The female smiled, turning from me. "Together, we shall find her a master as kind as you. I shall have a cage prepared for them."

The female moved away toward the metal enclosures, and the male pulled us toward the corner of the large room. Many eyes were upon us, most especially those of the males who were chained within the enclosures. Their need was strong upon them, yet were they unable to see to it, chained and pent as they were, and that was truly a waste. Many of them would have been acceptable in the home tents of the Hosta.

In the corner the male attached the chain to a circle upon the wall. He then walked to where Binat stood, drawing her closer to the wall, so that he might take a chain already set upon the wall and secure it to a small circle on the collar about her throat. Binat glanced toward me as she was taken and I shook my head very slightly. It was not the proper time to show what might befall a male who touched a Midanna warrior unbidden.

My warriors and I stood facing toward the wall, held in place by the chain to which our collars clung, our wrists still firmly closed behind us. I knew not whether the time was of light or of darkness, for there were no windows. I knew not where we were, I knew not of the presence nor lack of light; I knew only that we would again be free, or dead in the attempt.

A short while we stood in inspection of the wall, then there were steps behind us. A moment later, large wooden pots of water were emptied upon us, cold water which first shocked the body, then caused it to waken and tingle. I shook the water from my eyes, feeling nearly as refreshed as though I had stepped beneath a falls, and my warriors sighed in contentment at the touch of Mida's blessed wetness upon their bodies. Three times further were we treated so, but the last time was unwelcome. The water had been fouled with that which gave it a scent not unlike her of the orange and pink tent, and my warriors and I did not care for it. Angrily we stood, with hair and clan coverings dripping to the floor, much outraged that such a thing would be done to us. The Hosta, too, have at times taken prisoners, yet never have the Hosta subjected even blood enemies to such.

For perhaps two hind we were left to stand as we were, then we heard the approach of footsteps. The female known as Karil briefly touched the clan coverings and hair of each of us, then came her voice from behind.

"Their skirting has dried, Bariose, yet their hair remains wet," said she. "So long and heavy is it, it shall be wet some time yet. I do believe I shall have it combed now, then you may cage them."

"As you wish, Karil," said he called Bariose. "Their combing and skirting is beyond my province. Send your slave to me when the matter is done."

The female agreed. A moment later came quick, light steps, and a female with a collar about her throat and a heavy wooden comb in her hand approached Binat, and removed the war leather from her hair. The comb was drawn through Binat's hair, beginning low, the better to remove the snarls and tangles which had accumulated, then higher and higher till the slave-woman found it necessary to fetch a low, round platform upon which to stand, so that she might reach Binat more easily. When the combing was done, the war leather was replaced upon Binat's hair, which caused me to smile. City folk are ignorant in all matters, for one does not aid one's enemies in war preparation.

The hair of each of us was combed in a like manner, but the slave-woman had to fetch a piece of leather with which to tie Fayan's hair. I then recalled that Fayan's leather had been gone when we were taken by Pileth and his males, and I wondered what had happened to Fayan. She had not spoken of the matter, for there had scarcely been the opportunity, yet I believed that she chose not to speak of it, and I was disturbed by this.

When the slave-woman had retied Comir's hair, she lifted the platform and carried it away. Shortly thereafter came heavier footsteps, and three males appeared beside us. Two of the males began to remove the chains that bound us to the wall, and the third reached to the chain which held my collar. At the male's touch, the chain fell away, then he moved me to the right, the while my warriors were taken to the left. I did not care to be separated from them. However it was best that should one be taken, I be the one. My warriors had greater chance for escape if they remained together.

I was pulled perhaps five paces, to where he called Bariose and another male waited. Bariose held in his hand a coiled length of leather, covered most of its length, perhaps by cloth, perhaps silk. Bariose moved the coiled leather gently yet continuously against his leg as the second male came forward to grasp my arm. Between them I was taken to a wall, from which, high up and apart, projected two thin cuffs, flat to the wall, into which my wrists were locked. The cuffs forced me hard against the wall, and I was unable to stand flat upon my feet, needing, instead, to raise up upon my toes. I felt the chill of the pink smooth stone against me as the male to my left parted my hair as it lay in the leather, and pushed it forward across my shoulders so that he might knot it below my chin. With this done, the two males departed.

"You now receive your first punishment, slave," came the voice of Bariose from where he stood. "Consider the cause of it as the lash reaches you, and perhaps it may not be necessary for the lash to reach you again. A slave must obey in all things, else is she punished."

Then I was struck with such force that the blow drove me closer against the wall and farther up on my toes. My breath sucked in at the fire which flared across my back, a fire which stretched from shoulder to waist. My hands grasped uselessly at the wall, seeking to hold to it against the fire, but there was nothing to hold to nor grasp. Then came a second blow, sharp against the first, adding its fire to the flame which already consumed me, and a third, and a fourth. My body shook to the pain I felt, yet was I Jalav, war leader of the Hosta of the Midanna. Hard against the wall was my cheek, my fists clenched in the cuffs, my eyes closed tight, yet not a sound did I make to shame myself before Mida.

Barely did I know when the fire no longer reached me. Pain covered me as darkness covers the forest, and all had receded before it. I was aware of no part of me save my back and shoulders, aware only of the wall where I hung. It was a moment before I realized that the males were again beside me, releasing the wall cuffs, and I was not able to stand against such abrupt release. To my knees by the wall did I go, attempting to deny the pain, yet it would not be denied. It burned at me ceaselessly, turning me sick with its strength, helpless in its grip. My hands at my middle, my head low, I knelt by the wall, clinging to the light against darkness only by will, and my arms were again forced behind me, and again held by unyielding metal. Hands upon my arms forced me to my feet, and I was taken, half dragged, half stumbling, from the wall and across the floor.

Slowly I was aware of the silence of the room; mistily did I see the eyes upon me. Those within the enclosures and without looked upon me in my pain, but without ridicule. I attempted to straighten myself and walk as a warrior should, but could not. Trembling like a kan beside a gando, I was taken by the males to an enclosure, within which stood my warriors. Their eyes were wild with fury, but they were still bound with metal, and enclosed behind the metal of city males. A door was opened in the enclosure by the male to my right, and easily were my warriors pushed aside so that I might be thrust within among them. I stumbled but a pace or two before I fell, landing hard upon the metal floor upon my side. My warriors came and crouched above me, anxiously asking after what pain I felt, and the demands of the flame could no longer be denied. The light drifted from me, as though loath to depart, yet depart it did before the soothing darkness.

6.

The display—and an escape is planned

I could not bear the enclosure. I sat cross-legged before the metal which pent me up, and stared at those who walked about without. I would have killed without stop, male and female alike, to be free of the enclosure, but my wrists were held behind me with metal, my weapons gone I knew not where. Therefore I could only sit and stare, caring naught for the discomfort I caused in those who read my stare.

"Jalav, what are we to do?" asked Fayan as she sat beside me. She, like the others, felt as I did, a wild, unreasoning desire to be free. A bit larger than three paces by three was the enclosure. We had each paced it off, over and again, in our impatience to be free.

"I know not," I said, staring from the enclosure. "Yet Mida has not forgotten her warriors. An opportunity shall come."

Fayan then asked, "How is the pain?"

"It recedes," I said, straightening a bit. When I had awakened in the enclosure, I had been stiff and sore from that which had been done to me, and filled with fury by it. To treat a war leader of the Hosta so, and then permit her to live, was an insult the like of which had never been given. My battle skill was thus spat upon and dismissed, for these males to care so little for my vengeance. As my warriors and the others of the room slept, I struggled to my feet and held my head high, asking Mida in silence to grant me the favor of a sword in my hand and Bariose armed before me. To send him to Mida's chains would be worth my life to me, perhaps even my honor. Those armed males who stood beside the entrance to the room looked upon me, yet did they remain where they were and say nothing. Then I paced off the enclosure before sitting to stare.

Bariose and she called Karil, with a number of males, arrived together. My warriors had already awakened, and sat watching as did I, as the slave-women were released from their enclosures and set about various tasks. Some saw to a huge metal pot which hung upon an arm of metal above a fire in the wall far to the right, some took large wooden pots of water and cloth rags with which to wash the floors and walls, and some used other cloth, tied about the end of a length of wood, to wash the insides of each of the enclosures. The slave-woman who came with lowered eyes to wash our enclosure paused before us where we sat, raised her eyes slowly to mine, shuddered at what she saw there, grasping the length of wood convulsively, then hurried to the next enclosure. My warriors and I sat as we were, awaiting what would next eventuate.

A terrible odor arose from the pot above the fire, and when those who had seen to the washings had finished, they hurried to the fire with small, round, wooden pots. The small pots were filled by those who tended the huge, metal pot, and the slave-women washers took the wooden pots to the males and very few females who remained in the enclosures. A hand of pots were brought to us by slave-women who did not raise their eyes, and these pots were hastily thrust through a long gap in the metal of the enclosure, which was low in the wall to our right. Those females retained in enclosures wore no chains, and therefore raised the pots to their lips, yet the males, chained as we were, knelt before the pots, lapping at what they held like children of the wild. Even had the contents of the pots, a loose mixture of what seemed to be over-ripe fruit and rotted grain, not been so vile, Hosta would starve before they fed so.

The slave-women of the pots then partook of the mixture themselves, after which the wooden pots were again collected. I myself felt no regret at their being taken. The odor had been foul enough to fell a gando. Quickly, then, were all of

the pots cleaned and restored to that place from which they
had come, and the slave-women hurried to stand before their
enclosures, their hands clasped before them, their heads
bowed and eyes low. Four of the armed males then approached the females, and took them, some few at a time,
through a closed door in the far wall to the left. The males
returned each time to fetch further females, yet there was no
sign of what befell those who had already gone.

The males came at last to our enclosure, but we were not
all taken at once. First Fayan and Larid were taken, the
Binat and Comir, and lastly they returned for me. My arms
each held firmly in the grasp of a male, I, too, was taken to a
large, circular space which held many doorways in its walls,
and I was pleased with the doorway they chose. That doorway led to Mida's light, beneath a sky which sparkled in its
blueness. The air was a gift of love to my breath and skin. So
delighted was I to be free of walls again that I nearly missed
the sight of what awaited me. I struggled in the grips of the
males, yet were forced up and within the narrow enclosure,
whose door was quickly closed upon me. The space was
barely wide enough to turn in and was lifted by thin, metal
legs, the height of my knee from the ground. I threw myself
against the wall-door of the enclosure, yet were my actions in
vain. I stood within an enclosure not a single pace in width
and depth, barely high enough for me to stand erect, which
would not release me no matter how violent my efforts. Some
few of the slave-women knelt in the grass, before the high
wall which surrounded the open area, under the eyes of two
of the males, yet all the rest, my warriors included, were pent
in enclosures such as that which held me. The sweet air
turned sharp in my throat, and sight of the skies filled me
with bitterness. It is evil enough to enclose a warrior born to
freedom, yet to enclose her beneath the openness of the sky is
unspeakably worse. Vile and unspeakable were those of the
cities, fit only to die by a warrior's hand. Silently, I spoke to
Mida, and begged that the hand might be mine.

All of us were at last enclosed beneath the skies, then two
gates in the surrounding wall were opened, one to either side
of the area. Males and slave-women entered eagerly when allowed to do so, moving slowly from enclosure to enclosure.
Some continued past us without pausing, yet many stopped
before my warriors and myself, the eyes of the males showing
heat, the eyes of the females disapproval. One rounded male,

despite the urging of his slave-woman, remained standing before me, his face full of desire, his eyes filled with decision. He raised a hand and made a noise with his fingers, and a moment later, an armed male appeared beside him.

"I would buy this one," said the rounded male, his eyes still upon me. "I offer two silver pieces."

"Her price is forty silver pieces," replied the armed male, grinning. "Could she be had for two, she might long since be found in my own quarters. It stirs a man's blood merely to gaze upon her."

"Forty is too much!" protested the rounded male, turning to frown at the armed one. "I am only able to offer five at the most!"

"Forty is her price." The other shrugged. "Set personally by the High Seat. It shall not be lowered."

The rounded male turned again to me, his eyes desolate with deprivation. He gazed but a moment longer, then moved away, his slave-woman following after sending to me a hate-filled look. The look amused me, and I smiled, for I would not have had her male even had she begged it. She was welcome to him, such as he was.

Within the enclosures were we kept till the light was at its highest, and many were the city folk who came to stare. Some few males arrived with notice taken by the armed ones, and these males were attended by the slave-women who had not been enclosed. The slave-women trailed the males closely, eager to be sent running for drink or wet, sweet-smelling cloth. At times it was they, themselves, the males desired, their bodies touched familiarly as the male strolled from enclosure to enclosure. Each of these found interest in my warriors and myself, yet were they displeased with that which was termed our "price." One protested that his profit would be too long in coming at such a price, but the armed male with whom he spoke merely laughed. I understood none of what they spoke.

With the light at its highest, those before the enclosure were hurried out of the area, the gates being closed and barred behind them. Then were the slave-women removed again, those who were unenclosed being taken first. Of my warriors, first were taken Binat and Comir, then Larid and Fayan, I, again, being left to the last. The males led me through the doorway to the large area, but I was not returned

to the room of enclosures. In its stead, I was taken to a doorway on the left, where waited she called Karil. The female
stood happily, a smile upon her face, her hands clasped joy-
ously before her.

"The display shall be excellent!" said she as I was brought
to her, great gladness in her voice. "The brown-tressed ones
ringing the group, then they of the red and golden hair
closest to the center, and at the center, *you*, my girl! Those
who pay their coppers for the display shall not be disappointed! Bring her in."

The males followed after the female, stepping carefully to
avoid the slave-women sho sat here and there upon the dark
floor cloth, a length of leather running from their collars to
circles fast in the floor, which held them in place. The room
was perhaps seven paces by seven, hung with golden silks, lit
by torches in silver sconces, yet it was worse than the deep
place of darkness where we had at first been chained. To the
rear of the room were my warriors, and those slave-women,
six in number, who had been kept enclosed while the others
had washed and cooked. The slave-women wept, my warriors
fought, yet all were held fast in place by metal and leather.
In half circle upon platforms of various heights were they set,
three slave-women to either outside end, all brown-haired and
all dressed in long, slave-woman coverings of white cloth,
then one at each side, were Binat and Comir, they also being
brown-haired, though they had still their clan coverings.
Beside Binat was Fayan, beside Comir was Larid, between
the platforms of those two, an unoccupied platform which
completed the half circle. I, too, fought as I was drawn forward, for each of them, slave-woman and warrior alike, had
been placed upon her platform in a manner which invited
touch and use by a male. Arms were arranged above heads,
wrists set in cuffs, throats tied fast with leather, knees bent at
various angles, ankles well apart and secured by other cuffs.
With all of my strength I struggled against being placed upon
the last of the platforms, yet my strength was not great
enough to equal that of the two males. I almost gasped as my
back was pressed to the silk covered platform, as leather was
drawn about my throat to hold me in place, but I was able to
keep silent even as my arms were fastened in cuffs. I kicked
at the males when they reached for my ankles, catching one
on the chest, with a grunt from him as result, yet nothing else

did I accomplish, for I was then closed in the cuffs, unable to draw my legs together.

She called Karil walked about, lifting the covering of two of the slave-women a bit, moving the hair of Comir and Larid, stopping before me to straighten my life sign. Truly pleased was she as she glanced about, and then she clapped her hands.

"Our patrons shall begin arriving very shortly," she said to the males who stood about the room. "You may now prepare them."

She then left the room with head held high, and the males grinned broadly and came forward, nearly two hands of them, to my warriors and me. Three stopped beside me, one of them being he who had said he would have owned me, and they ranged themselves upon either side of the platform. He who had spoken with the rounded male stood alone above me, his hand beside my leg.

"I regret I may not complete that which I now begin," said he, his eyes hungry and burning, "yet would such a thing mean my life. Perhaps you may sometime be removed from display, and then I shall see to you properly."

I did not know the meaning of his words, but his intent became apparent. His hand moved from the platform to my leg, his fingers stroking in a long, slow, upward line. As my thigh was reached, I shivered, and then did the other males touch me as well. On my thighs and breasts was I caressed, and so, too, at the center of my being, the intent, perhaps, to drive me insane. Nearly were their intentions realized when, as I moaned in the metal and leather, the males ceased their caresses and walked from me. Though my need was great, I held to myself, and did not cry out when the males stopped beside the slave-women upon their platforms, and did to them as they had done to us. Small sounds only did I hear from my warriors, for they, too, were Midanna, yet the slave-women had not such strength to draw upon. They wept as they were touched softly, lingeringly, and then screamed and begged the males to return when they were abandoned. Their screams and tears availed naught, however, for the males did not return to them. The males did each choose a seated slave-woman, and with them did they ease the strain which touching us had put upon them. The sight of this added to the fire in my blood, yet soon had they seen to their need and returned to their places about the room. We upon the platforms writhed in silence or with sobs, for the males had seen to their needs.

Directly had the males finished with the slave-women, the door to the room was thrown open by one of them to allow the admittance of the female Karil and a large group of males. She led them within the room with a flourish, gesturing about herself.

"A field of flowers, my friends," said she, "each waiting to be plucked so she may give up her essence. Please feel free to look about yourselves."

The males, of many sizes and shapes, separated to move about the room, some few looking closely upon the slave-women who sat upon the cloth. These slave-women who were so looked upon immediately placed themselves upon their knees, heads bowed, eyes down, their fingers laced before them. She named Karil, however, spent no time on these, moving, instead, to the platforms, her head high, a smile upon her lips.

"These are my best," she said to the males who stood about inspecting us, her arms sweeping open to indicate the platforms. "My lovelies toward each end may be had for a mere ten silver pieces each, and worth twice that. See how eager they are to please you."

A male stepped to a slave-woman on her platform, and placed his hand upon her. She writhed at the touch and wept, begging to be taken, and the male laughed. "This one is hot enough," said he, raising her covering to see the more of her. "I might offer two silver pieces."

"Impossible," laughed she called Karil. "I could not part with her for less than eight."

"Her skin is passably smooth," mused the male, moving his two hands over the slave-woman, who sobbed with her pain. "Four silver pieces."

"Come now," smiled she called Karil, going to the male and placing her hand upon his arm, "think of the pleasure she may give you, being unable to refuse you. She need not even be clad, should that be your wish. Surely six silver pieces is not too great a price for such delights."

The eyes of the male were still upon the slave-woman of the platform, the tension of his body speaking well of his desire. Again did he place his hand upon her, causing her to weep the louder, then said in a hoarse voice, "Five."

The female Karil smiled a knowing smile, and then re-moved her hand from his arm. "I see she does not please you as greatly as she might," said she, stepping back a bit. "Per-haps you would care to examine my flowers of the carpet? They may be had for as little as a silver piece each."

As she began to turn away, the male grasped her arm in anger. "Very well!" said he, his lips tight, his eyes flashing. "Six silver pieces! Though did you not speak with the voice of the High Seat. . . ."

"Yet, I do speak so," laughed the female Karil, and then clapped her hands. "The guard shall release her, and you may have her papers from Bariose, who is also to be given the silver. I wish you much pleasure with your purchase."

Her head nodded toward the male, then did she take her-self off, to join a male who found interest in another of the platform slave-women. The angry male waited in silence as an armed male released the slave-woman from the platform, first taking the leather which had held her head in place, and knotting it to the circle of the collar she wore. The angry male was given the leather, and once freed, the slave-woman was pulled by the male from the platform, and dragged from the room behind him. She still wept, for she still felt her need, yet had she seemed fearful as well. The angry male could not vent his anger upon the female Karil, yet he would have to express it. The slave-woman would not find her lot an easy one.

Another two of the platform slave-women were taken by males, then the female Karil came to stand beside a male who stood above me, one who had stood above me for some time, his arms folded across his broad chest, his masculine face entirely without expression. The sight of him had stirred me, yet I had been able to conceal my need. The female Karil smiled at me, then clasped her hands before her.

"Is she not lovely?" asked the female softly, her words very nearly a sigh. "A desirable child indeed, and one who also desires to please."

The male's lips moved in the faintest of smiles. "Do you think me blind?" asked he, his deep voice slightly amused. "Those black eyes are not the eyes of a slave eager to please. She has held my gaze as long as I have stood here, not once thinking me her master. She does not feel herself slave."

"But, of course," laughed the female, gazing fondly at me.

"It has been left to her master to teach her that she is slave. It shall be a great part of his pleasure with her, yet does she ache to be had by a man. Have you tried her heat? If not, do so, and see that what I say is truth."

The male's smile deepened somewhat, and his hand reached toward me, his eyes still holding mine. His touch was that of a male to a slave-woman, and a fury rose with my heat. Was I, a war leader of the Hosta of the Midanna, to be touched so?

"See her eyes now!" laughed the male, his hand still upon me. "She would have my life, were she able to take it! This one is worth the ten you ask. Have her uncuffed and leashed."

"Alas, my friend, at ten I am unable to do so," sighed the female, reaching forward to stroke my hair. "Her price is a firm forty, set personally by the High Seat. Is forty too much to ask for such fire and beauty? For the pleasure of teaching her to kneel at your feet, obedient to your will? See how she responds to your touch, and think how great her desire to please would be, should she be denied for a time! Buy her, and make her yours alone!"

The male touched me once again, and then sighed. "I would," said he heavily. "had I the forty. I would give that and more to own this female. There is no possibility of the price being lessened?"

"At this time, none," responded the female sadly, her hand still upon my hair. "And I did so wish to see her with the proper master!"

"I wish but one thing," said I with difficulty, holding the female's bright blue eyes with mine. "Should I ever again hold a sword within my grasp, I would wish to see your insides upon the ground before me. Then would my denied desires be fulfilled."

The female gasped and paled at my words, then she snatched away her hand as she stepped quickly back from my platform, and the male laughed in pleasure. "Filled with fire, indeed," said he, folding his arms once more. "Should I ever have her price, it would be wise to add the price of a lash to it. She shall not be easily tamed."

"The ungrateful savage!" snapped the female, her fists held in fury before her. "She shall be punished for speaking so to me, and punished well!"

She then whirled and marched away, her back straight in

its long, city slave-woman covering of pink silk. The male watched her go, then turned to me with a grin.

"I fear you shall regret your words, girl," said he, and then he reached out to touch my breast. "It would be a crime to mark a body such as yours, yet have you great need of the lash. I, in their place, would take care to give pain alone. Hopefully, they, too, shall see the wisdom in such a course of action. Be brave, but learn from the error."

He then turned from me and left the room, looking briefly at those who sat upon the cloth. My body burned from where his fingers had touched, and the misery was not yet at an end. For many hind did we lie upon the platforms, suffering the stares and touches of those who came to us, but not a one was able to meet the demands of the black-haired female. She had once again become sweet-tempered and friendly, yet was there a coldness in her eyes when she looked upon me, and many were those whom she urged to "test my heat." I would have tossed about upon the platform had I been able, therefore did I grow to be grateful for the metal and leather which held me. I would not have writhed in my need before her.

The light must have been low when at last the door was closed upon the final males. More than a hand of the slave-women upon the cloth had been taken, as well as four of the platform females. Comir and Larid, the only ones of my warriors within my sight, seemed as played out as I, myself, felt. I was weary of being bound and touched, and would have taken any opportunity to escape, even had I known that such attempt would be fore-doomed. Far better to be in Mida's Realm, than to be treated so.

And Mida's Crystal! How was it to be recovered if I lay there a prisoner, my warriors beyond the walls of the city, the thieves moving ever farther away from the sword of vengeance? And then I recalled what I had told Gimin. A hand of feyd, I had said, wait no longer. Had she obeyed my word? Had the hand already passed? I could not know, yet must the Crystal be recovered! My fate was in Mida's hands, therefore must my warriors continue in search of the Crystal! I resolved to find some manner in which Larid and Fayan and Binat and Comir might elude those who held us, and thereby see that my word was obeyed. But how? How were they to be freed of the metal upon them?

Long did I think upon the questions, even to the time we were returned to the larger enclosures, yet little had come to me. My warriors must be free of metal and enclosures. However, only those slave-women who washed and cooked were freed, and of those, only the most attractive to males were freed to the open air. Far more attractive were my warriors than those who had been free, but how were they to be freed to begin with?

I sat in the enclosure, seeing the ache my warriors yet felt—as did I—and feeling upon my wrists the metal which had been replaced before I had been freed from the platform. Larid and Binat sat as I did, their backs against the metal of the enclosure, their legs straight out before them. Fayan walked the enclosure restlessly, as weary as we, yet unable to remain still. Comir sat alone, her face to the metal, her legs folded before her, her shoulders bowed. She had been much disturbed by the happenings of the fey, by the feelings she had been made to feel, by the shame that had touched her. Very young was she, too young, perhaps, to have accompanied me. I should have thought of the dangers, and left her to grow a bit more.

Again were the reeking bowls of mixture brought to us, and again we ignored them, yet this time it was not to go unnoticed. Bariose halted before the enclosure, frowning at the untouched bowls, then he raised his eyes to us.

"Why have you not yet eaten, slaves?" he demanded. "Come here and do so at once!"

My warriors looked to me, and I merely shrugged. "We do not feed upon that which seems trodden under foot," I informed Bariose. "Nor do we feed as children of the wild, with our arms bound behind us. Should you wish to release us and offer meat, well and good. If not, you may depart."

"May I, indeed!" said he with cold indignation. "It seems learning comes to you slowly, slave! You shall eat this moment of your own volition, else shall you be fed! Will you eat?"

Calmly I gazed into his angry, dark eyes, and simply said, "No."

"Very well," said he, then motioned to him two of the armed males. He raised his hand, indicating me, and said, "Feed her." Then he turned and walked away.

The armed males looked upon one another, shrugged their shoulders, then entered the enclosure, pulled me to my feet, and removed me. I was held by one of them while the second male fetched one of the hand of pots from within the enclosure. He it was who had spoken to the rounded male in the open area, he also who had been first to touch me. He returned, grinning, with the pot in his hand.

"Never before has it been necessary to feed a female slave," said he, rolling the mixture about in the pot. "It took only the sight of the lash to have them swallow the gruel as though it were their favorite of dishes. I believe, my lovely, that I shall enjoy feeding you a good deal more than I enjoy feeding male slaves. Hold her."

The first male grasped my hair and pulled, forcing my head back somewhat, then he held my nose closed with his fingers. The second brought the pot to my lips, forcing my jaw open with his free hand, then spilling some of the vile mixture into my mouth. I struggled in their grip, unable to breathe, and then I forced my throat to swallow while holding the mixture in my mouth. He with the pot, thinking I had swallowed the mouthful, released my jaw so that he might pour more of the mixture into me, and then I spat the mouthful back at him, catching his face and spattering his covering. The male jumped back with a shout, too late, by far, to protect himself, and he who held me roared out his laughter, as did my warriors and many of the male slaves. The bespattered male wiped his face slowly with distaste, and flung what had been on him to the floor. His cleared eyes glowered at me as he stood there, and quickly a female slave hurried to him with a moistened cloth. He wiped the mixture from him, then took the pot again and approached me with heavy steps.

"For that, you shall eat this bowlful and a second," said he, no longer seeming amused. "Would that you were mine to punish as well as to feed!"

He then emptied the mixture into me, allowing no further opportunity for a repetition of what had at first occurred. True to his word, a second pot was brought, and that, too, was forced upon me. I struggled to the last, half suffocated and completely nauseated, yet was there no way of avoiding the mixture. My warriors, too, at the word of Bariose, were fed the vile creation, they, too, struggling as I sat within the enclosure, feeling as though I would lose the whole of it. When all had been fed, again was the chain attached to our collars, and again were we stood at the wall to be wet with

pots of water. In truth, we were nearly as badly in need of it
as we had been before, the sweat of the fey and the spilling
of mixture combining to make a more than unpleasant
aroma.

Upon completion of the combing of our hair, again I was
separated from my warriors to be taken before Bariose. The
female Karil stood beside him, her arms folded in satisfaction, as he once more swung the coiled, covered leather
against his leg. They both regarded me as I stood before
them, and Bariose gestured with his hand. The two males
who gripped me then forced me to my knees, so that I must
look upward toward the male and female.

"You are to be beaten, slave," said Bariose, with a look of
stern disapproval. "The beating may be lessened, however,
should you show proper regret for your words and actions.
You may begin with words of apology for your Mistress here,
and then you may address me."

"Jalav regrets only the loss of her weapons," I said, aware
that again the fire would touch me, and I spoke to Mida in
my heart, asking that I be spared the shame of showing
weakness before my enemies. "City folk have not the courage
to face her in honest battle."

The male and female were angered at my words, and
quickly I was taken to the wall and bound there, my arms
high and wide, my wrists gripped tight, my body raised upon
my toes, held close to the cool, smooth, pink of the stone. I
pressed my cheek to the wall, awaiting the first of it, holding
tight to the remembrance that I was a warrior. My back, although uncut, was yet ridged and sore from the earlier efforts
of Bariose.

Two hands of fire did I count before darkness claimed me,
in great pain, yet unshamed by the utterance of it. Naught do
I recall between the last of it and awakening in the enclosure,
bound as always, my warriors about me. Movement was agony, my attempts to sit in vain. I lay upon my right side,
feeling the sickness and loss of strength, cursing those of the
city as I had never before cursed an enemy, and Fayan spoke
to me.

"Jalav, they are the spawn of darkness!" said she, her voice
low, yet filled with bitterness. "They degrade us by their every action, and beat you as though you were theirs to own!
We must escape them!"

"Fayan, you speak truth," I said with difficulty, attempting in some way to ease the pain; my thoughts were unusually clear. This time, I knew, they had drawn blood, and perhaps it was that that had aided me. "There is something we must try."

"Attack!" Fayan breathed, the prospect lighting her eyes; Larid, Binat and Comir stirred with pleasure.

"We may not attack," I said, wishing it were not so. "To die by the swords of the males would be sufficient escape, yet must the Crystal of Mida be remembered. The Hosta must ride in search of it, no matter the fate of their war leader."

My warriors were silent then, knowing from my words that I would not accompany them. I had realized that such a thing would not be possible, for never would Bariose and the female Karil see me unbound. I would wait to know that my warriors had truly regained their freedom, then would I, with great pleasure, take the remaining avenue of escape—to Mida's Realm.

"We shall make the attempt with the new light," I continued, "for, although we cannot see it, we know of its presence when all are awakened. You have seen those slave-women who walk about in the open, unchained and unenclosed, so that they may accompany males. Upon the new fey, those slave-women shall be my warriors."

I explained then how it would be done, which greatly displeased and disturbed them, yet am I war leader, and to be obeyed. When the matter was clear, I bid them rest and remember, and then asked Mida's blessings in their attempt. Despite the still-burning torches, they were quickly asleep, gathering their strength for the new light. I, too, attempted sleep, unsuccessfully. The pain in my back was not easily ignored, and many thoughts chased each other about in my head. That my warriors would be gone gladdened me, yet did I also feel a coldness that I would be alone, bound among my enemies, perhaps unable to find my own escape. To continue such an existence was unthinkable, but it might happen. My thoughts then went to her who bore me, whose blood I had not been able to avenge. That others would find the vengeance rightfully mine was some comfort, yet how would I face her spirit, should these city enemies succeed in shaming me? I was a war leader of the Hosta of the Midanna, denied the right to die with due dignity. Would they take everything before allowing me release? Where, then, would my soul go, for never then would it belong among those in Mida's blessed realm! Long did I think upon such matters, and soon was the pain of my back as though naught. The greater pain of confinement fended off sleep.

7.

Escape—and a price is met

My eyes opened quickly to the arrival of Bariose and the female Karil, to find that my warriors already sat awake and alert. Stiffly, I struggled up that I might sit, seeing Larid, Binat and Comir together by the wall of the enclosure, Fayan a distance apart from them. No word did we speak to one another, for all had already been said.

The released slave-women went quickly about their work, their reduced number affording more tasks to fewer workers. We sat and watched and waited, and soon there came the reek of the mixture, heated within the large, metal pot. When the small wooden pots were brought to us, I continued to sit as I was, yet did Larid and Binat and Comir, in obedience to my instructions, glance at one another, and then rise hesitantly to make their way to the mixture. As though angered by their actions, I, too, rose to my feet, and stood stiffly.

"What do you do?" I demanded coldly of them, causing them to pause before the pots. "Such as that is not to be fed upon!"

"But, Jalav, our hunger is great!" pleaded Larid, whose liking for pretense was deeper than that of the others. "Surely, naught save the leather shall be gained by refusal to feed!"

"We shall not do as they bid us!" said I, firm in my beliefs. "Return to your places, and do not leave them again!"

"No!" Larid cried, and then fell to her knees before a pot. "I must feed!"

121

She turned to the mixture as Binat and Comir, nodding in fearful agreement, also knelt. In a rage, I sprang to them, kicking them from the pots as they begged and pleaded to be allowed to feed. The armed males were already at the enclosure, already entering it, before I understood that Fayan, rather than joining my other warriors in supposed rebellion, was instead at my side, aiding me in keeping them from the pots. Too late, then, was it for her to be removed with them, too late that she might also escape.

An armed male placed himself before me as another aided my warriors in leaving the enclosure. I attempted to pass him, in my anger, to reach those who would feed upon the offerings of enemies, but his outstretched arms restrained me. He laughed at my struggle, placing himself so that his body touched mine, yet not putting his hands upon me. Fayan merely stared in fury, and soon were she and I alone in the enclosure. Larid, Binat, and Comir knelt without, at the feet of Bariose, and wept in their misery as they had seen slave-women do. Tears come hard to Midanna, yet in the service of Mida, all things are possible.

"I would know what was done to you," said Bariose to them, a frown upon his face. "Fighting between slaves is forbidden!"

"She would not allow us to feed!" wept Larid, her face raised to his. "I do not wish to be beaten, yet she will not allow us to obey you! We fear her anger and may do nothing against her, but I do not wish to be beaten! Protect me, and I will obey you as you ask!"

"Do these others feel the same?" asked Bariose, thoughtfully. At the urgent nods of Binat and Comir, he, too, nodded. "Very well," said he. "For my protection, I shall have obedience in all things. You shall kneel in my presence, and kneel, also, to your Mistress. You are to obey her now, and later there shall be other things for you to obey in. Go now to her, and beg to be put to work."

Gratefully did Larid, Binat and Comir rise to their feet and hurry to the female Karil, kneeling before her. They would do what was required of them, no matter how debasing, for I had explained that Bariose, thinking them eager for his protection, would likely use them to please those males of note who came to the open area, pleasing himself, too, in the thought of their capitulation to him. Should it not happen this fey, it would happen the next, for I was certain that it would happen. Should it not happen within three feyd, they were free to act as they would.

Bariose looked upon me with satisfaction, thinking that he had stolen my warriors from me, and I did not disabuse him. He and his males turned to other things then, and I looked upon Fayan, who stood innocently by my side, avoiding my gaze.

"The word of the war leader no longer has weight?" I asked quietly, studying her innocence. "What do you do here, beside me, rather than with your sister warriors?"

"Surely, Jalav has forgotten!" said she, her eyes wide with sincerity as she turned her face to me. "Your word was for the others, and I was to remain with you! Thus would the matter seem truer to the enemy, and therefore strengthen the chance of the others! Does Jalav think I would disobey the war leader?"

I smiled and looked toward my warriors who knelt before the female Karil. Their wrists had been unbound by males, and refastened before them, so they might work at what tasks were given them. Even so small a thing was victory, and perhaps Fayan was right.

"No," I said softly, bringing my eyes again to Fayan. "The warrior Fayan, in her courage and pride, would not disobey the war leader. I am pleased to have you beside me, sister."

"It is my proper place," said she very simply, a smile in her eyes. We moved from the metal then, seating ourselves without speaking, and soon, perhaps, Fayan regretted her choice. Four males came to again force the mixture upon us, and the struggle was not pleasant. I found much pain in the grip of the male who held me, for I was held with my back against him. Almost did I feel relief when the last of the mixture was within me, and I was returned to the enclosure. Fayan's face showed her disgust at being forced to swallow the vile concoction, and I would have smiled at her expression, had mine not matched hers. Larid, in her role playing, came to laugh at our discomfort, her wrists held plainly so that we might see her partial freedom. Her laughter held more true amusement than I cared for, as she and the others seemed to have been overlooked with regard to the mixture, therefore was I pleased when a male passed behind her and struck her sharply below the small of the back, to remind her of her work. She almost turned on the male in anger, yet remembered in time what she was about, and then followed

meekly after him. Fayan and I laughed then, and heartily, for
such actions needed not be ours.

Soon came the time that we were removed from the enclosures, and nearly did I watch with hope as my warriors
were led through the door. When the males came for Fayan
and me, I fought as though reluctant to be put again within
the tiny enclosure, although truthfully I was desperate to see
what had befallen my warriors. I could not halt to look about
as I was dragged to the enclosure and thrust within, yet when
I turned, furiously straining against the metal, there knelt my
warriors before the wall, wrists tight before them, heads
down, shoulders bowed—unenclosed! Surely, Mida had seen
our plight and had answered her daughters!

The hind passed as had the others, with many coming to
stare at what was held by the enclosures. Again did some offer a "price," which, I gathered at last, was an attempt to
trade for me, yet none could see the matter done. Males of
note had come too, and my warriors accompanied them as
though loath to be parted from them. Pleased were these
males by their presence, and pleased, too, were the males of
Bariose by their actions. They ran, and knelt, and smiled, as
though true slave.

The light was almost at its highest when the moment came.
The last male of note departed the area, a familiar touch
upon Binat marking his departure, and all of my warriors
now knelt by the wall, none save two armed males within
reach of them. They raised their heads to seek my agreement,
and I nodded, silently wishing them Mida's favor. Larid and
Binat rose slowly, leaving Comir to stand as though unde-
cided, and quietly they each approached an armed male. The
males gestured impatiently for them to return to their places,
but were watching those who walked before the enclosures;
my warriors seized the swords of the males before the males
had knowledge of it, and, but an instant later, the males lay in
their own spreading blood.

Screams and shouts arose, city folk ran hither and yon,
armed males found their movements blocked by those who
screamed and shouted, and my warriors turned and raised
their bloody swords and arms, shouted, "Jalav!" then quickly
disappeared through the gate to the left. Their salute pleased
me nearly as much as their escape, for they would now attempt to move as the zaran moves through the forest, silent
and deadly and unseen, finding or forcing a place to hide

themselves till the darkness, and then they would make their way over the wall to true freedom. I threw my head back and laughed, Fayan joining my laughter, and laughed even further at the fury which gripped Bariose. He shouted to his males to pursue nearly frothing like a well-run kan, and then drove the city folk from the area, seeing the gates locked once more. Few were the armed males remaining behind, and those few replaced us all in the wide enclosures, none being allowed their freedom, none being placed upon the platforms. Fayan and I were well pleased, and sat within our enclosure patiently, waiting for the passage of the hind. Should my warriors remain free till the fall of darkness, none there would see them again.

The return of the armed males—weary and alone—gave me cause to thank Mida for her kindness. My warriors had regained their freedom, and the Hosta would now surely continue in search of the Crystal. Larid carried my final word to Gimin, should the new war leader not yet have departed, and all would be seen to. The males were angered and concerned with their own feeding, and no slave-woman was released to tend the great, metal pot, therefore were we spared the necessity of swallowing any more of the mixture. The slave-women of other enclosures wept and begged to be given the opportunity to feed, yet were Bariose and the female Karil too wroth to heed them. They and their males departed, much agitated, and Fayan and I composed ourselves for sleep, pleased that our own capture might soon be ended. The deaths of two of their number would be remembered by the males, and quickly would their blades strike in retaliation when Fayan and I chose to press them. That sleep I dreamed of the Realm of Mida, and was much gratified.

When Bariose and the female returned Fayan and myself were awake and awaiting them. The slave-women were released to see to their duties, and quickly indeed were those duties seen to. As the slave-women scurried about, hastening to the time that they might heal their hunger, Bariose came to our enclosure and halted before it. No trace of his fury remained, and he smiled coldly at me.

"I regret to inform you that your traitorous friends were unfortunate enough to be found," said he, and folded his arms. "They were dealt with as are all escaped slaves, and now lie beyond the wall, feeding the creatures of the forests and fields. You may now tell yourself that their deaths are upon you who urged their attempt. But for you, they would still live within these walls."

"I thank you for your words, male," said I, surprised that he would honor me as the cause of my warriors' freedom. "Perhaps I have misjudged your actions in the past. I am pleased to be told of my warriors, and shall repay the favor, should I find myself able to do so."

"What words do you speak?" he demanded, the smile gone, confused. He grasped the metal of the enclosure. "Do you not understand what I say? Those others have been found and killed!"

"Your words are clear." I nodded, frowning. "My warriors now stand with Mida. May they shine forever in her presence."

"Truly are you savage!" he said, staring in disbelief. "You care naught even for your own kind!"

He then took himself swiftly away, seemingly disturbed over some matter. Perhaps it rankled that my warriors were no longer within reach of his leather. Fayan and I looked at each other, then bowed our heads in memory of three fine warriors who had escaped their enemies.

Not long were we left to memory, for the mixture was brought and again fed to us. The males were impatient, considerably harder than they had been in their handling of us. No understanding had I of their actions, nor had Fayan. Had not the spilled blood of their brothers been avenged?

The light was sharp when we were placed within the enclosures in the open space, yet was I easily able to see that no slave-woman knelt by the wall. Fayan and I grinned at one another, in amusement at the foolishness of males, who believed that slave-women might emulate the actions of warriors. Soon were those at the gates allowed entry, and then began another time of examination.

Long since was I without patience for the mindless city folk who walked and gawked, and was attempting to see what there was to be seen from the gate to the right, when Fayan's gasp riveted my attention. She stared toward the gate to the left, her eyes and mouth wide, and when my gaze followed hers, I, too, felt a bit open-mouthed. Striding in was a pleasantly unconcerned Nidisar, yet that was not what surprised me. Beside Nidisar, as though friends of long standing, walked the sthuvad of the Hosta home tents, he of the red-gold hair called Telion, and the unnamed, dark-faced, light-eyed leader of the hunters, who had been in the capture of my warriors! The three came directly toward our enclosures, wide grins upon their faces. They came to gloat over the capture of Jalav, I knew, and therefore I stood a bit straighter in my enclosure. I would not lower myself before them and add to their pleasure, yet did Fayan seem pale where she stood, though her head was high. That she was disturbed, I could well understand.

The three males stepped closer to our enclosures, Nidisar before Fayan, the others before me. The dark hunter, I saw, was nearly of a size with the sthuvad, yet I had not known that. The times I had seen him, he had either been sitting down, lying down, or standing alone. Now he stood beside this Telion, and they both inspected me closely.

"A fair piece of female flesh, Telion," said the hunter, regarding me critically. "What think you of her?"

"Passable, Ceralt," nodded the sthuvad, also eyeing me. "A bit too spirited perhaps, yet passable."

"I rather fancy this one," mused Nidisar, his attention close upon Fayan. She calmly returned his stare, her face still pale.

"Shall we buy a woman to serve us?" asked the hunter, Ceralt, of the sthuvad, Telion. "There is a thing or two I might find to occupy a slave."

"Perhaps it would be best to look farther," responded Telion doubtfully. "Surely, she is not the best to be had among the lot. In her youth, she would doubtless faint at the demands a man would put to her."

No wish had I to give sign that I had heard him, yet did my head come up even farther at his words, in anger. Ceralt, the hunter, merely laughed.

"I feel sure," said he, "that she is capable of learning to please a man. Yet, perhaps, in fairness to ourselves, we should look farther. Do not stray, pretty bird, for we may yet return. Do you accompany us, Nidisar?"

"If you wish," nodded Nidisar, "although I have found the slave I shall buy." His eyes returned to Fayan, and he grinned. "Await me here, golden slave, for I shall return shortly for you."

The three males strolled away, carefully examining the female occupants of enclosures, and I watched but a moment before turning to Fayan. I expected to see in her the same fury I, myself, felt at their ridicule, yet was she following

Nidisar with almost-frightened eyes, her back hard against
the rear of the enclosure.

"Fayan, what ails you?" I frowned, not understanding her
behavior.

"Jalav, he must not return for me!" she whispered, clearly
upset. "I could not bear it!"

"They merely make sport of us," I said, beginning to feel
concern for her. "I am sure they have not the—price—with
which to trade. Fayan, has something occurred of which you
have not spoken?"

"Something, indeed," replied Fayan heavily, her head and
eyes low. "When we were taken by the males in that place of
hunters and renth, my sword did not drink beside yours,
Jalav, for my sword was no longer mine. It had been taken,
with me, by this Nidisar."

Surely was it a fortunate thing that I could not then speak,
for my words would have done credit neither to myself nor
to Fayan.

"I knew not what would befall me, till it had occurred,"
she continued miserably. "I stood with a pot of renth in my
hand, laughing at the thought of throwing daggers, as both
male and warrior were near to being unable to see the wall
which was to be thrown at, when I was seized from behind. I
thought to teach the male who held me the folly of touching
a warrior without her permission, but I was unable to free
myself from his grasp! Never had I thought that a male
might be possessed of such strength! I was carried, unable to
reach my weapons, through a doorway and to a very small
room, where my sword and dagger were taken from me.
When released, I turned quickly to see who the male might
be, and was angered to observe this Nidisar, sliding a bolt of
metal which held the door closed from within."

Her eyes again raised to mine, and she pleaded for understanding. "Jalav, I fought him!" she said with intensity. "I
fought him as best I could, yet did he see to me easily! He
took my clan covering, and threw me to the lenga pelt, and
when I continued to attempt resistance, he slid a small part
of the wall aside, and withdrew a configuration of chains,
which he then forced upon me! In Mida's name, I swear it
was impossible to resist such a device! He held to it as he
took me, forcing me with pain to move as he wished! Never
have I felt such terrible pain, not even when clawed once by
a lenga when on the hunt! I—obeyed his commands to keep

the pain from me, rather than endure it as a warrior should. I am not worthy to be called Hosta, for I have shamed myself and my clan. Should he return for me, I shall force the males to slay me, rather than be shamed again."

Her eyes were again upon the floor of her enclosure, her pain and shame easily felt. I longed to have my arms free, so that I might place a hand of encouragement upon her shoulder.

"Fayan, a warrior may not be condemned for something she cannot change," I said softly. "Mida is able to see within us, and surely she has seen your strength. You may reclaim your honor with your death—should that be necessary."

Her head raised again, confused. "You speak as though you think the act unnecessary." She frowned. "As I have been shamed, how would it be unnecessary?"

"I have little true understanding," I said thoughtfully, merely a strange feeling. Mida allows that which she wishes, and always for purposes of her own. Could this, all which has befallen us, be in accordance with Mida's will, to achieve her purpose? Have we, her warriors, been demanded service of, service which would not ordinarily be given?"

"How may one know?" asked Fayan. "Should such be the case, we are not free to allow our lives to be taken!"

"There is one way to know." I grinned, pleased with the possibility. "Should further service be required of us, Mida will not allow us to be slain."

"Truly spoken!" laughed Fayan, seeing the self-evidence of this. "We have merely to try, and should we fail, we shall know that we have succeeded in answering our question!"

"We must try when we are returned to the large enclosure," I said. "No longer is there reason to remain here, should it not be Mida's wish."

Fayan nodded, no longer disturbed by shame, and I looked high, to see the position of the light. Shortly would we be returned to the closed-in area, and then we would find the means to attack.

Abruptly were my thoughts taken from the skies with the return of the three males, Nidisar, Ceralt and Telion, in the company of a fourth male, one who saw to those in the enclosures. The males stopped before us, and Ceralt gestured toward Fayan and myself.

"Have you no others aside from these?" he asked the male of Bariose. "I had heard that a full five were taken."

"The others attempted escape, and were slain," the male answered stiffly. "Are you merely curious, or do you wish to buy them?"

Ceralt, Telion, and Nidisar exchanged strange looks, and then Ceralt cleared his throat. "As the others are slain, we shall indeed take these," said he. "My friend and I wish the black-haired one, my brother hunter shall have the one with golden hair."

"Easily said," snorted the male, seemingly in annoyance. "Had I a copper piece for each of those who wished to own these two, I, myself, would have their price. They are set at forty silver pieces each, a price which is fast. Do you wish to look again upon the other female slaves available?"

"No," responded Ceralt evenly, to my surprise, and also to the surprise of the male. "We wish to buy these two, and have the price which was set. To whom must we speak?"

"I will show you to Bariose," said the male, his annoyance lost beneath a smile of pleasure. "He will provide their papers, and I will then personally see to their leashing. Come this way." The males then walked off, and Fayan and I looked upon one another.

"Perhaps they act unknowingly for Mida," she ventured, when I said nothing.

"Perhaps," I agreed somewhat doubtfully, "though such is certainly not my hope. They have little love for Jalav, nor cause for such. We must make our attempt as soon as may be."

Her agreement was heartfelt and complete, and we awaited what would next eventuate. The city folk within the area were escorted to the gates, the gates closed behind them, those within the enclosures removed, and still we were not approached. I began to think that we would be left as we were, when the armed male who had left earlier reappeared, in the company of three other armed males. They carried lenghs of leather, and approached our enclosures directly.

"You are now the property of others," said the first male, as he and another opened the enclosures. "May they find as much pleasure in forcing gruel upon you as we have."

As his hand reached up for my arm, I borrowed the attributes of my life sign, the hadat, and snarled and leapt. Fayan, with the swiftness and ferocity of her own life sign, that of the keren—a child of the wild which often stood upon two legs to hurl its mighty mass in attack—kicked at the opening door of her enclosure, and sent the male before it sprawling to the ground. Swiftly we were among the males, attacking with teeth, showing no mercy, and surely, had not otherwise been Mida's will, we would have been as swiftly slain. Filled with fear were the males, yet were their hands stayed from their weapons. We were struck, each of us, with the hilt of a dagger, hard enough to daze, yet not so hard that death would surely result. The males, breathing heavily, then pulled us from the ground, attached the leather which they carried to the collars about our throats, and tied the free end of the leather to the legs upon which my enclosure stood. The leather was tied so closely, however, that Fayan and I were forced to remain on our knees, a bit bent over. We raised our aching heads to one another, our bodies scratched and bruised from the stones of the ground, and then grinned broadly. Mida watched her warriors closely, so that further service might be rendered.

A mere handful of reckid was it before footsteps heralded the approach of others. Fayan looked past my shoulder and nodded, indicating the presence of the three who had come to claim us. The footsteps stopped, and an exclamation of surprise came from one of the males.

"What has been done to her?" demanded the voice of Telion, so close that his shadow fell upon me.

"She was beaten for disobedience," responded the voice of the armed male, he who had spoken with them earlier. "The lash was covered, therefore shall the welts fade quickly. It is now your decision as to whether her future whippings shall mark her or not."

"I shall not use a lash on a mere girl," said Telion stiffly. "A strip of leather will suffice for any disobedience she may care to attempt."

"You are a fool!" The male laughed bitterly. "A fool in thinking she is a girl, and a fool in paying good silver for her! Those two are savages, and, like savages, shall tear your throats out! I would not have them as a gift!"

"They were not offered you as a gift," came the calm voice of Ceralt. "You may now open the gates for us."

The male made a sound of disgust and moved away, and Fayan and I were untied from the legs of the enclosure. Ceralt held the leather to my collar, Nidisar taking that of Fayan, and Nidisar looked upon Fayan's back as he pulled her to her feet. Pleased did he seem that no welts marked her, and

she looked upon him curiously, as well one might when looking upon a tool of Mida. Telion grasped my arm firmly in his
hand, and thus were we taken to the opened gate and
through.

Many were the city folk we passed, as we walked from
way to way among the dwellings. I had thought anything
preferable to the enclosure I had been kept in, and truthfully,
the ways did seem broader than previous, yet did the feel of
a city seem wrong to me, so close and crowded and dirtied
was it. We came to a way narrower than most, dirtier than
most, and more peopled than most, and ragged city males
came forth, holding up various objects to be seen, urging
those objects upon the males who led us. The males cared
naught for these objects, cuffing away those who offered
them. Others came too, to be cuffed away in turn, yet these
others offered nothing in their outstretched hands. A deformed lot were they, some without eyes and some without
arms or legs, and they lacked more than eyes or limbs. Once
had I fought Lidin, famed war leader of the Summa clan, bitter blood enemies to the Hosta. Lidin had fought well, nearly
taking my life, yet had I succeeded in taking her sword arm
with my blade. She had stood before me, her arm and sword
on the grass between us, her blood pouring forth to feed
Mida's ground, a smile upon her paling face.

"You fight well," she had said, her head held high. "I
salute you, war leader of the Hosta."

Then had she gone to her knees, her wound taking its toll,
yet had she lost none of her dignity. Had she lived, though
possessed of but one arm, still would she have been a warrior
of note, for she retained her dignity. Those about us, with
hands outstretched, would surely have been deformed even
had they all of that which they lacked—for they lacked dignity
most of all.

At last were we urged within a dwelling upon that way, a
small, dirty dwelling, one among many. The opening door
showed us a dim room, no more than seven paces by eight,
which contained naught save a few platforms, with lower
platforms beside them. The bare wooden walls contained few
candles, and none save two large ones were lit. Nidisar led
Fayan to one of these platforms, Ceralt and Telion close behind him, and Nidisar seated himself upon one of the lower
platforms.

"Kneel there," said Nidisar to Fayan, pointing to the floor

by his feet. Fayan looked upon him in confusion, yet Ceralt nodded in agreement.

"And you," said Ceralt to me, seating himself as had Nidisar, though opposite to him. "The floor is a fit place for a slave."

Briefly I studied Ceralt as Telion took his place at the platform to the left of Ceralt, and then I shrugged. As I had no wish to make use of the platforms, I crouched where I stood near Fayan, but this was not what Ceralt wanted. Hard did he pull upon the leather tied to my collar, and I fell to my knees, nearly pitching flat upon my face, for my wrists were still bound behind me. Ceralt held tight to the leather, nearly crushing my throat with the collar, so that I had to kneel.

"That is the position you are to take," Ceralt informed me evenly as I knelt upon the filthy floor, facing the platform. "I shall be pleased to give you whatever instruction you require, so that you may become an obedient slave."

"Well spoken," cackled a voice as I glared up at Ceralt in a rage. An aged, unbelievably obese slave-woman waddled to the platform, her yellowed-gray hair cut shorter than a male's, her head nodding in approval. "So spoke my man, bless him, when he lived," she cackled again. "Many was the time he gave me what-for, for daring to give him backtalk. I was as wild as that one, and aye, as pretty, too, yet he tamed me proper. The first time he bedded me, I knew him for more than my match, and how fine it was, having him prove it. Now, young men, what may I serve you?"

"Renth," answered Ceralt with a smile. "Three flagons of the best renth you possess."

"And two bowls of water for the slaves," added Nidisar, pulling Fayan down to her knees beside me. "We would not wish to forget the slaves."

"Indeed not." Telion grinned, leaning forward to inspect me. "There are many things concerning the slaves which we would not wish to forget."

"To which of you does she belong?" asked the slave-woman of Telion and Ceralt, scratching at her side. The two males laughed, then Ceralt reached forward to take my face in his hand.

"She belongs to both of us, old mother," said he clearly. "My friend and I own her, share and share alike. We have many things in common, we have found, therefore do we own her in common."

"That is not wise," clucked the female, her head shaking as she turned to leave. "Two men may share many things, yet a woman is not one of them. I shall fetch the renth."

Slowly then did she make her way across the floor and to a doorway. "This establishment is excellent for private discussions," said Nidisar in a low voice as the female disappeared through the doorway. "Few come here any longer, and the old mother dozes when she does not serve. We may have the rooms on the floor above for a few coppers, and may leave the city with the new light with little difficulty."

"Which brings us to the question," said Ceralt, looking sternly upon me, "of where those females of yours might now be. I shall have the truth from you, Jalav, so do not think to put me off!"

"The hunter has seen them much more recently than I," I commented, returning his look in sudden amusement. "Why does he not return to where they were?"

"I have!" Ceralt shouted, his fist clenched, and then he regained control of his tone. "I have," he repeated more softly, "in the company of fifty hunters from this city! They were not where I had left them!"

"Nor was there sign upon the ground to show where they had gone," put in Nidisar, somewhat in annoyance. "I find it difficult to believe that five score of women and a score of captured hunters may disappear as easily and completely as that."

"They are warriors, not slave-women," I laughed to Nidisar, pleased that Gimin led my warriors well. "You would find no sign were there twice the number of Hosta and captives." Then I looked again at Ceralt. "How is it that you were released?" I asked. "I do not believe you were able to escape."

His face darkened a bit, and his hand gripped the leather more tightly. "I was released upon the whim of the girl Gimin!" he snapped. "She informed me that she was not able to send her women to the city, but there was nothing to prevent her sending *me* to inquire about you! She also gave me her word that should I betray their position, I would never again see the men of my hunting party! When I returned, quickly and with suitable numbers, they were gone!"

"Would you have had them await your attack?" I asked in amusement. "Rest assured that you were watched closely, and that your return was well noted. My warriors are no longer near Bellinard."

"Of that I am already aware," said Ceralt, slowly and angrily. "What I wish to know is where have they gone? Have they returned to their home?"

"Or have they continued on to Ranistard?" put in Telion, his face also tight with anger. I smiled faintly.

"Gimin is now war leader of the Hosta," I informed them. "Therefore, the movements of the Hosta are now hers to discuss. I have no knowledge of them."

Fayan made a small sound of amusement, yet were Telion and Ceralt taken with rage. Ceralt slid his fist along the leather to my throat, and pulled me closer to him, so that I might more easily see the blaze in his light eyes.

"Do not toy with me, girl!" said he, a rasp in his voice, his face very near to mine. "You are now my property, and none may interfere with whatever I do to you. I will know the whereabouts of my men, or you shall know the meaning of true pain!"

"Ceralt may do as he wishes," I said huskily, finding it difficult to breathe with his hand within the collar. "I know nothing of the whereabouts of the Hosta, and I am prepared to join those of my warriors who earlier found freedom from this city."

Ceralt was silent a long moment, then his hand withdrew from my collar. Released, I fell back upon my heels and knelt there, breathing more easily than I had been able to. When I looked about, the males seemed more than sobered, and Nidisar's hand touched Fayan's hair.

"Are they truly slain?" asked Nidisar of me, his eyes serious and filled with pain. "Larid, and Binat, and that infant Comir. How could such come to pass?"

"They were fortunate enough to escape the walled area," I said. "The male Bariose later informed me that they were found and slain. That they were not recaptured shows that Mida cares for her warriors."

"Such talk is for ignorant savages!" snapped Telion. "Far better that they were recaptured and sold, than that they lie dead and unmourned! I can scarcely credit the heartlessness of the Guard of this city, Ceralt! To slay mere girls, so coldly and out of hand!"

"Their heartlessness is not in question," said Ceralt thoughtfully. "I have heard many things said of this Bariose, and kind-heartedness was not one of them, yet neither was wastefulness. It has come to me that should the girls have been retaken, they would have been well lashed before the other slaves, as a lesson and warning. To merely slay them not only served no purpose, but was wasteful as well. Their prices are now forever lost."

"Then that may mean—they still live!" said Nidisar, his face now creased in smiles. "They live and have escaped!"

"And Bariose seethes," also laughed Telion. "He has claimed their deaths to save himself the embarrassment of admitting their escape!"

"It seems these Hosta females are the cause of much embarrassment everywhere," observed Ceralt, as Fayan and I looked upon one another in gladness. Our sisters had escaped, and still lived to serve Mida! "However," continued Ceralt, "I know of two Hosta females who shall no longer cause embarrassment." Again I looked toward him, and he leaned forward a bit. "With the new light, Jalav, do we travel to Ranistard, for there I believe I shall find your females— and my men. We shall then trade your lives for theirs, your freedom for that of my men. You had best hope they still live when we reach there."

"We go to Ranistard?" asked Fayan, looking from one to another of them. When Ceralt nodded, she threw her head back and laughed as though touched, and I, too, laughed so, for we had discovered that our enemies were determined to force us to that place where we most fervently wished to go! Truly, Mida watched over us, directing our steps and allowing us to serve her!

"You'd best see they get none of this renth!" said the aged female, returning with a board upon which stood three tall pots. She looked upon Fayan and myself in disapproval, disapproving, also of the bewildered expressions upon the faces of the males. "I know not what you have been giving them, yet there are limits even with the use of slaves! Slave or no, such innocent young girls should not be taken advantage of!"

The males, too, burst out in laughter, which further annoyed the aged female. She was about to turn and leave in indignation, when Nidisar spoke.

"A moment, old mother!" he called, his face flushed with laughter. "We apologize for our behavior, and give you our word that no renth shall be given to these—innocent young girls. Are we forgiven?"

"And how may I not forgive three rascals such as you?" quarreled the aged female. "Was my man not one such as yourselves? I shall now fetch the water for the slaves."

She again took her leave, and the three males fell to their renth. I, myself, would have done well with a swallow or two, though that was not forthcoming. The males often moved their eyes to us, yet Fayan and I were offered none of the renth, nor was the leather attached to our collars forgotten. The ends were tied to the legs of the taller platform, thereby allowing the males greater freedom for drinking.

Deep pots of water were brought for Fayan and myself, which we ignored, yet were we not to be left in peace. The aged female paused behind me briefly, then waddled out, only to return, long reckid later, with a wooden pot of something that had a strong herbal odor.

"Her back must be seen to," proclaimed the female, standing above me. "The welts are bad enough, and the cuts must not be allowed to fester. Who is to do it?"

"I shall see to it," replied Ceralt. He rose from the platform and took the pot, then moved behind me.

The touch of his hand nearly made me gasp, for what the pot contained burned against my back. Quickly I shifted about, sitting flat upon the floor, to face Ceralt. The hunter was annoyed by my abrupt movement, yet the aged female placed her hand upon his arm.

"The salve is not soothing," said she, no smile upon her heavy, wrinkled face, "yet must it be applied. You may weep as you need to, girl, but you may not refuse it."

"I do refuse it," said I, not kindly. "I wished nothing from city folk, yet have I received much. I am as I am, and would continue so undisturbed."

"Your wants are no longer to be considered," said Ceralt, and he crouched before me. "Turn again, so that the salve may be applied."

I regarded him as steadily as I had regarded Bariose, though I knew that this time the lash would touch me deeper. Almost did I regret the need for further service to Mida, as I responded, "No."

Ceralt was annoyed, and sounds of vexation came from the aged female and the sthuvad, Telion. The aged female stepped a bit closer, to peer down at me.

"My man would have had her howling for a hin," said she

with a shake of her head. "As she is the belonging of you
two, young men, which shall it be? A beating or the balm?"

"The balm," said Telion without pause, rising from his
place at the platform. "Let us tie her to a bench, Ceralt."

"A good thought," said Ceralt, rising from his crouch, and
he and Telion moved a smaller platform closer from another
place. When the platform stood almost before me, the two
males pulled me from the floor by the arms.

"Lie face down upon the bench and grasp it with your
arms," directed Ceralt as he worked at my wrists. Even as he
spoke, the metal fell away from me, yet was I unable to bring
my arms forward, Telion, holding the leather to my collar,
took my left arm as earlier, the metal no longer there to prevent movement, and I was unable to prevent a gasp at the
pain.

"What is it?" asked Telion, a frown creasing his face.
"What caused you to pale in such a manner?"

I did not respond to him, shamed that I had given sound to
what was, after all, a minor thing, and Ceralt came and stood
beside him, also frowning toward me, thoughtfully.

"How long were you cuffed so?" Ceralt demanded after a
moment, his eyes narrowing. Telion seemed startled, and then
looked more closely upon me also.

"I know not," I responded, my shrug adding somewhat to
the pain. "What does it matter?"

"What does it matter, she asks!" exploded Telion to Ceralt,
gesturing with the hand about which was wrapped the
leather. "She thinks us like those of your High Seat's Guard!"

"One may say much and show naught," replied Ceralt with
a shrug. "Until my men are released unharmed, and your city
lies secure from attack, we *shall* be like the High Seat's
Guard. See to her left arm."

He then took my right arm, moving it slowly yet deliberately forward, and began to rub it, causing the feeling to return with a rush of stabbing needles. Telion did the same
with my left arm, and I was unable to pull away from the
pain they caused. They held tight to me and rubbed, more
and more vigorously, and I saw that Fayan received the same
from Nidisar. Fayan struggled in Nidisar's grasp, yet the
hunter with the reddish hair rubbed her arms with a will,
using the leather from her collar to assist him in holding her.

When my arms could again be moved somewhat, Telion
and Ceralt led me to the low platform they had prepared,

and forced me down upon it, my cheek to the smooth wood. The leather to my collar was wound about the platform and my neck, holding me tight in place, and other leather, brought by the aged female, tied me to the platform at waist and knees, insuring that some effort would be necessary before I might free myself. My arms were left unbound, yet little good did it do me. My arms were still weak, and the eyes of Telion and Ceralt did not leave me.

Ceralt applied that which was in the pot to my back, then did he and Telion return to their platform, leaving me as they had placed me. My back again burned with pain, yet this time I had not shamed myself. Nidisar spoke with the aged female of rooms to be had, and Ceralt spoke with her of food to be had. In all things was the aged female agreeable, and she brought a large, tall pot of renth from which the males might pour for themselves, conversing pleasantly as they awaited their provender. Nidisar had not rebound Fayan's arms, therefore did he keep one hand tight in her hair as she knelt, in anger, beside him.

The hind passed slowly and fruitlessly, although I learned the how and why of the males being together. Nidisar, as a brother hunter of Ceralt, had accompanied him, with others, as they sought my warriors. Upon their bitter return to the city, they had learned of the presence of a stranger, one who asked of strange-seeming women, large, armed women, who wore almost no clothing. They had found the stranger, he being Telion, and had been told that Telion sought these women he spoke of because he believed they intended attack upon his own city of Ranistard. He sought them in Bellinard, for he had heard mention of Bellinard before the departure of these women from their tents, and wished to see if he might stop them before they rode upon Bellinard.

Nidisar knew the whereabouts of my warriors and myself, for he had been fully informed of it after Pileth's males had taken us. He had not been upon the scene to see the thing for himself, for he had attempted to keep Pileth's males from taking Fayan, and had therefore been rendered unconscious by them. He had been of a mind to come for us when we had been declared slave, yet even the trade of his precious wristlet had not produced enough of the silver pieces to meet the price of more than one of us. Telion, however, with the bright stones given to sthuvad upon their release, and Ceralt, with a lenga pelt given him by Gimin for trade, should it be

needed, had small difficulty in securing sufficient of the silver
pieces to meet the price of each of us. It was in their minds
to trade my warriors and myself for Ceralt's males, plus an
assurance that Ranistard would be left untouched, and they
had been surprised to find three of my warriors gone. They
still thought to use Fayan and myself for the same purpose,
but they did not know how Midanna think. My warriors
would not turn aside in their search for Mida's Crystal
merely for the life of their war leader, and none of the
Midanna would expect them to. In truth, should my warriors have done so, I would have spat upon them, and no
longer called myself Hosta.

Darkness was close to descending when the aged female
appeared with food, and surely did my mouth water at sight
of the roast lellin, awash in its own grease, as it was placed
before the males. Other things were they given as well, such
as vegetables cooked in a broth, and dark slices of ground
and baked grain, and the males fell upon it all with relish.
Fayan and I watched as they feasted, for none was offered to
us to feed upon. The males finished most of it, then were
they reminded of the presence of others. Nidisar leaned back
from the platform in satisfaction, gazed fondly upon Fayan,
then took a piece of the lellin between his fingers.

"Nearly did I forget my golden slave," said he, reaching
toward Fayan with the lellin. "Here, little slave, now you
may eat."

He put the lellin to Fayan's lips as she opened her mouth
silently, and then he howled and snatched his hand back as
Fayan's teeth sank, not into the lellin, but into his hand. My
warrior had done as I would have, and Telion and Ceralt
were greatly amused.

"Do not forget that their meat need not be cooked,"
laughed Ceralt to an angered Nidisar, as Nidisar attempted to
shake the pain from his hand. "Perhaps uncooked flesh truly
tempts them more greatly."

"I, myself, am greatly tempted," said Nidisar, gazing
darkly upon a smiling Fayan. "When last I was so tempted, I
could do naught for it, yet now the female belongs to me."
He then released the leather to Fayan's collar from the platform, and took her by the hair as he stood. "Come, little
slave," said he, pulling Fayan from the floor by her hair. "We
have a matter to see to, you and I, and when next you are
fed, you shall know which the food is."

He pulled her from the room, she struggling futilely in his grasp, and Telion and Ceralt laughed at their departure, and then looked upon me.

"You may not eat save from the hand of Telion or myself," said Ceralt, sipping at his renth. "Will you eat so, or do you prefer going hungry?"

"Hunger is no stranger," said I, unable to move even slightly upon the platform. "I am no slave-woman, to feed from the hand of a male."

"We shall see what a closer acquaintance with hunger does for your views," said Ceralt, and then turned to Telion to ask, "Shall we throw for first?"

"I was about to suggest the same, myself," answered Telion with a grin. "Thus far, we have had no service from our slave."

"That shall not continue," said Ceralt, as he and Telion rose from the platform. The two approached me and removed the leather from waist and knees, and then was I pulled to my feet, and tied to the wall. My hands, for the first time free since I had been taken, immediately went to my throat and the metal of the collar. Ceralt saw the movement and smiled.

"You may pull at the collar as you wish, girl," said he, looking down upon me. "It shall open for none save your masters."

He and Telion then each produced a dagger from a sheath worn at his belt. "Do not move, girl," cautioned Telion, "else the blades shall reach you rather than the wall. Take first cast, Ceralt."

"With pleasure." Ceralt grinned, then sent his dagger flying toward me. I stood as I had stood during the clan test for warrior courage, neither feeling nor showing fear, and the dagger took the wall beside me to the left, less than a male's hand from my head. The two males laughed then, with pleasure and approval.

"Well thrown," said Telion, his hands upon his dagger. "And well stood, too. Now comes my throw."

His blade flew to the other side of my head. Upon the sound of its meeting the wall, Telion laughed again as Ceralt frowned.

"Yours is clearly the closer," grumbled Ceralt, his fists upon his hips. "First use is yours."

"I have waited long for this," said Telion with satisfaction, and then I turned quickly and reached for Ceralt's dagger to my left. My hand, wrapped about the hilt, had scarcely drawn it from the wall when the males were upon me. Ceralt held my left arm as Telion took my right, and a twist from his hands caused the dagger to fall from my grip.

"Slaves do not touch weapons," said Telion, his hands still hard upon my arm. "There will be punishment for the attempt."

"Jalav is no slave," said I, returning his look. "There shall be other daggers."

"Not for Jalav," said Ceralt, reaching up to release the leather that bound me. "Take her now, Telion. Full darkness has fallen, and we must be away with the new light."

"So we must," agreed Telion, taking the leather from Ceralt. By the collar about my throat was I pulled along behind him, the collar which would not remove itself at the urging of my fingers. Not since it had first been placed about my throat had the collar felt so tight.

Telion pushed through the door which the aged female had used, and I saw a small area with two farther doorways and steps to the left. Up these steps did the male pull me, to a very dim place of another two doorways. We entered the second. Within was a small room, perhaps three paces by three, which contained a single small candle upon the left wall, a window closed tight with wood in the far wall, and a very wide mat upon the floor to the right. Telion pulled me from the doorway by the collar, and then slid a bar of metal across the door, which allowed it to swing neither in nor out. Then I was taken to the mat to the right, and pushed to the center of it. Above the center of the mat, quite low on the wall, there protruded a circle of heavy metal, to which Telion tied the leather of my collar. With this done, Telion stood again above me.

"You took great pleasure in denying me your body," said he softly as he began to remove his covering. "Of all the females presented me, it was you I most wished to have. Now you may not deny me."

The feeble candlelight glinted upon his red-gold hair as he moved, and the metal would not allow me to slide my hand free. "Jalav has not given you her body," said I, "nor shall she."

Telion laughed quietly as he bent again to the mat, the muscles beneath his skin moving smoothly to his motions. "It is not necessary that you give," said he, grasping my ankles to pull me flat. "You are a girl, and young, and have much to learn of men. It is the male, not the female, who is best at taking."

I fought him as I could, yet was my clan covering removed, baring me to his eyes. The sight pleased him mightily, the sight of Jalav, helpless beneath his hands. Beyond my control did he heat my blood, gloating as I writhed before him. His hands and lips upon my body brought moans from me, yet beneath it all, there was deep misery within me. A war leader must not receive from a male, yet must I now receive, to further serve Mida's demands. Oh, Mida! You truly ask much of a daughter you love! Telion cried out, and then took me, the weight of his body crushing me to the mat. Never before had I felt a male's body so, the strength of him taking all I possessed, his arms tight about me, his lips hard against mine. Again and again did he take me, as though still in the grasp of the sthuvad drug, and when at last I was released, truly might it be said that I was well used.

Telion rose to his feet, replaced his covering, and then unbarred the door and left without comment. Little strength was there left to me, as I lay upon the rough mat, my hair, which had been released from the war leather, spread out about me. Much had Telion joyed in my hair, stroking it with his fingers, grasping it in his fist. A woman's hair was made for the touch of a man, he had said, and then had he buried both hands within it, holding me so for his lips. Had my hair not grown to the glory of Mida, surely would I have shorn it to less than that of the aged female.

There was again a sound at the door, and my eyes beheld the entrance of Ceralt, who paused to slide the bar in place before coming to stand above me by the mat. I stared up at his sober face, and silently begged Mida to spare me further shame.

"I see no warmth in your greeting," said Ceralt, his hand slowly opening his covering. "Have I a stone before me, who must be warmed to life?"

I made no answer to his question, and he threw aside his covering, and sank to his knees upon the mat.

"You are truly lovely," said he, as he knelt above me. "In the forest, I dreamt of seeing you so, open and soft before me. Yet I now see that you have been hard used, Jalav. Ask that I leave you unmolested, and perhaps I shall."

I could not clearly see his eyes in the dimness, yet I knew that they rested square upon me. I swallowed the sour taste within my mouth, and forced myself to silence.

"Very well," he said, and then lay himself beside me to take me in his arms. "Perhaps this is best, for I have heard it said that captives must be much used by their captors. You shall be much used, Jalav, for that you have my word."

His arms were strong about me, his body hot upon mine, and I found I could not resist him. He brought forth my heat again, raised it high, then quenched it with his own. His word was good, and much used was I by him, far beyond my own need. When he was done with me, he rose to unbar the door and extinguish the candle, then he returned to lie beside me in the darkness, his arm about me as he prepared for sleep. Strong was the odor of him upon me, and still could I feel the manner in which he had taken me. Tightly did I hold to the memory of the Crystal of Mida, for without it, surely would I have shamed myself further. I had cried out to him as he took me, and he had laughed at my weakness, and then had taken me more fully. Ceralt's breathing grew even in sleep, and I moved as far from him as I might, wishing myself again in Bariose's keeping. Bariose, though hard, had only used leather upon me.

A short time later the door was again pushed open, and the form of Telion entered quietly. In the darkness he made his way to the mat, removed his covering, and also lay beside me. His hand touched me briefly before he lay still to seek sleep, and my eyes closed in misery, caught there as I was, between my enemies. I knew not what would be required of me in Ranistard, yet Mida knew, and also did she know my strength. Surely she would not allow me to be used beyond my strength. Surely it would not be so! My eyes did not wish to open again, therefore did I, too, seek sleep.

8.

A journey—and a meeting in the forests

I was already awake when Ceralt and Telion opened their eyes. In the near dark of the room, faint light coming from between the wood upon the window, I had untied the leather from my collar, and was then attempting to force my hand free of the metal upon my wrist, as the metal had refused to yield to my attempts to open it. With some pain did I pull my hand against it, willing, even, to break the hand, should that free me of the restraint.

"I believe our slave is attempting escape," came Ceralt's voice, lazy, still, with the sound of sleep to it.

"I believe so," agreed Telion with a yawn. "Perhaps she does not care for our company."

I turned my head, and in the dimness could see them, studying me where I knelt by the wall, working upon the metal. The Mida-forsaken metal lay close upon my wrist, the circle of it wide enough for my wrist, yet too small, by far, for my hand.

"Are you not able to escape, slave?" asked Ceralt, his fingers upon the back of my leg. "It is only metal upon you, the metal of men. Surely the metal of men is inferior to the leather of women."

"All things of males are inferior to those of warriors," said I, kicking at his hand. "Had I the physical strength of males,

145

I would find no need for the use of metal! Yet what may one expect from those who have no souls?"

"Our souls are quite as fat as yours," said Telion, striking me sharply with his hand, as Larid had been struck. I turned and kicked at him as well, yet did he move from range of my foot, and stand to stretch broadly. "I could do with a bit to eat, Ceralt," said he, with another yawn. "What say you?"

"Definitely so," agreed Ceralt. Then he rose to one knee, and struck me as Telion had, before stepping from the mat. "Are you prepared to travel, girl?" he asked, reaching for his covering as I clenched my fists. "We have a distance to go, for Ranistard is not near."

"A warrior is ever prepared to travel," I said, remembering, as I watched them dress, that Ranistard was more my goal than theirs. When their coverings were upon them, Ceralt threw mine to me, and both watched as I replaced it about my hips. When it was secure, Telion approached me. First, to my fury, was the leather reknotted to my collar, then I was released from the wall. As I rubbed my now free wrist, I thought upon that small piece of metal that released the bonds and saw that Telion placed it within his covering. One would do well to try the small metal before one resorted to breaking one's own hand.

I was once more taken to the room below, Ceralt following behind. Barely had the sky begun to lighten, yet were Nidisar and Fayan already there before us. Nidisar sat at the platform as he had the fey previous, and Fayan, too, knelt as she had, yet with head down, and anger in the set of her shoulders. Telion pulled me to the place beside Fayan, and I was thrust to the floor, the leather then being easily tied. On all fours did I kneel, again filled with fury, and my hair fell about my arms to frame my face as the two males did lazily take their places at the platform.

"Share my food, friends," invited Nidisar pleasantly, gesturing toward the boards of meat upon the platform. "The old mother prepared this upon my request, therefore it is fresh and hot."

"And welcome, as well," said Ceralt as he and Telion chose cuts of meat for themselves. "I do not care for the acquaintance of hunger, and the sight of good food sets running the juices of my appetite. Have you ever seen that the exertions of darkness give better taste to the first food of the new light?"

"I did so notice," laughed Nidisar as Telion grinned. "And exertions there were aplenty. Here, Jalav. You may use this." I raised my head to him, and saw that he held a wooden comb in his hand, which he proffered to me. "Fayan has already used it," said he, "for I dislike dishevelment in a woman. Your hair, too, should be seen to."

Fayan's hair lay neatly combed and unbound by war leather. My war leather, too, was gone, and when she did not raise her eyes to mine, I understood. Instead, I looked upon Nidisar and folded my arms.

"You now show better sense in choosing combs, Nidisar," said I with an approving nod. "Perhaps you, unlike other males, possess the ability to learn." I then unfolded my arms and extended my hand. "Give it here."

Nidisar frowned, yet before he was able to withdraw the comb, I took it from him as though he had obeyed my word. Fayan burst out with uncontrollable laughter, and I smiled upon Nidisar, reminded of the time we had thrown spears together. Perhaps he, too, remembered the time, for a grudging smile touched him before he laughed full out and shook his head.

"Ah, Jalav, you are a terror, indeed," said he, looking fondly upon me as I combed my hair. "I would not have the ownership of you for all the silver in Bellinard."

"Yet, perhaps you would care for the use of her," murmured Ceralt, who had not been amused by the exchange. Telion had smiled with Nidisar's laughter, yet Ceralt had been annoyed. "You may have her, come darkness, if you wish, brother," said he. "She must learn the proper manner with men."

I looked upon Ceralt without expression, not ceasing in my combing, yet surely was he able to see the hatred in my eyes as I said with unconcern, "The touch of Nidisar would be most welcome—after what has already been offered me."

Ceralt, with true anger, made as if to rise, though Telion's hand held fast to his arm. "She is but a child, Ceralt, and knows no better," said he softly. "Take the leather to her, if you must, but see her as the foolish child she is."

"She is no child," growled Ceralt, his eyes still upon me, "yet foolish she most certainly is." Then he turned again to his meat. "The leather is a good thought, Telion," he continued with a mouthful. "It would take much of the bite from the she-hadat. What think you of my offer, Nidisar?"

"I shall consider it," said Nidisar with a grin for me. "Perhaps in return for the use of my comb. And the leather is most effective, Ceralt. Look here."

Nidisar then took a bit of the meat in his hand, and held it out to Fayan's lips. I thought him most foolish to do so, as Fayan only pressed her lips together in refusal. Her anger was strong, then, yet she did not meet his eyes.

"So you see," grinned Nidisar, removing the meat from before Fayan's lips. "She has learned the meaning of her actions, and what they will bring. By the next light, she will nót refuse the meat."

The other males laughed in appreciation of Nidisar's accomplishment, yet did Fayan's head lower further in misery and shame. I knew not what Nidisar had done to her; my hand, now free, was not kept from her shoulder. She was sister to me, and now was shamed for no reason other than that she had chosen to stay by my side. The shame was more mine than hers, and I begged Mida to make Fayan know this. Fayan's eyes turned to me, and I was pleased to note that some small understanding was with her. When we might speak together alone, the understanding would grow.

The males finished their meat and baked grain, and downed short pots of steaming liquid. The sight of the meat did not disturb me as it had, for most of the pain of hunger had left me. In a short while, the pain would be completely gone. Ceralt and Telion offered me none of the meat, yet were pots of water placed before Fayan and myself. I was of a mind to refuse the water as well, when I saw that Nidisar prepared to command Fayan to drink, therefore I lifted the pot to my lips and drank, Fayan doing as I did. The water was tepid, and tasted as though metal had soaked in it, but I drank it without comment for Fayan's sake.

We did not see the aged female as we left the dwelling, yet must she have heard the din that preceded our leaving. When I had finished the water, Ceralt rose from the platform and took a long strip of leather, ordering me to present my wrists to him. I gazed upon him coldly, refusing, even, to speak, and he reached down impatiently to take my wrist. As I still held Nidisar's heavy wooden comb, I thought it only proper to rid myself of it, and therefore threw it hard at Ceralt. At so close a range, it was scarcely possible to miss my mark, and Ceralt withdrew with a loud oath, his hand to his head where the comb had struck, his light eyes blazing in anger. I attempted to rise to my feet, the better to defend myself, yet was unable to do so, for the leather at my collar did not allow that. Telion quickly held me from behind so that I was unable to move. His hands forced my wrists together despite my struggles, and Ceralt quickly bound me with the leather, knotting it tight with an angry set to his lips. Then he roughly pulled me to my feet by my collar. Ceralt said not a word, yet his demeanor promised a reckoning on the matter. I, myself, cared naught for his reckoning.

Quickly was Fayan treated as I, and briefly did we wait, Fayan held by Telion, as Nidisar departed for a number of reckid and then returned. When we emerged from the dwelling, there stood before it three kand, which the males mounted. Our kand we had not seen since we had been taken, nor was I to see them again. Telion held the leather to my wrists, Ceralt the leather to my throat, and thus, between them, was I led along the way, Nidisar with Fayan afoot behind, riding before us.

The gates to Bellinard stood opened, yet were we not to merely ride through. The males with leather and metal walked before us, demanding papers of some sort, which Nidisar, Telion and Ceralt produced. The papers were examined and returned, the males stepped aside, and then were we permitted to leave the city. The males in leather and metal were not those who had been there upon our entry, and Pileth was not among them, yet Fayan and I were looked upon as though we were known to them. It was another thing I did not understand.

Upon leaving the gates of Bellinard, the males rode east till the city was lost from sight, and then turned north. The light grew strong above us as we went, the air was fresh and clear, the ground firm and clean beneath my feet. Much pleased was I to be free of Bellinard, yet not as pleased to be tethered to the males. They kept the leather taut between us, allowing no slack which I might put to use, and in the passing hind, the pace began to tell on me. The sweat ran down my body as I fought to match the kand, determined that I would not be dragged by the leather at wrists and throat. My hair, once combed, was now sweat-soaked, flying, again and again, into my mouth and before my eyes. Fayan, I saw, fared not much better than I, and perhaps a bit worse, for she seemed near to the end of her strength. Neither of us spoke of our difficulty, yet when the males stopped in a sunny glade, I found I

wished to throw myself.to the ground, and refrained from doing so only with a great deal of effort. Fayan stood nearly
atremble, her head down, her breath coming hard, and I well
knew that had we not been warriors, we would have been
shamed. The males had set a cruel pace, one, I was sure, that
was meant to break us. They did not know that Hosta are not
so easily broken.

Fayan and I were tied by the side of the glade, our wrist
leather tight to a rotting log, our throat leather taut to the
low branch of a tree. We could not lift our hands, nor lower
our heads, and thereby were the males assured that our teeth
could not be used upon the leather to free us. We had been
placed upon our knees before the log, a position most unten-
able, for we were unable even to sit upon the ground. The
males had inspected us after placing us so, Telion and
Nidisar with frowns, Ceralt with no expression, yet had
Fayan and I neither spoken nor looked upon them. They were
males and naught else might a warrior expect of them. At
last they left us, to do by the kand I knew not what.

For some reckid was Fayan silent, then she looked at me
with concern. "Jalav, were they hard with you?" she asked
softly. "I feared they might do you harm."

"They are males," said I, my eyes and voice lowering of
themselves. "No longer am I fit to be called war leader."

"That is not so!" she insisted quite harshly. "What they do
is at the urging of Mida, therefore has it no meaning! You
are war leader, and I am—" Abruptly she broke off, and
turned from me.

"What has he done?" asked I, as softly as she had. For a
moment she made no answer, then her voice came, low and
bitter.

"He beat me with leather," she whispered, "yet not as you
were beaten. He took my pride as he gave me pain, and then
did give his word to beat me so before the others, should I do
again as I did. The pain has little meaning, Jalav, and I
would not be further shamed before the others, yet am I unable to see which is the greater shame—to obey him, or be
beaten so before the others."

In truth, I knew not how to answer. To each of us is
shame composed of a different thing, in some places
touching, so that all sometime do feel shamed at once, and
then does it move apart, so that what is shame to one, is

naught save the usual to another. I could not council Fayan
in her actions, for I knew not how the shame touched her.

"Perhaps you might weigh one against the other," I suggested weakly. "See the one which would shame you more
before Mida, and choose the other."

"Before Mida," she repeated thoughtfully. "I had thought
only of my shame before the males, yet is it Mida I must truly
be concerned with." She smiled faintly. "It is often hard,
Jalav, to be so well-loved by Mida. Perhaps I am not
worthy."

"I, too, have had the thought," I sighed, "Yet Mida knows
what we do not. We can only act as we are, therefore that
must be what Mida wishes."

"There is much to think upon," said she, also with a sigh,
"and gladly would I do so, were I not so befogged with lack
of strength. When I spoke of Nidisar as pure sthuvad, surely
Mida whispered in my ear. Through most of the darkness did
he use me, and again before he arose." Her eyes closed
briefly, and her smile widened. "Much would I enjoy having
that one in the Hosta home tents. Disallowed of the balance
of his habits, he would give constant pleasure in the sleeping
leather."

"There is ever a bright side," I laughed at her smile. "Perhaps I should hope he seeks payment for his comb."

Fayan, too, laughed at the thought, but our laughter was
not long in continuing. The males approached us to release
the leather, therefore did we prepare ourselves to continue
the march. However they were not of a mind to do so. Fayan
rose to her feet with some difficulty, and Nidisar frowned
down upon her.

"I do not care for the look of her, Ceralt," said he, his
hand below Fayan's chin. "I will see some food in her before
we continue."

"This one looks no better," Telion frowned, taking my face
between his two great hands. "When last did you have the
taste of meat, Jalav?"

"In the darkness," I informed him, attempting to pull my
face free. "Beneath the dwelling of great size. I slew the creatures of the darkness and fed. It was sufficient."

"Those!" exclaimed Telion, his face and eyes, for some
reason, ill. Nidisar, too, seemed sickened, his eyes upon
Fayan, who shrugged and nodded agreement, showing that

she, too, had thus fed herself. Ceralt alone showed no disgust, though he seemed much disturbed.

"They shall both be fed," proclaimed Ceralt, holding fast to the leather of my collar. "They have not the wit to see properly to themselves, therefore must they be seen to."

"Scarm!" said Telion with a shake of his head. "She eats scarm, and considers such sufficient! Bring them along before I lose what *I* have eaten!"

Telion walked first to the kand, from the folded leather upon which he drew forth a portion of nilno. Nidisar brought Fayan, and Ceralt took me, and when we had reached Telion, he handed a slice of nilno each to Nidisar and Ceralt. Ceralt turned to me, and held the meat to my lips.

"This shall do for you for now," said he. "Too much will sicken you." As I made no move to touch the meat, he frowned, and ordered, "Eat!"

"Jalav does not feed from the hand of a male," said I, holding his eyes. "Do what you will."

"You are being fed, not punished, you she-lenga!" said Ceralt in high exasperation, his eyes angry, his fist tight upon the leather. "Is there no understanding within you?"

"Of a certainty, I have understanding," I nodded. "I understand that Jalav shall not feed from the hand of a male."

Ceralt closed his eyes, attempting, I thought, to hold back his rage. Nidisar, too, was angered, for Fayan also refused the nilno, then did Ceralt's eyes open, and he looked upon me once again.

"In the Palace of the High Seat, you were punished for disobedience," said Ceralt, still angry. "Should the need arise, I am able to do as they did. You shall eat at my bidding as you did at theirs, else shall I match them blow for blow."

I felt the fire touch me in memory, and turned from Ceralt that my eyes not betray me. "Do as you will," said I again, standing as straight as I might. "I shall not feed from your hand."

"Very well," agreed Ceralt evenly. "What number of blows were you given before you obeyed? Five? Ten?"

No answer did I make, being fully occupied with the need to gather strength, therefore did Fayan speak for me. "The war leader Jalav was given four hands, then three," spoke my warrior proudly, "and still did the city males find need to force their vile creation upon her! She does not fear you, male!"

Ceralt's hand grasped my arm and again turned me to him, his face showing great disbelief. "Thirty-five?" said he in a choked voice, his light eyes wide. "With the lash?"

"The last hand of them were unfelt," said I. "You need not taunt me with my weakness. This time, I shall be stronger."

There was a deep silence, and I looked up to see that all eyes rested upon me, Fayan's with pride, the males' with—I know not what. A curious look was upon the faces of each of them, a look of disbelief, and hurt, and anger as well, that I did not comprehend.

Ceralt was first to act. By the arms did he take me, and quickly seated me upon the ground. "Sit!" said he very shortly, then he placed the nilno in my hand. "Now, eat!"

He crouched beside me with his arms upon his thighs, a stern look to him, and only when the first of the nilno was in my mouth did he grunt in approval. Telion came to crouch by my other side, making no sound, yet did he watch me carefully as I chewed, angry as well. Slowly I fed upon the nilno, understanding naught of what had occurred to so change their position. Males are strange creatures indeed.

Fayan was pleased that it seemed I was not to be beaten, and she watched but a moment before turning toward Nidisar. "I, too, shall accept the nilno," said she, her bound arms outstretched, one hand open. "Give it here, male."

"Shall you, indeed," murmured Nidisar, a thoughtful look about him. "I do not recall offering it to you, slave."

Fayan closed her hand and withdrew her arms, her back stiff and her head high. "A Hosta warrior is well able to do without," said she coldly, and then turned from him.

"Nor do I recall saying you were to do without," said Nidisar, taking her by the collar to turn her to him again. His hand raised with the nilno, and flatly did he say, "Eat, slave."

"Fayan is no slave!" hissed she, her angry eyes flashing upward toward his. "You are only a servant of Mida, and may not speak so to me!"

"I may speak as I wish," said Nidisar, annoyed. "It is you who may not speak so. Do you obey me, or must you be punished again?"

"No!" cried Fayan, struggling to escape him, though his fist was tight upon her collar. As she could not free herself, she raised her right foot and kicked with strength, sideways, catching him just below the knee. Nidisar grunted with pain, and true anger flooded him. He thrust Fayan off balance, and then struck her resoundingly upon the back of her clan covering. The force of the blow sent her, with a cry, flat to the ground upon her bound arms. Before she could rise, Nidisar was quickly beside her, his hand upon her neck, his knee in the small of her back.

"Now, slave!" said Nidisar to an immobilized Fayan, "is it to be the punishment?"

"No!" cried Fayan again, in true distress. I attempted to rise and go to her aid, but Telion and Ceralt prevented me. The broad strength of their hands held me fast as Fayan choked out, "I shall feed."

"On your knees, then," said Nidisar. Briefly did Fayan hesitate, then she raised herself slowly from the ground to her knees, her hair falling about her arms in disarray, her shoulders rounded in defeat. Her eyes lifted miserably to Nidisar as she knelt there, and he held the nilno to her lips again, so that she might take a bit of it. She did so without commenting, chewing in a manner which showed she would have been happier without such. Nidisar's face held no expression, yet were Ceralt and Telion smiling in amusement. I bit again from the nilno, looking not upon Fayan's shame, knowing that she did as she did for Mida's sake.

When Fayan had finished the portion of meat, Nidisar drew her to her feet by the leather at her collar. "You have been a good slave," said he in approval. "For good behavior, you are to be rewarded." He drew her quickly toward him, his lips dropping to hers. She struggled at the unexpected touch of him, yet were her struggles not long in continuing. Surely was she remembering the pleasure he had given her, for her body moved toward his, her bound wrists held high between them. Nidisar held her so for unhurried reckid, then released her abruptly.

"Should your behavior continue in good form," said he, grinning at her flushed confusion, "the darkness shall find you further rewarded. Now we travel." He then took the leather of collar and wrists, and pulled her with him to his kan. Furious was Fayan at being treated so, yet did she hold her fury within her. Again Ceralt and Telion laughed, then they pulled me after them to their kand so quickly, barely had I opportunity to rise to my feet. A water skin was passed about, to Fayan and myself as well, and then we continued upon our journey.

The pace was slower than it had been, yet had we covered

a good distance of ground by the coming of darkness. We traveled upon a road, of a width sufficient for three kand to ride abreast and then some, which wound through a lovely forest well peopled by the children of the wild. All three of the males carried sword and dagger, and spears were borne by Nidisar and Ceralt as well. Telion alone carried a bow, unstrung and bound to the side of his kan beneath his left leg, a leather quiver before his knee to the right. I had wondered upon the unstrung bow, thinking, perhaps, that Nidisar and Ceralt would spear-hunt, yet had it not been so. No hunting had the males attempted, nor did they seek a place where the darkness might be spent. It seemed they meant to travel without stop.

Darkness was complete when we left the road, moving through the forest to the right. Fayan and I stumbled often, the darkness being too deep to see well in. However, it was a mere matter of reckid before I knew our destination. Far ahead, through the trees, were bright campfires, speaking either of a large number of unconcerned travelers, or a small number of foolish ones, and toward these fires we moved. We had nearly reached them, when the bushes before us moved, and six males, armed with bows, stepped in our path. Immediately we halted, and one of the six males spoke.

"What do you do here?" he demanded from the darkness, the others holding steady with their bows. "This camp is a private one!"

"We have taken passage with the caravan," said Ceralt without anger, "and your master expects us. Our pavilions should stand waiting for us. I am Ceralt of Bellinard, of the brotherhood of hunters."

"Indeed." The male nodded, gesturing to the others to lower their bows. "We were told to expect you, Ceralt of Bellinard. You may enter the camp."

Ceralt urged his kan toward the fires. The males stepped aside to allow our passage, looking upon Fayan and myself with wide grins. One placed his hand briefly upon me, patting deliberately, and the others howled their laughter. As the leather pulled me ahead, I could not turn upon him, and truly great was my fury. When next I stood before a male, a sword firmly in my grasp, each insult that I suffered would be avenged.

We halted by the largest fire, before which a male awaited us. Short was that male, and narrow of chest, yet did he hold himself with pride, and wear a swordbelt with familiar ease. He nodded pleasantly toward Ceralt.

"Well met, hunter," said he, his voice warm with greeting. "You are here sooner than I had expected."

"We left not long past your time," said Ceralt. "The slaves were coaxed to a fair pace, therefore are we here. It is fortunate you halt early the first fey from Bellinard."

The male chuckled as he looked upon Fayan and myself. Slumped did we stand behind the kand, road-weary as never before. Walking to the urging of leather is difficult, for the leather allows no rest nor change of pace. A warrior is able to march far afoot, yet not when bound in leather.

"You slaves seem well-coaxed," commented the male, and then he raised his arm to his right. "Your pavilions stand there, the red and the yellow. Roast trencha has been placed within, for we knew not when you would arrive, and renth, as well. We break camp at first light."

"Till first light, then," said Ceralt, raising his hand in farewell, then turning toward the tents the male had spoken of. Large were the tents, of red silk and yellow silk, and Nidisar took Fayan toward the red one, as Telion and Ceralt halted by the yellow.

"We shall rejoin you at first light," called Nidisar, dismounting by his tent and tying the kan. "I must now see if I possess a slave who wishes to be rewarded."

He then pulled an outraged Fayan within the tent, to the accompaniment of laughter from Telion and Ceralt. They, too, dismounted and tied their kand, and I was taken within behind them. Five paces by five was the tent, floored with lenga pelts, and softly lit with candles within boxes. At the center of the rear wall a narrow wooden post had been placed in the ground, and there was I taken, to be placed again within the metal by my left wrist, the other end closed about the high post. The leather was left upon my collar so that Telion and Ceralt might fall upon the meat left for them upon a cloth, and I sat without strength by the post as they fed and drank of renth, then did I take the meat which was given me by Telion. Ceralt looked upon him with curiosity.

"I would know," said Ceralt, "why you insist that we join the caravan upon its way, rather than while still in Bellinard. And also why we ride east, rather than north, from the gates."

"I dislike leaving a city in caravan," said Telion as he

stretched out upon his side on the lenga pelt. "The dislike is irrational, I know, yet there is little I may do. As for the direction in which we rode, I considered the possible presence of certain of that one's females, watching to see if she were taken from Bellinard. It would be to Ranistard's benefit, did the gaggle of them ride east in search of her."

"An excellent point," said Ceralt, reaching for the skin of renth, "yet I fail to see how I may trade for the release of my men, should Jalav's wenches ride east. I go to Ranistard solely for that purpose."

"That had not occurred to me," said Telion, then he grinned at Ceralt. "Happily, I saw no sign of watchers, therefore all should be as we hope. We will find the females somewhere about Ranistard."

"Or, so we hope," corrected Ceralt with dryness, and then did he drink from the skin. He had scarcely removed it from his lips, when the silk of the tent was moved aside, and Nidisar entered, carrying another skin.

"As the kand have been seen to by the caravan slaves," said he, smiling pleasantly about him, "I have come to visit a short while. Your meal is over?"

"It is," said Telion, looking about behind Nidisar. "You came alone?"

"Indeed I did," said Nidisar, walking over to join the other males by the cloth. "My slave was careful of her behavior, and thereby earned a reward, yet did she refuse to request that reward. I have therefore left her within the pavilion, suitably warmed, to reconsider her position. Should she request her reward upon my return, she may receive it."

"The wench deserves her anguish," laughed Ceralt as Telion grinned. "When she says, 'male,' she might the well say 'slave.' Perhaps you would now care to reconsider my offer, Nidisar. Jalav would keep you well primed against your return."

"I had not remembered that," said Nidisar slowly, turning to gaze thoughtfully upon me as I sat with the meat part way to my mouth. This male was to torture my warrior, and then come to me for release? He grinned and put down the skin of renth. "I do believe," said he, "that I shall accept your offer."

He then came to stand above me, and I looked upon him in irritation. "*I* have not completed my meal," said I, "therefore may Nidisar look elsewhere. Preferably, in a pen of gandod, which is surely his proper place."

"Such a temper," laughed Nidisar, and then did he crouch before me. "I see, Jalav, that you sit cross-legged to eat, as before. I have not allowed this to Fayan, for a slave must kneel in the presence of her master. Your masters are kind indeed to allow you such liberty."

Easily did I see that he attempted to incite Telion and Ceralt against me, therefore I smiled faintly. "Beware your actions and words, Nidisar," I warned him softly. "None may know the intentions of Mida, and should the spear be cast again, who knows who will then be slave and who free?"

"Yet, this spear cast is not done with," said Nidisar with a grin. "I also do not allow Fayan her skirting when alone in my presence. Clothing makes a slave feel less a slave, and therefore more prone to rebellion."

"That is a point I have heard mention of before," said Ceralt thoughtfully. "Our slave, Telion, is extremely prone to rebellion. What say you?"

"Such rebellion should be stemmed whenever possible," agreed Telion soberly. "She should be made to earn her bit of cloth."

"It is agreed, then," said Ceralt, and Nidisar's grin grew broader. "Slave, remove your skirting."

It is said that there are many ways to take the pelt of a lenga, yet are certain ways more pleasant than others. To do battle, unarmed and chained, with three males, each of whom was larger than I, would be tantamount to hunting the lenga in a like manner. When a warrior is unarmed, she does well to lure the lenga to a trap.

I threw the balance of the meat left aside, uncrossed my legs, and lay back in the deep furs, and then said, "Perhaps Nidisar would be good enough to do so for me. I have not yet thanked him for the use of his comb."

Nidisar looked startled, Telion seemed surprised, and Ceralt frowned. My eyes directly upon Nidisar, I moved my hips in the furs as the female of the pink and orange tent had moved within her silks.

"Is a Hosta warrior to neglect thanks due?" asked I, the words of Fayan returning to me, and making me unreluctant for Nidisar's touch. "Come, Nidisar," I urged, raising my left wrist slightly, "I cannot escape you, for I am chained here. You may do as you will."

It has been shown by males that I was pleasing to their eye, and so was it then with Nidisar. He went to one knee beside me, his hands moving toward my covering, his eyes taking in my form. I raised my right hand to his broad shoulder, thinking to draw him closer—and Ceralt took my wrist while placing his own hand upon Nidisar's shoulder.

"She must not be rewarded for taking such a manner with men, brother," said Ceralt to Nidisar. "She has disobeyed an order, therefore must she be punished."

"I shall punish her as soon as I am done with her," mumbled Nidisar, attempting to lean farther toward me against Ceralt's restraining hand. His eyes blazed hot, and eager indeed was he for the nearness of Jalav. Ceralt, however, showed by his stern look that that was not as he wished.

"No, Nidisar," insisted Ceralt, moving him yet farther away by the shoulder. "A slave must be disciplined quickly, else the action loses meaning. Surely you understand?"

Nidisar groaned with feeling, his eyes closing briefly, then he looked away from where I lay in the fur. "I understand only," said he to Ceralt as he rose to his feet, "that my own slave had best be prepared to request her reward. Else I shall beat her."

He then retrieved his renth skin from the fur by the cloth, and hurried from the tent to the accompaniment of chuckling from Telion. I attempted to raise myself once more to a sitting position, but Ceralt prevented me.

"As for you, slave," said Ceralt angrily, "you shall not be allowed to disobey me." He then turned me in the fur face down, and removed my clan covering. I struggled uselessly, and his hand returned to find that I had had some interest in Nidisar. He turned me from the post again, saw the anger in my eyes at his actions, and his own anger grew stronger.

"This time, first use is mine," said he, his voice low, his hand upon my thigh. "I shall ever see you well used, Jalav, no matter that you prefer the touch of another." His hand moved around and about my thigh, causing me to strain to keep a groan from escaping, and then he ceased abruptly, seized the leather trailing from my collar, and tied it close to the post. "You shall, however," he added as he stood from me, "await my pleasure. There is yet renth in the skin."

I snarled as he turned from me, and then attempted to remove the leather from the post, but it was well beyond my reach. I lay upon my back in the fur, my throat and left wrist held close to the post, my fury high, my body bared to the inspection of Ceralt and Telion, who reclined in the fur at their ease, drinking renth. Slowly did they drink the renth, commenting upon various parts of me, till Ceralt wiped the renth from his mouth with the back of his hand, rose again, and approached me. He did not remove his covering to take me, nor did Telion take his eyes from us. Well used was I before Telion, then was well used again by him and before Ceralt, and that was the bitterest to bear. Each saw the shame of my use by the other, each gloating over my debasement before and by him. At last were the candles extinguished and the males placed themselves to either side of me for sleep, and truly was the darkness welcome. It occurred to me that perhaps I had offended Mida in some manner, and was to be punished and shamed before being allowed to serve her once more. If that was the case, my punishment was full, and my shame complete. Again had I cried out to Ceralt, and would not again be able to meet his eyes. I was indeed well shamed and punished.

9.

The traveling set—and
a discovery of interest

Slow was the movement of the covered conveyances, though not so slow that the march was over-easy. Again I walked behind the kand of Telion and Ceralt, Fayan a small distance from me, behind the kan of Nidisar. We had looked upon one another briefly when first brought from the tents, and then had returned to our own thoughts and miseries.

When the new light had first begun to appear, the males had risen from their sleep to relight the candles and hand about portions of the meat we had eaten the fey previous. Telion had released the leather from the post so that I might feed, and I did so in vile temper, for the leather had kept me from reaching to Telion's covering as he slept, for the small bit of metal.

When we emerged from the tent, the kand of the males waited, as did a large number of other males, some of whom wore chains. Those with the chains quickly folded up the tents and placed them upon a conveyance which had no top or cover. The post from the rear of the tent had first been removed, and was also placed within the conveyance.

In the strengthening light, it was easily seen that more than six hands of tents were so being removed from the ground about us, and the fires were each being quenched. Many city folk moved about, some armed, some not, and better than thirty paces from us were a number of young slave-women being urged within the rear of a covered conveyance. Upon completion of the folding of the tents, the conveyances, drawn by kand, were sent upon their way, the kand ridden by males preceding them, following them, and moving beside them. The male slaves were chained to conveyances which bore tents, thereby made to walk beside these conveyances, and many were the stares sent from them to Fayan and myself.

The light from behind thick clouds was gray, and also gray was my humor. Fayan and I traveled toward Ranistard, yet our captivity grated upon me. What was to be accomplished with Jalav in leather and metal, captive to males, who gloried in her shaming? If this was the purpose of Mida, already had it been brought about. Fayan looked not upon me, not I upon her, and so it would go, seemingly forever. The stones of the road now bruised my feet, and I had barely the strength to ignore it.

When the light was highest, the conveyances halted, and Telion and Ceralt dismounted by a tree, tied their kand, and then found a tree to which my neck leather might be wound, I being placed so that I knelt before it, my back hard against it. The leather to my wrists was looped about my ankles, allowing me to raise my arms no farther than waist height. Then did they remove themselves to a distance, where they sat with Nidisar and fed from the meat they had fetched with them.

Fayan had been placed as I was, before another tree, perhaps five paces from mine. Why we had not been placed together, I knew not, yet I did not really regret it. Little encouragement had I to give her, and none to give myself. For perhaps two hands of reckid did I kneel so before the tree, and then did sounds draw my attention. First I heard the sound of a lellin, scolding harshly at some menacing presence, and then came the call of a high-nesting wrettan, its sweet tones adrift upon the forest air. At first, I thought myself deceived, that the calls of the feathered children of the wild were accident, then did I hear them again, changed slightly as they should be, and great joy rose within me.

I looked toward Fayan, and saw that she, too, had heard and understood. Strongly were her eyes upon me, therefore did I lift my bound wrists as high as they would go, and in the silent hand-gesture speech of Midanna, I asked "Do you see?"

Fayan read my words, and raised her right hand to answer,

"No." We both had heard the identifying call of Hosta, yet neither of us saw sign of them. I longed to see again the brave sight of my warriors, but knowing of their close presence was enough to dispel the gray of the skies. Mida had not abandoned us, and there was purpose aplenty to our captivity!

The males had neither heard nor seen, and came shortly to Fayan and myself with meat. Telion released the wrist leather from my ankles, amusing himself briefly, to my discomfort, as he did so, yet did I barely notice the playful touch, for I feared that Fayan, knowing herself watched by Hosta, would refuse to be shamed and inadvertently betray their presence. Fayan was, however, a strong and loyal warrior, refusing to betray her sisters even at the cost of her pride. She knelt before Nidisar and fed from his hand, reluctantly yet without struggle, then suffered his extended "reward" with eyes closed. When we were once more upon the road, I was relieved.

The conveyances were again stopped with yet a hin till darkness, and the tents were erected in their previous order by the male slaves. I hoped to be tied to a tree, so that in the confusion of erecting camp, one of my warriors might make her way to me unseen, yet was this not done. Telion took his kan and those of Ceralt and Nidisar, and disappeared from sight upon some errand, and Ceralt held the leather close about his fist till the tent stood, keeping me close by his side. Many times that fey had he looked upon me, yet had I not returned his looks, and once again did he seem angered.

At the departure of the male slaves I was thrust within the tent, and once within, Ceralt looked upon me. "You do not kneel to your master, slave," he observed, "nor do you remove your skirting as you were bidden to do. You are not as satisfactory a slave as the other."

"Jalav is no slave of any sort," said I, meeting his gaze, as I knew I would soon be shut of him. "The hunter must truly fear Jalav, to ever keep her bound in leather or metal."

"That may be a strong point in your training," mused Ceralt. "You feel yourself feared, therefore superior. You must be taught otherwise." He then reached toward me, and first removed the collar leather, then unbound my wrists. As I rubbed my wrists to restore life to them, he removed his sword, tossed it to the side, and looked toward me again.

"Now, slave," he said, folding his arms, "remove your skirting and kneel."

"I obey immediately," said I, and then darted swiftly toward his sword. Almost did I have my hands upon it, yet Ceralt reached me before I reached it. His arms wrapped about me and bore me to the ground, his well-muscled form holding me easily just past arm's reach of the sword. No farther did he move me from it, but kept me tantalizingly near as his hands ignored my struggles and removed my clan covering, then made free with my body. Maddened was I by his play, maddened by the nearness of a sword, and then he did that which I had never conceived possible. With his arm about my waist, he raised me to my knees, at the same moment forcing my head to the furs by a handful of hair, and in such a humiliating manner did he take me. The power of his maleness could not be escaped, and he made full use of me so before returning me to my back and using me again. Free was I of leather and metal, yet held helpless by his strength, and his laughter at my futile attempts at resistance smarted. In full heat was he in possession of me, and he laughed again as he used me.

"Your face shows you think yourself punished, Jalav," said he to a much dismayed warrior, "yet such is not so. Now you receive your reward and upon completion of being rewarded, shall you be punished."

I had no wish to know his meaning, though when he was well drained, his words became clear. Bested by him had I been, with neither leather nor metal to aid him, yet was I to be further reduced in my own eyes. He took me by the hair to where the leather had been left, bent me far over, and beat me with the leather across my hips and thighs. Painfully did the leather sting, but the pain was not a consideration. To be taken as I had been, then beaten in such a manner, showed the lowly position of her who was so used and beaten, and the superiority of him who held the leather. With my warriors within hailing distance was I treated as a slave-woman, as helpless as they to aid myself.

Ceralt beat me soundly, then was I stood straight again by the hair. "Take yourself to the post, slave," said he, the leather in his hand, "and kneel there as your master orders."

Numbly did I go to the post and kneel as bidden, the pain given me by Ceralt felt fully within me. The male nodded in approval at my actions, then stretched himself out in the fur at his ease, while I knelt and thought upon the wisdom of Mida.

Easily might it be seen that most males are superior in strength to females. I, myself, had been shown that, stripped of my sword, I was as helpless before a male as any slave-woman. Long had I wondered at Mida's reasons for allowing her warriors none save an occasional sthuvad, yet no longer did I wonder. Were her warriors to remain warriors, they must face males in no way save as captors or with sword in hand. Shamed had I been by Ceralt, and bested by him, and my life was his to end. Such was Midanna law, and such was that which I had lived by, and now wished to die by. Mida would not wish the services of one such as I.

Telion returned not long after, with a renth skin, and paused just within the silk to gaze upon me but I did not look up.

"My congratulations, Ceralt," said he, moving closer to the hunter. "Our slave seems most proper now, and quite a bit subdued."

"A woman need only be shown her master," said Ceralt, his voice filled with satisfaction. "I wager she obeys in all things now, and is much the better for it. How went your investigations?"

"Most interestingly," said Telion with a small laugh, seating himself beside Ceralt. "The lovely ladies travel to Ranistard, sponsored and protected by their fathers, and there shall suitable marriages be made for them. As few as are the females who remain in Ranistard by cause of the plague, they shall be welcomed by each man able to move, and offered one dowry after another. He who arranged for their fathers' agreements shall be a man of wealth, with commissions from both father and groom due him."

"We would have done well purchasing female slaves to the same end," said Ceralt. "Do you know the man who arranged for the brides?"

Telion hesitated briefly, then answered, "No. He is not a warrior, I know, and I have never met him. However, we shall have little difficulty arranging an introduction or two among the ladies. I have let it be known that I have acquaintances in the Palace of the High Seat."

"I shall not ask after those acquaintances," laughed Ceralt. "I do not wish to press you on matters which should best be left unmentioned—if we are to meet the ladies. I shall enjoy the company of a lady again, even though it be here in the wilderness."

"A lady is ever a lady," agreed Telion. I heard the words they spoke, yet it made little sense. Much occupied was I with preparation for death.

In a short while, a slave brought a large portion of roast meat, and a cloth to set it upon. Ceralt and Telion began to feed, and I remained upon my knees, head down, admitting to Mida and those Midanna who came before me all my lacks and omissions. The burden of spilled blood unrevenged was a heavy one, yet my soul would not have to face that of her who bore me—my soul would not enter the Realm of Mida. Heavy, heavy, heavy, was my despair at my failure, and nothing was left save the final cleansing. I then reached up and touched my life sign, stroking it a final time before removing it from about my neck and placing it upon the fur before me. Then was I truly readied.

Telion eventually rose from his place and approached me, and then crouched before me. "I would now see the obedience of our slave," said he lightly, a grin upon his face. His hand rose before my lips, a bit of meat there held, and he said, "Eat as does the other, slave."

I neither moved nor spoke.

"I seem to lack your facility, Ceralt," said Telion ruefully, looking back at the hunter across his shoulder.

"It is easily done," laughed Ceralt, also rising to join us. He took the meat from Telion, said, "Your master demands that you eat, slave," and held the meat to my lips.

Naught save death might I accept from him who had bested me. It was the law.

"Not as easily done as you thought," murmured Telion, his eyes narrowing as he inspected me. "Does she seem—different—to you, Ceralt?"

"Nonsense!" laughed Ceralt uneasily. "She merely sulks from her punishment! Here, slave, take the meat. I shall allow you to feed yourself this time."

Oh, Mida! My greatest failure was to you! You saw me to the glory of winning the place of war leader, and I was not worthy of the position! How bitter must be your disappointment!

"There is something wrong!" insisted Telion, a frown upon

his face, his eyes troubled. "She has—withdrawn from us! And the bit of wood! Where is the bit of wood?"

"Here," answered Ceralt low, raising my life sign from the fur. "Jalav, speak to me," said he, his voice concerned. "What has happened to make you act so?"

"She may not even hear you," said Telion. "I do not know what ails her, but perhaps the other may tell us."

He then rose to his feet and hurriedly left the tent, and I was left with him who had bested me. His hand moved to touch my face, his other hand a fist upon my life sign. I waited only for the touch of a blade.

Telion returned, Fayan and Nidisar with him, and the males came swiftly before me, yet Fayan saw clearly that my final farewell had been spoken. Unbound in leather was she, therefore was she able to halt three paces from me, a great sadness upon her, and sink to her knees so that her head might be bowed in memory.

Nidisar looked back to see that Fayan had not followed, therefore did he return to her side. "Fayan, what ails Jalav?" he asked softly, his hand upon her shoulder.

"Jalav awaits the final death," said Fayan, her voice filled with grief, her head low. "She has removed her life sign so that her soul shall be unguarded when it leaves her, and therefore disappear forever! Nidisar, she does not wish to enter Mida's Realm!"

"But, why?" demanded Nidisar, turning with pain-filled eyes to Telion and Ceralt. "What has been done to her?"

"What could be done to a girl child who has withstood thirty-five blows of the heavy lash?" asked Telion in a strangely cold voice, his eyes hard upon Ceralt where he crouched before me.

"It could not have been what I gave her!" said Ceralt, in dismay. "I merely removed the leather from her, used her, and punished her with the leather for attempting to take my sword! I have used her before—we both have!—and a hiding with the leather is fit for a true child! It could not have done this to her, not if Bariose's lash did not!"

"The war leader Jalav awaits the death stroke from your hand, male," said Fayan quietly, rising again to her feet. "Be merciful, and strike quickly!"

"You are mad, wench!" cried Ceralt, rising to his feet with incredulity as Telion and Nidisar exclaimed sharply. "I do not mean to slay her!"

"You must," explained Fayan patiently. "You have bested her, and now must take her life."

"Fayan, we do not understand," said Nidisar. "Naught was done to Jalav that has not been done to you! Why does she await death when you do not?"

"Jalav is war leader," said Fayan, her voice weary. "To free her and do as was done is to best her, and a war leader who is bested must be slain. It is the law of the Midanna. Her shame must truly be great, for her to wish her soul lost." Fayan's voice grew faint, and her eyes closed. "I, myself, await only the release of Mida to seek the cleansing of death. I thank Mida that I am only a warrior, for I have not the courage to remove my life sign."

"They both await death!" shouted Ceralt in a high, wild voice, as Nidisar stared upon Fayan as though he had been struck. "I have had many women, and—Aye!—punished a few as well!—yet never has the female then expected me to slay her! A few tears, perhaps, a respectful fear of my wrath, yes, but—death?" Swiftly did he come to me then, and down upon his knees, so that his hands might bite harshly into my arms. "Jalav, I shall not slay you!" he rasped, shaking me as I knelt. "Do you hear? You were merely punished! There is no need for death!"

The light eyes in the dark face were touched by tragedy, though I knew not why. Is one to take the pride and heart of another, and then expect not to take the life as well? Is it possible to be so cruel, even for one without a soul?

"Fayan, you cannot truly wish death," said Nidisar to my warrior, deep pain in his voice. "For a woman to be taken or punished by a man is no shame! It is the natural way of things!"

"For a warrior's pride to be sullied is deep shame," said Fayan. "Much pleasure have I found in Nidisar's touch, yet have I also been much shamed by him. The shame I have accepted for Mida's sake, but I may not carry it forever. Upon release by Mida, my blood shall wash away the stain upon my honor."

"No!" cried Nidisar, throwing his arms about Fayan and crushing her to him, his face twisted with grief. "I shall not allow such a thing! It is barbaric!"

"As are they," said Telion heavily, his face lined with strain. "They live amid heavy, dark leather, bound by cruel, unrelenting laws. Their lives are short, and perhaps that is a blessing."

"This is insanity," said Ceralt, "and we are fools for discussing it as if it were to be!" With a stern look he lifted my life sign from where he had dropped it in the fur, and slipped the leather over my head. "You are not to die, Jalav, nor is your soul to be lost," he said. "I will have no more of this foolishness, else you shall find the leather taken to you again!"

My hand went to my life sign, to remove it once more, but Ceralt's fist closed over my hand. I raised my eyes to his. "Is Ceralt without honor?" I asked quietly. "Surely, he will not refuse to take the burden of my life? A war leader who has been bested is naught, to force her to retain life is despicable. You have shamed me and bested me, Ceralt, now my life is yours to take."

Again I attempted to lift my life sign from me, yet Ceralt's hand was not to be moved. "Aye, Jalav, I have honor," said he, soberly. "I amused myself at your expense, thinking to repay you for your treatment of me in the forest by taming your fire somewhat. I wished to see you call me master with tears in your eyes, and obey me for fear of a hiding. I did *not* wish you to yield up your life to me, yet now that you have, my honor forbids that I refuse it."

"It is well," I smiled, pleased that he who had bested me *did* have honor. "Sword or dagger, the choice is yours."

"The choice is indeed mine," said Ceralt in annoyance, and still he did not allow the removal of my life sign. The other males looked upon us with concern as Ceralt lifted my hair through the leather tie of my life sign, so that it rested once more against my neck. "As your life is now mine," said he, "you shall live it at my direction."

Telion and Nidisar laughed with pleasure and relief, yet I looked to a bewildered Fayan, who also did not understand Ceralt's words. My life was his to take, not keep!

"Ceralt, you misunderstand what I say," I began. "By the laws of the Midanna, you must . . ."

"No!" he said angrily "I am not bound by the laws of the Midanna, for I am not of the Midanna! I have accepted your life, and shall see that you live it!"

"Such may not be done!" I protested in confusion. "When I became war leader, with my own hand did I slay her whom I had bested! You may not. . . ."

"I may do as I wish!" he snapped, again standing erect to place his fists upon his hips. "Do you wish to challenge my authority?"

"I do not understand," I said faintly, looking from one of the males to another. Nidisar stood beside Fayan, his hand upon her neck below her hair; his eyes sparkled with amusement. Telion crouched a short distance away, also amused. Ceralt himself stood tall and angry, his broad shoulders thrown back, his dark head high and proud, and to him I said again, "I do not understand. Am I to face you with sword?"

"No sword, wench," snorted Ceralt, then did he bend to grasp my arms and lift me to my feet. "I see now that it was cruel of me to take amusement from you, for you are only a savage, and I shall not do so again. From this moment you shall be treated as no more than a captive, to be traded for my men. I shall do what I may to civilize you till then, but not again will you be shamed. Do you agree, Telion?"

"Completely," said Telion, glancing up from where he crouched. "My injured pride has been avenged, and I would see my city safe. There is no need for your death, Jalav, and much reason to avoid it. Your Mida shall understand."

"And I now understand certain things, too," said Nidisar, gazing upon Fayan. "Come, captive, let us return to our pavilion."

Fayan looked confused as he took her hand and gently led her from the tent, yet was her expression deep understanding when compared with mine. I knew not what these males were about, and knew not why honorable death was denied to me. In misery I stood within the tent, at the mercy of those with no souls and no honor.

"You seem weary, Jalav," said Ceralt, brushing my hair from about my arm. "Do you wish to eat before you sleep?"

I shook my head, wishing only an end to my captivity by the living, and Ceralt took my arm gently and moved me closer to the post, where the chain was this time put about my left ankle. I sank to the fur, sitting and watching as he and Telion then moved about the tent, wrapping the meat, sharing the last of the renth, and lastly, extinguishing the candles. I waited for the males to lie beside me, demanding that I allow myself to be used, but that was not forthcoming. At a distance they lay themselves upon the fur, and soon were there sounds of sleep. This, least of all, did I understand, for had they not named me captive? Perhaps they did not wish to be near one who had been bested, and for this they could not be faulted. All alone, I lay down upon the fur by the post, to sleep as best I could.

10.

Mida's visit—and
a meaning is found

I awakened much awed, for in my sleep Mida had come to
me. My eyes had been blinded by her brilliance, and I had
turned away in misery, attempting to hide myself from her
sight, yet how may one hide from Mida? Her gentle presence
had drawn closer, and I found myself comforted and reas-
sured.

"Do not agonize, Jalav," she had said softly. "The war
leader of my Hosta has not been bested."

"I have!" I cried, shame forcing me to speak the truth.
"The male called Ceralt has bested me, yet he will not obey
your law! Is there naught you may do to sway him, Mida?"

"All has already been done," answered Mida, laughing
lightly. "The males do act as I have demanded, yet they
know it not, and the male called Ceralt does not disobey my
law, for he is not of the Midanna. The law is for Midanna
only, for males stand outside of it. Did you think, war leader,
that I would ask you to stand unarmed against a male, and
demand your victory? Am I not aware of the greater strength
of males? It shall be when you stand with sword in hand that
I shall demand your victory, be it male or warrior you face.
And soon will be the time you stand so, therefore you must
take heart. My Crystals must be recovered."

"I hear, Mida," I had acknowledged humbly, knowing that
what had befallen me had been by Mida's will. I did not
know the why of it, yet might it one fey be clear. To be

172

bested by a male, then, did not have the weight of being
bested by a warrior, unless the male held weapon in hand.
Though this was exceedingly strange, Mida's word was not to
be doubted. I opened my eyes to find Mida gone and the
males awake, putting flame to the candles against the coming
of the new light. I accepted the meat when it was offered me,
and chewed the overdone stuff with determination. Were I to
further serve Mida, my strength would be required.

Again we marched till the light was high, though this time
there were differences. Gone was the leather from my wrists
and Fayan's, it being replaced with the linked metal cuffs,
for, so said Ceralt, the strength of metal was needed to keep
his captives from escaping. Though I said naught, I knew that
was foolishness, for the leather had done well preventing escape till then. I suspected that Ceralt wished Fayan and myself to think ourselves more dangerous, yet did I fail to
understand this. Surely there are few things more dangerous
than an armed Midanna warrior; however Fayan and I were
still unarmed. How, then, could we think ourselves dangerous
to the males?

Such made little sense, but it made more sense than the humor of Fayan. She, as well as I, was drawn along by the collar leather, yet did she seem far removed from the warrior
who had so recently spoken of cleansing her honor with
death. She gazed upon Nidisar with a look which brought a
puzzled frown to me, a look not unlike that of one who has
seen the glory of Mida's Realm. She had stood beside the red
silk tent with him before the march, he holding her collar
leather, she presenting her wrists to be cuffed, and both had
gazed upon one another in like manner. Afterward, they
seemed nearly in a daze, he often turning on the kan to look
at her, ever finding her eyes already upon him. I failed to see
what captured her interest to so large a degree, and once,
when she chanced to glance in my direction, her face
reddened and her head had lowered, only to be drawn up
again in a moment to further contemplation of Nidisar. She
and I had both had opportunity to comb our hair before the
march, yet I failed to see, too, what Nidisar found so com-
pelling in her.

When the light was highest, we halted for a meal, and Telion rode back to our vicinity to join us. The leather of my
collar had been held by Ceralt, for Telion had been off about

other matters, and had Mida not told me that the males
served her purpose, I would have been easily away. There
would have been little difficulty in holding the leather taut
with one hand as the other unknotted it from my collar, yet
had I decided it to be unwise to rejoin my warriors just then.
Mida had placed me with the males for a purpose, and I
would do well to discover that purpose.

Telion dismounted as Ceralt did, and he laughed lightly as
he tied his kan. "The young ladies are somewhat eager to
reach Ranistard," said he to Ceralt. "Of course, they would
not admit it, but they wish to see those whom their fathers
shall choose. I had a delightful time."

"The next delightful time must be mine," laughed Ceralt as
he removed the wrapped meat from the back of his kan. "It
is time I thought more seriously of taking a wife, and a man
must look about him before he may choose."

"I sometimes believe the looking about to be superior to
the choosing." Telion grinned, taking the portion of meat
handed him. "How has our captive been behaving?"

"Quite well," said Ceralt, handing to me a cut of the meat.
"You seem much refreshed, Jalav. I trust you have gotten
over whatever disturbed you?"

"Indeed." I nodded, examining the meat with distaste. "Telion was right, for Mida does indeed understand."

"I somehow felt she would," commented Telion as he
chewed his meat. The thought came that he made sport of
me in some manner, but it was unimportant. He, like the others, acted only as Mida demanded.

We each crouched a short distance from the kand and fed,
Ceralt with the leather to my collar in his hand. Nidisar and
Fayan sat a short distance away, also feeding, yet also gazing
upon each other as they had done for hind that fey. So rapt
was Fayan, that she failed to hear the Hosta call sound again,
though I heard it quite clearly. I wished to acknowledge it in
some way; however, since the males were close beside me, I
could only stand slowly and stretch, holding my cuffed wrists
high so that they might be seen by those who watched. The
angry scolding of the lellin came again, quite briefly, and
much pleased was I. My gesture of acknowledgment had
been seen.

I brought my arms down again to find the eyes of Ceralt
and Telion upon me, yet neither male moved or spoke. After
a moment, Telion cleared his throat.

"It would not be difficult to find further pride to be avenged," said he, rather weakly. "Think you, Ceralt, it might be possible to. . . ."

"No!" said Ceralt firmly. His light eyes were pained as they rested upon me, and then did he look away and stand. "We have given our word, Telion, and may not reclaim it."

"I deeply regret being a man of honor," sighed Telion as he, too, rose. "A scoundrel's life would be much more convenient."

"Aha!" said another, higher voice. "I shall not forget that I heard you yearn for the scoundrel's life!"

We all turned to see a hand of the females who rode within the conveyance which was covered. They wore long, slave-woman coverings of various colors, and she who had spoken was as black of hair as I, yet was her hair bound tight in twists and knots, and held in place with bits of metal. Small were these females, and almost of a size, and all smiled upon Telion, who also smiled.

"Halia!" said Telion, a pleased sound to him. "I had not known that you stood there. May I present my friend Ceralt of Bellinard, of the brotherhood of hunters?"

"I am honored, ladies," said Ceralt smoothly, performing a small bow. "It is a pleasure traveling in your company."

The females looked upon one another and laughed strangely, a high, shrill laugh I had not heard before. The laughter seemed to please Telion and Ceralt, for they grinned at one another, also in an odd manner. The female Halia looked upon Ceralt, and brushed the skirt of her covering to and fro.

"I have heard many terrible things said of hunters," said this Halia with her head to the side. "Is it possible that they be true, Ceralt of Bellinard?"

"Not at all!" said Ceralt in amusement. "Hunters are fine fellows! To prove it, I shall also present my brother hunter, Nidisar." Then did he turn his head and call, "Nidisar! Come quickly to assist me in the defense of the brotherhood of hunters!"

Nidisar looked about at the call, saw the females, and rose to his feet with a small laugh. With Fayan's collar leather in his hand, he walked to join us, saying, "Shall I fetch my spear, Ceralt? Defense of our brotherhood is a serious matter."

Again the females laughed that laugh, and Ceralt and Telion laughed as well. "Your spear is not necessary, brother," grinned Ceralt, gesturing toward the females. "These are the critics we must defend against, for they have heard slanderous lies about hunters. In truth, now, are we not fine fellows?"

"Definitely the finest of fellows," said Nidisar with a grin. "A young lady might do no better than to be paired with a hunter."

"She would do equally well with a warrior," said Telion firmly, which comment again caused laughter among the females. "A warrior," said Telion, "is no whit less a fine fellow than a hunter."

"I fear you are all terrible fellows," said the female Halia, her eyes low, a small smile upon her face, "yet what may a woman do? She shall be given to him her father chooses, and she may say naught on the matter." Then her eyes raised, and looked upon me. "She may even be given to one who holds a slave in so awful a manner. Have you no shame, to dress them so?"

The males looked upon one another in discomfort, for the female's disapproval was strong, yet did I find the matter amusing. "Hosta warriors dress as they wish," I informed the small city female. "To feel the caress of Mida's air is no shame, as you might find should you attempt the matter."

"How dare you speak to me so?" gasped the female, color rising to her cheeks, anger strong in her eyes. "Never would I so display myself to the sight of men! It is shameful, especially so for one as overendowed as you!"

"Now, Halia," began Telion in upset, and, "Jalav, do not ..." began Ceralt, yet did I throw my head back and laugh.

"Now do I believe I see the reason for such coverings," said I to Fayan. "Mida has given them none of that which Midanna possess, and therefore must they disguise the lack! The displeasure of city males is now explained."

Fayan, too, laughed heartily, yet were the females in a fury. They stood with fists clenched angrily, and the males groaned as though in pain. Nidisar attempted to quiet Fayan's laughter, Telion attempted to speak soothingly to the females, and Ceralt briefly attempted to hide his face in his hand. The females muttered among themselves despite Telion's attempts, and the female Halia took an angry step closer.

"Beat her!" demanded this undersized female of Ceralt, furty ablaze in her eyes, her voice a hiss of hatred. "No slave may address me so, and I demand that you beat her!"

"Allow me to apologize for her!" said Ceralt, his smoothness dotted with desperation, his eyes nearly pleading. "Surely, the words of a slave have no ability to affect one of such excellent breeding! It is. . . ."

"Beat her!" screamed the female in a frenzy. "If you do not, I shall!"

Ceralt stood in wavering confusion, looking upon Telion, who shrugged his own helplessness, and the female Halia waited no longer. She bent resolutely to the ground, grasped a large, broken branch which lay at her feet, straightened again quickly, and brought the branch swinging hard toward my head. I raised my cuffed arms in immediate defense, and the branch merely struck against my left forearm, for the attempt had been clumsily executed. The female had swung with only her arms, using none of the weight of her body to aid her.

Ceralt angrily caught at the branch, twisted it from the hands of the female, then turned quickly to me, his arms up as though to intercept me, should I have thrown myself toward the puny female. I, however, stood as I had stood, my arms again lowered to where they had been.

"She must be beaten!" insisted the female Halia, as Ceralt's eyes gazed upon me in puzzlement. "She is a miserable slave, and I do not fear her as you seem to! There is little she may do, chained and leashed as she is!"

"Why do you do naught, Jalav?" asked Ceralt of me, taking no note of the female's words. "I had not thought you would allow yourself to be treated so."

"What may a warrior, in honor, do against one such as she?" I asked in amusement. "Am I to hurl the ability of a war leader of the Hosta of the Midanna against a sorry city female? There would be little glory in such an act." Then did I look at the female where she stood, and I was no longer amused. "Though, should the female wish to take sword in hand," I informed her coldly, "her challenge would be happily and quickly met. As have other challenges before hers."

The female paled at my words, her eyes wide. The other females seemed frightened as well, and all moved a step farther back from me. Then they saw that Ceralt's hand re-

mained tight upon the collar leather, and a new courage
possessed them.

"Slave!" taunted one, her hands upon her hips, her face
pushed insolently toward me. "Slave on a leash! Plaything of
men! Naked, naked, slave!"

The others were pleased with the words of the first, and all
took up the chant, "Slave, slave, slave on a leach! Slave,
slave, slave on a leash!" Halia was first in the set, laughing
and chanting with glee. I felt my chin rise high at their ridicule, and a low growl came from my throat. Little glory
would there be in besting such females, yet the pleasure
would indeed be great.

Fayan, in indignation, attempted to scatter the females,
but Nidisar restrained her. Telion frowned in disapproval as
Ceralt's face darkened, and he who called himself warrior
stepped forward.

"Enough!" ordered Telion coldly, gazing sternly upon the
females. "Have you no dignity about you, that you act so?"

"It is *she* who has no dignity!" said the female Halia,
pointing toward me with a casual finger. "How may a woman
possess dignity with no clothing, and hair free to her thighs?
She is fit to be naught save slave on a leash and plaything of
men! Should you wish the company of true women, you may
come, henceforth, to our wagon! Not again shall we return to
be sullied by the presence of slaves!"

With heads high the females then took themselves off, back
toward the conveyance from which they had come. Telion
and Ceralt looked upon one another in annoyance, and Telion took a breath which he expelled slowly.

"So much for our delightful time," said Telion with a
shake of his head. "Now must we visit them there, beneath
the eyes of their fathers. Hardly as amusing as here."

"I found small amusement in their visit," said Ceralt
sourly. "They are young, I know, yet they appear to have
little sense. Perhaps it would be best to seek elsewhere."

"Such as where?" asked Telion, equally sourly. "In Ranistard, they will be the best to be had."

Ceralt nodded his head. "Perhaps you are right," he said to
Telion. "We must attempt to repair the damage done, but
that would best be left till their anger has cooled. Perhaps we
may make the attempt later."

"Most definitely *without* the presence of Jalav," said Telion, frowning toward me. "It is little wonder that they be-came so outraged, being told to remove their clothing. They are gently reared, and are not used to being addressed so."

"Obviously not." Ceralt nodded in agreement, then he looked sideways at Telion. "Do you think, perhaps, that that *is* the reason for such long, high—"

His words abruptly ceased as Telion looked startled, then the two males laughed uproariously, slapping their own thighs and each others' shoulders. I, however, felt little amusement. The puny city females had made sport of me, yet was I for-bidden by Mida to walk from them, and forbidden by honor to cause them harm. Naught else was there to do save suffer the abuse, though I liked it not. Fayan, who had been upset by the incident, was further upset, for she stood a distance away with Nidisar, he speaking angrily she listening sullenly with eyes downcast. Then did her eyes raise in indignation, and with a toss of her head she turned from Nidisar, willing to listen to no more of his words. Nidisar, in annoyance, at-tempted to turn her to him again, yet did she keep her face averted. At last did Nidisar cease in disgust, and angrily pull Fayan by the collar leather to his kan, where he mounted in preparation for continuing the march. Ceralt and Telion, still chuckling, also mounted their kand, and once again did we take to the forest way.

As the fey previous, the march halted with a hin of light still to be passed, and male slaves began the replacement of the tents. Nidisar stood beside his kan, his hand tight upon Fayan's collar leather, impatient for the completion of his tent. Fayan had refused to look upon him for all of the march, and his anger had grown with the passing hind, till barely was he able to contain it. Ceralt had led me to a tree, pushed me to the ground before it where I might lean back, and had tied me tightly in place. Then had my arms been cuffed behind the tree, which had allowed Ceralt and Telion to ride away, satisfied with my immobilization. I sat and watched the progress with the tents, glad of an opportunity for rest.

With the tents finally as they had been, Nidisar handed the lead of his kan to a slave, and pulled Fayan within the red silk. The slaves looked upon each other with laughter, though they were forced by the armed males surrounding them to continue with their work. Nidisar's kan was led away, and I glanced back toward the red silk tent to see that a small fold of the silk allowed a narrow field of vision within the tent. Partially did I see Nidisar speaking to Fayan, and again did Fayan turn haughtily away from him, whereupon Nidisar grew truly angry. Quickly did he seize Fayan and bend her as Ceralt had bent me, then heatedly applied a loop of the collar leather to her clan covering. Dismayed, Fayan struggled, yet was the leather repeatedly applied to her, finally causing her to wail in a manner most unbecoming to a warrior. Nidisar did not cease swinging the leather at the wail, but continued till she blurted indistinct words, whereupon he ceased immediately, and stood Fayan to face him. Sternly did he speak to her then, seemingly asking a question, and miserably did she nod, her eyes downcast, her head lowered. Nidisar's hand gently raised her face to his as he spoke yet other words, and again did Fayan show the strange look she had worn much earlier, and her lips rose to those of Nidisar. With much heat did he take her lips with his own, and then he put his arms about her to throw her to the lenga pelts. The movement carried them from the opening of the silk, and I was much puzzled. What had Nidisar done to force my warrior to such strange behavior? I wished very much to speak with her, yet knew that Nidisar would keep her well occupied for some time. Naught was there to do save sit where I had been placed.

"Mida's blessings, Jalav," came a whispered voice from behind me. "How do you fare among the males?"

"Not as well as you have fared, Larid," I whispered in return, grinning. "You and the others are well?"

"Well and free," came Larid's amused answer. "There was little difficulty in avoiding those of the cities, and once over the walls, we followed the sign left for us by Gimin. Once with our sister warriors, Gimin had certain of the captured males release us from the metal. The others are a bit more than a fey before us, I alone remaining to bring you word. Gimin would know if you wish us to fall upon these males and free you."

"That, though pleasant to contemplate, may not be," I said in annoyance. "Mida has appeared to me, and demanded that I remain among the males. I know not why, but I may not disobey. Carry to Gimin the word that these city folk do travel to Ranistard, and therefore may the way be more fully known. Also, that warriors must be placed secretly within its walls before the arrival of this set. Once there, Ceralt and Telion shall be quick to speak of impending attack, and then shall their guard be alert."

"I hear, Jalav," whispered Larid. "I shall carry your word to Gimin, and then shall return against your need of me."

"Do not return!" I whispered sharply, attempting to move my throat within the leather which bound it to the tree. "You need not place yourself in jeopardy of capture, and Gimin shall require each sword available to her!" Silence greeted my words, and I whispered, "Larid, do you hear?" but the silence remained. Angrily I pulled upon the metal which held my wrists, for too often had my word been ignored by my warriors. With Jalav bound in metal, all went their own way, secure from the wrath of the war leader. Soon, soon! must I be released, to see once more to the discipline of the Hosta!

Slowly did the light withdraw from the skies, and still did I sit, my arms chained about the roughness of the tree, my throat held tight by leather to it. More clearly could the campfires be seen, and the smell of roasting meat wafted itself to me upon the breeze. Lightly, also, came the sound of laughter, that of males and females together. I wondered what amusement they shared, and unbidden came to me the memory of the dwelling within Bellinard, the place of hunters and renth. Laughter, then, had warriors shared with males, and the time had been an oddly pleasing one. Often had I found joy in battle and the hunt, yet joy of a sort there had also been in the dwelling. No sound was there from the red silk tent, and the darkness deepened.

Full dark was about all things when I heard the sound of footsteps. I could not turn to see who approached, yet the forms quickly stood before me, and then crouched in a half circle, three armed males, guards, by the looks of them, of the set with which we traveled. They gazed upon me with amusement, and the one in the center put forth his hand and stroked my breast.

"A fascinating slave," said he with a grin for my anger. "A slave any man would be eager to own. See how she moves against the leather, brothers. She would warm a man even upon the ice of Sigurr's Peak."

"What do you do here, little slave?" said the one to my right, extending his hand to me as well. "You travel far from your land, and we do not care to see such as you. Have you merely been taken and enslaved as you should be, or do you follow where only death awaits you?"

I did not reply, but I felt a great, bloody joy. These males knew well the sight of a Hosta warrior, and knew, too, the home place of Midanna. Though I had thought them to be well ahead of the chase, those who had taken the Crystal and lives of my warriors were before me! Ah, Mida! Clear is your sight, and deep is your understanding!

"The wench does not wish to speak," said the one to my left, raising a dagger from the sheath at his belt. His face was light-boned and delicate, like that of a girl, and his smile made him seem prettier still, like a young warrior returned from her first battle. He turned the dagger about, and then pressed its point to my breast. "Perhaps she must be persuaded," said this male, leaning the point a bit more into my flesh. "Speak to us now, wench, and speak of that which we wish to hear."

Well I knew the pain must be borne without a sound, for the lives of these males were mine to take when I was freed. The male moved his dagger about somewhat, then he in the center made a noise of vexation.

"She is as stubborn as the other," said he. "Present your dagger to her more delicate softness, and perhaps she may find her tongue."

He with the dagger removed it, but before it could touch me again, the male was pulled roughly to his feet and shaken as though he were child, clutched in the furious fists of Ceralt. The other two made as if to rise, yet were halted by the blade of Telion, it being free and near to their throats.

"What do you do near my slave?" demanded Ceralt of the male, who had dropped the dagger in his shock. "For what reason do you touch her so?"

"She—she savaged me!" screamed the male being shaken, fearful of the larger male who held him captive. "She, a mere slave, refused to beg my caress, therefore did I caress her with my blade!"

"It is not your caress she must beg!" growled Ceralt in disgust and anger. "Should I again find you near her, the caravan shall be lacking a guard! Take you hence, and your filthy friends with you!"

Roughly did Ceralt throw the male to the ground, and hastily did the male raise himself again and stumble away, the other two being driven off behind him by Telion. A moment Ceralt and Telion watched their departure, then they turned to me in the darkness.

"Tied fast to a tree, and still does she find trouble," muttered Ceralt in annoyance. "Had I not my brother hunters to consider, I would rid myself of her as quickly as possible."

"As you do have your brothers to consider," said Telion as he sheathed his blade, "it would be wisest to bring her now to the pavilion. The newly roasted meat will soon be brought."

Ceralt grunted an agreement, and walked behind to release my wrists as Telion made for the tent. The candles glowed within the tent as the last of the leather was unwound from my throat, and Ceralt pulled me to my feet by it, and took me behind him through the opening in the yellow silk. Once within, he turned as though to speak to me, but his eyes went instead to my breast and an exclamation escaped from him.

"By Sigurr's fetid breath, see what was done to her!" said Ceralt, stepping closer to grasp my arms. "I should have broken the craven's neck while my hands were upon him!"

Telion stepped to us quickly, in cold anger. At four points did blood flow from my breast, yet the cost was small for the knowledge of the faces of those who had been at the Tower. Never would those faces escape me, and, Mida willing, neither would the males themselves.

"Not a sound did she make!" said Telion in upset. "Not a sound from her lips nor a tear from her eye!"

"She is a—warrior!" said Ceralt in anger, and then did he take me by the arm and seat me upon the lenga pelts. "Hear my words, O warrior of stubbornness!" said he, crouching before me. "Should you ever again be approached by those who would offer harm, you are to raise that throaty voice and shout for assistance! Not again are you to suffer such treatment in silence!"

"For what assistance would I shout?" I asked in confusion. "My warriors are not near enough to hear me."

"You would shout for me, child of idiocy!" shouted Ceralt in a rage. "For what other reason would I instruct you to shout?"

I did not understand what he meant, yet Telion seemed amused. "He thinks only of his hunters, of course," chuckled the male who called himself warrior. "For no other reason does he alone wish to be called."

Ceralt's face darkened somewhat, and he straightened and turned from me. "Of course, I meant that Telion should also be called," said the hunter as he strode to the waterskin

which hung from the tent wall. "The other was merely a slip
of the tongue."

"Certainly." Telion nodded, still in amusement. "And when
is the miserable slave to be beaten?"

Ceralt stiffened before the waterskin, yet did not turn. "I
do not take your meaning," said he a bit faintly.

"My meaning is simple," answered Telion most affably.
"The lovely Halia has decreed that the slave is to be beaten,
else are you to be banished from the light of her presence. I,
myself, heard her pronounce the decree to you, and most soft
were her tone and manner. Did you then not agree to do so?"

"I—may have said some such," acknowledged Ceralt fee-
bly, his voice low, his back still turned. "It is all foolishness,
and best quickly forgotten. By the new light, the thought will
be gone from the wench's memory. Have you anything to
wash the wounds?"

"I shall fetch a cloth," said Telion, and then he strode
from the tent. Ceralt turned toward me, seeming to search
for the words he would say. I looked upon him briefly, in bitterness and anger. Again did he use me for purposes of his
own, as he had attempted to use me to free his males in the
forest, as he still meant to use me to trade for their release.
To promise the puny female my pain was to add to the
shame he had already given me. Always was I to be used by
him, my value in trade foremost in his mind. I sat in silence,
the pain of my wounds a throb in my mind.

Telion returned quickly with a cloth in hand, and Ceralt
poured water upon it to moisten it, then did Telion approach
with the cloth where I had put myself in the fur. He
crouched beside me, and a gentle smile touched his lips.

"If you wish, Jalav," said he, "I believe I might find another to assist you with the cloth."

His glance had gone to Ceralt, who still stood beside the
waterskin, yet for what reason his glance moved so, I knew
not. Ceralt wished naught from me save use, in one manner or
another.

"I wish the assistance of no other," said I to Telion. "Are
we not both warriors?"

"Indeed." Telion nodded a bit sadly. "We are indeed both
warriors." He put the cloth to me, and I closed my eyes,
barely hearing the departure of Ceralt through the pain I felt.
The dagger had bitten fairly deep, and the touch of the cloth
was no small thing. By the time the blood had ceased to flow,

I no longer had stomach for the meat which had been brought. Telion insisted upon my drinking of the renth, then I lay once more in the fur, a heavy toll taken of my strength. Vaguely did I hear the return of Ceralt, who stood briefly above me before going to his sustenance. No words were exchanged by the males, and easily then did I sleep.

11.

Shaming by a male —and a life is saved

I awakened to find myself locked by the ankle to Ceralt's belt. Too distant had I been from the post, therefore the hunter secured me in such a manner. He and Telion awakened then as well, released the metal from my ankle, and offered me a portion of the meat. I accepted it from Telion, wishing none of it, yet knowing that I must feed to regain my strength. Happily, the portion given me had escaped much of the overeager fire of those who had cooked it, and was far more edibile than the meat I had previously been offered. After having swallowed from the water skin, I angered Telion by refusing to allow a cloth to be put upon the tracks of the dagger. Midanna only bind a freely bleeding wound, for how may Mida aid in its healing, should it be kept from her sight? The marks were small, only slightly to be seen now, and I wished them to heal quickly so that I might feel them as little as I saw them. Telion strode away with the cloth in resignation, and once more I was led through the forest behind Ceralt's kan.

Ceralt had spoken no word to me, though he had words with Telion. Telion, having seen my pain and weakness of the darkness, had wished me to ride that fey, but Ceralt refused to hear of it. Jalav was merely a captive, he insisted, and captives were not to ride. Telion argued somewhat, then he capitulated in disgust, saying he, himself, would not hold the collar leather. Ceralt was then forced to take the leather, which he did without looking upon me. My wrists were again held before me in metal, and I followed without comment, for little else had I expected of the hunter Ceralt.

Fayan, this fey, rode behind Nidisar, and in misery refused to meet my eyes. She and Nidisar had been told by Telion of what had befallen me in the darkness, and Nidisar had been enraged that I had not called to him, he being so near. For long did he storm about and shout at me, yet had Fayan been reduced to deep shame. Her war leader, bound and helpless, had been in need of her, and she had lain all unknowing, but paces from the incident, sporting about with a male. She wore only the collar leather, and when Nidisar had called her to his kan, she had not wished to go. He, however, had refused to accept her refusal, and had swung her to the kan behind him. Then had she placed her arms about him in misery and clung to him, unspeaking yet feeling her shame. I still had no understanding of her actions; however I would wait to hear her explanation before condemning her.

For two feyd I was led about by Ceralt, and not merely upon the trail. He took to leading me about at every halt of the set, most often to the conveyance of the city females. There would the females, from the safety of their conveyance, laugh and call me slave on a leash, plaything of men. Although I felt much anger toward them, I ignored their chant so that I might search for a glimpse of the ones who had been in the Tower of the Crystal. Many males were about, and they looked upon me, but the three that I sought were not to be seen. Ceralt found great amusement among the females, most especially with the one called Halia, but Telion had ceased attending them. For many hind would there be no sight of him, yet I had the feeling that he was not far. The two males spoke rarely, and merely shared the tent to take their food and rest. Always did Telion see that I fed, as though he felt that Ceralt would not do so. Ceralt made no comment to this, and always did *he* see that I was secured for the darkness. Neither male attempted use of me, and so it went, in silence, through the darkness and light.

Upon the third fey I decided to search more earnestly for the males who had been to the Tower. That Larid was soon due to return was a great factor, for I would then send her for Gimin and my Hosta, to halt the set I traveled with and free me. Then, then! would the three males be questioned, of the location of the Crystal and of those others who had ac-

companied them. Their questioning would be short and
pleasant to them once they learned their fate, and great care
would I take that their fate was exacted in full. Death would
not rob them of their pain, not till my warriors had been well
avenged!

Also that fey, had Ceralt done much to enrage me. He had
again, with the light at its highest, led me before the females,
where they sat upon the grass beside their conveyance. He,
too, took seat upon the grass, and then pulled me to his lap,
to be held in his arms. Much amused were the city females
by my struggles, and they clapped their hands and laughed
shrilly, urging Ceralt to show them full use of a slave. Ceralt,
too, had laughed to begin with, yet with his fist in my hair,
and his arm pressing me close to his chest, his amusement
left him. His light eyes sobered, and very light did they appear below his dark, unruly hair. Then had his lips come
swiftly to mine, the lips of the male who had bested me and
shamed me, he who moved to the demands of Mida. Hard as
metal was his arm about me, harsh and demanding were his
lips on mine. Surely did I wish to struggle further, yet Mida's
hand must have restrained my struggles, for I did not refuse
his lips, nor did I ignore their demands. For many reckid was
I held thus, and then did the female Halia cry out in delight.

"Use her now, Ceralt!" urged the female, her hand upon
the hunter's shoulder. "Teach her her place as a slave! Use
her as the plaything she is!"

Ceralt turned his head from me, and saw the look upon
the female's face. Overbright and excited were her eyes. She
looked upon me with gloating, wishing with every part of her
that I be shamed before her eyes.

Ceralt was silent a moment, then quietly did he ask, "Have
you then never been bedded, Halia?"

The female flushed further, and quickly did her eyes dart
to the hunter. "What has that to do with the matter?" she demanded shrilly. "Use her, Ceralt, use her!"

"You, too, shall soon be used, Halia," said Ceralt with
gentleness, "and her use will not take the place of your own."
Then a grin flashed across his face. "And I would also not
care to face your fathers, should I do such a thing before the
eyes of innocents. I think it best that we leave now."

To the accompaniment of long drawn "ohhh's" from the
females, Ceralt pushed me to my feet, then rose himself. The
females still laughed as they looked upon me, yet the female

Halia sat slumped with head down, her eyes lowered in misery. The puny city female was disturbed in some manner, yet could it not have been important. City females have naught of importance with which to concern themselves. Ceralt reclaimed his kan, and soon were we again on the move. Not again, though, had Ceralt returned his gaze to me.

Much angered was I with Ceralt for treating me so before the females, yet pleased was I, too, with his lack of attention. When we halted for the raising of the tents, I found no eye upon me, therefore did I carefully unknot the leather from my collar and retie it to a branch that hung nearby, then slipped into the woods.

Though my wrists were still bound in metal before me, I gloried in the freedom of the forests. Quite easily could I have continued on in the set's direction, seeking the sign to be left by Hosta for their sisters. Much did I wish to do so, yet I had been forbidden such by Mida, and, too, Fayan and the males of the Tower still remained. Fayan was of little concern, for Nidisar saw to her constantly; however she was still a sister warrior, and not to be abandoned. The males, however, held me more closely than the metal of an enclosure, for I would not depart and leave their blood unspilled. Sooner would I deny the word of Mida, and before that, would I see my soul unalterably lost.

The leaves of the trees caressed me as I slid by, hidden in their foliage. Armed males had been set about the camp, searching for those who would enter their area unbidden, yet it was simple to bypass them without notice. Some small knowledge of the woods had they, but as those who often pass through, not as they who have dwelt therein. Each of these males did I gaze upon, seeking the three of the Tower, yet each had the look of a stranger, not of those I sought. Armed males, too, directed the efforts of slaves throughout the camp, and these, too, appeared innocent. Well I knew that hunters roamed about for the camp in general, and much did I hope that the males of the Tower were among them. That they should have fled the set and the area was not to be borne.

I circled the camp completely for sign of those I sought, and also for sign that Larid had returned. I found no sign of Larid nor the males, yet another sight was presented me. The clutch of city females stood, surrounded by many males, awaiting the completion of their tents, and one stole away from them to the woods, looking again and again past her shoulder, to be sure that she was unobserved. She halted among the bushes and trees, at the edge of a tiny clearing, and beat at the tree in frustration. Still was the female Halia disturbed, and well might she be disturbed, for the woods were not for those who knew them not. Much sign had I seen of a hunting hadat, that swift and terrible embodiment of my life sign, and there, but three paces from the tiny clearing, could I smell the presence of hadat, near and on the move.

Coolly did I watch the female Halia as she wept against her arm, her misery great over some matter. Sounds came from the direction of the camp, shouts from few and then from many. The shouts roused the female from her weeping, her face turned toward the camp, then did she turn resolutely from the tree as though to move farther into the woods, yet was the sight before her tear-filled eyes one which halted her completely. The hadat had come upon the clearing as she wept, and now it stood, joying in the sight of that which it would seize. The hadat, light red in color, stood swishing its tail, its head at least the height of my shoulder, its short, soft pelt all aquiver with anticipation. Slowly, very slowly, did it move toward the female, its fangs just bared, a croon in its throat. There had been those who thought the hadat tame, those who had been deceived by its croon of capture; however, they had not survived, for the hadat gave no quarter. Only when upon its victim did it scream victory, to declare itself unbeaten and sole possessor of its prize. Soon would it scream so above the female, its claws upon her broken, bloody form.

Then did the female realize what stood before her, her eyes wide, her hand to her mouth, and a single, terror-filled scream erupted from her throat, as though she knew there was little time for more. The shouts of the camp suddenly turned to our direction, and I became disturbed. The hadat, once in possession of its prey, would not again quickly leave it, and those from the camp would surely arrive to slay it. This female, this city woman Halia, would thus be the means by which the embodiment of my life sign would be slain, taken ignominiously by the males of her city. The hadat was woods-wise, and not easily hunted, and should it escape, the set's hunters would not soon find it again. I then determined that the hadat would not be taken, and swiftly moved toward the clearing where it stood.

The hadat was little more than two paces from the female when I entered the clearing, hearing the rapid approach of those from the camp. The female's eyes were held fast to the promise of death before her, and the hadat held her gaze with its own. Deliberately then, did I sound the furious hiss of another hadat, raising it quickly to the scream of rage and challenge. The hadat, with the speed of thought, turned with its own scream and raced for me, furious that its hunt had been challenged. In such a way will the hadat guard its victim from another, the two hadat leaping together in the air, fangs and claws flashing with kill lust, each determined that the other shall not survive. So, then, did the hadat leap for me, yet was I no puny city female, to be taken by the mere sight of my life sign. As the hadat leaped, so did I, too, leap, yet not to meet it. I threw myself swiftly to the ground, rolling beneath the claws which reached for my blood, using the instinct of the hadat which had sent it to the air, even before it fully realized that I was no hadat. With a great howl of fury did the hadat alone reach the trees beyond the clearing, and then were the sounds of many shafts leaving their strings. The hadat snarled its fury as it turned, unwilling to face the numbers that confronted it, and I sat upon the ground and watched it gone, the shrieks of the female Halia sharp as a blade in my ears.

I turned to the running footsteps then, and beheld Ceralt before the rest, pounding toward the screaming, weeping Halia, as she waited to be grasped and held against her terror. Up to the sobbing female did Ceralt run—and past her to where I sat upon the ground. His face an unreadable mask, he pulled me from the ground and threw his arms about me, his hand pressed hard to the side of my face, my metal-bound wrists lost between us. He held me so for a long moment, my cheek upon his chest, and Halia stood with widened eyes, her screams and fear forgotten, in disbelief. Many males ran to her then, and quickly was she taken in the arms of one who had often been beside her, yet she stood numbly against him, receiving none of the comfort she had craved.

Then Ceralt's arms released me, his hands taking my arms instead, so that he might shake me. "Now shall you truly be beaten!" growled the hunter, enraged, his fingers like metal upon me. "To call upon yourself the hunting hadat, merely to save the life of one who has given you only grief, is the act

of a veritable idiot! Do you not know that you could have
been killed? Have you no sense within that great, empty
head? Will you never learn to care properly for yourself?"

His hands shook me, his voice raised high in deep-felt
outrage. I did not understand his actions, yet was I unable to
ask of it, nor explain my true purpose in luring the hadat to
me. Question upon question did he shout, demanding answers, yet allowing for none, till the male who had held the
female Halia came to us, and placed a hand upon Ceralt's
shoulder.

"Gently, hunter, gently," said this male. "Well do I know
your feelings in the matter, yet must it be remembered that
my daughter's life would have been forfeit save for her. I
would offer my thanks to her before you beat her for her
foolishness."

"You may thank her," said Ceralt with anger, "yet beaten
she shall be, and soundly! Also for having run from me, for
had she not run, she would have been in no danger!"

"Truly, for the moment I had forgotten," said the male.
"She is slave to you, is she not." The words were not a question, and the male looked at me, then at Ceralt. "I would buy
her release from you, hunter," said the male very simply.
"Speak her price."

Ceralt held the male's eyes as he stood there, his hands yet
upon my arms, though he shook me no longer. "Her release
from me shall never be bought," he murmured, "for her price
is beyond any who might wish to meet it. She is mine, and
mine she shall remain."

"As a slave?" asked the male beside us, as Ceralt looked
softly down into my eyes. There was a hint of amusement to
the male's voice, and Ceralt smiled faintly.

"If need be," said he very gently, and then did he swiftly
bend and lift me upon his shoulder. Never had such a thing
been done to me, and through my outrage came Ceralt's
chuckle. "She has not yet learned to obey me," said he quite
briskly. "If you will excuse us?"

Amid the hearty laughter of those all about us, Ceralt carried me from the clearing. I beat at him with the metal of the
cuffs, yet was he not to be deterred. Unhurriedly, steadily was
I carried to the yellow silk tent, the candles having already
been lit against the slowly falling darkness, and then within.
Once he stood upon the lenga pelts, I was again placed upon
my feet, and the metal was removed from my wrists. When

the second cuff was open, Ceralt took the metal and threw it from him, then he did the same with his sword. Uneasily I stood and watched him, for once before had he freed me and disarmed himself. The hunter saw my wary look, and laughed lightly.

"You are correct," said he with a grin, chucking my chin. "I do indeed mean to take you again, in relief over not having lost you forever." He paused by the waterskin, and turned to look back at me over his shoulder. "Do you object?"

By his single question was I rendered speechless. Of a certainty, I objected! Was I not a warrior of the Midanna, war leader of the Hosta? Could a warrior, in all honor, accept the touch of a male who simply announced that he meant to take her? Would Mida not see the shame in such a thing? Surely the male had been touched with madness. Narrow-eyed and quite suspicious, I asked, "Why would I not object?"

Ceralt laughed quite heartily at that. "The answer to your question, my girl," said he with a grin, "must be yet another question. You were free from the leash for quite some time, yet you did not lose yourself in the forest. I know full well how easily you would fare on your own, therefore do I ask: why did you not go?"

"I could not abandon my warrior," said I, finding it unnecessary to speak of other matters. "Fayan is yet held here, and I shall not leave her."

Again Ceralt laughed, and placed the waterskin at our feet. "Fayan is held through her own desires," said he, his hand gentle upon my shoulder. "She has given her heart to Nidisar, and holds his in its stead. All who have seen them know the truth of the matter, and you, too, have seen them. I know why you remained, Jalav, and I am filled with happiness." Abruptly were his arms about me, and he held me to him. "You cannot bear to part from me, just as I cannot bear to part from you!"

"That is madness!" said I in shock as his lips began to lower to mine. "Most happily shall I part from you as soon as may be!"

"Women," muttered Ceralt in annoyance, raising his head once more. "Be they civilized or savage, all must be coaxed—or captured. Look you, Jalav, can you not merely admit that you wish to be mine? As I wish you to be, and intend for you to be?"

"Be yours?" I repeated in outrage. "Never shall I be yours! I am a warrior of the Midanna!" I pushed from his arms, and wearily did he release me.

"Very well," he sighed resignedly. "I see you cannot yet admit it, therefore must I continue to hold you captive till the fey you may no longer deny it. Till then shall you remain my possession."

"And mine," came Telion's voice from the tent flap. We turned to see him, his face amused, and Ceralt frowned a bit.

"In truth, I had forgotten that," mumbled Ceralt. "Telion, my friend, I would buy your partial ownership of her."

"Partial?" inquired Telion with raised brows. "Surely you recall, friend Ceralt, that my ownership is equal with yours?"

"True," responded Ceralt most soberly, "yet have I the greater claim. It was to my city that she first came."

"It is to my city that she meant to go," replied Telion with equal sobriety. "My claim should then be the greater."

"I was captured by her clan and held for many feyd," said Ceralt.

"I was captured by her clan and held quite briefly," mused Telion, and Ceralt brightened, yet Telion then added quickly, "yet was I captured first!"

The two males then glowered at each other, and I merely stood to the side and examined them. Not the least idea had I of the point which they debated, and seriously did I doubt that they, themselves, could have told me. Mida, perhaps, understood, but none below her.

Another moment of glowering passed, then Ceralt firmly folded his arms. "I," he announced in icy tones, "feel deep love for her!" He stood and waited then, his eyes fast to Telion, and Telion also folded his arms.

"I," announced Telion as Ceralt stiffened, "have grown fairly fond of her!" Ceralt's mouth opened in huge surprise, for surely had he expected other words from Telion. Telion laughed at Ceralt's look, strode quickly to him, and then clapped him on the shoulder. "Ceralt, my friend," he said, "that was the telling point. I did not know if you would admit it."

"I must admit it," Ceralt made answer ruefully, and then he too, laughed. "How else am I to purchase your—*partial* ownership of her?"

"That will not be necessary." Telion laughed. "I give my

ownership—of whatever size—as a gift to you. Long have I known that it was in you she found greater interest."

"No interest have I in *any* male!" I informed them indignantly, yet was I completely ignored, perhaps wisely. For a warrior to be so foolish as to say she finds no interest in males, is hopefully a lie—and tragically not.

"I have also secured another pavilion," continued Telion. "It stands there, to the right of yours."

"You are the most understanding of friends," said Ceralt with a grin. "Had you not thought of it, I would have suggested it."

"It was not understanding that prompted the action," said Telion with a sly look. "There is true need for another pavilion, and happily will I show it to you."

Telion then left the tent, and Ceralt turned to me with a questioning look, as though I would understand. So long had it been since I had understood things, I no longer felt surprise at the unexplained. I merely attempted to ignore them, in the fond hope that they would suddenly cease to be, and need no explanation. Should matters continue us they had gone, Mida would require all of eternity to rid herself of my First Question.

"I took myself hunting," said Telion as he returned, "and see what fell to my trap."

"The luck of the inexperienced!" laughed Ceralt with fists on hips, and I groaned with a great deal of feeling. Over Telion's shoulder, bound wrist and ankle with leather, was Larid, struggling futilely to rid herself of the cloth which kept her from uttering a sound. Truly, Mida was making her task most difficult, and briefly did I wonder upon the possibility of her having changed her mind regarding return of her Crystal. Should that have been so, it would have been well to have mentioned it.

"I have not yet questioned her," said Telion to Ceralt, "thinking that you, too, might find some interest in her words."

"I shall know after her words are heard," said Ceralt, and then did he gesture toward the lenga pelts. "Put her there, and then we may listen at our ease."

Telion placed Larid on the fur, and then untied the cloth from her. Furious was Larid at having been treated so, and she glared quite strongly at Telion. Telion did not seem to see the glare, for he sat beside her and smiled in a gentle manner.

"We are extremely pleased to see you, girl," said Telion mildly to Larid. "Where are the others of your wenches?"

"The Hosta are all about you!" answered Larid forcefully, her eyes ablaze. "Release me now, and you may keep your lives!"

"That is extremely kind of you," nodded Telion with a smile, "yet do I believe that we shall hold you for a while longer. Might I ask exactly *where* about us the Hosta are?"

"*All* about you!" replied Larid with a toss of her head. "Should I not return within the hin, they will attack immediately!"

"Then we have only a hin to wait," remarked Ceralt with a yawn. "It will take very little time to don my sword, so I need not hurry."

"I already wear my sword," said Telion, "therefore shall I have to occupy my time in another manner." He paused to think a moment, then his face lit up with inspiration. "I have it!" he announced with pleasure. "I shall fetch from the caravan slavemaster his heavy whip, so that should the attack not take place at the specified time, I shall be able to properly punish a wench who dared lie to me."

Slowly did Telion begin to rise to his feet, and Larid took on a look of fear. "Wait!" she gasped, and then bit her lip. "Perhaps I was mistaken as to the actual moment of attack. It may not come for, oh, all of the darkness!"

Telion, who had settled back upon the fur, nodded his head most soberly. "That presents no hardship," said he. "I shall still fetch the whip, and merely hold it for use for the new light."

Again he made as if to rise, and truly frantic was Larid. "No!" she pleaded in great upset, her eyes large and helpless. "I—I did not speak the truth a moment ago! I—do not even know where the Hosta are!"

Telion and Ceralt exchanged looks of satisfaction, and I seated myself upon the fur, my hand before my mouth so that my amusement would not interfere with their interrogation. Larid was once again indulging her fondness for pretense, and had now led the males to believe that she knew naught of the whereabouts of the Hosta. As the information had had to be forced from her, there was no doubt but that they believed her.

"These are serious matters!" Telion frowned sternly upon a thoroughly cowed Larid. "You must speak the complete truth, else you shall be well beaten!"

"I do not wish to be beaten!" begged Larid earnestly. "I will speak the truth!"

"Very well," said Telion coldly. "I would first know how you came to be here."

"I wished to free Jalav," answered Larid miserably. "I waited without the city after the others and I had escaped, and followed when I saw her taken from there."

"You are one of those three!" said Ceralt in surprise. "How did you rid yourselves of the slave metal, and where have the other two gone?"

"At swordpoint did we force a city male to remove the metal," said Larid smugly, yet a glance at the disapproval of the two males before her cowed her once more. "Binat and Comir went in search of the Hosta," she added uncomfortably, "and I remained in hopes of sighting Jalav and Fayan."

"Then you must be—Larid!" said Telion. "Tell me, Larid, where did the others go to seek the Hosta?"

"Toward Ranistard." Larid shrugged quite openly. "We do not know its exact location, yet do we know it lies to the north. Come one light or another, it shall be found."

Telion and Ceralt looked upon one another again, and then Telion indicated that Ceralt was to join him at the far side of the tent. The males walked to the side and began conversing quietly, and Larid moved dancing eyes to me. Seeing the attention of the males elsewhere, I placed my fingers to my lips, then lowered the hand, palm upward, to my lap. "Good," I had told Larid in the silent speech of the Midanna, and her dancing eyes sparkled with pleasure before assuming again a look of cowed misery. It then occurred to me that Larid may have come with a purpose, but I was unable to ask the question, for Telion and Ceralt chose to return to her then.

"We shall, for the moment, accept your answers," Telion informed Larid sternly from above her. "Should we find, however, that you have lied, the whip will be fetched so that you may be beaten!"

"I have not lied!" sobbed Larid with great fear, writhing in her bonds. "Please do not beat me!"

"We shall see," said Telion, then he crouched before her

and lifted her face with his hand. "Do you recall who I am?" he asked rather mildly.

Larid seemed puzzled, yet she answered, "Of course. You are the last sthuvad of our home tents."

"Good." Telion smiled. "And do you, by chance, recall what occurred in a room in a large, stone tower?"

Larid parted her lips to reply, yet was her voice stilled as a wary look entered her eye. Telion grinned as he saw memory return to her, and he nodded quite slowly.

"I see you do recall," said he, reaching behind Larid to remove the war leather from her flaming red hair. "A captive was used by a warrior without the captive's permission. I somehow feel that the incident is shortly to be repeated—with yet another captive and another warrior."

Larid frowned and glanced worriedly toward me, but there was nothing I could do. Had she come with a purpose, her predicament was unfortunate, yet had she come in disobedience to my word, her predicament was well earned. In either event, the predicament could not be avoided.

"I believe she may now be returned to your pavilion," said Ceralt to Telion with a laugh. "The meal should soon be brought, and I would see Jalav's wound washed before then."

"Wound?" frowned Telion, looking toward me, yet I, also, knew naught of such.

"From too close an association with a hadat," said Ceralt, striding to me and taking my leg in his hand. There on my left calf, till then unnoticed by me, was a small cut, surely no longer than a finger. The bleeding had long since ceased, and I had not even felt the faint throb of it.

"Ah, yes," said Telion, and then he shook his head. "Had I not seen it with my own eyes, I would not have credited accounts of it."

"I still do not credit it," said Ceralt sourly. "And all for the sake of that foolish Halia."

"By now, a well punished Halia," laughed Telion. "When you carried Jalav off to your pavilion, Halia seemed to be seized by a fit. She screamed and wept and threw herself about, the gist of her ranting composed of equal parts of her refusal to be given to any man, her heated desire to be carried off only by you, and her deep conviction that Jalav is the sole source of her ills. Her father took up a strong, supple branch, and then firmly led her toward their pavilion. As I passed, her shrieks were already well in evidence."

"Perhaps it may do her some good," said Ceralt as he shook his head. "I, myself, would not wish her for wife."

"Nor I," agreed Telion, then did he raise Larid to his shoulder once more. "I shall see you again come the new light."

"Certainly not before," laughed Ceralt with a glance toward me, and Telion left the tent with a laugh of his own. Larid, upon his shoulder, outraged and worried, also seemed upset that we had not spoken. Truly, her presence there was for a purpose.

"Turn your leg," directed Ceralt from beside me, for he had moistened a cloth and brought it to me. I did as he directed, and slowly, carefully, he washed the traces of blood from the scratch. His hand was upon my ankle as he did so, his eyes intent upon the motions of the cloth, and surely was his presence felt most strongly by me. Such broad shoulders had he, such well muscled arms, and large hands. In the home tents of the Hosta, easily could he become, even among many others, one of my true favorites. Perhaps the Harra were right, and captives might in honor be kept past initial usage. I would have to think on it.

The meat and a cloth to place it upon were brought by a slave, and the slave looked upon me most curiously. Ceralt laughed softly as the slave departed, then did he cut a portion of the meat for me. We fed in silence, seated side by side at the cloth, however Ceralt refused the renth to me. He, himself, drank sparingly from the skin, his eyes directly upon me. In my annoyance, I cared not where he looked.

Upon completion of the meal, Ceralt rose and began to extinguish the candles, therefore I rose also and walked to the post, there to seat myself once more. Ceralt turned from one of the candles, and seemed surprised.

"What do you do there?" he asked, as though no reason could occur to him.

"I wait to be chained as always," said I, finding it odd that he would not remember.

"I see." He nodded quietly, the one remaining candle throwing shadows about him. "And for what reason would you need to be chained?"

I then stared at him, wondering how long such questions would continue to come from him. "Why, to keep me from escaping," said I, thinking that perhaps the answer had not been as obvious as I had thought.

"There is chance of your escape?" said he, full innocence upon him. "When now we hold not one, but two of your warriors?"

I had not considered that, but he had spoken truly. The Crystal must be considered above any of the Hosta, yet had I still to hear what word Larid brought. Should I depart the set I now traveled with in hopes of rejoining the balance of my warriors, indeed might I find that they had gone where I could not easily follow. I did not know what news might have come to Gimin, and I would truly be foolish to depart without first speaking with Larid.

"I hear no answer from you," said Ceralt, and then he placed himself beside me on the fur and laughed lightly. "Perhaps that is because the true answer is that you cannot run from me. As I shall never allow you to run from me."

Deliberately, then, he removed his covering, and removed, as well, my clan colors. I did not know how to answer his strange comments, yet did Mida make it that answer was unnecessary. His arms about me again showed his strength, and easily did the rough, hairy touch of him heat my blood. He held me to his chest till I was mad to take him, and indeed did I attempt to do so; however, with a laugh from him was I thrown to the fur and taken instead. As a war leader, I could not approve of being done so, though Ceralt's actions were in accordance with the will of Mida. For Mida's sake, then, did I abandon my objections, and accept all that Ceralt brought to me. Blessed is she who follows Mida's will without question.

12.

A message—and the spilling of blood

I was not pleased. Sooner would I have walked the forest road at the end of a length of leather, yet Ceralt would not hear of such. Before him on his kan had he placed me, his arms about me as though I had never before taken seat upon a kan, as though I were city slave-woman. My two legs brushed his left one, and so, with humiliation, did the journey continue.

Fayan, behind Nidisar, seemed both pleased and amused by what had been done to me. Although she still avoided my eyes, now it was mainly her amusement that she wished to hide. Should she and I ever again face one another alone, her amusement would be well seen to. The warrior Fayan had been greatly surprised by the appearance of Larid, seemingly very well used, her wrists bound behind her, her throat held tightly by a length of leather, but Fayan had said nothing. Just then did she meet my eyes, and though the contact was brief, I had little doubt that Fayan would continue to say nothing. Possessed in some manner or no, Fayan was yet a Hosta warrior.

Larid looked to me occasionally as she stumbled behind the kan of telion, and a grimace from her told me that Telion had done well with avenging his pride in the darkness. Ceralt, too, had not been idle, for after he had used me, great amusement had he found in pursuing me about the tent. Each time he had closed with me, sharply was I struck with his hand, below the small of the back. With each blow, was I told, "You shall not again do as you did this fey!" and I found that I could not avoid him. Desperately had I attempted escape from the tent—impossible. Again and again I was cornered and struck, till wildly had I thrown myself upon Ceralt, attempting attack with teeth and nails. The hunter was taken by surprise at the attack, and briefly was I able to appease my fury, yet all too quickly did he rally from the surprise and force me from him, striking me the harder. For close to a hin had this continued, I, stumbling about, knowing the blow was soon to reach me, nearly crying out when it did, he, doggedly pursuing, allowing me no rest, no corner in which to find a haven, saying all the while that I was not to do again as I had done that fey. When at last I had dropped to the fur, thoroughly winded and obviously bested, soundly beaten and deeply humiliated, he had again taken me in his arms. Thus had I passed the darkness close beside him, my cheek upon his chest, his fist wound tight in my hair, and the strong male smell and warmth of him had done much for the chill of the darkness. I knew not what to make of his actions, yet was reluctant to have them repeated. Truly must I have angered Mida for her to have allowed the male such doings.

The meal stop, though of no particular interest to me of itself, provided an opportunity for speaking with Larid. Telion joined Ceralt and myself to feed, leaving Larid bound to a tree, and once the meat had been seen to, I stood before her with arms folded beneath my life sign.

"So," said I quite coldly. "A Hosta warrior comes to free her war leader. Very well, then, warrior. Proceed to do so."

Larid, her red hair free about her bound arms, looked woefully ashamed. "Forgive me, Jalav!" she pleaded most piteously in a small voice. "I know not how the male surprised me so!"

"Perhaps he flew upon the wings of a lellin," said I, crouching down before her. "It would be best, I feel, if we were together to ask Mida's forgiveness for your shame."

"I hear, Jalav," Larid acknowledged miserably. The males, knowing nothing of our customs, would believe that we spoke with heads bowed to Mida, when in truth, a warrior who called to Mida stood straight and proud, as Mida wished her to be.

Larid's head did not raise itself, yet in a moment her whisper came. "They no longer watch us, Jalav. Did they truly believe me?"

"I feel they did," I murmured. "What word do you bring from Gimin?"

"We have captured two males," whispered she. "They knew the look of Hosta and attempted battle, but we were able to take them without spilling much blood. Upon questioning them, we learned that they were indeed a part of those who stole from the Tower, yet they knew not the location of the Crystal. Those others who had been with them, save for one who still travels with your set, have all continued on to Ranistard. Two hands of them, in all, there were."

"These two," I murmured, feeling a great elation in that we moved closer to the Crystal, "was one a male with the look of a young girl?"

"No," Larid whispered. "They both were as most males appear. He who yet travels with your set is one who brings slave-women to Ranistard, to be given to males within Ranistard."

"I know him," said I, recalling the look of the one who had brought the city females to travel with the set. Broad was he, and tall, yet lacking the height of Telion and Ceralt. Many times had he gazed upon me, yet now did I understand the meaning of the look upon his tight, hard face.

"Gimin would know if she may begin to deal with the males she holds," whispered Larid. "Much pleasure did we have in their questioning, yet does she feel it unwise to bring them still living to Ranistard. Binat now watches from the forest, her gando and mine not far off, and easily might you join her, should you wish to do so."

"So you thought to change my capture for yours," I mused. "Is that why you fell to Telion's trap?"

She, too, smiled faintly. "Almost did I find the need to take him by the throat," said she. "He watched you from the forest, thinking himself well hidden, yet had Binat and I small difficulty in seeing him. I could not speak with you without his knowing of it, therefore I decided to allow him to bring me to you. Had he not been one of those you traveled with, I would have spilled his blood in silence, yet I knew not what you wished done with him. I had nearly stepped upon him before he saw me, and most difficult was it pretending I saw him not."

"These males know little of the forests," I murmured. "Did he treat you harshly because of your doing in the Tower?"

"Most annoyed was he at the memory," said she. "I was much used by him, yet the sight of tears affects him strangely. I shall have to attempt to produce more of them."

Inwardly I smiled, knowing Larid well able to see to her safety, and said, "I shall not return to Gimin with Binat. I shall continue on with this set to Ranistard, for there, I believe, the Crystal lies. Also, should this male from the Tower attempt to depart the set before it reaches Ranistard, I would know of it and be able to follow. Do you wish me to free you so that you might return?"

"The males would not be pleased with such an action," mused Larid. "I would not have you given pain through their displeasure, therefore shall I remain also. Binat awaits your word."

"Very well, warrior," said I with a sigh. "But you must bear in mind that the choice was yours."

Larid frowned with lack of understanding; however, rather than enlighten her, I stood and walked from her. Perhaps Larid would not be shamed as Fayan and I had been, and I did not wish to speak of it with her. One who has not experienced such would find difficulty in its comprehension.

I paused to one side of the road, some few feet from where Larid sat upon the grass, bound to a tree, and gazed casually into the woods. A lellin scolded in the near distance, just before me, therefore did I move my arms about as if stretching, then bring the finger away from my lips, my palm up, to give a sign message. The lellin scolded again, then was there silence. I crouched where I stood, pulled a piece of grass upon which to chew, and smiled faintly, pleased that Binat had read the silent speech. "Tell Gimin yes," I had said, although I used the sign for Gimin, rather than her name. Had Binat not been able to read my words, the lellin would have cried twice.

I crouched before the woods, chewing upon the grass, for no more than a moment or two before a hand touched my shoulder. I turned my head to the left and saw Ceralt, who grinned slightly.

"There are those who would speak with you, Jalav," said he in some amusement. "I have told them that you would be pleased by their visit."

Again I stood straight and looked past him, and saw the

females who had delighted so in chanting at me, yet Halia
was not among them. They stood perhaps ten paces up the
road, all in a tight clump, most moving nervously, their eyes
everywhere but upon me. A grimace creased my face, for I
wanted none of them, and Ceralt laughed.

"It will cause you no harm to speak with them," he said
firmly. "Should you not wish to approach them of your own
accord, gladly shall I aid you by tying the leather again to
your collar." His fingers reached out and lightly touched the
circle of the collar which still held my throat. "A leash is a
great convenience when a man must deal with a woman."

Coldly did I look upon him, for I had not forgotten his actions of the darkness, then did I stride toward the waiting females. Upon the recovery of the Crystal, Ceralt would again
be given to my warriors, and only if he begged it of me,
would he be returned to my sleeping leather. His captivity
would be long indeed, and as humiliating as possible. The
hunter would learn the weight of the wrath of Jalav.

I halted before the city females and folded my arms
beneath my life sign, saying no word. Almost completely
without hearing are those of the cities, for the females knew
not that I stood there, till one chanced to look toward me.
Then she jumped as though struck by the venomous sednet,
and uttered a startled, "Oh!" as she stared up into my eyes in
fright. The others quickly turned to me as well, and sickly
smiles grew upon their faces. One, of light brown hair, took a
hesitant step forward.

"We wished to say how brave we thought you to be," said
this female timidly. Then did her head drop, and she twisted
her hands at her waist. "Also," added the female with some
difficulty, "we wished to apologize for what was said to you.
Your act was a noble one, completely undeserved by the past
actions of Halia—or any of us."

"Yet, had it been me who was saved from the beast," said
another, one with tightly bound, light gold hair and large
eyes, "I would have been filled with a gratitude the like of
which has never been seen! Halia feels no gratitude, and refuses even to speak a word of thanks! Her father should have
broken two switches upon her, rather than just the one!"

"Indeed he should!" they all murmured with angry indignation. Seemingly, they all felt outrage toward the female
Halia, which, in itself, was amusing.

"The female Halia was saved through the actions of Mida,

not mine," I informed them mildly. "Also, Mida demands
that each of us act according to her nature. To do so, no
matter what such nature might be, is to act in accordance
with Mida's will. No one may be faulted for obeying Mida's
will."

"You are far too generous in your beliefs!" said the light-
haired female. "Had Halia treated me so, I would have
scratched her eyes out!"

As I frowned in lack of understanding, she of the light
brown hair pointed toward my throat. "Look!" said she in
disbelief. "Still she wears a collar! Has that Ceralt not freed
you as yet?"

"It is monstrous!" said another indignantly, one with hair
of dark brown, "How does he dare to keep you a slave?"

"I am no slave," said I, seeing that they had no understanding. "Jalav has never been slave."

"But—but—the cuffs, and the leash, and the leather!" protested another. "He holds you as a slave, and calls you his!"

"It matters not what others believe." I shrugged. "Jalav
knows herself to be free, and that is sufficient. The hunter
holds me captive, yet the state shall not continue forever."

"You are magnificent!" said she of the light-gold hair, ado-
ration clear in her tone. "You are a woman, like us, yet you
are truly free! Even held captive by a man, are you nevertheless free! How I wish I could be like you!"

"Especially as we, too, shall soon be held by men," said
she of the light-brown hair. "Our fathers shall choose them to
whom we are to be given, and we shall be slave to them in
all but name. For us, there is no escape."

"How do you remain untouched in your captivity?" asked
the one of dark brown hair in curiosity. "Should it be possible, I, too, would learn the way of it. I have no desire to be
touched by a man."

The others agreed with firm enthusiasm, and again was I
puzzled. "The hunter uses me as he wills," said I, seeing the
shock and reddening grow upon their faces. "That is to be
expected, for my warriors and I used him well when he was
captive to us."

With mouths gaping they stood, and she of the light-gold
hair recovered her tongue first. "You use men?" she gasped
quite shrilly. "With none to force you to it?"

"Strong males give a warrior much pleasure." I smiled,
amused by their innocence. "There is no shame in the enjoy-

ment of a male. For what other reason would Mida have provided them?"

They looked upon each other helplessly, unable to answer my question, and she of the light-gold hair waved a hand in vague gesture. "But we have ever been told that we must not allow the touch of a man, for it is evil!" said she. "Our fathers have told us this always, that only he to whom we are given may touch us! I have never quite seen why the one should be an exception, but I do truly believe the act to be evil, and my mother has ever held it so. Is it not evil?"

"I have found no evil," said I slowly, feeling a great sadness for these city females. To be taught to find no pleasure in the touch of a male is an abomination. And how is a male to find his own pleasure, with a woman raised to loathe his touch? Telion and Ceralt, when first they used me, found much excitement of their own in the excitement they caused me to feel. Had I not responded so, they might the well have acted alone, in a corner. "I have found no evil," said I again, "nor has any of my warriors. Have you never looked about you, felt the draw of a male, imagined him prepared to give you pleasure?"

"I have," said she of the reddish-brown hair, a bit hesitantly. "I had thought it wrong, but why should a man expect to be given pleasure, yet expect to give none in return? I think perhaps I might enjoy such pleasure."

The others seemed doubtful, yet did she of the light-gold hair, who was smaller than the others, square her shoulders in determination. "I do not know if I shall be able to do it," said she, "yet I shall attempt to see it that way. I had thought that I was destined to be dirtily used by men, and the thought that I, too, might use, intrigues me. What might be a way to begin this, Jalav?"

They all looked to me as though I had words from Mida for them, yet truthfully, I knew not what to say. How does one instruct in the way the look of a male, insolent in his prime, fires a warrior's blood? "You must examine males, and see if they please you," said I, groping for the proper phrases. "The set of his shoulders, the manner in which he holds his head, the look in his eye. Does he feel strong in his own being? Does he carry himself proudly? Does he meet your gaze evenly? A male such as that may give much pleasure, for he is untamed."

"Ceralt and Telion have such a look," mused the female of

reddish-brown hair, studying the males from where she stood. "Do they give pleasure, Jalav?"

I turned to also study the males, Ceralt where he stood beside his kan, inspecting the leather seat of the kan, Telion where he crouched by Larid, putting meat into her now unbound hands. I studied them briefly, then did I smile. "Indeed those males know the way of giving pleasure," I murmured. "My warriors had much use from each of them, and Mida willing, shall have the same again. They are males with much to give."

"I think I should enjoy seeing men bound and helpless," said she of the reddish-brown hair, still studying the males with a thoughtful swing to her body. "I would then beat them if they did not please me."

The other females laughed at the comment, nodding in agreement; I shook my head. "Males as captives must be bound," said I, "yet a warrior finds greater pleasure in a male who is not bound so. And a male who would please you only if beaten is not a male at all, but a slave. Only those who are slave themselves, would enjoy the use of a slave."

"Those two seem pleased with each other," said she of the light-brown hair, nodding toward Nidisar and Fayan where they sat, somewhat apart, speaking softly and laughing much. "Nidisar keeps her leashed close, yet she does not seem to mind."

I made no answer for I had none, and she of the dark-brown hair mused, "What would it be like, I wonder, to be leashed by a man? Should it be done to me, would I struggle, or obey him? If I did not obey him, would I be beaten? What is it like to be truly beaten?"

"Jalav knows," said she of the light-gold hair most soberly, her large eyes filled with sadness. "Telion did say that she was beaten in the Palace of the High Seat, for she refused to obey them. Why did you not obey them, and avoid the beating, Jalav?"

"A warrior does what she must." I shrugged, feeling the answer inadequate. "Much pain was there from the lash of Bariose, yet not as much as would have come from the discarding of dignity. My dignity may at times be taken from me, yet never shall I give it of myself."

"Dignity," said she of the light-gold hair. "I had thought that I possessed dignity, yet now do I see that I do not. I shall also attempt to attain what I may of that, for true freedom, I feel, lies in dignity."

Each of the females greeted this in silence, their eyes turned inward toward their own, deep selves, and the sudden appearance of Ceralt caused them annoyance.

"How do you fare, ladies?" asked the hunter with lightness, a grin upon his face as he placed his hand upon my back beneath my hair. "Have you spoken to Jalav of the ways of civilized women, ways which she, too, may learn?"

"Indeed we have spoken with Jalav," said she of the light-gold hair quite coldly, looking upon Ceralt with disapproval. "Have you no care for her dignity, that you paw her? She is no slave, that she may be treated so!"

"I feel that this one has much heat in him," said she of the reddish-brown hair, carefully inspecting Ceralt, whose jaw seemed unhinged. "You are a man—a *male*—of some interest, Ceralt. Would you care to call at my pavilion come darkness? I would see you compared with other males who are about."

Ceralt's jaw moved up and down, yet no sounds emerged. She of the dark-brown hair stood herself before him, her arms folded, and laughed lightly. "You look foolish, Ceralt," said she, "I do not believe one so foolish looking is at all capable of giving much pleasure. Let us seek further, girls, for there are many to choose from."

Firm nods and forceful agreements came from the others, and they then took themselves away, pausing at conveyances to carefully inspect the startled males upon them. Their actions were amusing, for they sought to emulate warriors, though their understanding was still far from complete. Ceralt's hand upon my back did naught of a drastic nature to my dignity, yet did it sorely put my reserve to the test. No wish had I to reward him for his treatment of me, yet I also had no wish to deny myself.

"What have you done to them?" asked Ceralt weakly, staring with dismay at the strolling females. "They seem so . . . . What have you done to them?"

"I did nothing," I responded truthfully, and then shrugged. "It was, after all, you who insisted that I speak with them."

"So that they might instruct *you*!" said Ceralt angrily. "Not the other way about! I see that for their sake, I shall have to keep you from them in future! Come, it is time to continue on the way."

He urged me to the kan once more, and seated me again as I had been. I was still much displeased with the position, most especially so as Larid, too, found amusement in the hunter's arms about me, his face often buried in my hair. There was much for a war leader to think upon, yet serious thought deserted me at the playful touch of Ceralt's hands and lips. When I attempted to return these touches, he would not allow it, laughingly holding my wrists between his hands so that I might not reach him. In a fine fury was I when the set halted at its campsite, and Ceralt was exceedingly amused. Had I been able to free myself from his grasp, I would have taken to the woods on the moment; that must have been clear to him, for he held me fast till the tent stood again, and then was I thrust immediately within it.

"Should you be wondering," said Ceralt mildly when I stood angrily upon the lenga pelts, "you are being punished for urging those innocent young girls to emulate savages. Savages deserve no consideration, and when I find you behaving in such a manner, so will you be treated. It shall not be enjoyable to you."

Then he seized me and lowered me to the fur, and began to encourage my ardor. Much encouragement was not needed, yet on and on did he continue, caring only for lighting the fire, naught for cooking upon it. Truly beside myself was I in my need, yet he only laughed.

"I was carefully instructed when I purchased you," said he, moving his hand in a manner which caused me to moan. "A woman told me that I was to be sure to deny you quite often, after first having aroused you, and you would quickly learn to beg me for release. Are you yet prepared to beg for release?"

His eyes watched me with amusement, and most desperately did I need release, yet the words were impossible to speak. Clearly did I recall the touch of fire given me by Bariose, and my eyes closed so that this pain, too, would more easily pass. My body shook in his arms, and I attempted to stiffen myself as against a blow, for a warrior must be strong enough to stand against all that is done to her. Then Ceralt opened his arms and moved from me, for a slave brought the freshly roasted meat. Ceralt went to it and began to feed, and I lay on the lenga pelt, willing myself not to writhe.

"Come and eat," called Ceralt, his mouth full. "It is nilno, and quite tasty."

The lenga pelt was smooth and soft beneath me, and I could almost feel individual hairs. I rolled my cheek to it, grasping it in my fists, feeling it bunch silkenly in my hands, surrounding and caressing my cheek with its sleek warmth. There was no pain, there was no need, there was only the lenga pelt beneath me.

"Jalav, do you hear?" said Ceralt from a distance. "Come and eat with me."

The lenga pelt caressed me at many points, whispering to me and touching me, allowing no rest to my body. A small whimper escaped me, for the fur spoke as leather did not, and I could not silence it. Small hairs rushed to my nose and mouth as I breathed, wishing to touch me within as well, then was I again abruptly seized, and held tightly to Ceralt's chest.

"Jalav, forgive me," said he in upset. "I thought to give you only discomfort, not true pain. That sound you made— once I saw a falth near death from a spear wound, and its pain must truly have been great, yet it made no more than the same sound. A sound of pain to be endured and not acknowledged." In silence did he hold me for a moment, then he sighed deeply. "There is but one manner in which I may make true apology," said he, and then did he release me, remove his covering, and place himself flat upon the pelts. "I am the cause of your pain," said he. "Come and use me."

Wearily did I gaze upon him, and as wearily turned away. To be given a male out of pity is worse than no male at all, and should it be the male himself who thus gives, it is the worst of all.

"You find no interest in me?" came Ceralt's voice from the fur. "How is it you are able to resist so fine a fellow as I? Do you mean to say I am unappealing?" Suddenly, he pinched me hard, and when I rounded on him in fury, he laughed and said, "Or do you merely mean to say you fear me?"

True fury did I feel then, and upon hands and knees I advanced upon him. He lay somewhat raised up on one elbow, amused, then when I placed my hand and weight upon his throat, forcing him flat once more, his amusement changed to frowning surprise. He seemed about to protest, but I was quickly in possession of him, for a warrior has much skill in such things. Possessed and used did he suddenly find himself, not at his own bidding, but at that of a warrior. He seemed shocked at the speed of the thing, and I smiled, for he had

forgotten his time in the woods with the Hosta. Then the
memory returned to him, and he pulled me close, his hands
spread about me, his lips raised to mine. Much pleasure did I
take from him before he could hold himself back no longer,
and then our places were reversed. He then used me well, and
much pleasure did I receive from him as he took his own. The
nilno grew cold before he was able to return to it.

I laughed. I threw my head back and laughed so heartily
that Ceralt took my arm and shook me angrily. "There is
nothing amusing to be seen there!" he hissed, turning me
from the sight he had pointed to. "The thing must be
stopped!"

"I see only females with their hair unbound." I chuckled,
still amused at Ceralt's distress. "From the manner in which
you spoke, surely did I think to see them armed upon gandod."

"That is not far from occurring," grumbled Ceralt, and
again he pointed. "Do you see no more than that their hair is
unbound?"

Again I studied the females, the self-same females who had
come to speak with me. This fey was their hair unbound, yet
little more did I see from our vantage point in the trees.
True, they walked about and openly gazed upon males, and
now that I thought on it, their gait did indeed appear strange.
They seemed to swing their bodies as they walked, the step
composed of glide, pace, and stride. Truly, it was most difficult seeing how they retained their balance.

"Why do they move in such a manner?" I asked with a
frown. "Have they been injured in some way?"

"Aye, injured," Ceralt replied disgustedly, shaking his
head. "Can you not see, child of the forests, that they attempt
that hadat-like stride of yours? Yet, while yours is strong and
graceful, they in theirs appear injured!"

"It is merely a mannerism from stalking on the hunt," I
shrugged. "You wish me to correct their errors?"

"No!" he came close to shouting, but kept his voice down.
"I wish you to have them cease such behavior! Their fathers
have all come to me, for they find themselves frantic! The
threat of a hiding means nothing to them as they are, and the
hiding itself seems to strengthen their convictions! They have
announced that they shall wed no man whom they, them-

selves, do not approve of, and their fathers are beside themselves. So invidious is the infection that others of the young ladies are beginning to follow the lead of these!"

"There is nothing I can do," I informed him, amused by the situation. "I did not suggest such behavior, therefore I may not stop it. A pity they are too old to begin training with a sword."

"A pity it would be inconvenient to wring your neck!" said Ceralt from between his teeth, and then he paused. "How are they too old?" he asked in curiosity. "They are no older than you."

"Think you I have held a sword but moments?" I asked with a laugh. "I was many kalod from womanhood when my hand first touched a hilt. It seemed so large and heavy then that I felt sure I would never do well with it, yet was I to grow and best many, warrior and war leader alike. As well as male."

Ceralt studied me briefly. "Nidisar said three guardsmen were slain when you and the others were taken," said he hesitantly. "You slew one of the guardsmen?"

"I slew two," said I. "Pileth, too, would have fallen before me, had I not been struck from behind."

"But—Pileth is a Captain of the Guard!" said Ceralt in shock, looking upon me strangely. "He is one of the finest swords in the city! You could not seriously have thought to challenge him!"

"Do you forget that I am a war leader?" I asked in annoyance. "Pileth would have fallen as did the others."

"The others were undoubtedly new recruits," said Ceralt firmly, "unused to blades, and hesitant about striking at a female! Pileth would not have been of the same caliber, and he would have trimmed you properly! I had best never see you foolish enough to draw sword against a true warrior—a *male* warrior—else I shall take the blade from you and thrash you soundly with it! Now, let us return to the current problem. What are we to do about those silly wenches?"

"The problem is not mine," said I shortly, angered that he thought so little of the war leader Jalav. "They are not my warriors, therefore I have nothing to do with them."

I turned and walked from him then; he quickly matched my stride and took my arm. "As it is you they fashion themselves after," said he sternly, "the problem is indeed yours!

You shall seek a way to return them to their former sanity, or else I shall act upon the matter! You had best bear it in mind!"

I did not reply to him, and we returned to the others in silence. The feeding of the meal stop had already been attended to, and Telion sat speaking with Nidisar, Fayan close beside them. Still Fayan refused to speak with me, but now she was often deeply in sorrowed thought. I felt it best to leave her as she was, hoping that in time she would once again be the warrior I had known. Larid sat upon the grass to the side of the road, her wrists unbound, yet with leather still upon her throat. She pulled at the grass absently, almost angrily, for this fey, she, too, had ridden, although Telion had chosen to emulate Ceralt rather than Nidisar. Larid rode before Telion, as I rode before Ceralt, and she was much annoyed at the position.

Ceralt joined the other males, so I walked to Larid and seated myself upon the grass beside her. My face showed no hint of a smile, I knew, yet Larid frowned.

"There is no cause for amusement!" said she in an angry whisper. "I truly regret not having spilled his blood when the opportunity was presented me!"

"Merely for riding you before him upon his kan?" I asked with amusement, stretching myself out in the grass.

"That is the least of it!" she snapped, her eyes flashing. "He expects from me the actions of a slave-woman, and beats me with leather when I will not obey! And I must still pretend fear of the heavy whip, else he shall begin to doubt what was told him! When may I have his blood, Jalav?"

"Take it now, if you wish." I laughed, enjoying the touch of the grass upon my back. The sky was clear above the trees, Mida's light warmed me, the children of the wild spoke softly about me, and soon I would be within reach of those who had taken the Crystal. In those things I found much pleasure.

"I find little humor in your jest, war leader," said Larid bitterly, her eyes bleak. "My sword and dagger are well bound upon his kan, and attempting to take *his* weapons only earned me the leather! If matters are to remain so, we might as well bind our hair and smother our bodies as true slave-women!"

"Matters shall remain so till Ranistard is reached," said I

most comfortably. "It is there that the Crystal lies, and our duty with it."

Larid drew in her breath sharply, and a glance at her face revealed pained memory. "Forgive me, Jalav!" said she earnestly. "The capture of the two males drove the thought completely from me! There is yet other news which you must hear."

I raised myself to an elbow, no longer amused, and Larid continued.

"Rilas sent a messenger," said my warrior seriously. "The Keeper's Attendants visited the Tower of the Crystal which the Silla guard, and there were refused entry. The Silla were respectful of the Attendants; however, they were hurried away from the Tower, and away from the Silla home tents. The Keeper Tanir, of the Silla, was reportedly unavailable to speak with Rilas's Attendants, and Rilas believes that the Silla no longer possess their Crystal, but that it was not stolen."

Much disturbed was I by this news, for although the loss of the second Crystal was by no means unexpected, it now seemed that the Silla approved of its having been taken. The Silla were less than falth, full blood enemies of the Hosta, yet I knew not how it was possible for Midanna to give up Mida's Crystal while they still lived!

"Was Gimin able to learn the reason for the Crystal's having been taken?" I asked Larid.

"The males knew of no reason for what they did, other than the payment of much metal," said Larid. "We thought perhaps the metal was desired for the construction of some object they coveted."

"Who may know the desires of those with no souls," said I in disgust. "Now are both Crystals in the grasp of those who should not even be permitted to gaze upon them! When the Crystals are again in the hands of Midanna, the Silla shall not again find themselves honored!"

"Never have I truly understood why the Silla are so honored to begin with," said Larid in anger. "Never have Hosta and Silla faced one another with aught save hatred and bloodshed. Perhaps we will be fortunate enough that the Silla will come seeking their Crystal when they learn of its ultimate location."

"Perhaps." I nodded then laughed. "That would be a Mida-sent gift of pleasure."

"Pleasure indeed," agreed Larid, also with a laugh.

"They speak of pleasure," came Telion's voice from quite near, and we looked up to see the warrior and the hunter regarding us. "Think you they speak of us, or rather what we may be foolish enough to purchase for them in Ranistard?"

"Undoubtedly both," Ceralt decided without hesitation. "The female mind is completely capable of considering two thoughts of such a nature."

"I agree fully." Telion grinned, then he reached down to grasp the end of the leather which circled Larid's neck. "Come with me, little flame," said he to an indignant Larid, who was pulled unceremoniously to her feet. "I feel an urge to walk in the woods, and therefore shall you accompany me. Ceralt, see that my kan is left tied where it stands, should the walk go beyond departure time."

Ceralt nodded with a hearty laugh, therefore did Telion start for the trees, nearly taking Larid from her feet with his pull on the leather. Larid grasped the leather in her hands, attempting to pull it from Telion's grip, unsuccessfully, and in his track she stumbled along, led by the throat into the woods.

"I feel their walk shall occupy them for some time." Ceralt grinned, looking down to me where I sat in the grass. "The thought is an interesting one, and well worth serious consideration. Much pleasure may be had from a walk in the woods."

His eyes spoke clearly to me, yet had I other matters to consider, matters of greater weight, therefore did I rise to my feet and shrug. "The woods hold no interest for me at the moment," I informed him, brushing my hair back from my arms. "How soon does the march continue?"

"Soon enough," he grumbled, appearing most displeased, then did he eye my collar. "Perhaps it would be well to reattach the leash," he mused. "I should not like you to be thought of as less desirable than the other two wenches."

"The thoughts of others do not concern me," said I, folding my arms beneath my life sign. "Ceralt is too often concerned with others."

"That is necessary when one must live among them," rejoined the hunter dryly. "Jalav would do well to do the same."

"Jalav does well serving Mida," said I quite firmly. "Naught else need she consider."

"Jalav had best consider Ceralt," said Ceralt, his eyes stern. "Have you yet thought upon what may be done with the young ladies?"

"Should they please Mida, she shall see to them," said I with satisfaction. All problems have their answers, should one seek earnestly enough.

"I have little intention of waiting for your Mida to act," said Ceralt in annoyance. "Come the new light, either you shall have thought of something, else shall I lead you to the wenches' midst, and prove to them that the mighty Jalav is naught save a wench herself—who may be punished as easily as they. Come, the caravan now continues."

We again mounted Ceralt's kan and followed the road, and I gave little thought to the city females. Much more pressing was the question of why the city males desired Mida's Crystals. The Crystals had naught of the look of the shiny stones males cared so much for; indeed were they cloudy within their facets, at times aswirl with movement, and never a glint to be seen. To some fell purpose did the city males wish to put them, of that was I convinced, although their purpose was beyond me to conceive of.

By the passage of two hind had Telion and Larid rejoined us, Telion seeming quite pleased, Larid awash in smugness and contentment. The leather, I saw immediately, was no longer about Larid's throat, and when she caught my gaze, one eye did she close in satisfaction. I knew not what she had done to the luckless warrior this time, yet was she now completely unbound, and Telion pleased to have her so! Larid had bewailed the loss of her weapons, but it seemed quite clear to me that she had little need of them.

The next fey brought little light, for Mida's tears fell quite heavily upon the set and ground over which it traveled. The males put upon themselves skins to ward off the wetness, and to the outrage of my warriors and myself, they insisted that we do the same. To say that the tears of Mida were a blessing, one which boded well in next battle for her who bathed in them, did nothing to sway the intentions of the males. Firmly we refused such coverings, for even Fayan stood with us on the matter, and gladly did we stand upon the mud, glorying in the wetness, yet were we savagely seized and tied, then thrust within the hated coverings. Struggle availed naught, for the males were truly set, and so did the journey go, throughout the fall of the tears. One benefit did, however, accrue, or so Ceralt felt. A male who accompanied the city females rode to Ceralt, and informed him that the rain was truly a blessing, for it and it alone had kept his female and others from attempting to adopt the Midanna manner of dress. So incensed was this male in his anger toward me, that I could only laugh. My wrists bound tightly at my back, the smell and feel of the covering sickening me, I laughed at the upset of the male, at his fury at the attempted escape of his female. Ceralt quickly clapped his hand to my mouth, saying that the rains had addled my wits in some manner, and most fervently did the male agree before he turned and rode to his original position. Most wroth was Ceralt with me for my laughter, and most sharply did the leather of his anger sting, but he could not lessen my amusement.

Three full feyd did the tears of Mida fall, soaking all it touched. Unlike the welcome rains of our home, this wetness brought a chill upon the winds which whipped it about, forcing the kand to plod unhappily against it. The trees bent and moaned; little was heard or seen of the children of the wild, and no fires were then built. The meat which we ate was at long last acceptable, bloody and raw rather than burned to leather, yet had the excess, already cooked meat, been taken for the city folk. They, it was said, were unable to eat raw meat, and none save the hunters of the set, my warriors and myself, and the three males who traveled with us, ate it.

Upon the fourth fey bright light at last returned, and we and the children of the wild stretched in pleasure. Not again would the hated skins cover us, and no longer was it necessary that we be bound. Although the air of the light now held a chill which only the darkness had heretofore had, my warriors and I were pleased to be free once more. The fey passed easily, the kand disliking the mud of the road, yet preferring it to the blasts of the rain.

The set had halted to make camp, and we stood awaiting the completion of our tents, when the sounds of a disturbance reached us from the area of the conveyance which carried the city females. Filled with curiosity, we, along with others, approached the area, and the sight which greeted us caused a groan in Ceralt, and chuckles in Nidisar and Telion. My warriors and I were amused, for the city females, to the fury of their males, had altered their coverings so that they now were little longer than clan coverings, and obviously meant to remove the tops of the coverings as well. Red-faced, the males shouted at them, yet the females, though taken a bit with nervousness, stood firm in their resolve.

"Now see what you have done," muttered Ceralt to me, as my warriors and I stood watching with interest. Even the male slaves had ceased in their labors to laugh, and the guards did not beat them, for the guards laughed as well.

"The doing is not mine," said I quite firmly. "Should they take spear in hand, and enter the woods to hunt, would the doing be yours merely because you are a hunter?"

"The point is not the same!" replied Ceralt with equal firmness. "Take yourself to them, and see that they cease their foolishness!"

I began to inform him that never would I attempt to so order the life of another, when the hordes of darkness fell upon us. From the trees about the camp they came, too swift to number, males upon kand, their swords swinging. Screams and shouts of terror erupted from the city folk, curses from the guards who had not taken their posts, and abruptly shortened wailings from those armed males who were struck dead without chance for defense.

"Brigands!" shouted a male, he who was called caravan master. "Defend the caravan!"

Those who were able freed their blades, and my warriors and I found ourselves elbowed aside by Ceralt, Telion and Nidisar, who quickly stepped to do battle. Many were the males about us, and never shall Hosta stand about when there is blood to be spilled, therefore we made our way to those who no longer needed the blades they wore. The females, frightened to screaming, had been returned to their conveyance, and male slaves crawled beneath the conveyances in an attempt to save their miserable lives. My fist closed about the hilt of a sword, and once again did Jalav, war leader of the Hosta of the Midanna, glory in the world about her.

Quickly I turned to the battle, and just as quickly threw myself to the ground and rolled, thereby avoiding the slashing attack of one of the mounted males. His kan thudded by, carrying him past, and I leaped to my feet again to rejoin my warriors. Many of the attacking males had abandoned their kand, perhaps wisely, for they seemed not well used to battle

from the back of a mount. They fought their way across the
now littered ground, and high did the battle lust blaze within
me. With the battle cry of the Hosta full upon my lips,
echoed by my warriors, we charged to the midst of the attackers, and caused our blades to sing. To left and right did
we lay about us, our edges taking arms and eyes and heads,
and blood aplenty. Cries of anguish arose from the males we
faced, and much fear was there in their eyes; however Hosta
never give quarter in battle. On and on we pressed, barely
seeing that the males of the camp had fallen back, for the
pleasure of battle-glory had too long been denied us.

Three males were then before me, desperation in their
stance and manner. Surely they wished their blades to drink
my blood, yet was it I who charged with full eagerness, well
upon them, my sword cutting toward them. The one in the
center backed with a cry, his blade held before him to ward
off attack, and swiftly I slashed that one in the neck before
his sword could cover his unprotected side. The one who had
backed away moaned in anguish, for it was his retreat that
had left his fellow open, but the time was past to repair the
error. The one on my right thrust toward me with an oath,
thinking to spit me; however my blade was quickly there,
turning his thrust and returning it with strength. Surprise and
horror covered his face as my blade went into his belly, and a
scream was torn from him as I also tore my blade free. His
body fell to the reddened ground, his life already fled, and
then there was but one further male to deal with.

The one who had retreated now stood alone, his sword still
held before him. Slowly I stepped toward him, joy upon my
face, the capture croon of the hadat in my throat, and slowly
his head moved from side to side, denying the fate that was
his. He was of a size with me, yet were his shoulders wide,
his arms stronger than mine. Had we two stood unarmed,
surely he could have bested me, yet he had chosen a weapon
that I knew full well the use of, that I had learned to wield
with strength and sureness. My sword gripped tightly, I
moved upon him, not to be denied my victory.

As the chosen prey of the hadat comes to knowledge, so,
then, did this male see his end before him, yet were my hopes
of further battle dashed to naught. With a cry of terror this
male threw his sword from him, and fell upon his knees before me to beg for his miserable, useless life. With great dis-

gust I stood above him, sickened by his groveling and mewling, and then I raised my sword and, two-handed, removed his head, so that Mida's ears need not be further fouled by his pleadings. His body fell silent to the ground, and I turned, to seek more of the enemy.

Many were the dead upon the ground, and my sword dripped red from many of them, and now a silence of end of battle had fallen. The attackers had all been seen to or made to flee, and my warriors stood but paces from me, their heads held high, their blades dripping from the thoroughness of their efforts. No others were there to stand before us, therefore did we raise our bloody swords and arms to Mida's skies as I shouted, "For your chains, Mida! Accept these worthless males from your Hosta! Always shall we spill blood to your glory!"

"Always!" echoed my warriors with their arms high, and then we turned, full pleased, from Mida's skies. The armed males of the set stood about in small groups, their swords still grasped in their hands, their eyes wide. My warriors and I laughed in our pleasure, and Fayan and I took swordbelts from those we had bested, cleaned our swords in Mida's sweet ground, then donned belt and sword. No longer were we unarmed, and not again would I lose a sword as easily as I had. I took, too, a dagger from the one who had sought to spit me, and placed it in the leg bands which I still wore. The dagger snuggled in its proper place, a now-filled void that had too long remained unfilled.

Slowly sound returned to the camp and its people. The males who had stood about with sword in hand now cleaned and sheathed their weapons, though somewhat reluctantly, and still did they glance strangely at my warriors and myself. The females did not emerge from their conveyance, but sat clustered about its opening instead, their arms about one another, their faces pale and filled with sickness. To the rear of their conveyance stood the male who had arranged for their journey, the sole remaining male of the Tower, and now that I thought upon it, I did not recall seeing his sword bared with the others. He stood with his hand upon the side of the conveyance, his eyes upon me, and slowly I raised my head and folded my arms beneath my life sign, for he and I had unfinished matters between us. As our eyes met, his body stiffened angrily, then was his hard, broad face gone from my sight, his steps carrying him away behind the conveyance. Then I heard the sound of laughter.

"You did not acquit yourself badly, male," said Larid to Telion as I turned. She stood proudly displaying the sword-belt she had taken to replace her own. "With a bit of effort," she laughed, "you might yet earn the name of warrior."

"I have already earned the name of warrior!" Telion snapped in annoyance. "Should you sometime look about you, wench, you will learn that there are other means of using a sword than all-out attack!"

"Hosta know of no other means," laughed Larid. "So have we ever entered battle, and so shall we ever do. It is our means to victory."

Telion made a sound of disapproval, and then I saw Nidisar and Ceralt, some paces behind Telion. Nidisar looked upon a radiant Fayan, for Fayan had cleansed much of her shame in battle, yet it seemed that he was not pleased for her. She moved toward him, joy upon her face, but he turned away from her and strode quickly away, without a word. The joy fell from Fayan like too much oil from a sword blade, and she seemed grieved. Stiff and proud she stood, as a Hosta warrior should, yet had the heart been taken from her more cruelly than with the slice of a sword.

Ceralt looked after Nidisar a moment, then slowly approached me. "Truly is the war leader Jalav most skilled with a sword," he whispered. "I offer my apologies—for all things."

Then he turned and strode after Nidisar, his head somewhat down, his pace somewhat hurried. I did not understand why he acted so, nor did I understand his words, but as Telion abruptly moved after him, another male voice spoke.

"You have seen," said the male to the city females within the conveyance. "You wish to speak as they do, and dress as they do. Do you also wish to do as they do?"

The city females, each with a shudder, removed themselves from the entrance to the conveyance, none having spoken in answer, yet all having, nevertheless, answered. The male then turned away from the conveyance, but in place of the satisfaction I thought to see upon his face, a great sadness showed. Larid stood beside Fayan, and I then went to join them.

"Jalav, what ails Fayan?" Larid asked softly, her face concerned. "I spoke to her, but she does not hear my words."

Although Fayan stood with head high, her face, so lovely in laughter, seemed sad. "Fayan has felt a wound," said I, my hand upon Fayan's shoulder, "a wound which the Hosta have heretofore been blessed in avoiding. It is not a wound a warrior should be made to feel. Let us return with her to the tents."

Larid, in silent confusion, assisted me in urging Fayan slowly forward. Fayan moved as we bid her, although her eyes were elsewhere. Slowly we made our way to the tents, but Telion stepped before us at the yellow tent, barring the way to the red.

"It would be best if she slept in the yellow pavilion this darkness," said Telion, much concern and sadness upon his face. "Nidisar—is not well, and he would not disturb her sleep."

Telion's eyes met mine; I nodded. "The warrior Fayan is ever welcome to share my roof," said I, and with Larid's aid, helped Fayan within the yellow tent. Fayan sat in the fur as we bid her, and then I turned again to Telion, who had followed us within. "Ceralt will not object to her presence?" I asked him.

He looked sad. "Ceralt—feels it best that he stay with Nidisar," he said without inflection. "To give him aid, should he require it. They are hunters, and brothers. Not warriors. Larid, would you honor me by sharing my pavilion?"

Larid, in frowning confusion, looked toward me, and I nodded to her. She seemed uncertain at my decision, yet was I, once again, proven war leader of the Hosta. Telion held open the tent flaps, waited for her slow, hesitant exit, then followed behind her.

Soft yellow, in the candlelight, were the tent walls, and shadowy golden were the pelts upon the floor. Fayan sat where she had been placed, rocking gently to and fro, as tears flowed silently from her eyes. I did not understand why Nidisar had not spoken to Fayan, and I did not understand why Ceralt was not to return. So many were the darknesses we had passed together, and I searched my words and actions to see where I had given insult. None did I find, though again and again I searched, reflecting, even, that of late, I had not even attempted to use him, allowing him, instead, to use me. Where, then, did the insult lie? I did not know, for I knew nothing of the thoughts of city males, little of the thoughts of any male. Then Fayan began to sob, weeping like a city female, yet unlike them as well. Deep, deep, were her sobs, twisting her body as she lay in the furs. With tight fists she held to the fur, giving to it the wetness of her body, the agony of her soul. Briefly I stood watching her torment, then I walked slowly to the rear of the tent, seating myself by the post that stood there, leaning my shoulder and face upon it. Quite late was it when the roasted meat was brought, yet neither Fayan nor I were asleep.

13.

Ranistard—and an
enemy is found

Fayan, Larid and I, in the company of Telion, rode at an
easy pace toward Ranistard. The set was nearly there, for in
the distance, the walls of Ranistard rose to proclaim its
presence. The road had left the forest early that fey, and now
we rode the gentle hills that surrounded the city. The kand
my warriors and I bestrode were those brought by the attacking males of the fey previous, our lawful spoils, and no longer needed by those who had been left for the children of the
wild. Deep into the darkness had the slaves labored, taking
the bodies a distance from the campsite, and theirs was a
strange labor. Deep into the ground had they dug, and into
the holes thereby made had they placed the bodies of those of
the set who had fallen. The bodies were then covered again,
stones set to mark the places, those of the set in attendance
during these actions. I wondered briefly why they did this,
then dismissed it from consideration. That city folk honored
their attackers by allowing the children of the wild to feed
upon their bodies, yet denied the selfsame honor to those
who had been of their set was merely as one with the rest of
their actions.

During the darkness, Fayan had returned to herself, silent
yet dry-eyed, and we had shared the meat brought to us earlier. We had then blown the candles out and slept, awakening
again at the appearance of Larid. The new light had not yet
come, yet Larid had wished to share with us a thing told her

by Telion. Fayan and I listened to her words, angrily spoken, and then we took the leather she had brought to us and used it as war leather. Neither Fayan nor myself had commented on the thing told Larid by Telion, and I understood little of it, although it filled me with fury.

Nidisar, and Ceralt as well, had been horrified at the sight of Hosta in battle. That we fought well, and fought to slay those who would challenge us, seemed most unnatural to them. The hunters had thought to see us stumble and fall before males and their swords, crying out for assistance against superior enemies. Ceralt had recalled the number of Hosta I had led against him and his hunters, and had concluded that such numbers had been used for no other reason than that fewer Hosta would not have been able to take them. He had not known that such numbers had been used so that they might be taken *alive*, for he knew naught of the loss of the Crystal. Now the hunters carried the sight of victorious Hosta before their eyes, and the sight sickened them. So much for the worth of *any* city males.

The hunters had stood beside the red silk tent when we had emerged to claim our kand. The caravan master saw the weapons we wore and had had the kand brought. No one of the city folk had spoken to nor approached us; the females now wore their coverings and hair as they had previously done, and the male slaves, wearily working to fold the tents, had looked at us with a good deal of fear. My warriors and I had removed the leather seats of the kand, had mounted, and then had waited for the march to begin. Telion, when he came, had silently removed the collars from about my throat and Fayan's, then he waited with us, his head high and proud, not ashamed of being in the company of—savages.

At the meal stop, Fayan took herself into the woods, to return shortly with a small polt, which she had slain with her dagger. Quickly did we skin the furry animal, then we passed portions of it about among ourselves. Polt is not as toothsome as nilno, but was most satisfactory. Telion, though he sat with us, was offered none, nor did he request a portion. Upon the meat of the previous fey did he feed, saying nothing of our choice. As the march was once more to begin, the hunter Ceralt took a step toward us, as though he would speak, but we had no interest in the words of a city male. Briskly my warriors and I mounted our kand and rode off, to be joined, once again, by Telion.

The gates of Ranistard eventually lay open before us. Much alike were these cities of soulless ones, yet did city folk pass within the portals unhalted by the armed males who stood about. Our set was also allowed entrance, to the cheers of many males who waited just within the gates. Grinning and eager were these males, and quickly they surrounded the conveyances which held the city females, causing them to halt. The females were then urged, with much laughter, from the conveyances, and the sounds of approval from the males increased considerably. The females seemed somewhat at a loss, finding themselves the objects of such appraisal, and Halia had had to be forceably removed. She stood, her hair in disarray, not far from those who had attempted the appearance of warriors. Slowly did Telion ride through the masses of males, my warriors and I following, and the males showed much approval at the sight of Hosta. With grins did they attempt to move toward us as they had moved toward the city females; however our hands upon sword hilts halted them somewhat. Though they still grinned in pleasure, they kept respectful distance. Halia had turned from the conveyance to gaze upon me with hatred, but she of the light-gold hair put her hand out as we approached.

"Jalav, forgive us!" she called in misery. "We cannot gain dignity in the manner that you do! We cannot so easily take the lives of others!"

I halted my kan. "One need not take lives to possess dignity," I informed her. "Dignity depends upon self, not upon others." Then I urged my kan to motion once more, following the track of Telion, my warriors behind me.

Ranistard had the look of Bellinard, with cobbled ways and high dwellings, yet it seemed somehow empty. No more than a handful of slave-women were to be seen, and deep was the hunger with which the males looked upon us. Many were the males upon the city ways; however, their movements were slow and ponderous, as though they moved through memory rather than from volition. They stopped to stare as Telion led us from the gates, and though none attempted to approach, a stirring flashed through them, restoring, somewhat, a semblance of life. I knew not what ailed these city males, nor did I care. I gazed upon the dwellings about us with loathing, and thought only upon the location of the Crystals.

Through the city ways we rode till we came to a broad

way, such as that of Bellinard, and indeed could a dwelling
of unreasonable size be seen at the end of it. Overlarge dwellings stood to either side of this way, also as in Ballinard, and
also did these dwellings possess males in leather and metal
before them. Telion, without hesitation, rode toward the immense dwelling, and I disliked the thought of his destination.
As we drew nearer, I recalled that other immense dwelling,
and therefore slowed my kan. Telion, in glancing back, saw
that he was closely followed no longer, and he slowed his kan
as well.

"Jalav, there is naught to fear," said he, moving but slowly
forward. "This is not Bellinard, and you shall not be treated
here as you were there. For this you have my word."

"The word of a city male carries small weight," I said. "I
prefer to camp in the open."

"You cannot!" replied Telion in anger. "Too easily, then,
might you be—" His words broke off, seemingly in vexation.
"The men of Ranistard have been deprived of women for too
long," he said. "Should you and these others remain in the
open, the men will find themselves unable to control their
desires. Many will go down before your blades, yet will you
and Fayan and Larid eventually be taken. Do you wish to be
used by half a city of desperate men? Take my word as a
warrior that no harm shall come to you should you accompany me!"

My warriors only awaited the word of their war leader.
Had I been alone, my decision would have been different, but
I was not alone. Again I looked upon Telion, and said, "We
shall accompany you."

Telion nodded, with relief, I thought, then he continued
on, leading us to the immense dwelling. There we dismounted, tying our kand, as Telion tied his, to the rail beside the
steps. Closely were we studied by the males in leather and
metal who stood about the entrance; however, the path to the
interior was left unblocked, and we entered within behind Telion.

"This way," said Telion, and warily we again followed.
The cloth upon the floor was as fine as fur, a deep blue cloth,
pleasing to the eye beside the walls of pink stone. Silks of a
similar blue hung upon the stone of the walls, torches stood
tall in large, silver sconces, and many platforms of various
sizes and shapes were to be seen standing upon the blue
cloth. Many males moved about, all seeming curious as to

our presence, and a number of females were to be seen as well. These females were clad in blue silk like that upon the walls, and all wore metal collars about their throats. Telion, seeing my gaze, smiled faintly.

"The sole remaining female slaves in Ranistard," said he, nodding toward the females. "Their presence is essential, for the Palace of the High Seat must be looked after, and the Guard of the High Seat must be seen to. Their lot is hard, yet with so few females about there is no help for it. I shall find rooms for you, then I shall see about a bath for me. Never have I felt so in need of one."

"There is a stream or river close by?" Larid asked him. "I saw naught of it as we approached."

Telion halted abruptly, then laughed. "No, little flame," said he quite softly. "There is no river or stream. You may bathe within your room, and this, too, shall I see to. It is past time for you to learn the ways of civilization."

He then touched Larid's face briefly, and again led the way, this time to a wide, very high set of pink stone steps, which he began to climb. Larid shrugged, as though to say, what may one think of the actions of city males? I, too, had little hope of understanding, and we followed without comment.

The end of the steps revealed a long, clothed area down which Telion strode. Doors there were to either side, doors of intricately carved wood, and candles within boxes hung upon the silk-covered walls, illuminating the area quite well. To the center of the area was a low platform, about which knelt four collared females in blue silk. To these females did Telion stride, and quickly they bent low before him.

"I wish three rooms for my companions," said Telion. "They are to be made as comfortable as possible, and baths are to be drawn for them. See to it."

"Yes, master," said one of the females, who then sprang to her feet and clapped her hands. The other three rose and ran to doors on the right, each past another, and held these doors wide. She who stood beside Telion seemed startled at sight of my warriors and myself.

"The slaves shall fetch whatever you require," Telion said to us. "I shall return for you when it is time to take a meal, and you may rest yourselves till then."

With a smile he left us then, walking quickly back as we had come. I did not care for the feel of the dwelling, so close about us, no windows in view, yet was there little to be done just then. Come full darkness, with all in the city asleep, the males who stood before the gates would be persuaded to open them, and then would the full numbers of the Hosta enter, to question as many as need be to find the location of the Crystals, and those who had stolen and slain. Not much longer would we have to bear the strangling closeness of the city.

"Please to enter, Mistress," said the slave-woman to me, gesturing toward an opened door. I nodded to my warriors to take the others, then I walked to the door which was to be mine. The small slave-woman shrank back a bit in fear, thinking, perhaps, that I would devour her as I passed. Little patience had I left with slaves; however I ignored her fear and her presence and looked about at the room which had been offered me.

Large and high, it possessed four windows which stood from floor to roof, hung with silk, of an inner, sheer white, and an outer heavy red, held in place by metal. Silk of a pale pink covered the walls, a deep soft cloth of red, pink and white covered the floor; large candles hung in white sconces about the walls, and to the right there was a large unlit fireplace with wood laid in. To the left stood a strange-seeming platform, raised from the floor to perhaps the height of my knee, and then, by four poles, of carved wood alone, it reached toward the roof. Easily was it the width of three warriors side by side, a length longer by more than a head than my own height, and the poles which reached to the roof bore a contrivance of metal and cloth, also of pink, red, and white, which stretched fully as long and as wide as the lower portion. Silks and cloths in various shades of pink and red covered the lower portion, and large, stuffed squares of white silk were strewn about upon it. To the left of this odd platform, nearer to the corner where the walls met, stood a small, flat-topped platform which bore tiny pots, large combs and brushes, and a wide polished square which repeated whatever it saw, much as a calm run of water does, though clearer. To the right of the odd platform was a high, sectioned contrivance of white silk, which hid what stood behind it from view, and to this contrivance did the small door slave scurry. Easily was the thing moved aside, and behind it stood a large, round, stone—pot, it might perhaps be called. It stood to my thighs from the floor, was nearly the width of my body height, and was of the pink stone of the walls. Once having revealed this large pot, the slave again scurried, this time from the room.

Curious, I walked across the cloth, passing two small, Keeper-like seats which stood near to the fireplace, and paused before the windows to see what might be seen from them. I saw males, in leather and metal, walking about upon the ground below. It was clear that they stood guard about the immense dwelling, and that the large, stone dwelling directly before my eyes was the object of their attention. There, too, were leather and metal clad males, yet fewer in number, and lightly did my left hand rest upon my sword hilt. Perhaps there would be the pleasure of battle to be joined that fey, before the entrance of my warriors. It would pass the time most pleasantly.

Soon the small slave-female returned, in the company of two others. I turned from the window to see them bearing three large, wooden pots, which they carried to the very large stone pot. The wooden pots, filled with water, were emptied into that of stone, then did the females again hurry from the room. In a hand of reckid they returned, again bearing full wooden pots, and again were they added to that which had been put within the stone pot. All three females then scurried forth once more, yet she who had held my door returned immediately, bearing a thick fold of cloth, and quickly did she close the door sliding a bar across to disallow its swing, then turned to me.

"Your bath is prepared, Mistress," said she, her head and voice low. "Would you now care to enter it?"

At last seeing the point to the thing, I strode to the large stone pot and looked within. Indeed, a goodly amount of water had been placed therein, yet I laughed. Only city folk would prefer to bathe within walls in a pot rather than taste of Mida's sweet streams and rivers. How was one to swim and dive in such a pot?

"I shall use the water," I said to the female as I began to remove my swordbelt. "I am Jalav."

"Yes, Mistress," said she, with eyes down and head low. "I am to assist you."

"Jalav needs no assistance," said I, placing my sword within easy reach of the pot, then removing my dagger and leg bands. "Why do you stand so, girl? Think you Jalav shall find reason to attack?"

"Oh, no, Mistress!" she said, fearfully. "It is merely that I

have never seen such a woman as you! Had I been such a
woman, never would I have fallen slave!"

"To fall slave may happen to any," I said. "To remain
slave is yet another matter."

I turned to step within the stone pot, finding the water of
an unexpected warmth. How frail these city folk were, to
heat their washing water, and not heat their drink! Firmly, I
lowered myself, to see that the female had stepped closer.

"May I not aid you?" she asked, seeming most anxious to
do so. "I would find it an honor rather than a duty."

I shook my head. "I require no aid," I informed her, seeing
her disappointment. "I shall not be long, for I dislike the feel
of this water. It does not refresh as would unheated water."

Wordlessly did she sink to her knees, head down, obedient
to my word. Obedient, too, were the Hosta to the word of
Jalav, yet was the obedience of another order. Never would
the Hosta bend their knees, not even to their war leader. For
such an act would Mida cast them out. Thoughtfully, I lowered myself into the water, my hand reaching a bit of it to
my throat and neck. Easily did my fingers find the chafe
marks of the collar which the hunter had thought so well of.
All males should be placed within collars to know themselves
the feel of it, the constant awareness of it, the inability to rip
it from one's flesh. Should they be unable to swallow easily
because of it, tear their fingers upon its unyielding metal,
then perhaps they may be less willing to place it upon others.
Such is a lesson sorely needed by certain males.

I brought the wetness to all of me by briefly submerging
beneath the water, then did I rise and step from the pot. The
water fell from me as it was wont to do in the forests, yet
was this unacceptable to city folk. The collared female rose
also and hurried to me, the thick fold of cloth now opened to
a large square, and the drippings were caught within the
cloth, and taken from me by its touch. So, too, was my hair
done, much to my annoyance, though protest was not worth
the effort. I did, however, laugh most heartily when the female produced, from beneath the low platform of the reflecting square, a slave-woman covering of yellow silk. To think
that the war leader of the Hosta would don the color of the
Helda was most amusing, more so even than the thought of
the covering itself. With chuckles I replaced my own clan
colors, then leg bands, dagger and swordbelt. The small female, once again seeming frightened, bent quite low to me

then removed herself, an action which did not displease me. With comb from the small platform I seated myself upon the cloth, and saw to my hair, then I waited. To her hunters, has Mida taught much patience.

Darkness was very near when Telion entered the room. He looked about in the gloom, saw me where I lay upon the cloth, then shook his head. "For what reason are the candles unlit?" he asked as I rose to my feet. "And for what reason do you choose the carpet over the bed?"

"The candles are unlit," said I, "for the simple reason that I have no 'flamemaker. I do not know the meaning of 'carpet' nor 'bed.' "

Telion again shook his head. "Ah, Jalav, you are most difficult," said he. "A carpet is what you stand upon, a bed is what one sleeps upon. Yonder is a bed." His hand waved toward the large, odd platform, and I frowned. One was to sleep raised up so high above the ground? One might as soon sleep upon the back of gando or kan. "Also," said Telion, "a flamemaker may have been had from the slaves. You had only to send one for it."

"I dislike slaves," said I, walking to where he stood, "and therefore would have as little to do with them as possible. Are we now to feed?"

"Eat," said he, holding the door wide, "and yes, we are now to eat. Let us fetch Fayan and Larid."

He then led the way to the area beyond the room, past the slaves who knelt in the candle glow, to the next door from mine. A push upon it took him within, yet did he stop abruptly with a low exclamation. I stepped beside him so that I, too, might see, yet naught was there to so startle him. In the room, like mine save for the colors of yellow, gold and white, stood Fayan and Larid, the candles having here been lit. My warriors had turned at the sound of Telion's entrance. It was clear, from the dagger in Fayan's hand, and the position of Larid's dagger, that they had been casting at the tall, carved post of the odd platform. Larid's dagger stood straight from the center of the narrow post, and I had not seen how excellent a target it made. Should one wish to strike the post at all, one's cast must be truly accurate, yet was this of no concern to Telion.

"What do you do here?" he demanded of my warriors, his hand still upon the door. "Do you think yourselves in a tavern or the forest?"

"There was nothing else to do to pass the time." Larid shrugged, then retrieved her dagger. "A pity," said she, her back to us, "that all may not cast at so excellent a mark. Perhaps the eye of those of the cities would improve somewhat."

As her hand raised toward her dagger, another dagger struck the post above hers, quivering in the thick wood. I had seen Telion's hand move, and with Larid's laughter did my own amusement grow, for she had sought to lure him to the mark, not having missed the disapproval in his tone. At Larid's laughter did Telion know himself gulled, and surprisingly, he laughed as well.

"Larid, you are an imp of Sigurr," said this male who was a warrior. "The mark is indeed worth reaching, but you should not have tempted me so. Such actions are improper within the Palace of the High Seat. Come now, for food awaits us."

Larid fetched both her dagger and Telion's, and returned the male's with a grin. That she now approved of the large, red-gold haired male could easily be seen, and I looked toward Fayan with a smile for the change, yet Fayan wore no similar smile. Her dagger had been returned to its leg bands, and most distant did she seem as she approached us, much like a warrior who bears her wounds in silence. Telion glanced upon her and lost his amusement, then did he silently lead the way from the room. There was little to be said to Fayan the warrior, and that little must come from Mida herself. As I walked beside Fayan, I knew again how small was the worth of a city male.

We descended the steps from the area of our rooms, and then were led again to the left, across the blue cloth—called carpet—toward large doors set side by side. Before these doors stood males in leather and metal, who stood aside with faint grins so that we might pass. Large were these males, and attractive, and Larid looked upon them, then glanced toward me with a grin of her own. Much pleasure would my warriors find after recovery of the Crystals, though none of the males would be taken with us when we departed. City males were best left where found.

The large doors, pushed open by Telion, showed a room fully twice the size of that in which I had waited. Torches along the walls lit the room, and in its center was a large platform, in a square, with many Keeper's seats placed about. At one side, seeming far too few in number for so large a room, stood three males, tall and well made, all in leather and metal, the leather and cloth of the one in the center turned to the blue of the wall silks and floor coverings. Dark of hair and eye was he of the blue leather, with hair of a length with Telion's, and a grin showed upon his face as he saw my warriors and myself. The other males, too, seemed pleased, and he of the blue leather nodded and grinned as Telion approached him.

"I must send you forth more often, Telion," this male said with amusement. "Had I known of your fondness for returning with mementoes, I should have sent you much sooner."

"The acquisition of mementoes such as these are much easier than their keeping." Telion laughed, pausing before the blue-clad male to bow somewhat. "There is little that I may report, Galiose, for so long an absence."

"For now, it is enough that my brother warrior has returned," said the male Galiose, placing his hand upon Telion's shoulder. "That you came from Lodistard for the sole purpose of aiding me places me gladly in your debt. I would not have upon my hands the blood of one beside whom I have fought. Though I now be High Seat in Ranistard, I have not forgotten the life of a warrior in Lodistard."

"It was for a similar reason that I came." Telion placed his own hand upon the shoulder of Galiose. "As often as my life remained mine through your efforts, how could I do otherwise? As Ranistard is now yours, so is it mine."

"And ever shall you be welcome," said Galiose warmly. "Now, brother, you may introduce these toothsome wenches, then we shall all take seat and dine."

Telion turned to my warriors and myself and gestured toward me. "Galiose," said he with a grin, "I would have you know Jalav, war leader of the Hosta of the Midanna, and her warriors, Fayan and Larid, three wenches of extraordinary ability."

"Warriors?" said the male in blue leather, with a smile. "I see they bear arms, yet—warriors?"

"We are not warriors such as males are wont to speak of," said Larid. "We know the *proper* method of wielding a sword."

Galiose threw back his head in laughter, joined by the two males who stood beside him. I, too, laughed, and even Fayan smiled; however Telion found little amusement in the point

which he and Larid had contested. He grimaced sourly and
Larid laughed.

Galiose of the blue leather continued to chuckle as he motioned toward the large square. "Let us now seat ourselves,"
said the male, "for I feel I have been well put in my place.
The food has been prepared, and awaits only our convenience."

Galiose took the seat at the center of the square side, indicating with a small bow that I was to take the seat to his
right. I did not care overmuch for its appearance, but such
odd seating was clearly custom. As we partook of the provender in the dwelling of Galiose, little was there to be done, so
I walked to the seat and lowered myself, finding difficulty in
the placement of my sword. Then did a gap in the seat to the
left accommodate me. Telion seated himself beside me, Larid
to his right, then the first of the other two males, then Fayan,
then the last of the males. All sat to the right of Galiose, and
this, too, seemed the custom.

Immediately slaves appeared bearing tall, metal pots which
were then filled with renth. I welcomed the mild drink, and it
easily flowed down my throat. Galiose, who had been studying me most carefully, sipped at his own pot and grinned.

"I am pleased to see the renth has your approval," said
he, motioning to a slave that my pot was to be refilled. "I
should, however, caution you that the beverage is somewhat
potent. Pleasant though the thought may be, I cannot be
silent on the matter."

His large, dark eyes, amused, looked at me as though I
were city slave-woman, therefore I shrugged and broke custom. "Renth," said I most pointedly, "has less potency even
than unbrewed daru, which is fit only for males. You need
have no fear."

Instead of showing anger at the disparagement of his
provender, Galiose laughed. "I see you each have tongues as
sharp as blades," he said. "I do not believe I have ever heard
speak of daru."

Telion leaned toward Galiose. "Daru is fit for a warrior's
palate," said he, quite innocently, then added, "Unadded to,
that is."

The dryness in his tone brought forth laughter from Larid
and myself, and most quizzically did Galiose look upon Telion, but there was no further opportunity for discussion.
Many slaves entered bearing food; one would have thought a

clan was to be fed. Meat there was, of four varieties, roots and berries, both swimming in drippings and unadorned, baked wheat both light and dark, fruit from the trees, birds from the skies, fish from the rivers. Confections were there as well, of a sweetness to tempt a child and sicken a warrior grown, and all manner of flat, metal boards, square with edges slightly raised, upon which the provender was to be placed. Much confusion was there with slaves moving about, males helping themselves, and the like, therefore it was a moment before Galiose looked up to see the leather and metal clad male who stood before the far side of the square, one who had earlier stood without the room.

"Yes, Captain," Galiose said, nodding toward the male.

"Blessed one, there are those without who would speak with the warrior Telion," said the male stiffly. "They insist that their presence is no intrusion, and refuse to await meal's end. Shall I see to their arrest?"

Galiose looked toward Telion, who smiled faintly. "Allow them entry," said Galiose, and the male bowed and returned to the door.

Scarcely had the door been pushed to opening, when Ceralt and Nidisar strode through, angrily. Nidisar's eyes were drawn to Fayan, while Ceralt, with a strange glance for me, looked directly at Telion.

"I see," said Ceralt to Telion, "that you do, indeed, have acquaintances in the Palace of the High Seat! I would know what is to be done about my hunters!"

"Little at the moment," said Telion, choosing a small fruit. "Perhaps the High Seat may be persuaded to extend his hospitality to two impatient visitors from Bellinard."

"There is sufficient for two others," agreed Galiose most judiciously, inspecting the hunters coolly. "Seat yourselves there, men, and join our repast."

Ceralt was truly angered, but appeared unwilling to insult Galiose. "We thank you for your generosity," he replied in a choked voice, adding a bow, then he angrily sat at the square, directly across from our position. After a brief hesitation, Nidisar, too, sat.

Slowly did the feeding progress, and never did the renth cease to flow. Most amusing was this Galiose of the blue leather, and much was the laughter he caused to be—among those to his right. The hunters, though well served, were not looked upon by him, nor by any other. Once, when leaning forward for a fruit, I glimpsed Fayan where she sat. Quite coldly did she swallow renth, caring naught for the gaze of Nidisar, which was still upon her, and pleased was I to see that. Ceralt glowered at me, yet was he to be disappointed in his wishes. Sooner would I fall beneath thirsty blades than again be handed to him as item of trade.

At last came a time of no further serving, the slaves having all departed and not returned. Galiose, asprawl in his seat, waved toward Telion. "Now I would hear of your journey, brother," said he most comfortably. "A tale is best told upon much food and renth."

"It is a tale of some fascination and many questions," said Telion, with a pot of renth in hand. "As you bid me, I traveled in the wake of Vistren's man Arrelin and his ilk, who were, ostensibly, to ride only to Bellinard to arrange for the dispatch of marriageable females. One of these did indeed halt at Bellinard, yet Arrelin and the others continued on, to what destination, I knew not. Curiously I followed, to the Dennin river and beyond, and there discovered the existence of the Midanna."

Telion paused to drink of his renth, and Galiose said not a word, yet seemed no longer amused.

"The Midanna, I found," continued Telion with a smile, "were a sort of wench I had not before encountered. Close upon the trail of Arrelin, soon to know his destination, I was rudely taken captive and—uh—persuaded to entertain their host. When at last released by these females, Arrelin had long since departed the area."

Telion paused to drink, straightening himself in his seat. "I again rode for Bellinard," said he, bringing his eyes to me, "for I not only hoped to there find Arrelin; I also hoped to find one Jalav of the Midanna, who had briefly spoken to me of a loss. Certain of her females had been slain, and that which had been in their keeping was taken. Certain was I that Arrelin had done the deed, at the bidding of Vistren. Once in Bellinard, I discovered the whereabouts of this Jalav, and also that of Arrelin, who was soon to take caravan with the brides who had been arranged for, therefore did I, with Jalav and others, also join the caravan and make for Ranistard. As we are now safely in Ranistard, I should like to ask my first question. Jalav: what manner of thing was taken from you?"

Closely did Telion look upon me, nor was he alone in his

interest. Galiose, too, stared from beneath lowering brows, and Ceralt and Nidisar as well. Slowly I said, "Where might he called Vistren be found?"

Telion grinned, and Galiose laughed aloud. "Extraordinary wenches indeed!" said Galiose. "I trust, Telion, you did your utmost to—entertain them. Hear my words, lovely Jalav. This Vistren is my enemy, for he would be High Seat in my stead, though he is only cousin to my family. He now prepares some manner of devilment, the knowledge of which I must have to see him undone. I give you my word that your possession shall be returned to you as quickly as I have settled with Vistren." He then leaned forward placed his arm upon the back of my seat. "Now, wench," said he. "What manner of thing was taken?"

"The matter is one for none save Hosta," I informed him most courteously, "and this Vistren, too, is marked as theirs. Best you not attempt to stand between us."

Galiose frowned mightily at my response. "By the four part tail of Sigurr the dark!" he shouted, striking the platform before him with a fist of outrage. "The wench thinks to warn *me* off!"

Telion then leaned forward with half-hidden grin. "There is yet another point which should be mentioned, brother," said he, somewhat apologetically. "The wench had a somewhat larger force to begin with—approximately one hundred fighters on gando-back. They now roam the forests hereabout and seek the location of Ranistard so that they may enter and take the city."

"Take the city?" roared Galiose, enraged. "What nonsense do you speak, Telion?"

"I merely report their intentions." Telion shrugged, no whit upset. "They also hold some twenty hunters of Bellinard, the men of Ceralt, there. Ceralt thought to locate the horde before their attack on Ranistard and barter his men's freedom for Jalav's."

"Twenty hunters, eh?" mused Galiose, no longer enraged. He leaned away from me and stroked his chin in thought. "It is a point to bear in mind," said he. "I ask you again, girl. What is it that Vistren thinks to use against me?"

"It is nothing a male may use," I said, finishing the last of the renth. "It will be quickly removed from this Vistren, along with his life, though the second not as quickly as the first."

"Vistren now knows of their presence," said Telion. "Three of the hirelings of Arrelin, in the guise of caravan guards, attempted to force Jalav to speak of her purpose here. Ceralt and I appeared before too serious harm was done, and thereafter did I keep watch upon her, to see that no others attempted the same. Not again was there such an attempt upon her, for Arrelin dismissed the three, and sent them on ahead of Ranistard. I surmise their destination, yet safely so, for shortly before the last darkness was the caravan attacked by brigands—who seemed most intent upon reaching Jalav and her wenches. Had these selfsame wenches not been most skilled warriors, surely their blood, rather than that of the brigands, would have flowed to the ground."

Galiose, appearing thoughtful, murmured, "That Vistren wishes their lives may be easily seen. I would know why."

"Perhaps," suggested Telion, "Vistren does not wish the nature of what he holds known. Remaining silent under such circumstances merely aids an enemy."

Again they turned to me. "It may also be," said I, "that this Vistren knows his fate with my presence. Well might he fear the arrival of Hosta."

A sound of annoyance came from Galiose. "You are a stubborn one," said he, "and no mistaking it! Did you not hold the word of my brother, Telion, I should be much tempted to—" His words ceased. "Well, no matter," said he with a wave of his hand. "As you remain my guest, perhaps I shall be able to convince you to speak through more pleasant means. There shall be amusement in the trying, eh?"

Again he leaned more closely toward me, this large, well made male, and abruptly Ceralt rose from his seat.

"I demand to know," said Ceralt quite angrily, "what is to be done about my hunters! I must have the wench to trade for their release!"

Galiose looked toward Ceralt in annoyance. "You have not the slightest knowledge as to their whereabouts," said he to the hunter. "How may one trade with those who are not present?"

"And," added Telion to Ceralt, "what is there to cause you to believe that your trade will be accepted? Perhaps such is not done among the Hosta."

Lightly did I laugh then, and surely did Ceralt know the truth of Telion's words. The hunter looked at me angrily and I laughed the harder.

"The wench is mine!" Ceralt shouted in rage. "As slave did I purchase her, and never have I released her! I demand that my property be returned!"

Galiose considered these words soberly, then turned to me. "What say you on the matter, Jalav?" he asked. "Are you slave to this man?"

"Jalav is slave to no living being," I said, regarding Ceralt coldly. "Were I not guest within your dwelling, the suggestion of slavery would have been sufficient to cause my blade to drink deep. As captive, there may be need to endure such words, yet I am no longer captive."

"You hear," said Galiose to Ceralt. "He or she who would fight for freedom may not be called slave."

"She is mine," repeated Ceralt coldly. "A fool was I to see her as aught save a wench with blade, for easily may a blade be kept from her reach. When next I have her in my possession, she shall not escape me."

He glared at me, then turned and walked from the room, followed by Nidisar, who had not spoken since his arrival.

"Well," mused Telion, "Ceralt seems most adamant in his stand."

"Ceralt is a fool in truth," I said, feeling the closeness of the room because of the renth.

"Many men be fools," said Galiose, rising from his seat, "yet not all have the wisdom to see it in themselves. Come, pretty Jalav. I would pursue the questioning of you in more comfortable surroundings."

With a grin he led me from the room, his hand upon my arm. I cared little for what questions he would attempt, for there was a great need within me. Silently, I mounted the steps beside him, his males in leather and metal behind us, and we walked a good distance before arriving at an over-large door, before which stood more armed males. Those in our wake joined those at the door, all standing aside so that Galiose and I might enter.

Two collared females knelt within the large room, which was of many shades of blue. The females rose quickly at sight of Galiose, and hurried to him to assist in the removal of his blue leather and metal covering. A large fire burned in his fireplace, and I stood before it, pleased that no candles burned as well. Many things was it necessary for me to do, yet my thoughts roamed many places. Foolish, indeed, was Jalav of the Hosta, for drinking so much of the renth.

"Surely you may now remove that blade," said Galiose
from behind me, and I turned to see him with eyes upon me,
in his blue cloth covering alone, the collared females having
gone. For a moment, I was reluctant to remove my swordbelt, then, almost in anger, I threw it from me. The arms of
Galiose circled me then, and his lips were hot and moist
upon my body. Great was my need, and great was my desire,
yet I found I would have fought his strength, had I been able.
He pressed me to the cloth beneath our feet, close before the
fire, and there did he use me. Though I struggled against his
use, struggled to reach my dagger, yet were the arms of Galiose hard about me, preventing me. Much pleasure did the
male take, and some pleasure was I given, although the
pleasure touched my body alone. I felt no pleasure in use by
a male, no pleasure and much bitterness. Perhaps in such use,
with bitterness, was the evil once spoken of to be found.

Long did Galiose spend in his pleasure, before he fell
asleep upon the cloth by the fire. For a moment I lay beside
him, then I rose and retrieved my sword, carrying it silently
out the door. No bar had Galiose placed across the door, for
no bar was necessary. Those without had seen that none disturbed us. Wordlessly I passed these males in leather and
metal, and wordlessly I searched out the area of the room
which had been called mine. The collared females slept upon
the cloth about the small platform, and none stirred as I
walked to the rooms of my warriors.

The room nearest mine was that of Fayan, and she sat full
awake by the fire. She rose quickly to her feet at my
beckon, and silently followed to the door of Larid. Larid, too,
sat awake by her fire, and the shadow flames leapt on the violet and lilac of her surroundings. Despite the white mixed in,
the violet seemed the color of dried blood.

"Telion was not pleased that I chose another of the males
this darkness," said Larid with something of a smile when
Fayan and I sat ourselves before her fire. "His actions when
angered amuse me, yet was I foolish to release him. The new
male was pleasant enough, yet not so superior a sthuvad as
Telion. I shall have to reclaim him for our stay here."

"Our stay here is at an end," I said, and Larid ceased grinning. "We now know where the Crystals lie, therefore shall
we reclaim them." I rose again and walked to the window,
gazing upon the structure to be seen in the near distance.
"There is the dwelling of he called Vistren," said I to my

warriors who stood close beside me. "Earlier I saw the way the males gazed upon it, as if it were the dwelling of an enemy. You are both to seek the warriors whom Gimin has sent within these walls, and together shall you all see to the opening of the gates for our host. I have little doubt that Gimin observed our arrival this fey, and waits even now for the opening of the gates."

"Larid may easily see to such a thing, Jalav," said Fayan from beside me. "My place is beside the war leader," said she, "and there I shall stay."

"No, Fayan," I denied, gently yet firmly, my hand upon her shoulder. "I shall see what may be seen of yon dwelling alone, for should Larid be unable to locate the others, your blade shall be needed by her at the gate. First, before all else, must the Crystals be considered."

She seemed pained at my words, yet she knew she must heed them. Fayan nodded silently, and therefore did I leave the window. The cloth beneath our feet was soft to step upon, and more silent still did it cause the tread of a Hosta to be. Like the zaran in the darkness did we move, silent and swift, although there was no need for deadliness. Before the entrance to the dwelling of Galiose stood many armed males, yet did the lower area contain a window which stood slightly ajar. Through this window my warriors and I went, into the bushes before it, and the darkness about it. Many had seen the arrival of three Hosta, but none noted their departure. Through the cloaking darkness we moved from the dwelling of Galiose, and in the darkness my warriors and I parted, they to see to the admittance of their sisters, I to see to the male who had caused shame and pain and loss of glory to the one who had borne me.

14.

The dwelling of Vistren
—and a meeting with darkness

Quite chill was the darkness, and damp was the grass I lay
upon. The Entry to Mida's Realm had not yet appeared in
the skies, therefore I was unseen by those who stood before
the dwelling of Vistren. Never before had I felt such icy
sharpness to the air, never had the grass held so penetrating a
dampness. I wished to refuse contact with it all, but that was
impossible. Carefully I moved through the grass and
darkness, showing no trace of my presence, for though the
dwelling itself lay bathed in torchlight, and no bushes or trees
surrounded the area, still did I have the darkness and the
grass through which to move.

Slowly, silently, I made my way about the dwelling, seeing
the positions of all armed males. Not as large was this dwelling as that of Galiose, yet was it of sufficient size to require a
good number of armed males, some of whom stood within
the torchlight, and some of whom walked about, attempting
to search the darkness. Without hearing and sight both are
those of the cities, therefore was there little difficulty in approaching a darkened corner of the dwelling. This corner lay
to the left of the well lighted entrance, and turning the corner
showed one a distance of perhaps thirteen paces, all in
darkness, before a small doorway might be reached. This
doorway was lit by a torch, and was guarded by a single
male. Closely did I regard this male from little more than
two paces from him, yet he knew not of my presence. I

waited patiently for the moment when those about us had attention elsewhere, then I stole up behind this male, with dagger in hand, thrust up his covered head by the chin, and plunged my point down into his unprotected throat. No sound was made as he died, and no sound was made as I pulled his body to the shadows and there left it, to guard as well as it had before the door.

The door was unbolted, and I was quickly within the dwelling. Darkness filled the area I had entered, for torches hung unlit upon the walls, therefore I paused to allow the dark to lighten somewhat before moving softly from the door. Far to my right, somewhere beyond walls, was the large entrance to the dwelling, and little interest did this entrance hold. That which I sought would not be found by the entrance. To the left I moved, through an archway, to a wider, unlit area. Farther to the left was a slash of light, from which came a murmur of voices, and to this I went.

I eased the door open slightly to see the presence of a hand of males. To the left of the door were they grouped, before a wall draped all in blue silk, before which stood a large seat also of blue silk. In the seat sat a male, sword and dagger about his waist, thin and long of leg, sharp-faced and narrow-eyed, his dark hair mottled with gray. About his neck, hanging at his chest upon his light blue covering was a silver chain, from which depended a silver square, the representation of an opened eye upon it. To the right of this male stood one I knew, he of the traveling set, he who had visited the Tower. Arrelin, had Telion called him, he who had not drawn during the attack. The two males looked at three who stood before them, on a lower step. To right and left were the males in leather and metal, yet he in the center was held in chain, his wrists tight behind him. Familiar seemed the male in chain, though my attention was taken by the voice of the one in the seat.

"It was foolish of you to attempt resistance," said the male to the chained one. "I required your presence, and what I require is always brought me."

The captive stood straight in his bonds and said nothing.

"There is a matter of business I would discuss with you," continued the thin male. "There is that in the Palace of the High Seat which I would have, in return for which, I am prepared to pay a price of your own setting. You have proven access to the Palace, therefore the task should be a simple one for you. What say you?"

Again the male in chains spoke not.

"Come, come!" snapped the thin male. "You may be a man of great wealth before the new light, should you see reason! You owe no allegiance to the High Seat! Riches are yours, should you bring me the black-haired savage slut! It is. . . ."

A snarl came from the throat of the captive, and he attempted to throw himself upon the thin male, but he was held in place by those males beside him. As he continued to struggle, Arrelin laughed harshly.

"The fool is heated by the thought of the bitch, lord Vistren," sneered this Arrelin, "though the why of it is beyond me. His oiling of her during the journey from Bellinard seemed sufficient to bore any man with the thought of further use."

Arrelin laughed once more and looked down upon the captive with contempt, and the captive, who, with his struggles, had revealed himself to be Ceralt, quieted himself once more and returned the gaze.

"Do not be within reach when I am released, Arrelin," said Ceralt coldly. "It would give me great pleasure to see to you with my hands alone."

Arrelin snorted, still with contempt, and Vistren waved a hand in annoyance. "Enough of this foolishness." snapped Vistren. "I shall have the she-savage, hunter, make no mistake in that! Five hundred silver pieces may be yours for the deed, and pleased you should be to see the matter done so! Arrelin tells me she has spurned you, refusing, even, to notice your presence. Would vengeance not be sweet? If you wish, you may even have full use of her the while I hold her here."

"Neither five hundred nor five thousand would tempt me to bring Jalav to you," said Ceralt, his head high. "She is worth ten of any of you, even with all of your silver!"

Arrelin stiffened in anger, yet Vistren merely pursed his lips thoughtfully, his hand reaching up to stroke the small square of silver. "I shall have to investigate the lure of this savage," said Vistren. "Her power to bewitch men seems great, and I would learn from where it springs." He then regarded Ceralt quite coldly. "I shall have you placed in a cell," said he to Ceralt, "and see if close confinement, no food, and beatings do aught to bring you to reason. I care not how I have your word upon the matter, so long as I have it."

"Do what you will," said Ceralt, almost in a growl. "I shall not bring you Jalav."

"We shall see," said Vistren, and then he motioned with his hand. Those beside Ceralt roughly took his arms to force him from the room, and I moved quickly back in the darkness, to the archway, and through. Barely had I placed myself so, than they with Ceralt appeared, he attempting to struggle. Roughly was he thrust through the archway, and as roughly taken to the left, away from me. Again I moved toward the slash of light, where again the murmur of voices was to be heard. Behind the door were Arrelin and Vistren, they whom I had come to find and slay. Most easily could I have entered then, yet no hesitation did I feel. Silently, I moved past the slash of light, in the wake of those who held Ceralt.

Perhaps twenty paces directly ahead was Ceralt taken, then all three males turned a corner to the right. I, too, reached the corner rapidly, in time to see the males enter a doorway, three paces farther along. Torchlight spilled out from this doorway as the door swung, and as I reached it and eased it open a bit, I heard coarse laughter.

"The torches are bright, are they not?" asked one of the males of Ceralt. Indeed, the glare from the many torches of the otherwise bare room stabbed at my eyes, causing them to tear. In pain, I averted my gaze, and heard, to the accompaniment of chain sound, the further laughter of the male. "The torches are never extinguished," continued the male, "and indeed are replaced as often as required. One quickly comes to beg for the soothing of darkness."

Ceralt did not reply to the male, and softly did I move again from the door. Within the room would I quickly be blinded, prey for those who chained the hunter. When the two emerged, they would be blinded, and then they would be mine. I moved from the door, not quite to the corner, and there waited, dagger in hand, for the appearance of the males. Shortly they emerged, and turned at the door to grope for a bar which was slid across the door. Silently, I approached from behind them, and he who stood closest was first to die, as had the guard without the dwelling, my dagger deep in his throat. The second turned at the sound of the body's fall, and him I greeted with my point in his eye, for he it was who had laughed at the brightness of the torches. A scream this one began, yet was it a scream which was never completed, and he, too, slid to the floor in death. A moment I stood, listening to the darkness, and then I cleaned my blade upon the second one's covering, replaced it in the leg bands, and moved to the door.

The bar slid aside quite easily, and I partially opened the door, so that my sight might accustom itself to the blaze of the torches. As the pain eased a bit, I entered, looking about. To the right of the door, chained fast by ankles, wrists, and throat to the wall, stood Ceralt, his eyes upon the door, struggling uselessly against his capture. At sight of me, he gasped in surprise, and wide indeed were his eyes.

"Jalav, what do you do here?" he demanded in a hiss, outraged. "Do you not know this Vistren seeks your capture?"

"I know," said I, approaching him more closely.

"Then why do you merely stand there?" he demanded again, moving his wrists in the cuffs of metal. Tight to the stone of the wall were his wrists held, to either side of his head, and close, too, was his throat grasped by a collar of some width, the chain of which fell briefly to the torn front of his covering before rising to pass his shoulder. His ankles were enclosed in cuffs which also led to the wall, their chains short, yet thick. "Look you there," said Ceralt with an upward movement of his head, "to the wall beside the door. There hangs the key to these misbegotten gifts of Sigurr. Bring it here and release me, and we may both depart with haste. Vistren thought himself clever, hanging the key to my freedom within sight, yet out of reach. We shall see how clever he feels himself upon discovery of my escape."

"I shall gladly release you," said I, a strange, quiet feeling within me, "yet I may not depart with you. I have matters to settle with those males called Arrelin and Vistren."

"All may be seen to in company with the High Seat's Guard!" said Ceralt angrily. "I shall take you to the Palace, and return with the Guard, a thing which the High Seat shall be pleased to order upon learning of Vistren's intentions to invade the Palace! Such a thing in itself is sufficient for Vistren's exile. Now, fetch the key!"

I turned and saw the bit of metal he spoke of, thin and of the length of my finger. I went to remove it from its place upon the wall, then did I return to stand before Ceralt. So tall and broad was the hunter, so very much male, yet when I looked upon him, feelings other than of desire touched me. I knew not what these feelings might be, and in truth, I feared them somewhat. Slowly, I approached and circled his chest with my arms, pressing myself to his flesh through the torn covering, raising my lips toward his. Startled did his eyes appear as they looked down upon me, then did he lower his head so that our lips might meet. Sweet was the touch of him, and deep did my lips drink, and then there was no longer time. With great reluctance I released him from my arms, and stepped back so that I might place the bit of metal within the inside pocket of my covering, where once I had held bright stones for the soothing of males.

"Jalav, what do you do?" whispered Ceralt, his voice husky and low. "You must release me!"

I did not reply to him, for surely I knew I must not release him. He would have demanded that I depart with him, and no weapon could I have used to dispute him. His male strength would have carried me off, my obligations unseen to, the Crystals unrecovered. The cell would see him kept from harm, for Vistren would find no opportunity to plague him, and later, with all seen to, might he be released. I quickly turned to the walls, and one by one, removed most of the torches, plunging them briefly in a large wooden pot of water. With this done, I turned to see the shock upon his face, for surely he knew he would be left.

"Jalav, do not go alone!" said he, a tightness in his tone. "Seek out the others of your Hosta, and return when you have found them! You cannot face these men with no one beside you!"

"Mida stands always beside me," said I, then I departed, a final glance at Ceralt a thing I could not deny myself. I paused beside the dead to slide the bar upon the door, then sought the room of Arrelin and Vistren.

Almost did I reach the door before the thing occurred. Other dark doorways did I pass on my return, and all seemed as silent as they had earlier been, yet from one, standing fully ajar, came a very faint rustle. Instantly did my sword whisper from its scabbard, its blade eager to meet the softness of flesh, yet was there none to be met. From behind and above me did the net fall, like that of the males who fished in the Dennin, yet heavier was this net, and more thickly made. My blade fouled as I struggled and attempted to cut myself free, and the weight of the net held it firmly about me. Then did the males in leather and metal appear, their swords drawn, points pressing in toward me. One of these males reached and knocked my sword from my grip, bending then, to lift the bottom of the net to hastily take it. Also was my dagger taken, then was the net removed, yet not so the sword points. Close did they circle me, no whit uncertain, and then was I ordered, by gesture, to continue as I had been going. Little choice had I in the matter, therefore did I continue on, ringed by the males and their metal.

The doorway which I had been seeking was passed, as were others, till we reached a large room, hung with yellow silk. Wide platforms and small were there, upon a yellow floor cloth, and several wood and yellow-silk seats, yet none of this drew my eyes as did those who stood within. Arrelin and Vistren were there, and another younger male as well, yet beside the younger male stood Zolin, she who was war leader of the Silla. Large was Zolin, of a size with me, possessed of brown hair and malicious brown eyes, eyes which ever sought the harm of others. The red of her clan colors was the red of blood, and she laughed most heartily at the sight of Fayan and Larid, who stood bound before her. Armed was Zolin with sword and dagger, for easily might it be seen that she stood among friends, yet at my appearance her laughter ceased, and rapidly did her hand move toward sword hilt.

"Excellent!" exclaimed Vistren, his thin face seeming most pleased at sight of me. "Where was she found?"

"Within this very corridor," replied the male who had taken my sword. "Had we not found the body of the guard, lord, much mischief would she have been able to see to."

"Kill her!" hissed Zolin, her eyes bright with hatred upon me. "Heed me, Vistren, and have her slain this moment! Where Jalav is, the Hosta are not far to be found!"

"The Hosta shall not trouble us," said Vistren, his narrow eyes regarding me closely, a thin smile upon his lips. "I venture to say those two were to fetch them, yet my men apprehended them before any such action was possible. No, we have little to fear from the Hosta."

Fayan and Larid stood silent in their leather bonds, bloodied here and there from their capture, their heads bowed only a little. Failure had they found in the task I had set them, yet would I wager that they had given good account of themselves before being taken.

"There is ever that about the Hosta which an enemy might fear," said I to Vistren, folding my arms beneath my life sign. "Your life shall yet be of a sufficient length so that you may learn this."

"Insolent bitch!" snarled Arrelin, his face twisted with rage—and a good deal of fear. Though the armed males surrounded me with drawn blades, still he hesitated to approach me. Perhaps, in his mind, was a memory of the manner in which Hosta do battle.

"Insolent indeed," nodded Vistren, a coldness in his tone and look. "Yet even insolence such as hers may be overcome with the proper handling." Then he turned to the male beside Zolin to say, "Filinar, go to your brother and bring him here."

The male Filinar seemed puzzled, yet he replied, "As you wish, father," then turned to a door within the room, and disappeared through it. Zolin stood and regarded me as Silla and Hosta are wont to regard one another, and I rested my eyes upon her.

"I would know, Zolin," said I, "why your life sign is still upon your breast."

The males about us knew not the meaning of my words, yet Zolin knew. Pale did her face grow, and tightly did she grip the hilt of her sword where it rested within its leather scabbard. Fayan and Larid raised their heads and looked seriously upon her, and their solemn regard deepened Zolin's upset.

"It is not true!" Zolin whispered harshly. "Clearly did Filinar point out that Mida intended her Crystals to be used to the benefit of her Midanna! Many male slaves are the Silla to receive for their Crystal, males for use and service! The Silla shall be greater than the Hosta, greater than any clan of the Midanna! We are to be blessed by Mida!"

Her eyes demanded agreement from me, but I slowly shook my head. "The city males have spoken lies which the Silla wished to believe," said I, with no trace of feeling or warmth. "Had Mida wished her Crystals to be given to males, she would not have sent her Hosta to recover them. Remove your life sign, you who were once of the Midanna. No entry shall Zolin's soul find to Mida's Realm."

The males about us laughed as males are wont to do over things of which they have no understanding, yet did Zolin stand as though struck in stone, for greatly did she fear I

spoke the truth. Her hand crept slowly toward her life sign,
and then she turned from me, knowing she dared not believe
my words. Had I spoken the truth, her soul was forever lost.

The male Vistren had seated himself not far from where
he had stood, yet his eyes had not moved from me. Closely
was I regarded, and thoughtfully, though no words were spoken. Arrelin stood behind the seat of Vistren, his hard face
set with lines of anger. Many reckid was it left thus, and then
the door within the room opened, revealing three males. One
was he called Filinar, returned from his errand, the second
was he of the traveling set, he with the features of a girl and
a fondness for daggers. The hand of this second was upon a
third who was—

"Jalav!" the third cried, and ran forward to throw himself
to my feet. Openly did he weep, seemingly with joy, and well
did I know this male I had called Fideran. His arms circled
my legs, thrusting his body against me, and wildly enraged
was the male called Vistren.

"Fideran, for shame!" shouted Vistren, jerking himself
from the seat to stand erect. "She is a savage, a barbarian
slut! She is fit only to be your slave, not you hers!"

"I am forever enslaved to her!" cried Fideran, his back
bent, his head low. "I love her, father, and naught may
change that!"

"I wished her brought here for but one purpose!" snarled
Vistren, and then did he stride to me in fury. "I shall soon
show you the object of your love!" Wildly did he thrust
Fideran aside, and then did he strike me, full force, harshly
across the face. Again and again he struck, throwing me
from him only to pursue and strike again, and easily did the
blood flow from the corner of my mouth. To a wall was I
struck and thrown, and then did Vistren whirl from me
toward a weeping Fideran. "There!" shouted Vistren, pointing
back toward me, his eyes upon Fideran. "There cowers the
object of your love!"

Fideran raised his eyes to me, and then did he laugh
shrilly, insanely, and point also toward me, for Jalav did not
cower away from the blows, nor bow her head in shame.
Mida had taught her warrior that no shame was there to be
had in being bested by the strength of a male, that no victory
was demanded of a warrior then. Only with blade in hand
was victory demanded of Jalav, and no blade was there in
her hand. As yet.

Again Vistren turned to me, his eyes disbelieving that I stood as I had stood, straight and proud, yet filled with a fury that would soon reach out to him. His eyes met mine, and flinched from what he saw there, that which had sought him for so long. His narrow face grew further pinched, and harshly did he turn to address Fideran.

"My own blood!" said he bitterly to a now standing Fideran. "He who once called himself my son! Two sons did I send to win over the savages, yet did one only prove himself true! The other was himself won over, and made slave to a—*female!* For the sake of a glance from that female, he found himself willing to leave a priceless device of the Early Times to molder on its savage altar! I say now that you are no son to me, Fideran! To worship at the feet of a lustful, savage, pavilion-she, one who has been had by warrior and hunter alike, would turn the stomach of any true man!"

"That is not true!" cried Fideran, angry now. Vistren no longer looked upon him, yet did he speak to the stiffened back of Vistren. "She has not been had by others, father!" cried Fideran, his hands clenched into fists. "Only I have had her! Only I!"

Vistren turned his head to glance at Fideran in disgust. "I see you are a fool, as well!" said Vistren snappishly. "Think you the hunter and warrior she traveled with sought naught save a smile from her through their many feyd of—companionship? They passed the darkness within a single pavilion, Fideran, and you may be sure they each oiled her properly!"

"No!" screamed Fideran, wild in his denial. "It is a lie, a vicious lie! She is mine alone, I tell you!"

"Arrelin!" snapped Vistren, all patience gone away. "Tell this craven what was observed by you in the caravan! How that hunter carried her over his shoulder to see what all men knew she craved! Speak of your own knowledge!"

"I shall not listen to lies!" screamed Fideran even as Arrelin sneeringly prepared to speak. He who had been my male seemed to have lost himself completely. He stood upon the cloth of yellow, his shoulders bent, his fists clenched before him, his chin to his chest, his eyes shut tight. Strange was his behavior, for surely he knew he had not been the first male I had taken, nor would he reasonably be the last. Was a war leader to deny herself to suit a male's fancy? "She is mine alone," said Fideran, his voice now a mutter, and his head raised so that he might regard me with unusual eyes. "She is mine alone," he repeated, "and I shall see that she remains mine alone."

He began to walk to me, this male who had served so long in my tent, very slowly did he begin to approach me. I knew the male, knew his weaknesses well, knew that he was wont to obey me. Still unshorn was his hair, as he had worn it in the Hosta home tents, and surely was he a familiar sight.

Then from without, and all about the dwelling, came the sound of sudden shouts and screams, and above all could be heard the Hosta battle cry. Somehow had my warriors arrived, and surely now would the blood flow in vengeance for those lives taken in the Tower of the Crystal! A male burst through the door from the darkened area, a male in leather and metal, who marked his passage with his own blood. His hand held a naked sword, and his eyes sought out Vistren.

"Lord, we are under attack!" gasped the male, pale and trembling. "Females all about, ones who fight like Sigurr's legions! I must have every man here to defend the House!"

"Take them!" ordered Vistren, in anger and dismay. "Do not allow those savages entrance!"

"They shall not pass!" vowed the bloody male, and with a gesture he swept from the room those males who had netted me. Little good would his vow do; he would follow the others to a certain fate. Fayan and Larid stood showing pleasure, Vistren stared in the wake of his armed males, and Fideran, who had paused, now resumed walking toward me, his hands beginning to lift from his sides, as though to grasp something tightly.

I looked again upon Fideran, this male who had ever obeyed my word, and then did I whirl quickly, step two paces to Vistren, and take possession of his blade before he knew what was about. A wordless shout did Vistren utter, and jump away from the point that had been his, yet this Vistren was not my immediate concern. First had I Fideran to consider, a Fideran no longer as I had known him. Beware the strength of a male, had Mida taught me, do not face him with bare hand and expect victory. Fideran had roasted meat for me, had brewed daru for me, had been used many times by me, however, he was male, and to be considered as such. With deep regret did I move to him and slide my point through his unprotected middle, seeing the pain in his eyes, his hands attempting to grasp my throat. Although I understood little of males, I was able to see that Fideran was no

THE CRYSTALS OF MIDA

longer as he had been, and that his life must be forfeit if
Mida's Crystals were to be recovered. My point withdrawn,
Fideran collapsed to the yellow cloth, his face twisted with
greater pain than that caused by a sword. His hand raised to
me, reaching for a gentle touch, his voice whispered, "Jalav!"
and then did the final darkness claim him, taking him and his
pain beyond the reach of the living. I looked upon his body
with sadness, and did not dedicate his blood to Mida, for
there had been no glory in the deed, merely necessity. In his
memory I whispered, "Mida's blessings, Fideran. Perhaps we
shall some fey meet again," and then I raised my eyes to seek
those for whom I had come.

The room stood empty save for Fayan and Larid, still in
their bonds, and Zolin, who stood before the room's inner
door, her arms folded beneath her life sign. Gently did the
door yet swing, showing that the males had passed that way,
and so, too, must Zolin be passed if one were to follow. Hard
and cold was the face of Zolin, hatred in her eyes.

"I am pleased, Jalav," said she, "that the attack of males
upon your traveling set, which *I* recommended, did not take
your life. I have now the pleasure of facing you personally,
and of sending you on by the effort of my own blade."

"Face me, then," I said, stepping forward, "for I have
things which must be seen to. Mida's work has yet to be
done."

With a snarl, she drew her blade and moved toward me,
her eyes insisting that *she* did Mida's work. As our blades
rang in meeting, each warrior attempting to reach the other,
well did I know that truth would be proven at the close of
battle. She who stood in victory stood also in Mida's cause.
Zolin swung lightning quick toward my head, and not for
naught was she war leader of the Silla, but I moved with the
speed of the hadat in challenge, and bent beneath the blow,
sending my edge toward her thigh. My enemy jumped backward from my swing, but the point of my sword just caught
her, opening a line through which her blood might flow. Although the wound was slight, Zolin's eyes grew wide, for
surely had the hand of Mida not been before her as shield.
Onward I pressed, urged further by the sight of Silla blood,
and backward did Zolin stumble, her blade nimble through
habit rather than by volition. Harder and harder I moved
against her, swinging mightily in hopes of cleaving her, and
more and more difficulty did she find in parrying my thrusts,

till at last she was a shade too slow in moving, and straight through her heart did my blade plunge, to make one less of the damned Silla. Fayan and Larid raised their voices in salute, and I raised my sword and arms to Mida, and she who once was war leader of the Silla fell dead to the yellow cloth, her life and soul gone away together. Forever lost is she who turns her back on Mida's will.

"Jalav, release us!" called Larid, in exultation. "The males took to their heels through yonder door, and surely the Crystals lie somewhere within this dwelling!"

"We shall follow the males," said I, striding to my warriors and cutting the leather which bound them. "The males will lead us to the Crystals, else shall we have the pleasure of questioning them upon the point. Arm yourselves, and come along."

Fayan hurriedly took Zolin's sword, Larid her dagger, and we three walked in search of our enemies. Beyond the door lay a narrow area, dimly lit by large candles. No other doors broke the evenness of the pink stone, and little dust lay upon the gray stone of the floor. Farther on we walked, till a corner was turned and high steps were revealed. No other direction might the males have taken, therefore did we, too, mount the steps, in pursuit. Up and up we went, and then came an end to the steps with the appearance of a small space, which lay between the pink stone walls. A large wooden door barred further movement, and a touch upon the door showed it to be held firmly in place.

"They seek to escape their fate," said Fayan, examining the door. "Shall we search out another method of entry?"

Before I might even consider the matter, there came sounds from behind us, as of many feet mounting the steps. Quickly did we turn from the door, and Larid made a sound of disgust.

"Do they think us penned here?" said she, taking a tighter grip of the dagger. "Should they have gone round in some manner, they shall not be pleased with the results of their efforts!"

"They are merely males, and know no better," said I, pleased at the thought of further battle. I had not cleaned the blood from my sword, for I was not yet done with the spilling of it. Zolin would mingle with Arrelin and Vistren and the others in the most fitting manner for one's enemies to mingle—and when all was done, then might they all be cleaned from sight and memory at once. Fayan and I stood forward, for we two held swords, and Larid waited impatiently behind us till the moment she, too, might take sword from one who had no further use for it.

In little more than a moment did a male's face appear, and Fayan, Larid and I laughed. Only one male's face was there, the others in company with him being Gimin, Binat, Comir, and others of my Hosta warriors. The swords of all ran red with blood, as did the body of the male. Bound was he, and stumbling to the urgings of my warriors, and most amusing was the realization that it had been he who had vowed to Vistren that no entry would be gained by the dwelling's attackers.

"Mida's blessings, Jalav," called Gimin, with a wide grin. "I feel our goal has nearly been reached."

"Indeed, Gimin," said I, laughing lightly as I resheathed my blade, "and now may a question be more easily answered." Then I turned to the male and said, "There are other means of entry to this level, are there not?"

"No," denied the male, wearied and hurt. "There is but one entrance to the private area of Lord Vistren, and that before you is the one." His eyes met mine as he spoke these words, and no challenge appeared in them, merely defeat. It was possible that he lied, yet was I impatient to be on about my business.

"Send warriors to fetch something we can use to break the door," said I to Gimin. The warriors were dispatched, and Gimin came up to stand beside me.

"The dwelling is ours, war leader," Gimin said in satisfaction. "Our losses were small, yet few of the males who attempted battle still live. This one did we spare so that he might lead us to you, but the room was empty of all save the remains of the Silla trash. Again was the male persuaded to guide us, and happily did we find you here."

"And a pleasant sight indeed did we find you," said I, turning to look upon her. She had addressed me as war leader, therefore had she not as yet decided to give challenge for the position. That pleased me just then, for Hosta should not battle among themselves when an enemy is at hand. "I would know, Gimin," said I, "how you arrived at this place. We found ourselves unable to send word to you."

"That is both simple and complex," said Gimin, with a look of uncertainty. "We observed your entrance through the gates of the city, and observed, too, that you once more rode free, therefore did we gather by the walls at darkness, feeling you were sure to effect our entry. A number of hind did we wait with no sign, then one of the gates began to open slowly and silently. Thinking it the work of one of you, we moved forward and aided in its opening, only to find the presence of a strange appearing city slave-woman. Black was her hair, much like yours, Jalav, yet did she seem taken with insanity at sight of us. She screamed and threw herself about so, we found we must bind and gag her to silence her. All about on the ground, and in small dwellings to either side of the gate, were there males to be found, each one taken with such deep sleep that we were unable to waken any. The rantings of the slave-woman indicated that it had been she who had done a mischief to the males' drink to make them so, for some reason believing that the action would be taken as yours, and her disappearance, as well. She spoke of a thing called 'writing,' screaming that this writing would accuse the savage, Jalav, and the slave-woman's lack of presence would confirm it. We understood nothing of what she said, and put gag to her with great relief."

"Mida uses many tools," I observed, and laughed a bit at the thought of it. Halia would not escape the males who sought her, nor would Jalav be accused as she had hoped. Jalav stood behind the shield of Mida, a place entirely unknown to Halia.

"Then were we faced with indecision," Gimin continued. "We knew not where in the city our war leader might be, and did not wish to jeopardize her efforts by our untimely arrival. Nearly did we withdraw from the gates again, yet were we halted by the arrival of those warriors I had earlier sent over the wall and into the city. The hand of them had also observed your arrival, and had followed to your destination with little difficulty. At darkness they were able to approach closer, and easily did they see you three emerge from the enormous dwelling. They watched as war leader and warriors parted, and were about to approach Fayan and Larid, when armed males fell upon their sister warriors. Too brief was the battle to allow them to join, and though two males were left behind in the dirt, Fayan and Larid were quickly taken to the dwelling where Jalav had gone. In haste did the warriors decide to fetch the rest of the Hosta, and most surprised were they to find that there was no need to do battle with the males of the gate. We stood already within, and rapidly, then, did we make our way here. Upon arrival we attacked, taking the males by surprise, and making the dwelling ours. The rest you know."

"Indeed," said I, nodding in pleasure at the doings of Mida. Her aid was ever there when her Hosta truly needed it, and now was I sure that victory would be ours. Three warriors mounted the steps bearing a small but sturdy metal platform, and we by the door withdrew so that they might swing the platform at the door. Again and again did they swing, and the door, though well made, began to crack beneath the determined assault. Quite a dent had been made in the door, when a Hosta warrior hurried up the steps to Gimin and me.

"Your pardon, Jalav," she said with a nod for Gimin. "There are males without the dwelling who approached openly, saying they had no wish to do battle with us. They ask to be brought before Jalav, saying they are friends to Hosta. One of the males is he who was last taken to our home tents, that bright-haired sthuvad."

For a moment I considered these tidings, then I made my decision. "Have them brought here," I ordered my warrior, "and then see that those on guard are fully alert against surprise attack. They may think to distract us with their presence, while their host moves secretly against us."

"I hear, Jalav," acknowledged my warrior, and then she retraced her steps. Gimin and I glanced at one another, wondering at the ends the males hoped to achieve, yet neither of us spoke. In a silence broken only by the thud of the platform against the door did we wait, and shortly were the males brought before us. Telion and Galiose appeared first, a hand of Galiose's males behind them, and somewhat annoyed did Telion and Galiose seem. Not so the hand of males, though, for they examined my warriors who surrounded them with large grins of appreciation, much like the approval that my warriors showed. Briskly did they mount the steps to our level, a knowing glance for the efforts at the door.

Galiose shook his head at all about him, and then he looked upon Telion. "So they roam the forests hereabout seeking us, do they?" he asked of the warrior beside him. "It appears that their roaming has been quite successful, and the difficulty in locating us small."

"It is beyond my understanding," said Telion, upset. "We were definitely informed that the Hosta knew naught of the location of Ranistard, and that they must search for it! How their search was so easily culminated, I have no—"

Abruptly he ceased his speech, for Gimin and I wore broad grins. Telion frowned, and his gaze darted to Larid where she stood above us. Lightly laughing was Larid, and she closed one eye to Telion before turning again to watch the progress upon the door. Telion was then filled with rage, yet little was there for him to do. He had been gulled by Larid, and Hosta warriors now stood within the gates of his city.

"Were I you," said Galiose dryly to Telion, "I would make haste in repairing my sources of information. They leave quite a lot to be desired." Then he turned to me. "That you and your wenches stand armed within my city, lovely Jalav, I am prepared to forgive," said he with a bit of a grin. "I shall not, however, as easily forgive your continuing with that which my Guardsmen should see to. Withdraw your forces and allow my men entry, and the object you seek shall be returned to you when Vistren lies chained in my dungeons."

"Vistren is destined for Mida's chains," said I, looking down upon him, "and the Hosta themselves shall recover what is theirs."

"You damned, stubborn female!" Galiose growled angrily. "I attempted reason, now I shall achieve with force! Prepare your wenches for further battle, woman, for I shall return to give it them!"

Stiffly did he turn and prepare to descend; then, a gesture from me caused my warriors to draw their blades, preventing this. The grins they showed left no doubt as to their eagerness, and Galiose whirled angrily to me again.

"What means this!" he demanded in fury. "We were granted safe conduct!"

"And such have you had," I informed him. "Should you wish to continue in safety, you shall stand quietly where you are, and offer no difficulty. My warriors care not which males fall before them."

Truly great was the anger of Galiose, yet there was little that he, too, might do. He and Telion stood surlily beside one another, and their hand of males also appeared to have lost their amusement. I turned from them to see the progress upon the door, and discovered that it would soon be opened. Gimin, too, turned with me, and I was minded to ask her a thing.

"I take it," said I, "that the two captives of the forest were properly sent to Mida? Their journey, I hope, was not too swiftly over?"

"Their journey was long and filled with endless pain," replied Gimin, with grim satisfaction. "I regret you chose not to accompany Binat, Jalav, for much pleasure would the sight have given you. Too late did we discover the sign of a third who had been with them, yet somewhat behind because of difficulty with his kan. The third escaped us then, yet he shall not escape again, should he be found here."

"He is here," said I, recalling his presence in the lower room. "He is one with the look of a girl, and none shall touch him save I. It is he, I believe, who carries the life sign of she who bore me, and it shall be I who sends him to Mida's chains."

"One may safely assume that they have been in constant communication," said Galiose to Telion. "Secure as a slave was she brought here, alone and helpless, a wench to be pitied and aided! Poor, helpless female, forced to the bidding of two strong men, at their mercy in all things! Telion, should we both live through their presence and departure, I shall immediately seek a healer for you, for surely have your long travels upon kanback addled your wits!"

I glanced at the males, and Galiose gazed with withering look upon Telion, who stood slumped against the pink stone of the wall, his hand to his head as though he were in pain. I turned away again, with a smile, and patiently awaited the opening of the door.

Now much longer could the wood withstand the assault, and with a final, loud crack, it gave way. My warriors with the metal platform moved aside to allow others, with drawn sword, to precede them, then they carried the platform through and set it down. Gimin and I quickly ascended, the males behind us, to emerge within an area of blue silks and floor cloth. Exactly the blue of Galiose's dwelling was this blue, and the male looked about himself in anger.

"The check of the spawn of Sigurr!" Galiose muttered darkly. "To assume the royal color as though it were already his!"

Galiose was much disturbed; the thing had no interest for me. Swiftly I sent my warriors to left and right, searching for a barred door within the area, and as swiftly was the doorway found. Far to the right it lay, the farthest from the entrance doorway, and there did we proceed to move when all oher rooms proved empty. This doorway was but a pale shadow of the first, and a mere half dozen blows of the platform sent it crashing open, therefore did we enter with speed to find Vistren, Arrelin, he called Filinar, and the male with girl's appearance, all save Vistren with blade in hand. The male Vistren stood above a platform upon which was a device beyond description, a device of metal thick and thin, of small things round and square, and of an area above all such which seemed formed of golden air. Three distinct parts was the golden air divided into, and the parts to left and right held Mida's Crystals suspended, seemingly of themselves, with naught to support them. All halted to stare at this device, and Vistren raised to us eyes of triumph.

"Behold!" said Vistren, his visage full of gleeful satisfaction. "A device of the Early Times, one that shall call the legions of the gods to my bidding! A 'comm' was it called, and held much in awe by the Ancients, till the Crystals of power were stolen away from it. For many kalod I searched the writings of the Ancients, seeking a clue to the location of the crystals, and the locations of two did I find! The third remains lost, yet shall the two be sufficient to bring me aid against the puny swords of Guardsmen! The place of High Seat shall be mine, High Seat of the entire world!" A maniacal laugh came from Vistren, and his hand grasped a thing of rounded metal. Before any could halt him, he twisted the thing of rounded metal, and my warriors and I gasped as we were thrust at by swords unseen, sharp and hot and all about us, and again did Vistren laugh.

"It causes them agony!" he crowed, as we fought to retain our feet, fought to retain our grips on swords. Numberless flaming points stabbed about at me, and truly was the feeling agony. "Females feel it always!" laughed Vistren, his hand still upon the device. "With three Crystals in place is it merely painful, with two in place, full agony, and with only one, sure death. I had doubted the writings on this, and so tested the device with the one Crystal I had then. Almost every female in Ranistard died! It is the reason the females took the Crystals to begin with!"

Through waves of pain I saw the horror upon the faces of Galiose and Telion and their males, and Galiose stepped forward.

"You slew our women?" Galiose cried, his hands in fists.

"For the sake of your twisted dreams, hundreds of innocent women died? Cease the working of the thing at once! At once, do you hear?"

"I hear, yet shall not obey," laughed Vistren, and again he moved rounded metal. "In a moment shall the device be prepared, and my call shall be sent to the legions of the gods! You cannot stop me, Galiose, for it is far too late!"

Again did Galiose step briefly forward, Telion by his side, but that occurred which took my eyes despite the pain. The Crystals in the golden air had seemed as always, cloudy, roiling, uneasy, yet were they suddenly transformed. Before us all did they abruptly clear, then quickly darken further and yet further. So dark did they grow that never had I seen a darkness like it, thicker than the darkness after fey's light, deeper than the darkness of the dungeons, colder than the darkness about the Entry to Mida's Realm. An empty darkness had they become, and a darkness not empty enough, for in the cold, lightless dark could some presence be felt, a presence which filled one with a like empty coldness.

"Now!" shouted Vistren, and for a third time reached his hands toward the device, yet this time was his fate to meet him. A dagger flew, from the hand of a pain-filled Larid, I saw, and buried itself deep within his breast, in exact line of his heart. With a wide-eyed scream did he attempt to touch the device, yet Larid had thrown true, and his life flowed from him. As he fell to the floor cloth, Galiose and Telion leapt forward, and Telion's hand grasped the rounded metal, returning it as it had been. Almost instantly did the sharp points weaken, then fade to wherever they had at first come from. Two of my warriors fell to their knees then, with heads low, as though the points had held them in place the while. A moaning came from some others of them, and in truth did I, too, feel the need to moan. Haggard were the faces of my warriors, and they touched their life signs, their lips moving in thanks to Mida.

"Put down your weapons," said Galiose to the three males who still stood with drawn blades. "Your master is dead, and the world is well rid of him. Be wise and surrender to me."

The males looked at one another, and then threw their blades to the floor, and quickly did I move my still aching body to step between Telion, who also looked toward the males, and the device.

"The Hosta thank you for your assistance," said I a bit

hoarsely to Galiose, who turned to me with a frown. "Now we shall take what is ours and go."

"Girl, you seem barely able to stand!" protested Galiose as he looked upon me. "We shall deal with these slaughterers of the innocent, for that you have my word! Rest here till the strength returns to you, and then you may go!"

"The Hosta go now," said I, "and they go with what is theirs." Haggard still were my warriors, yet all stood straight with sword gripped firm, and therefore did I indicate the male Arrelin and the male with girl's features. These males paled and shrank away, their heads shaking in denial, yet did my warriors prod them to motion with their swords. Trembling were the males as they were taken from the room, and tremble they might, for they would pay for Vistren's actions as well as their own. Galiose and Telion watched them go with frowns; however, they sensed the mood of the Hosta and said nothing.

Then I forced myself to look again upon the Crystals in their golden spaces, and found with relief that the darkness was gone, the cloudy roiling having returned. I placed my sword upon the platform and reached up carefully to the Crystals, loath to touch them, yet knowing that to be my duty. My fingers had not yet closed upon them, when a flash of blue fire touched me, flowing from my fingers to the bottom of my soul, searing me with lightning from the skies. A scream was forced from my lips and I was thrown from the device, to writhe in the memory of great pain, upon the floor cloth. Mistily did I see Telion and Galiose reach for me, only to be thrust aside by my warriors, who came quickly to my aid. In the throbbing, trembling ache about me, I almost saw the brilliant form of Mida, standing before me, her head sadly shaking, in denial of my effort. Her Crystals had been placed beyond the reach of her Hosta, and this she well knew. Her arm raised and pointed south, willing us to return to our own lands, and this would we gladly do. My warriors helped me to my feet once more, and I stood a moment, with head down, to gather my strength, before I retrieved my blade and resheathed it in its leather scabbard.

"The Hosta go now," said I quite faintly. "Your city is again yours." Telion and Galiose gazed upon me almost with sadness, and a memory came to me. From the pocket of my covering I withdrew the bit of metal that I had placed there, and oddly did the bit of metal seem warm. I placed it in the hand of Telion and said, "Search the dwelling and release him." Telion seemed puzzled, yet had I no further strength with which to speak. I led my warriors from the room in silence, and we left the dwelling of death and darkness, hoping never to look upon it again.

15.

*The Hosta home
tents—and capture*

Most pleased were we all again to see the Dennin, for the sight of the river was a sight of home. In four sets did we again cross, I in the first set, as before. My strength and health were again as they had been, yet did memory of our departure from the city still disturb me. On foot had we crossed half the ways of the city, for my warriors had not brought their gandod fully within to their destination. We had taken the two males with us, and a sorry sight indeed did we present. Some of my warriors needed the shoulders of others in support, most stumbled with the memory of pain, and three had died, though no visible hand had touched them. Evil, evil were the cities, and never again would I think to enter one. Little understanding had I of the words of Vistren, yet I fully understood why it was a female who took the Crystals from males. Surely the female had been Mida in the guise of a living being, and she had taken them to spare her warriors pain. Sad indeed must she have been to see the Crystals once again in the grasp of males.

As I waited for the balance of my warriors to cross, I smiled grimly in memory of the fate of the two males we had taken. Once upon gandod, we had ridden from the city to the place Gimin had set her camp. There we paused just long enough to free the hunters and gather up the guards left over them, and then we rode for the forests. Through the darkness and half the light we rode, exhausted and pained, anxious to put distance between us and Ranistard. Upon halting, I set guards over the captives and ordered my warriors to sleep, for upon awakening there would be many things to avenge. Despite the coldness of the darkness, we all slept through it, and upon the arrival of the new light, we dedicated the males to Mida. The males screamed through four feyd and four darknesses, through travel and rest, through motion and sleep, and then were they denied that with which to scream. He with the features of a girl did indeed hold the life sign of she who bore me, the leather strung about his neck as though it were his to wear. Through his dedication did I see the life sign left in place, and I hoped that the soul of her who had borne me was pleased. The male with features of a girl had lived but nine feyd, and Arrelin had lived but twelve. The remains were placed beneath the ground, away from the sweet light of Mida, and at last was the matter over and done with. Though the Crystals had not been recovered, the lives of Hosta warriors had been avenged.

Shortly we passed the village of Islat, and as I had no stomach for the customs of visiting, I merely dropped the lenga pelt before the dwelling of Maranu, and rode on. The Headman of the village had pronounced himself satisfied with but two lenga pelts, yet had I promised the third should I be unable to return the kand in trade. I had not seen the kand since the time in Bellinard, therefore was a third pelt due Maranu.

The Hosta home tents were a fine sight, and gladly I entered the tent of the war leader. Gimin had told me that she had decided against the challenge, therefore I had only one further duty to see to. Rilas the Keeper was summoned and told the tale of our journey, and saddened indeed was she upon learning of the loss of both Crystals. It was necessary for me to sadden her further, for I explained that though some of my warriors, Fayan and Larid among them, had been with child, all had subsequently lost the quickened seed. Rilas cursed the device as the cause of the loss, and I had already concluded as much. Deeply hurt had Fayan been at the loss, and I knew the child to have been Nidisar's doing. Little had my warrior Fayan left to raise her, and had it not been counter to the ways of the Midanna, I felt that Fayan would have taken her own life. Perhaps all ways of the Midanna are not wise.

Upon the departure of Rilas, the Hosta again took up

where they had been upon the theft of the Crystal. A hand of feyd passed with little of interest, and then, almost at darkness, was a sthuvad taken. My warriors were pleased with the look of him, big and broad, and angered at being detained, and happily was he given the sthuvad drug, and then removed to the use tent. I found that I had little interest in him, and fetched daru to my tent to brew, for I wished no use from tho sthuvad. Memory was with me of another male, one whose lips were sweet, whose body was a burning in my blood, one whose like I might never again see. Fayan came silently to my tent, and Larid as well, as we three sat upon the black leather, saying no word to each other, sipping from many pots of daru. With difficulty my warriors left at last, and I, too, felt a good deal of dizziness as I moved from candle to candle to extinguish them. I had not thought my intake of daru excessive, yet did I nearly forget to place my dagger in my hand as I lay upon my sleeping leather, and quickly indeed did sleep find me.

Strange and unknowable are the workings of a warrior's mind. Long did I sleep; through deep mists I imagined that the face of Ceralt was before me, smiling down upon me. Then did it seem that he knelt and reached for my hand, gently removing the dagger from it, and casting the dagger aside. In full need did I move upon my sleeping leather, raising my arms to the phantom of my mind, and the phantom laughed gently and came to me, holding me close and placing his lips upon mine. Sweet, so sweet, were those imagined lips, yet when strong maleness was brought fully to me, it seemed a bit more than imagined. Great pleasure was I given by the phantom, and then was I held by him as sleep took me again. At no time had the mists cleared, yet this seemed unimportant.

Then I knew it to be full light, but I was unable to throw off the mists of sleep. Faintly, I recalled having swallowed a mixture somewhat resembling that which had been given me by Bariose and the female Karil, yet this time had it seemed to be Ceralt who had held the pot. I had not cared for the mixture, and had attempted to refuse it; however, Ceralt had spoken sharply and I had obeyed him. I also knew not why I had obeyed him.

It seemed that I sat upon a kan, leaning my body and face upon Ceralt's chest, his arms tightly about me. Other kand were there about us, one with Nidisar holding Fayan, one with Telion holding Larid, others with other males holding others of my warriors. From a distance, I heard the voice of Ceralt say, "We have them all," and the voice of Telion replied, "Let us leave, then."

Motion there was, with which I slept and wakened, yet never did the mists leave me. I slept for some time, it seemed, and then was the voice of Maranu close although distant.

"Where do you take them?" demanded Maranu, and never had I heard such coldness from him. "They most of them seem dead!"

"They but slumber from a drug placed in their daru," replied Ceralt, laughter in his voice. "We provided a captive for them, and most obligingly did they partake of the daru. They shall slumber till we allow them to awaken."

"I have still not heard their destination," said Maranu, no laughter within his voice. "She whom you hold is like a daughter to me, and I shall not allow her to be taken to slavery."

"There shall be no slavery," said Ceralt softly, and his lips touched my hair. "We take them to the city of Ranistard, there to civilize them and make them our women. Some of us are hunters of Bellinard, and some of us are warriors of Ranistard, and few are the women remaining in Ranistard. These shall find an easier adjustment there, and their life in the wilds is done. They shall have the company of others of their kind, for another group of us has traveled to the ones called Silla, the only other wild females we know of. The Silla, too, shall be taken, and once again Ranistard shall be filled with women."

"I see that you care for her," said Maranu as I moved in discomfort. There was a thought, an important thought, yet it would not come to me. "I am pleased to see that she shall have a man to stand beside," said Maranu. "I have often asked their Mida to provide one such for her, and perhaps her Mida has answered."

"I shall stand beside her always," said Ceralt, and again his lips touched me. So good was the feel of him against me, and then I slept again, pleased at his presence.

Some time later I found my eyes opened, the forest lost in the mists still about me, a great horror within me. We traveled to Ranistard, Ceralt had said. I feared the city and hated it, and did not wish to enter it again. We were to be made their women, Ceralt had said, city slave-women he had meant. And worst of all, Silla too, were to be brought there. The Silla and the Hosta were blood enemies, sworn to fight to the death upon any chance meeting! The ways of Ranistard would run red with blood! And the Crystals, the Crystals of darkness! Two awaited us, yet I could somehow see a third, much danger about it, even more danger within it! I moaned at the thought of the Crystals, and moved about in much upset.

"Hush," said Ceralt, taking me more tightly in his arms. "All will be well, my Jalav. All will be well."

Again I moaned, and moved in misery. All would be well, Ceralt had said. How little of things did males truly know! I attempted to speak to him, but this the mists would not allow, and again sleep claimed me, leaving my protests unsaid.

16.

The return—and a bitter truth is learned

Forever had I traveled through the land of mists, and now the journey was over. The mists had cleared with the newest light, and Ranistard lay in the distance before us. Again were my wrists bound behind my back, and for this had Ceralt professed regret, although he refused to release me. My warriors, each and every one bound as well, rode as did I, before a male and within his arms. Well pleased were the males with their actions, pleased, too, with the sight of their city, yet my warriors and I were filled with fury. Never had the Hosta participated in raiding, yet now had we, ourselves, been raided of our very freedom. Such a thing should not be, and now that it had been done, it must be avenged.

"We shall be there in a matter of hind," said Ceralt, self-satisfied. He and Telion rode side by side, and easily might it be seen that Larid felt as I did. Her arms moved against the leather, testing its strength, testing the knots, seeking a means of escape. I, too, had tested the leather; it had proven sufficient to hold me, and I was not pleased.

"Well in time to partake of a decent meal," said Telion, and he looked down at Larid. "The wenches, too, will do well with such. Though nourishing, the gruel is hardly their usual fare. A pity they could not be made to eat meat as easily as they swallowed the gruel."

"The drug allowed them little control." Ceralt shrugged. "That was necessary to keep them docile." Then he laughed

271

briefly. "Though there were many times Jalav's control was sufficient."

"Aye," laughed Telion in agreement. "I, too, found a sufficiency of control at certain times. Perhaps it would be wise for a man to put by a supply of the drug—for the times he desires only a docile and willing wench. Truly docile and willing was my small flame here—before she awakened."

The two males chuckled their amusement, for many times upon the journey had Ceralt used me well, and there was much reason to believe that Telion had also indulged himself so with Larid. I remembered much of the times with Ceralt, giving him pleasure at his direction, accepting all that he brought me. Most humiliating was such treatment of a warrior, and not soon would Jalav forget. I had as yet addressed no word to Ceralt, nor had I intentions of doing so till I had once again found my freedom.

Beyond Telion rode Nidisar, and little amusement did the second hunter find in the presence of Fayan. Quietly had he spoken to her when the mists had finally left her, yet did she refuse to acknowledge his existence. She did not ignore him, for that would, in its way, be an acknowledgment, therefore she made it seem that she rode alone, that no other shared the kan beneath her, and the hills about her. Untouchable and unreachable was Fayan, for Nidisar had tried, and the hunter rode in misery which had been well earned. Fayan truly wished to know naught of him, and was bound to keep it so.

The hind passed too quickly, for all too soon we reached the gates of Ranistard. The chill of darkness touched me in memory at sight of it, greater than the chill of the air about me, for well did I recall the presence of the Crystals and their device within the city's walls. My warriors, too, felt so, and many moved in anguish before the males, making no sound, yet attempting desperate escape. The males held them more closely, speaking soothingly; the males had not felt the agony of the Crystals, the flaming talons of a torture not kind enough to kill, and therefore knew naught of what they asked. To the gates of Ranistard we rode, and most menacingly did they lay open before us.

Within the gates stood many males, and other hastened from nearby ways to join them. They laughed and shouted with delight, the roar of their voices a painful greeting to the males who rode with warriors. These males grinned proudly

at their proven success in raiding, each raising an arm to acknowledge the greetings sent them. Cloth of many colors
hung from the dwellings within sight of the gates, as though
to say that the Hosta were now no better than any other, perhaps in truth, much less, for the other clans of the sisterhood
still rode free, while Hosta lay captive to males. Should this
be the thought which filled their minds, sorely would they regret it.

The city males lined the ways with their shouts and laughter, some running before our procession, some moving apace
of it, some darting in and out of dwellings to call others forth
to gape and laugh. Still were there very few slave-women to
be seen, yet these few stood here and there, behind the
throngs of males, and smiled quietly, thinking they now had
others to join them in their bondage. Little did they know of
the Hosta of the Midanna. Through the ways filled with mer-
rymakers we rode, and then to the way which led to the
dwelling of Galiose. All about had cloth and silk been hung,
and soon it was possible to see that the grass directly in view
of the entrance to Galiose's dwelling had been filled with a
straight, unbelievably long line of platforms, one beside the
other, no less than thirty or more paces in length. Upon the
platforms, which were covered in the blue silk of Galiose,
stood pot upon pot of foodstuffs, metal squares of baked
grain, tall pots empty, and taller ones which held renth. On
fires nearby roasted a full hand of nilnod, tended by female
slaves and turned by male slaves, and not far from these fires
we drew rein. Ceralt dismounted and lifted me down to stand
beside him, the other males doing the same with the warriors
they held. The crowds of city males which had accompanied
us stood about the outer edges of our set, and then Galiose
appeared from his dwelling trailing leather and metal clad
males, and strode to where we stood. He halted a short distance before me and looked about with a broad grin upon his
face, then he raised his arms.

"The city of Ranistard gives welcome to its newest cit-
izens," he shouted, and his words were greeted with raucous
approval by those males who stood about. "We are greatly
pleased to have the Hosta among us once more, and even
more greatly pleased that this time they hold no swords to
our throats." Laughter came then, from all in hearing save
Hosta themselves, for surely did we wish for swords. "You
wenches shall be given the freedom of the city," said Galiose

with a smile, "for all has been prepared against your coming. No weapon shall easily fall to your grasp, and heavily guarded are the gates and walls. You may roam as you please, learning of our city, yet may you not approach nearer to the walls and gates than a distance of two streets. Any wench found nearer shall be subject to immediate arrest and return to him who fetched her to the city, and any wench so returned may confidently look forward to a sound hiding as well. You have been fetched here to serve the needs of men, and here you shall stay. The men of our city shall henceforth see to your protection and requirements, and you need only serve them well."

A great cheer arose from the throats of the males, and Galiose looked about himself with much satisfaction as my warriors and I were freed of the leather which held our wrists. Neither sword nor dagger had we been left with, and we stood, rubbing feeling to our wrists again, as naught save captives within a hated city of males. Galiose nodded, and his arm swept toward the platforms of provender.

"For the Hosta has the High Seat declared a feast," said he, "and all men invite them to partake of it. Step forward, wenches, and eat what you will."

A pleasant murmur of anticipation arose from the males, some beginning to step forward toward the platforms, yet the eyes of the Hosta were upon their war leader, and Jalav merely folded her arms where she stood, therefore did they also remain in their places. Ceralt frowned at my lack of movement, and Galiose again looked about himself, this time with less satisfaction.

"Why do you wenches merely stand there?" demanded Galiose, his eyes moving about among my warriors. "Have you no understanding that you have been invited to table? The food is yours, come now to eat it!" Again there was no response to his words, and the males about us murmured quite differently. Galiose frowned, somewhat in anger, and his eyes came to rest upon me. "Lovely Jalav!" he called, a grin appearing. "Once before did you dine at my table, therefore shall you now show these others that there is naught to fear. Step forward, wench, and be the first to eat."

"The Hosta do not fear the city males," I informed him, taking no note of the hand which he held out toward me. "Warriors do not feed at the bidding of males, nor do they accept their captivity. The Hosta shall again ride free, be it this fey or the next, this kalod or the next. Galiose had best look to his safety, for it shall certainly be a sometime thing with the presence of Hosta."

Galiose placed his fists upon his hips in anger, and Telion came to stand with Ceralt, where the hunter gazed down upon me with angry disapproval. The male warrior shook his head in exasperation, and folded his arms across his chest.

"I now see the reason for the immobility of the others," said Telion in annoyance. "Should Jalav see fit to rise into the air, the others would attempt to emulate her. They obey her utterly, for she is first among them."

"I had not recalled that," muttered Ceralt, as Galiose came to stand before me as well. "I clearly saw, when held captive by them, that nothing was done save with the permission of the war leader. Now the war leader withholds her permission."

"Would that my warriors were as well disciplined as they," said Galiose, his dark eyes bright upon me. "I knew her to be high among the others, yet I had not known her to be war leader, and absolute in her power. How do you propose to see to this, hunter? I would not care to have them die slowly of starvation, like so many lellin in captivity."

"I know not," said Ceralt, and he rubbed his face with his large, male hand. "I had not expected her to refuse that which was freely given." He then placed his hands upon my arms and turned me gently to face him. "Jalav, I do not wish to see you suffer," said he, his voice soft. "The Hosta shall not again ride free, for men have claimed them as mates. You are mine to love and care for, and should you refuse to eat with your own hand and will, I shall feed you your gruel as I did upon the trail. Is this your wish in the matter? That you be fed against your will, with the fare of slaves?"

"Jalav is no slave," said I, looking away. "She cares naught for what a male attempts. Telion was taken, then allowed to ride free. Ceralt was taken, then allowed to ride free. Hunters were taken, then allowed to ride free. The city of Galiose was taken, and he as well, then all were allowed their freedom. City males come araiding for lifelong captives, for those they wish to make slaves. City males have no concept of honor, and a warrior does well to spit upon them."

Deep silence from the males greeted my words, and they each looked upon the other with discomfort, for surely they knew I spoke the truth. I attempted to move from Ceralt's hands, but he tightened his grip and drew me closer.

"Do not feel betrayed!" said he, his light eyes much disturbed beneath dark brows. "It is not as slave that you were brought here! My love for you is great, Jalav, too great to allow us to remain apart! You shall soon come to know the ways of a city, and regard them as your own. Then shall you see that what was done was kindness, not capture. We would teach you that life may be rich and warm, not empty and covered in blood. I now have no doubt that you return my love, therefore shall I keep you by my side. Join me at table, wench of my heart, for I would not see you hunger."

He attempted to place his arm about me and draw me with him, yet was I not to be moved. "In truth does Jalav hunger," said I sharply. "Jalav hungers for her freedom, and the sight of the Hosta home tents. She shall feed beyond the walls of this Mida-forsaken sinkhole, else shall she feed not at all!"

Again the males glanced at one another, and Telion sighed quite deeply. "She speaks of herself as Jalav," said he in weary tones. "Ceralt and I have learned, Galiose, that when Jalav is Jalav, naught may be done with her, and if Jalav does not eat, neither shall the others. So much for the feast and festivities."

Galiose then looked upon me quite sternly, no whit of approval remaining in his glance. "I do not care for stubborn wenches," said he, "and this one has too often refused my bidding. Beware the wrath of the High Seat, wench!"

I prepared myself to speak on how little the wrath of the High Seat concerned me, yet Ceralt's hand quickly clapped itself to my mouth. "She shall soon be taught a proper humility," said Ceralt, holding fast as I struggled to free myself from his grip. "I, myself, care little for the temper of a shelenga, and shall labor most earnestly to correct the fault."

"I wish you considerable success," muttered Galiose as I glared at him above Ceralt's hand. "Also, the blessing of the Serene Oneness, which I dare say you shall require in great measure. Let us now avail ourselves of the tables. As the young ladies feel no hunger, they may stand as they are and observe *our* repast."

The males showed agreement with these words, and all walked from me to the provender, the other males joining them as well. Full pleased was I to be free of Ceralt's hand, and his presence as well, for I did not care to be treated in such a manner, yet could not prevent it. I shall ever fail to see why males have been given such strength, when warriors, who have a far greater need of it, must do without. Surely, the matter was seen to without Mida's knowledge, for never would she have allowed that to be.

The males gathered about the platforms, each taking a square of metal upon which to place whatever he wished to feed upon. I looked slowly about myself, confirming the attention of my warriors upon their war leader, then returned my gaze to the males. The moment was nearly at hand, and the Hosta would move as one. I awaited only the first taste of the provender by the males, for one's body then expects a second taste, and is little prepared for movement other than that. The moment came when the jaws of the greater number of males worked upon what was placed between them, and then did Jalav move swiftly. I threw my left arm up and circled the air once, the Hosta signal to mount and ride, and then jumped to the leather seat of Ceralt's kan. The kan was in rapid motion even as I held to its mane to lean far forward to grasp the trailing rein, and my warriors were mounted and running behind me. Directly toward the line of onlooking males I rode, shouts and cries filling the air all about me, and wildly did the males attempt to throw themselves from the path of the thundering kand. Some found themselves able to accomplish this, yet many fought, tripped, and fell in my path, fearful fodder to be trampled underfoot. Considering the frailty of the legs of the kan, I thought it unwise to allow them to fall among the struggling mass, therefore I jumped the beast above them, touching not a single one, my warriors taking to the air in a like manner. Onward we rode, the shouts falling away behind us, the ways being hastily cleared before us, for we rode to the gates of the city, the gates of freedom.

Many of my warriors voiced the Hosta battle cry as we rode, passing happily both cloth-hung dwellings and staring city folk alike, yet was our happiness not to last long. Although the light of the fey was still strong above us, the gates to the city stood closed and barred, many males in leather and metal afoot before them. Even as we thundered up, reluctantly drawing rein, other males ran to stand beside those who already kept us from freedom, and I noted with sinking heart that none of the males were armed with even so much as a length of wood. How, then, were we to fight our way clear, if the males bore no weapons which we might take as our own?

My warriors milled about in uncertainty; however, we were not this easily defeated. "Hosta warriors!" I shouted, pointing toward the males. "Attack!"

With a howl of freedom frustrated, my warriors dismounted and raced toward the waiting males, following the track of their war leader. The males stood, hands up, grins upon their faces, happily anticipating contact with Hosta, till the contact proved less pleasant than their anticipation. With full weight of our movement did we fall upon them, bringing grunts of pain as our numbers drove them into the heavy wood of the gates. The male before me grasped me to him, attempting to hold my clawing hands and teeth from their targets, only to release me again as another of my warriors threw herself upon him with a will, attempting to take out his eyes. Shouts and cursing sounded all about us, as well as cries of pain and vexation, yet was I able, in a brief moment of peace, to examine the gate. Though the wide bar of metal had been run through its retaining slots, posing no problem of removal, it had also been secured with chain, the heavy links of which held the bar fast in position, the chain itself being clasped to the wood beyond the bar. Futilely did I pull at this chain, furious at its refusal to yield, then was I pulled from the chain in turn, by a male who then stood himself before the chain, determined to defend it. Over and over did my warriors and I attempt to pass the males, desperate to do battle with the gate itself, yet was this not to be. More and more of the males gathered, adding their strength to the battle, and then came the host of warriors and hunters whose mounts we had taken, and great, indeed, was the anger of these males. I knew naught of it till I was taken by the hair and forced from the gate, and then I saw that it was the fist of Ceralt which held me so, fury ablaze in his light eyes. Much did I wish to escape his hold and his fury, but this, too, was not to be. Stumbling and struggling was I taken from the gate, my warriors, by twos and threes, also taken, and not long was it before peace was restored to the area.

Galiose and his males had also ridden up, and he sat upon his large, black kan, surveying the battlefield that was, a grim look upon his visage. Many of the males from before the gates stood limply, their strength having been overtaxed by our assault, and not at all pleased was Galiose by their appearance. His dark eyes looked about at still struggling Hosta, and then finally came to rest upon me.

"The wenches act as one at the bidding of their leader," said Galiose in a loud voice. "Therefore does the High Seat decree that they be punished as one, their leader foremost in her punishment, and then all are to be kept from the others, till some measure of control has been established upon them. You men are to see to this, and right hastily."

Those with warriors in hand then made their way to the kand, and briefly did I see Telion struggling with a furious Larid, before Ceralt threw me to the leather seat of his kan. I attempted to free myself of his grip, a matter as futile as ever, and then we rode from the gates, my Hosta still captive within them. Surely would I have given my own freedom to assure that of my warriors', yet was my own freedom no longer mine with which to trade. Ceralt guided his kan upon the way, speaking no word, though his arms were hard about me, full evidence of his anger. We rode from my warriors, and that gave me little pleasure.

Fully to the broad way leading to Galiose's dwelling did we ride, yet were we not to continue the entire distance. A small dwelling stood to the right of the way, and to this dwelling did we go. The city folk we had passed stood with heads shaking with disapproval, yet did this seem most foolish of them. Were Hosta to be taken captive, then submit to their captors as though slave-women? Never had that been done, and never would city males see such an action, yet still did they show disapproval.

The dwelling was not so large as that of Vistren, indeed was it considerably smaller, though it was far larger than the home tents of the Hosta. Still without a word did Ceralt pull me from the kan, and his fist fixed firmly in my hair, was I taken within. Ceralt strode along with wide steps, and some difficulty did I experience in matching his stride. Up the steps to the entrance we went, through the door to the interior, left along the interior area to further steps, and again up these further steps as well. Such rapid climbing was forced upon me by Ceralt that I was barely able to take note of the female who had appeared at our entrance. An older female was she, though still blond of hair, and much surprise did she show as I was quickly taken past her. With the steps ascended, we again moved to the right, and Ceralt thrust me within the doorway to a room, then threw the door to behind me, with the sound of a bar being slid to rest coming last. The room was dark, no windows being in evidence, and I made my way back to the door to assure myself of its refusal to swing. No light came to me within the room, yet was I able to feel the softness of a cloth beneath my feet, smell the lingering odor of strange, sweet scents, and hear the receding footsteps of Ceralt. Much disturbed was I at this further captivity, yet I only seated myself upon the cloth, for nothing else was I able to do. I looked about at the darkness, and recalled the presence of the Crystals within the city, and there was a bit of chill to the darkness.

Not too long was it before footsteps came again, and Ceralt reappeared at the door, the strange female behind him. In one hand Ceralt carried a pot, the other hand being full of a small, slim torch, and the female drew the door closed again behind him, and barred it. By the light of the small torch did Ceralt place the pot upon a narrow platform, and then proceeded to light the candles which hung about the room. Much yellow silk was thereby revealed to me, it being hung upon the walls, and laid upon the large, odd platform which the room contained. Such a platform had been called "bed" by Telion, yet was this platform of a lesser size than the first, and also did it lack the contrivance above the other. To the right of this platform was a small, round one with reflecting surface, and combs and small pots adorned its top. The room, perhaps four paces by four, contained much of what was to be found in that of Galiose's dwelling, and I cared as little for it as I had cared for the other.

Ceralt finished with the last of the candles, and then he threw the slim torch to the room's fireplace before turning to regard me. His regard contained little warmth, therefore did I sit the straighter in my place, my head held high as befitted a warrior of the Midanna. A sound of vexation came from him, and he stepped closer to stand above me.

"I wager you await the punishment Galiose spoke of," said he, his head bent forward so that he might regard me. "I believe I recognize the fixity of purpose in your eyes, the determination to allow none of the punishment to reach you."

"A warrior of the Hosta of the Midanna cares nothing for the doings of city males," I informed him coldly. "Your beatings shall be looked upon as those of Bariose were, and accepted with a similar silence."

"That remains to be seen," murmured Ceralt, and then he

turned to the pot which he had fetched. He brought it to me
with a determined look about him, and easily did the odor of
it inform me of its contents. A broth of nilno it contained,
and though I wished none of it, nearly all was spilled down
my throat by Ceralt. I fought and struggled till the last of it
was within me, then did I feel the onset of a great weariness.
Ceralt had released me and moved from where he had
perched to pour the broth within me, and I attempted to raise
myself from the cloth, yet found such simple action difficult.
Dizzily did the mists swirl about me, to a lesser extent than
upon the trail, though with enough of a strength to drain me
of purpose and will. I shook my head in an attempt to rid
myself of the mists, yet they clung firmly about me, and Ceralt chuckled.

"The drug is an excellent one," said he, "much superior to
that which you wenches are fond of. It allows for a greater
range of activity, which you are now to learn of."

He stood again before me, and his words came clearly
through the mists. I lifted my hand, as though to hold him
away, but he bent and took me by the arms, and lifted me
easily to my feet.

"The first matter to be attended to is your feeding," said
he, his arms holding me to him, my head upon his chest.
With the coming of the mists, my reluctance to be touched
by him had departed, and much pleasure was there in being
held so. Deep within, I felt it as humiliation, yet was I unable
to deny the pleasure. "Lodda shall shortly bring your gruel,"
said Ceralt, "and when it arrives, you shall partake of it as a
good wench should. Nod your head to show that you shall
obey me."

Sooner would I have professed myself slave, yet, to my
horror, my head nodded as though moved by the word of
Ceralt! I knew not what was about, for my head had nodded
against my will, and a shadow of disturbance crossed my
mind.

"My good, obedient Jalav," Ceralt murmured in approval,
his hand stroking my back. "You shall eat your gruel, and
then shall you be punished. You have earned a good hiding,
have you not? Nod your head to show that you wish to be
punished."

Again my head moved of its own accord, up and down,
firmly agreeing to Ceralt's words. A small moan escaped me

then, for deep within the mists, I knew I did not wish Ceralt's punishment, and again Ceralt chuckled.

"The drug does not allow you your own will, Jalav," said he quite softly. "In all things you shall obey me, as though you were slave in truth. I have lessened the amount so that you may be well aware of all happenings, for this is to be part of your punishment. Study the happenings well, so that the memory of them may long remain with you. Ah! Lodda comes."

I was then aware of a sound at the door, and Ceralt turned a bit so that I might see the entrance of the unknown female. She carried a pot of the awful mixture I had been fed so often, and her face wore a smile of contentment. Briskly, she approached us where we stood, and her head nodded.

"Quite nutritious," said she, raising the pot toward us. "I had not thought it so, yet I now approve. Are you to feed her, or shall I?"

"I shall feed her," said Ceralt, moving to a yellow-silk covered seat, and placing me therein. "I shall not require your aid till the new light, therefore you may retire to your own quarters."

"As you wish," nodded the female, and then handed the pot to him. "Come the new light, she and I shall become acquainted. Though she appears rather larger than I had imagined, I anticipate little difficulty."

"I anticipate much difficulty," said Ceralt, his eyes again upon me, "though perhaps certain of it may be avoided. We shall see."

The female seemed puzzled by his words, but she shrugged them off and again departed the room. Ceralt took no note of her going, for he had pulled another seat before mine, and had seated himself, the pot held easily in his hands. The mists clouded my thinking, yet clearly did I see and feel, more clearly, perhaps, than usual. Ceralt sat upon the yellow-silk seat, his dark green covering sharp against it, his light eyes filled with an expression I could not read, his broad, dark face softened beneath his wild thatch of hair. Again did I feel for him more than desire, a feeling which filled me with fear as well. To no male might a Hosta belong, yet did I joy in the presence of Ceralt, rage though I did, deep within. Ceralt took a long, flat bit of wood from the pot, and stirred the contents a bit before raising it toward me.

"Open your mouth, Jalav," said he, "for your gruel is now

before you. My good, obedient Jalav shall eat her gruel properly, for she does not wish to disobey Ceralt."

To my fury, my mouth opened, and Ceralt placed the bit of wood therein, from which I took the gruel as bidden. Though with all of my strength did I attempt to refuse it, little by little was it fed me, Jalav doing naught save swallowing to the urging of Ceralt. Humiliating was his treatment of a Hosta war leader, and degrading through purpose, for continuously did he speak to me as though to a child or slave, and was I able to do nothing save obey. The gruel was given to the very last of it, and then did Ceralt put the pot aside with a smile.

"Such a lovely, obedient wench is Jalav," said Ceralt, as I frothed within, nearly with madness. "Yet Jalav is not always as obedient, therefore must she now be punished." His eyes came to me again, and had a stern look. "Jalav shall feel each stroke of her punishment," said Ceralt quite clearly, "and she shall cry out with the pain of it as would any other wench who is so punished. Nod your head to show that you shall obey me."

For a third time my head nodded of itself, and a greater horror possessed me. Could it be that by so offhand a manner, I would be made to cry out as any city slave-woman? I could not countenance the thought, yet was the reality an even greater horror. Ceralt fetched a length of leather, the like of which he had used upon me a number of times before, yet never before had the pain been so great. The strokes forced cries of anguish from my lips, and at Ceralt's command, tears flowed from my eyes as well. More than soundly was I beaten with the leather, cries and tears a constant accompaniment, till Ceralt finally released me, then held me to him for a moment. The beating had been a terrible thing, and my legs refused to carry my weight, therefore did Ceralt raise me in his arms. I wished to beat at him, push from his touch, run from the very sight of him, but the mists closed more tightly about me, holding me still, and thence to the darkness.

Quite slowly did I waken and stretch toward the fire which burned in the fireplace. I remembered the happenings of the fey previous, a memory which would stay till Mida called. Never before had I been made to feel such humiliation, and the rage I felt toward Ceralt was a burning thing, a burning which would best be cooled in blood. Perhaps not a pool of his lifeblood, yet a pool which would give him a taste of the pain I had felt, the pain given me at his hand. No male must be allowed to treat a Hosta so, and the light would come that Ceralt heartily regretted his actions. Jalav was no slave, that she might be treated so!

I stretched out flat upon the cloth, feeling the mists completely gone, and then shivered with memory of a previous awakening. Ceralt had felt the need to torture me yet further, for he had placed me upon the odd platform—called bed—where I might awaken with great fear. I had awakened with fear, yet had I been able to move quickly to the cloth before the fire, and had not cried out with the fear. I was pleased with this, pleased that Ceralt had not caused me to voice my fear, and pleased that I had been able to move to the cloth. My sleeping leather was long behind me, but the soft, yellow cloth was an adequate substitute.

I sat up by the fire, and wondered briefly as to the future of the Hosta. That Mida was displeased with her warriors was apparent; still I had no way of knowing whether her displeasure might in some manner be assuaged. Were it possible to do so, the Hosta might once again ride free, for never would the city males hold us against the will of Mida. I thought again upon the Crystals, and felt that perhaps it might in some way be possible to free them of the golden air. In truth, I wished to have nothing further to do with the Crystals, yet was I war leader of the Hosta, and bound to secure the freedom of my warriors, if that was possible. Should the opportunity arise, I would again attempt to free the Crystals, and put all memory of the first attempt from my mind. My hand quivered briefly, a thing which brought anger, and the anger did well to steady my hand. Anger was a more fitting emotion for a warrior, and Jalav was a warrior.

I then rose to my feet and searched for my clan covering; it was nowhere to be seen. It had been gone upon my awakening on the platform, but I had still been too deep within the mists to be concerned. Now I felt annoyance at its disappearance, and my hand raised to my life sign as I looked about the room, then did a sudden terror seize me, for my hand did not come upon my life sign! Quickly I stared down to where it should lie, but only my breasts and futilely grasping hand did I see! My life sign was gone, leather thong and wood alike, and I knew not where it had gone!

Frantically did I tear the room apart, throwing things

about in haste and misery. My life sign had never before been far from me, and my soul quivered with a fear which my mind echoed. How was I to find the Realm of Mida, should my soul be bereft of life sign? How was I to face an enemy sword, with my life sign not about my neck? What if I should now be called, and I unprotected by my life sign? A sob of hopelessness escaped from me, for my life sign did not seem within the room, and I knew not where it could be.

Then I recalled the battle at the gates, and thought, perhaps, that the leather might have parted there. The strip, though sound, had not been new, and not beyond thought was it that my life sign lay there. I determined to go immediately, and hurried to the door, fearing that it would be barred, yet did it swing wide at the touch of my hand. With much relief, I departed from the room, and quickly descended the steps. The entrance of the dwelling was before me, yet just as I reached it, the female Lodda was also before me.

"Has dread Sigurr taken your wits, girl?" she demanded, standing herself before the entrance. "You cannot prance about in only a smile of welcome! Return to your room, and I shall fetch clothing for you!"

I then recalled my lack of clan colors, and paused in annoyance. "I shall await my clan covering here," said I in decision. "Fetch it quickly, for there is something I must do."

"Fetch it quickly, indeed!" said this Lodda, her fists upon her hips in annoyance. Although she stood half a head below me, something about her suggested size. In truth, she was larger than other city females I had seen, and she seemed well aware of it. "You are not to order me about in such a manner, girl," said she, "for it is I who am here to instruct you! That bit of cloth shall no longer be worn by you, for it is extremely improper to appear so! Return to your room, and I shall bring a proper gown!"

Much angered did the female seem, with little reason for her anger; however, I did not lack reasons for the anger I felt. "The Hosta clan colors may be taken from a warrior's still body," said I quite coldly, "and in no other way! I shall see my clan covering returned—and in good order!—else shall I see the manner in which city slave-women bear their pain! Jalav shall not speak again upon the matter."

Again her mouth had begun to open in protest, but I wished to hear no further of her prattling. Impatiently, I brushed her from my path and approached the entrance;

however I was not to push without. Two arms encircled me from behind—Ceralt's. A chuckle came from him as I struggled, turning to gasp as my heel struck his ankle.

"None of that, wench!" said he quite sharply, and his arms tightened more closely about me. "Where do you think to go this moment, bare as a babe in the moment of birth?"

"I go where I must!" said I to the malo. "Release me immediately!"

"I fear Jalav seeks another hiding," said he, moving me from the entrance. "You may speak to me of your desperate errand, else you may return to your room for further punishment. Do you wish to speak?"

His arms loosened, and I turned to him to again demand release, yet the words were lost as my mouth gaped, and my eyes widened in disbelief. About his neck, upon its leather, hung my life sign, whole as it had been, and entirely unlost! Great joy filled me then, and relief as well, and I raised my hand to the guardian of my soul, saying, "Mida be praised! I had thought it gone! Give it here, hunter."

"I think not," said Ceralt, his hand quickly upon mine, disallowing the touch of my life sign. "It was explained to me, by a fellow not far from your camp, that Midanna may not stray from the presence of their life signs. Should you wish to be close to your life sign, Jalav, you must keep well within sight of me, for with me shall your life sign remain."

I could only shake my head at such a thought, and stare wide-eyed at Ceralt. Surely the hunter jested, for had it not been he who had returned my life sign to me when I had thought my life forfeit to him? Would he now, in the midst of my enemies, withhold the protection of my soul?

"Surely, you jest," said I rather shakily, overly aware of his hand upon mine. "The life sign is mine, and I would have it returned."

"I shall be pleased to do so," said he, most soberly. "Should I receive in its stead your word that you shall not seek escape, the bit of wood may be returned upon the instant."

Again I stared, for how was I to give my word in such a manner? I was Hosta, and Hosta may not remain captive to males!

"Perhaps you would care to consider the matter," said Ceralt, an oily smoothness to his tone. "You may join my meal the while, and think about which you would rather do without—your life sign or your word. Come with me."

He then urged me toward one of several doors in the area, and I, quite woodenly, accompanied him. The female Lodda stood aside indignantly, though I had little care for the city female. My life sign lay about Ceralt's neck, to be returned to me only should I give my word that I would not seek escape, yet to give such a word was impossible! Oh, Mida! Have you abandoned your warrior entirely? Is her soul to be lost through your anger? Such questions did I address to Mida, yet unanswered were they fated to be.

The room to which Ceralt led me contained nothing but red silks upon the walls, a large, square platform, and two seats before the platform, one at the left side of the square, one at its front. The seats, too, were of red silk, and Ceralt led me to that which stood before the square, himself taking the seat to the left. The platform bore pots and metal squares, each containing something to be eaten, yet had I lost all interest in such things. My life sign lay clear to my eye, yet how was I to reclaim it?

"Lodda is an excellent cook," remarked Ceralt quite casually, drawing the provender to him. "Should you wish to partake of any of it, you have merely to ask—in a proper manner."

My eyes raised to him, for his voice had changed, and he nodded with a grin.

"Quite right," said he, tasting of a meat which looked to be nilno. "You must ask politely to be allowed the food, else shall it be refused you. You must learn the manners of a proper wench, for now you be of the cities."

Miserably, I turned my eyes from him, reflecting that my sins must indeed be great. Had I erred in believing that Mida had sent me from her Crystals? Had I been bidden instead to free them from the golden air, even though my life be forfeit? Such must indeed be so, for now I was captive to males in an accursed city, bereft of weapons, life sign, clan colors, and soon, perhaps, my dignity as well. Mida's warrior had failed her, and now had the warrior been cast out of her shield, to die, ignobly, the final death. My soul had been found wanting, and soon it was to be no more.

"Here is her gruel," said the female Lodda, appearing beside me quite suddenly. She thrust a pot of the mixture before me, the sharpness of her actions an indication of her continuing anger. "I feel I must protest her undressed state," said this female to Ceralt, who continued his meal unconcerned. "Her appearance is most improper, and I insist she be properly clothed if I am to instruct her!"

"She shall be clothed when such clothing is requested by her," said Ceralt calmly, and he took a handful of temeer nuts. "Should she wish to leave the house, or remain when callers arrive, she shall be sure to request the clothing, else she shall be sent to her room. You are to begin with her when her meal is done, therefore I would have you prepare yourself."

"I am already prepared," said the female with a sniff, her head high. "She shall learn her lessons, as have others before her, have no fear of that."

"We shall see," said Ceralt as he had upon a previous occasion, his jaws busily working the temeer nuts. Long had it been since last I had tasted of temeer nuts, yet memory of their saltiness did not draw me from my misery to a wish for them. I wished only for my life sign and my freedom; neither was to be forthcoming.

The female Lodda departed once more, and Ceralt leaned forward to move the pot of gruel more closely to me. "Eat your gruel, Jalav," said he, "for there are many things which you must learn this fey."

"I wish none of it," said I to him, moving the pot again from me. "I have already learned many things this fey, and as my soul is to be lost, it is best lost without such as that."

"Your soul has not yet been lost," grinned Ceralt, his leg upon the arm of his seat. "You may eat the gruel of your own free will, else I shall see the drug within you again, though this time you shall not be controlled by me. Lodda shall see to your feeding and punishment, and sharply shall her leather be applied. She is a teacher of ignorant young ladies, and has little patience for disobedience. Do you wish to be done so, and before others as well? Lodda has told me that for a punishment to be complete and proper, it must be administered before as many onlookers as possible. I believe she had the city's center in mind. . . ."

Ceralt was much amused, and he laughed softly, and I was without the will even to feel fury. My honor would be taken from me by such an act, and I would be unable to reclaim it even in death. To see my soul lost then would be proper, yet did I know full well that Ceralt would not allow my immediate death. I had sinned greatly, and now Mida had declared my punishment, for I had not freed her Crystals with my life. I took the pot of gruel, and raised it to my lips, for my life and actions no longer had meaning.

"Excellent, Jalav," said Ceralt in approval, as I returned the emptied pot to the platform. "Go you now to your room, and Lodda shall be with you shortly."

Silently I rose to my feet, left the room, and ascended the steps with a slow, uncaring tread. For a warrior's life to no longer have meaning was a cold, empty thing, yet was my punishment well deserved. I had allowed fear to drive me from Mida's Crystals, fear of a pain the like of which I had never experienced, fear of a darkness the like of which I had never before seen. Fear was not a thing to be felt by a warrior, yet I had felt it, and scurried before it. Deep was my failure to Mida's will, and full, now, was my understanding of it. I was shamed, and empty, and ever would I remain so.

The room was as I had left it, and wearily did I seat my-self before the fire, so that I might contemplate its flickering depths. My knees drawn up before me, I studied the dance of the flickering flames, an orange and blue and yellow salute, its arms reaching upward to Mida with joy. Not again would the arms of Jalav reach so, for Mida wished none of her for-evermore. Empty was the life of Jalav, and empty, too, was her heart.

"What has been done here?" demanded the voice of Lodda. "Naught stands straight save the walls!" With angry step did the female enter, and walked directly to me. I kept my eyes with the fancy-free fire, and spoke to her not at all.

"Before all else shall this clutter be straightened!" came the female's voice from above me. "You do not now dwell in the caves from whence you came! Perhaps there was your sloven-liness tolerated, the filth and squalor your manner of living, yet here there are civilized folk, who shall have none of it! Up on your feet, girl, and I shall direct your efforts!"

The fire still drew me with the freedom of its movement, a freedom which was never again to be mine. How I longed for the woods and the Hosta home tents, the Tower of the Keeper, the laughter of the little ones in the care of the At-tendants. How round had the eyes of the warriors-to-be grown, when the war leader had ridden into their view! How eager were they to be taught the ways of the Hosta, so that they, too, might one fey be war leader! Now all, all was gone, the Hosta mere captives, their war leader done. Not again could I hold my head with pride, for Mida had withdrawn from me.

"Do you hear me?" demanded the female with vigor. "On your feet this instant, else shall I teach you the meaning of disobedience!" I still had no wish to speak with her, for I knew not what she was about, nor cared, yet did she fail to await an answer. "Very well!" said she quite rapidly. "As it is punishment you wish, it is punishment you shall have!"

Though her footsteps withdrew, what she would fetch made little difference. Ceralt had given me to her so that I might, with his approval, receive pain. Were I to attempt to deny this pain, the drug would be given me again, to make me slave to her. Already was there pain that Ceralt would do so, yet I had not released him from the chains of Vistren. The thought of this was surely with him, though I had somehow not expected—Ah, Mida. Your warrior is indeed a fool.

Briskly did the female return, and pause once more behind me. My hair was thrown to my right shoulder, then stingingly was I struck across the back with some manner of stick. "There!" said the female with a great deal of satisfaction as I straightened slightly at the blow. "Do you now wish to obey, or will you have more?"

The blow, though painful, was hardly unbearable, and as it was the wish of Ceralt that I be beaten, the matter would be seen to sooner or later. Little need was there for the female's pretense, and no need at all that I join her pretense. I therefore spoke not at all, and the blow was repeated, and repeated again, the pain that Ceralt wished for me coming quite freely. Without a sound did I accept the pain, so that I might be spared the shame of being made slave, and the female grunted with her effort. For many reckid did the blows come, and then was there again surcease.

"You are a stubborn young thing, that I'll grant," said the female then, somewhat out of breath. "Yet I have great faith in the power of the rod to drive the stubbornness from you. I shall return in no more than a hin, and should the room not have been seen to, you may expect a further acquaintance with the rod."

Her steps then took her from me, and I sat as I was without moving, for movement would have increased the pain. I had been well beaten by her, that I'll grant, and at last I lay my cheek to the cloth and stretched out full before the fire. I had wished to call to Mida when the blows grew heavy, yet had I refrained, for I knew my call would not have been answered. I lay alone before the fire, truly alone, and shivered somewhat despite the warmth.

Twice again did the female Lodda come to me, and twice again was I touched with pain. The second time she fetched with her something large and white, easily marked with charcoal. Meaningless lines did she make with the charcoal, insisting the lines held much meaning, yet was I beyond the ability to heed such nonsense. Silently did I turn my back upon her, and with much fury did she beat me, insisting that I would know the meaning of the meaningless, else would I know only pain. Pain was already well known to me; however it would become even more familiar, said this female, when Ceralt returned to the dwelling. He would frown upon my lack of obedience, and see me beaten further. "He shall use a lash!" said she, striking at me where I lay upon the cloth, my eyes shut against all sight. "Do you wish to feel a lash, girl? Obey me, obey me now!"

"Hold!" came Ceralt's voice, and the blows ceased to rain upon me. "What do you do here, woman?"

As I writhed upon the cloth, the female said, "I have been able to do nothing with her, Ceralt! Her stubbornness is beyond belief, and a lash will be necessary. Have you one of your own, or shall I have one purchased?"

No answer did Ceralt make, and then his hand was upon my arm. I moved as I had not intended, for his fingers had closed where the stick had touched many times, and quickly his hand withdrew.

"I was led to believe you used only the leather," said Ceralt, a tightness to his voice. "How many times have you done her so?"

"More times than with any other I was engaged to teach!" replied the female in annoyance. "But once was sufficient with the others, yet I knew full well that the leather would not do with this one! Even the rod has not reached her, therefore must it be the lash!"

"Must it indeed," said Ceralt quite softly, and then I heard his movement. "Take your things and leave at once," said he, "else I shall not be responsible for your safety!"

"How dare you address me so!" gasped the female in outrage. "Was I not engaged to teach her the ways of a well-bred woman? To be obedient and docile, to clean, to cook, to read? How else might such a thing be accomplished with an ignorant, filthy savage?"

"Another word," said Ceralt chokingly, "and I shall happily forget that you be female! This—filthy, ignorant savage—is more precious to me than my life, and surely it was at Sigurr's bidding that I gave to another to do what I was to have done myself! Now, get out!"

"Gladly," responded the female icily. "My time may be more profitably spent elsewhere! Allow me to say how well suited you and she appear to be!"

With angry steps the female departed, and once again was Ceralt beside me. "Jalav, forgive me," said he in a whisper, his hand upon my face. "Had I known she would treat you so—Ah, Sigurr take her, this is not what I wished you to learn! There has already been too much pain in your life, and the fault here is mine alone. Not again shall you be beaten, this I swear!"

I had no wish to open my eyes, for the sight of Ceralt was pain in itself. I lay upon the cloth, speaking no word, wishing with all my being that I might call upon Mida. My soul ached with the need to call, yet Mida wished no more of me. Ceralt sighed and rose to his feet, then he departed the room. I lay without movement till his return, then drank whatever he put to my lips. I did not care what it might be, though it was something I had never before had. Smoothly did it slide within me, and nothing else do I recall.

17.

Renth—and the
device is sought

I sat upon the red silk seat, awaiting the pot of gruel to be placed before me. Two feyd had passed from the departure of the female Lodda, two feyd in which I had not been allowed from my room. I cared little that I was kept so, and spoke no word to Ceralt when he came. The hunter had many times fetched a herbal mixture to be applied to my back, and had seemed quite distressed that I would not lie upon the platform called bed. Time and again had he placed me thereupon, and time and again had I removed myself to the cloth by the fire, where I might more easily watch the dance of the flames. The gruel had been brought to me also by Ceralt, yet was there a young female about, one who tended to the hunter's dwelling. No word had she addressed to me when in my room, and no word had I addressed to her. The pain of the beating had gone from me, yet the pain of emptiness remained, and no word did I wish to address to anyone.

Upon the third fey, Ceralt had come to take me from the room, and had led me to the place of red silk seats and square platform. Many and varied were the foods piled thereon, and a bloody chunk of nilno, as well. I sat upon the red silk seat as Ceralt had placed me, and awaited the pot of gruel that would be put before me.

"Now," said Ceralt heartily as he took his own seat. "See what we have here, Jalav! Hot bread, spicy pemma roots,

293

wrettan eggs—and nilno! Which of those do you wish to have first?"

I awaited the gruel and said nothing,

"See the wrettan eggs," said Ceralt, turning my face with his hand. "Almost were two hunters lost in the fetching of them. Clear to the top of a tree did we climb, risking life and limb, only to find that the wrettan had chosen to nest in the tree beside ours. Down we climbed once more, and up the proper tree, only to be set upon by the she-wrettan, returning to the nest! With much difficulty were the eggs at last secured, and carefully did we bring them, only to nearly drop them just at the gates! After such a perilous quest, surely you cannot refuse them?"

The hunter's eyes were entreatingly upon me, yet did I remove my face from his hand and say nothing.

"Jalav, you are merely a pale shadow!" Ceralt cried, turning my face to him again. "You say not a word, eat the gruel without protest, and grow thinner with each passing hin! The pain of seeing you so is beyond bearing! What may I do?"

There was nothing any might do, for who may speak with Mida of one from whom she had turned? Though my face was held tightly by Ceralt, my eyes dropped with sightlessness.

"Very well," said Ceralt with great sadness. "Sooner would I see you gone from me than dead beside me. You may have your life sign, your freedom, and a kan. I shall see you to the gates and release you."

Where once such words would have filled me with joy, then they brought only a very great pain. Where was I to be released to, with Mida's face turned from me? My failure was clear, my condemnation certain.

"Do you hear my words?" asked Ceralt with a shake to my face. "I have said I shall release you!" Naught save silence greeted him, therefore was I released again, and Ceralt leaned farther back in his seat. "By Sigurr's pointed ears, she hears not," said he in a mutter. "This must be seen to."

He raised himself from the seat and departed the room, yet was he to return quite soon. He then seated himself once more and stared upon me, and so did we remain for nearly a hin. I had found the light of Mida to be high when first I had entered the room, and now it receded toward darkness. The silence was broken by the arrival of Telion, who entered followed by the female bearing a red-silk seat upon which he might sit. The seat was placed at the square side to the right of mine, and the female wordlessly departed as Telion sat wearily in the seat and reached for a wrettan egg. I saw that he, too, wore a life sign, and knew it for Larid's.

"My apologies for not having come sooner," said Telion as he cracked the egg, "I was in the midst of a battle, and could not, on the moment, depart."

"A battle?" asked Ceralt with a frown. "I knew nothing of a battle."

"Would that I could say the same," sighed Telion, reaching now for some grains of salt to put upon the wrettan egg. "This fey was to be when my little flame would give over her bit of cloth for the gown of a civilized woman. The gown was a lovely blue, to match her eyes, and I had vowed that this fey would I see it upon her." Again he sighed, then tasted well of the egg. "The little flame liked not the gown, the blue, nor the concept," said he about a mouthful. "Roundly was I reviled for suggesting the color of the Hitta for a Hosta warrior, above the foolishness of so great and heavy a thing as a slave-woman covering. The gown was thrown about my head to accompany the abuse, and Larid now sits as Jalav does—save that Larid smarts quite a bit from a hiding. It has been my sincere hope that you have had some success with Jalav that I might emulate."

"I truly begin to believe that never shall there be success to be had with Jalav," muttered Ceralt, he being slid low within his seat, his legs out straight before him. "Would you care to speak with her?"

Telion's brows raised somewhat, and he turned to me. "Of what am I to speak with you, Jalav?" he asked.

I gazed upon the life sign of Larid and said nothing.

"You see," said Ceralt as Telion's brows lowered and knotted into a frown. "She has been so since the departure of that blood-kin to Sigurr whom I so foolishly engaged to instruct her. The harpy used a rod upon her, and she only lay there beneath the blows."

"Have you asked what disturbs her?" said Telion, peering more closely at me.

"As she will not speak," said Ceralt with some annoyance, "perhaps you would care to suggest how I might do that. She does nothing but eat the gruel given her, and stare upon the fire in her room!"

"She eats the gruel," Telion echoed thoughtfully. "I like

not the implications of that, yet perhaps it may aid us. Have you renth?"

"Certainly I have renth!" snapped Ceralt, straightening in his seat. "Do you think to find the answer in a flagon?"

"Not in one flagon," said Telion, resting his arms upon the platform as he gazed directly upon Ceralt. "In many flagons—which we three shall share."

Ceralt grinned and struck the platform with a fist. "An excellent suggestion!" He nodded as Telion grinned. "Perhaps, one might even say, inspired! Inala! Fetch three flagons, and a large pitcher of renth!"

The city female called Inala entered as bidden, bearing the renth and three tall pots. Ceralt and Telion seemed most pleased with the prospect of imbibing renth, for they rubbed their hands in anticipation, and eagerly poured the renth, then shared it. I, too, was given a pot they had filled, and as I cared nothing for what occurred about me, I drank the renth as Ceralt insisted. Again and again were the pots refilled, and as the hind passed, the males did, from time to time, attempt to speak with me—in vain. As I had not fed, I felt some slight warmth from the renth, yet the thin, weakly stuff did nothing else to lighten the burden of my life. By the coming of darkness, the female Inala had renewed the larger supply of renth a number of times, and the hunter and warrior seemed quite taken with it. Much difficulty had they in pouring, and much renth adorned the top of the cleared platform in pools. Finally had Ceralt most carefully filled his pot to the very top, and then passed the renth to Telion before placing both hands upon the pot, raising it slowly, and bringing it to himself in a manner most shaky. Telion sat, the renth unnoticed in his hand, and his eyes followed each of Ceralt's movements with fascination. In truth, I, too, felt curious as to what he was about, for his lips reached for the gently swinging renth, yet was it carried again and again, beyond their reach. With mouth ajar did he pursue the renth, and it was found to be continuously ahead of him. Telion made a sound of mournful commiseration, and then was his hand firmly before the pot, returning it in the direction of Ceralt. As a rushing river, swollen full with the growth of flood, returns to its bed and banks, so did the renth return to Ceralt, covering him with half its presence, yet was he then able to fasten his lips upon the pot and drink. Telion nodded happily, then he partook of the renth in his hand, disdaining the use of his own pot. I had but recently finished the renth given me, and it seemed I was not to be given more.

Ceralt replaced his pot upon the platform, dabbed gently at his lips with a cloth while seemingly unaware of the renth which soaked the whole of his covering, and then peered with difficulty upon Telion. "Has she spoken with you as yet?" he whispered rather loudly to Telion.

Telion took the renth from his mouth, expelled air sharply, then shook his head. "No," said he in the same manner of whisper. "Perhaps she is now too taken with renth to speak."

Ceralt blinked for a moment, then nodded once. "I shall see," said he most soberly, and his eyes attempted my direction. "Jalav," said he with a ghastly smile, "are you taken with renth?"

"No," said I, reflecting that it had been many kalod since even brewed renth had had the ability to best me. It has been said that my capacity for drink is Mida given, and perhaps this is so. Some few of my warriors do also possess the ability, yet truly few are they.

"She is not taken with renth," said Ceralt to Telion in the previous whisper. "Refill her flagon, and we may yet coax her to speech."

With a nod, Telion reached toward my pot with the renth, a similar ghastly smile upon his face. He poured quite carefully, spilling no more than a swallow, and then said, "Drink of the renth, Jalav. It shall do well for you."

"I do not feel the desire for more," said I, making no attempt to touch the pot, and then Telion gave me a stern look.

"You shall drink the renth as you are bidden!" said he, placing his arm in a wide pool of spilled renth. The stern look then turned sickly as he slowly inspected his dripping arm, yet he said in a mutter, "You must speak to us, therefore must you drink the renth. Should you fail to obey me, I shall take my leather to you as long ago promised."

"Never!" shouted Ceralt, jumping to his feet so rapidly that his seat flew away backward from him. "Never shall I allow her to be beaten again! Any who wish to beat her must first take *my* life! Draw your weapon, Telion!"

"I have no weapon," said Telion in distraction, seeking about himself for some manner of cloth to wipe his still dripping arm. "You are merely a hunter, Ceralt, and know not even when a warrior is disarmed. Remain with your spear and bow, and do not attempt the use of a warrior's weapons."

"Do you insinuate I know naught of a sword?" Ceralt demanded indignantly. "I am able to wield a sword as well as any warrior!"

"Hah!" shouted Telion, forgetful of his arm as he attempted to follow Ceralt's swaying movement with his head. "The hunter has not been born who is able to equal the meanest of warriors! The renth has obviously strengthened your self-image, and weakened your wits!"

"Weakened my wits!" echoed Ceralt, his eyes wide and disbelieving, anger growing within him. "For words such as those, you must pay with your blood!"

Telion's head had continued to follow Ceralt's movement as the hunter swayed to and fro, to and fro, and the male warrior seemed to pale somewhat from his efforts. "Do not—speak that word now," he said to Ceralt in a very low voice.

"Word?" shouted Ceralt angrily. "What word?"

"The—last word," responded Telion, swallowing heavily, sweat beaded upon his forehead.

Ceralt frowned a moment, then asked, "Do you refer to the word 'blood'?"

Upon hearing the forbidden word, Telion paled further, clapped his hand to his mouth, staggered to his feet, and hastened stumbling from the room. Ceralt frowned upon the abrupt departure, then muttered, "I fail to see the significance in the word blood. It is merely—" No further did he speak, for he seemed preoccupied with thought, then he, too, paled, and placed a shaking hand to his forehead. "Why must the room sway so?" he demanded weakly of the air, then he, too, made an abrupt departure. I watched him gone, then raised the final pot of renth and drained it slowly.

"Is it permitted that I now see to the spillage?" asked the female Inala from the entrance to the room.

I nodded my head without looking toward her, for I had a matter to think upon which had confused me. She moved silently to the platform and began to clean it, then she raised her head to grin at me.

"They are both in the midst of emptying themselves," said she with much amusement. "To see the city's chief hunter, and the High Seat's warrior advisor engaged so, is not usual. And it is surprising that you do not seem to share their urge."

"The renth lies heavy within me," I sighed, "yet do I feel naught save the need for sleep—though there is much doubt that sleep shall come."

The female lost her grin, and ceased in the midst of her cleaning. "You appear disturbed," said she quite softly. "I, too, am slave, yet would I offer what aid I may. Would you care to share whatever disturbs you?"

"The hunter, Ceralt, disturbs me," I said, my hand rubbing my eyes. "I have many times said that I have no understanding of males, and it seems that of Ceralt I have even less understanding." I hesitated briefly, then added, "Nor do I understand why I am speaking to you, a stranger, in such a manner."

"Each of us must have one with whom they may speak," said she, and I raised my eyes to see the seriousness within hers. She was no larger than other city slave-women, and now was I able to note the collar about her throat, the collar which had been hidden by her white, city-female covering. Her light brown hair found itself bound by small bits of metal, yet was she as untroubled as others by this. She stood, though clad in the collar of a slave, possessing a dignity which other city females lacked, and perhaps the renth aided in loosening my tongue somewhat.

"I—have strange feelings for Ceralt," said I, attempting to find the proper words, and also attempting to maintain a dignity of my own. "These feelings confuse me, for I am unable to know the reasons for what he does. There was, a city female before you, and Ceralt gave me to her so that she might cause me pain, yet was he prepared to do battle with Telion when Telion only mentioned the leather. I do not understand the desires and motivations of Ceralt!"

"There is little to understand," said the female Inala gently, and she came to place her arm about me. "I have heard what befell you at the hand of the mistress Lodda, and you are mistaken. The chief hunter Ceralt did not wish you beaten by her—that is why she was dismissed. The chief hunter has much strong feeling for you—and much gentle feeling. Already has he removed your collar, and I should not be surprised if he were to free you."

"I have not worn a collar," said I, my head shaking in the confusion about me. "I am captive to Ceralt, not slave, for surely Ceralt knows that Jalav may not be slave."

Inala's brown eyes seemed troubled. "I do not understand,"

she began, then she was lost in thought for a moment before continuing slowly. "Perhaps," said she, gazing into the distance, "perhaps the confinement and slave gruel and lack of clothing are only punishment. Yet for a man to treat a free woman so—" Her head shook. "Indeed, the chief hunter is a hard man. Have you no hope of appealing to the High Seat?"

"The High Seat Galiose has little reason to feel concern for Jalav," said I, much disturbed by what had been told me. Could it truly be that Ceralt had not wished for my pain at the hand of the female Lodda? That he was not concerned with my having left him enchained? The thought filled me with feelings I had little hope of evaluating, and weakly I said, "I do not understand why Ceralt challenged Telion. For what reason would he do so?"

Inala laughed softly. "Surely only a truly great love would cause a man to challenge so deadly a warrior as Telion," said she, much gladness upon her face. "Indeed, it seems that the captive has captured the captor."

My eyes closed briefly with the pain of such thought, and stiffly did I rise from the seat. "Such may not be," said I, looking down upon the female. "Even were it not contrary to the ways of Hosta, I am no longer of sufficient worth to be the concern of any, most especially not of one such as Ceralt." The female seemed quite saddened by my words, yet did a further thought come to me. I had failed Mida, and easily might it be seen that I must now attempt to repair the error. Should my life be forfeit in the attempt, my soul, too, would fade to naught, and that would be the best of the matter. No longer was I a proper Hosta warrior, for strange, unbidden feelings continuously presented themselves to me. Far better that Jalav be removed from the unknowable and exist no more.

I left the female and the room of red silk then, and ascended the steps to the room which had been given me. When I had pushed within, I became aware of a form upon the platform called bed. Ceralt lay there, deeply asleep, and haltingly did I approach him. He lay upon his side, his arm outstretched across the platform, his face unusually pale beneath the dark of his hair. I reached my hand out to touch his face, and he did not stir, not at the stroking of my fingers, nor at the withdrawal of them. So male was Ceralt, and so desirable, that a warrior found difficulty in keeping her hands from him, yet was he well taken by the renth, and therefore to be left untouched. I walked to the fire, and lay upon the cloth before it, there to pass the darkness, for with the beginning of the new light I would seek to do as Mida had bid me. Had I not had so much of the renth, I would have begun then, yet were some hind of sleep necessary to restore my thoughts to order. That I would pass these hind not far from Ceralt I had not dared hope, and well pleased was I to find it so. There was little to believe that my eyes would again touch him. I turned so that I might see him, and sleep found me positioned so.

The dwelling of Vistren seemed entirely untenanted, and silently empty before the pale beginnings of the new light. Carefully had I approached it, not caring to be seen by any who might be within, and now was there a door before me swinging easily to the touch of my hand. The same door I had entered once before gave me entry, and I was pleased to leave the heavy chill of the darkness without for the warmer darkness within. Truly had the chill intensified, and longingly did I wish for the warmth of Hosta lands. My clan covering, no matter how welcome its presence about my hips, did little to dispel the chill.

Still was the dwelling of Vistren, as still as Ceralt's had been when I had awakened. Ceralt had slept as soundly as ever, hearing naught of my departure, nor had the female Inala been disturbed by my searches. My clan covering was within the tiny, windowless room where she slept, among the bits and pieces of cloth folded in a corner. It was but the work of a moment to don it, and then did I leave the dwelling, my thoughts barely touching the life sign which hung about Ceralt's neck. I well knew that my soul was to be lost, and had come to accept the fact.

Vistren's dwelling contained naught of lit torches, yet had I little difficulty in recalling the direction. To the room of yellow silk did I go, and beyond through the farther door to the steps, and then to the floor upon which the device had been found. Neither ruined door had been repaired, and the second revealed the reason for such laxity. By the feeble glow of the small candle I had lit, was it easily seen that the device no longer sat where once it had been. Carefully did I seek about the room, yet was it nowhere to be seen. Deeply distressed did I feel then, refusing any relief, and then knew what was necessary. The entire dwelling must be searched.

Upon igniting a torch did I begin the search, to no avail. The device, in its cumbersome form, would not be easily hidden, yet nowhere was there trace of it. The new light was strong beyond the window beside the room I came to last, a room whose use was not easily seen. Bare of silks and floor covering was the room, the walls containing only paired metal cuffs, two hands of them, and very high. Then were the old traces of blood revealed by the torchlight, here and there upon the wooden floor, and no further explanation did I require. Vistren had held slaves, and well pleased was I that never again would he do so.

I extinguished the torch in a bucket of dirt, then seated myself beside the bucket, where I might take a moment to consider. The device bearing the Crystals could not have merely faded from view, therefore it must have been taken by someone. Vistren, dead, could not have seen to the matter, nor could those who had ridden from the city with the Hosta; however, there had been others within the room to learn of its existence. Telion had been there, and Galiose and his males, though Galiose seemed the most likely to have taken it. Galiose was leader within the city, called High Seat, and to his dwelling must the device have been carried. I cared little for the need, yet to Galiose's dwelling must I also take my search. I thought upon the wisdom of going with the light, then knew the effort would be futile. Much difficulty would there be with the males in leather and metal, and I, unarmed, would have small chance of besting them. Wisest would be to await true darkness, when the males found themselves touched by the wish for sleep. Then would their vigilance be less, and a shadow moving by them not be noted. I lay flat upon the floor, knowing the lack of all things edible within the dwelling and regretting it, and then forced myself to seek escape from chill and hunger within sleep.

Darkness was not far from coming when I awakened, therefore did I seat myself erect once more, and patiently await the passing hind. First came full darkness, then did the sounds from without grow still, and then did the Entry to Mida's Realm appear in the skies, and still I waited. When the Entry had once more departed, I rose to my feet, stretched briefly, then sought the door by which I had entered. The time had come to approach the dwelling of Galiose.

Many were the males in leather and metal about the dwell-

ing, yet were their eyes the eyes of city males and therefore
unseeing. To the bushes close by the dwelling I moved, passing near to a male who paused in his walk to stretch with
weariness before continuing on. Such a pause had been fool-
hardy, for it had been done in the darkness, between torches,
and had I had a weapon and wished his life, it would then
have been mine. Briefly I shrugged over the lacks of males,
then sought out the window which had once been left ajar.
What is done once is often done many times, and the window
did stand ajar once more, those within believing themselves
safe because of the presence of those without. Silently, I entered through the window, to find the blue cloth beneath my
feet and none about, therefore I hastened to the left, where a
long, darkened area was to be found, and began my search.

Again the hind passed, yet was the need for caution great.
No sign of the device did I come upon, and many folk were
about, at ease or asleep within rooms, for the most part, some
few walking about. At each sound of approach, I stepped
within shadows, those being caused by many of the torches
having been extinguished, and waited till the passerby had
gone his way. Once the passersby were two, a male of metal
and leather, and a female slave clad in the blue silk of Galiose. The male held the female by her wrist, taking her along
behind him as she attempted to fist the sleep from her eyes,
her steps hurried as she was made to match the pace of the
male. Neither saw me where I stood, yet was I able to see
that the male wore sword and dagger, and that interested me
greatly. Had I need of a weapon, I now knew where it was to
be had.

Each room of the lowest floor did I search, in some merely
glancing about, and then was I forced to the floor above.
Many rooms for sleep were to be found there, the slaves
asleep by their platform in the midst of the area, and quickly
I decided to seek elsewhere. Should the device be found in
such a place, surely it would be within the guarded rooms of
Galiose that it would lie, and should such be the case, I had
little hope of reaching it. Quickly, I passed the sleeping
slaves, for a farther set of steps was to be seen to the end of
their area.

Upon the third level was the floor cloth less grand, the silks
completely absent, and there was an air of use, rather than
neglect. Though the way was dim through lack of torches, I
was able to see the wood-covered walls, a smooth and pol-

ished wood, as I moved along. The air within a number of
rooms was heavily laden, filled with scents I could not iden-
tify, never before having come across them, yet was the
device not in view. Other things stood about on platforms,
items of glass and metal, some filled, some not, some con-
necting to another, others standing singly, and truth to tell, I
liked it not. Such things seemed unnatural, locked away from
the sight of Mida for fell purposes, and hurriedly did I leave
them to themselves. Again I carried a lighted candle, for a
torch was too difficult to extinguish, and I felt the presence of
others upon the level. Small murmurings came to me, of
voices from a distance, and most carefully did I move, so as
not to alert them.

Many reckid passed before I came upon the room, merely
one among others, yet lit somewhat by gently glowing
candles. My own candle I extinguished before moving inside,
and quickly was its presence in my hand forgotten, for to the
right, alone upon a wide platform, stood the device. Other,
smaller platforms stood before the wall, not far from it, and
upon these platforms were piles of leather and cloth. The
leather seemed to surround the cloth, perhaps protectively,
yet little thought did I give to it, for the end of my quest was
before me. The Crystals, cloudy in the golden air, drew me
toward them, and willingly did I go, at last raising my hand
to grasp one.

"No!" snapped a voice, and I whirled around. A male was
there, upon a seat behind a platform, and he gazed sternly at
me. An aged male was he, his hair gray above a sharp-fea-
tured face, his brows thick and gray above disapproving
black eyes. He rose from his seat and began to approach me,
and his green covering showed itself to be longer and fuller
than those of other males. It hung somewhat loosely upon his
tall, thin form, and his arms were covered by it as well.
Briefly, I saw a sign of metal upon a chain about his neck,
the sign of a single, opened eye, the sign which Vistren had
worn, and then he stood before me.

"Do you seek your death, foolish wench?" the male demanded in annoyance. "Secret fires guard the Crystals of
power when they are held so, fires which shall strike without
thought being given to whom they strike! Who are you, and
why have you come here?"

With disappointment I noted that the male wore no
weapons, yet he was aged, and perhaps without the strength

of others. "I come for the Crystals," said I, "for they belong to Mida. Do not attempt to interfere, for I shall have them!"

I turned from him then, and again reached toward the Crystals, but his hand closed upon my arm and pulled me from the platform. "You shall not touch the comm, young savage!" said he, his fingers upon my arm with surprising strength. He was still annoyed, but he only held my left arm, therefore I moved quickly toward him in attack, teeth and nails eager for victory. A muffled shout erupted from him as he struggled to fend off hurt, then his voice raised to a clear shout. "Guards!" he called breathlessly and anxiously. "To me, to me!"

Nearly had I driven the male to his platform, the snarl of the hadat deep within my throat, desperation clear upon his features. I thought to leave him and hasten to the Crystals before the arrival of others, yet was I unable to do so. The male had kept my teeth from him, though his hand still grasped my arm, disallowing my return to the device, and I was unable to free myself. Resolutely, I sent my teeth to his hand, and with a howl of pain from him I was quickly released, yet had the time fled to naught. Two armed males, in leather and metal, rapidly appeared then to bar my way, and firmly was I taken and held between them. My attempts at struggle were in vain, the device secure from reach beyond their broad, muscled backs.

"Hold her!" gasped the aged male, his bitten hand held to him by the other. "In the name of the Serene Oneness, do not allow her to reach the comm! The emptyheaded wench would throw her life away!"

With some difficulty the armed males drew me farther from the device, their hands upon my arms, their bodies behind mine, till we stood before the aged male, his disapproving eyes once more upon me. I breathed heavily from the struggle, yet was I still unbeaten. The Crystals lay not far from me, and my life was yet mine.

"Do not release her," the aged male ordered, his eyes unmoving from me. "I ask again your name, wench, and your purpose in attempting the theft of the Crystals of power. Know you not the gates of the city remain locked against all departures?"

Full straight did I stand in the grasp of the males beside me, and disdained to answer. To accuse one of the Midanna of theft of the Crystals of Mida spoke of foolishness beyond the norm, and there was nothing I cared to say upon the matter. The aged male's annoyance grew, and he nodded briskly.

"Very well!" said he harshly. "You may consider your reply till the new light, and then you may offer it to the High Seat! Place her in a retaining cell, and post a guard. The High Seat shall decide her fate!"

With nods the males pulled me from the room, and firm was their grasp upon my arms. I fully expected to be taken below, to the darkness in the ground; however I was forced to a new set of steps which we ascended. No cloth at all was to be found upon this next level, and the rooms were not rooms, but enclosures. The walls were unadorned stone of pink, the floors uncovered stone of gray, the doors not doors but lines of metal, enclosing rooms but leaving them quite open to view. Within such a room was I thrust, the light of a nearby torch casting shadowed illumination, and the metal door was closed behind, holding me captive within. The armed males grinned, and shook their heads before one took himself off, the other standing some paces from the room. The room itself contained only a narrow platform upon which was cloth somewhat like that of a platform called bed. I placed myself upon the gray stone of the floor, my shoulders against the pink stone of the walls, my head back, my eyes closed. Once again had I failed Mida, yet would I continue in my efforts till my life and soul had fled, naught less to halt me. With the new light would I face Galiose, demanding the return of the Crystals, else demanding his life in their stead. Naught was there to halt my final efforts upon Mida's behalf, for the Crystals must be freed. Perhaps then would my Hosta also be freed, to live as they had before my failure, for then would Mida be pleased. I sat beside the wall, my eyes closed, and awaited the new light.

18.

*Phanisar—and a
fool's tale*

Sounds of footsteps came from beyond the doorway, and I
rose to my feet, somewhat unsteadily, preparing myself for
the confrontation with Galiose. Much of the darkness had I
passed in sleep, and the demands of hunger had eased with
the passing hind, as they are wont to do, and fully prepared
was I to press my quest. The steps seemed to betoken the
presence of three males or more, and I placed myself before
the metal, to await their appearance. Earlier had the armed
male been replaced, the new male coming to grin upon me,
yet had none spoken or closely approached.

The steps resolved themselves to forms, and the forms
halted before my enclosure, true anger to be seen upon the
faces of three. Galiose, Telion, and Ceralt stood before me,
two armed males in leather and metal, seemingly amused, behind them. All eyes were unblinkingly upon me, and those of
Ceralt filled me with uncertainty, for their lightness was
chilled to a large degree. With some small difficulty I looked
from him, and gazed upon Galiose, called High Seat of Ranistard. This male's brows were low with anger, and slowly did
he shake his head.

"I should find little surprise at her presence within my
Palace," said he, "for surely has she been sent by Sigurr to
plague me for my sins! How obedient to your will she has become, hunter!"

Ceralt said nothing to this comment, yet his face darkened.

307

I disliked his gaze in its entirety, and looked once more upon Galiose.

"The Crystals of Mida must be released," said I to this male. "Neither they nor the Hosta are to remain in the grasp of city males, and Mida demands the release of all."

"Indeed!" said Galiose, surprised. "I would know the manner in which this revelation reached you—for I see no reason for agreement."

"All must be released!" said I quite sharply, my hands upon the metal of the enclosure, my gaze firm upon Galiose. "Should this not be in accordance with your wishes, gladly will I face you with sword in hand, and see the matter done when you have fallen."

"When *I* have fallen!" Galiose shouted, his face suffused with rage. "Truly do you require a lesson in manners, wench!" he shouted. "I am a warrior with a warrior's pride, and do not care to be mocked! Should you ever stand before me with naked blade, you shall quickly see who the fallen is to be!"

"You accept my challenge, then?" I asked, to the consternation of Telion and Ceralt. "To the winner belongs all, Hosta and Crystals alike."

"No!" shouted Ceralt and Telion as one, disallowing a reply from Galiose. Galiose seemed annoyed, and I, too, felt so.

"There shall be no battle!" said Ceralt quite sternly, his eyes ablaze like Galiose's. "A wench shall be punished, of that you may be sure, and no battle shall it be!"

"Jalav addresses Galiose," said I quite evenly to Ceralt and Telion. "Is he not to be allowed to reply of his own?"

"The High Seat refuses your challenge!" said Telion, once more causing Galiose's lips to part for naught. "Jalav shall not put hand to weapon, yet were she mine, she would find close acquaintance with the leather of punishment!"

"Have all now had their say?" inquired Galiose politely, looking from angered Telion to angered Ceralt. "No other wishes to relieve me of the tedious chore of deciding upon my own actions?" Telion and Ceralt flushed at these words, and again attempted to speak, till Galiose's hand raised to silence them. "Enough!" said he quite sharply. "Jalav addressed the High Seat, and to her shall the High Seat reply!" His eyes came to me once more, and a smile touched his lips. "Lovely Jalav," said he, his tone soft. "A warrior may not, in honor, raise sword to a woman, even though she be a woman such as yourself. The Hosta and the Crystals shall remain in the grasp of—'city males,' and there is naught you may do to alter this." Then did his smile slip away, and a hardness entered his tone. "Yet," said he, "there is a matter which must indeed be seen to by you! I shall have you brought before your wenches, and you shall instruct them against continuing as they have done so far!"

I found no meaning in the words of Galiose, and Ceralt and Telion frowned as well. "What has happened?" asked Telion of Galiose. "I have heard of no difficulty."

"Nor shall the word be spread," said Galiose in annoyance. "You know of the curfew declared against the wenches?" Telion and Ceralt nodded, and those males behind Galiose attempted to mask some amusement. "There is considerable reason for the curfew," continued Galiose, his eyes upon me. "Small packs of her females had taken to gathering at darkness, and by the new light were there many men of our city who had found themselves—persuaded—to please the females through the darkness! Yet the curfew has merely sent them to the shadows, and we have as yet to find the culprits! Jalav, their leader, shall order a halt to these doings, else shall she be punished in their stead!"

"Galiose, you cannot do so!" protested Ceralt, a tightness to his tone. "My wench has had no part in such doings, for she has constantly been with me!"

"So say each of the others!" snapped Galiose angrily. "They each would swear by the Serene Oneness that *their* wench be innocent! For now, I care not who has done and who has not! I simply wish to see an end to the matter! Jalav shall speak with them, and they shall cease, else Jalav shall suffer!"

"Jalav may do naught," said I with a shrug. "My Hosta have been taken from me, to serve the needs of city males, therefore may the city males see to their own safety. Am I to protect the servants of the thieves of the Crystals of Mida?"

"You dare to call me thief?" roared Galiose, beside himself with fury. His hands grasped the metal of the door, as though he would tear it from its place, and Telion closed his eyes as though in pain. Ceralt, I did not look toward, for I wished to use the High Seat's fury, and the hunter's presence disturbed me.

"Stolen were the Crystals and the freedom of the Hosta,"

said I with another shrug. "Should Galiose feel the accusation too deeply, he may perhaps find the stomach to face me. How say you, O honorable warrior?"

Galiose seemed unable to speak, so deep was his anger. He stared upon me with furious eyes, then he pulled himself from the metal and strode away, Telion immediately in his wake. Much annoyed was I that my challenge had been scorned, and I grasped the metal in anger, yet did I find my wrist grasped in turn. My eyes moved to see Ceralt, his large fingers tight about my left wrist.

"I shall gag you myself," he hissed, with eyes ablaze, "should I hear from you another word! You shall not face the High Seat in battle, even should he be willing to do so, for you belong to me, and I shall not allow it! Are my words clear to you?"

Clear were the words of Ceralt, and clear his disapproval, and I lowered my eyes and moved my right hand to touch gently the broad hand of him. Such strange feelings did he bring forth in me that I could not meet his gaze, yet was the sight of his hand upon mine no better, for his warmth reached through my skin and touched me deep. Dark was his hand, and dark the hair sprinkled upon it, so strong the fist, and almost smooth to my finger's caress. His hand trembled slightly at my touch, and more tightly was my wrist held in his grasp.

"Jalav, I had thought you gone!" he whispered raggedly, his left hand reaching within to stroke my back. "Why did you run from me, and what do you do here?"

"I must recover Mida's Crystals," I whispered in turn. "Ceralt must not care for Jalav, for Jalav is bound to do Mida's bidding—and belong to no male. Almost do I wish it were not so."

"It need not be so!" he insisted, drawing me to him though the metal stood between us. "There is naught you may do to free the Crystals, and the Hosta do now belong to the men of Ranistard! You are mine, Jalav, and so shall you continue to be, though you run from me a thousand times!"

"It may not be so," I sighed, "for Mida demands the return of her Crystals. May I—have my life sign when I am to face Galiose with blades?"

"No!" he shouted angrily, and the skin tautened upon the fist which held me. Again I sighed, for I had hoped that my soul need not be lost, yet did Ceralt still move to the bidding of Mida. My soul was to be the cost of my earlier failure, and naught was to change that. "No!" Ceralt shouted again, and his hand grasped my arm to shake me. "You shall not do battle, Jalav, therefore have you no need of your bit of wood! Do not speak of it again!"

My head lowered somewhat, knowing the futility of speaking of it again, and then footsteps reapproached. My eyes raised past Ceralt's arm, and Galiose and Telion did I see, coming once more to stand before me. As I did not wish him to, Ceralt did not release me, and again did Galiose smile slightly.

"We must turn your interest to things other than battle," said Galiose to me, "and I am pleased to see that that is not far from being done. Perhaps some words with Phanisar shall convince you that the Crystals of power may not be returned to the Hosta. Guard! Unlock the cell."

Ceralt and I parted so that the enclosure might be opened, and I was pleased at this turn of events. Should Phanisar be the aged male in whose keeping were the Crystals, still might I find opportunity to seize them. Down the area from the enclosures did we walk, Galiose and Telion before us, Ceralt beside me with hand upon my neck, the two males behind us. Still amused did these armed males seem, and that was also pleasing. Should the need arise, their weapons would not prove difficult to take.

But one level lower did we descend, to the level of the Crystals; however, we were not to enter the room which held them. Another room did we enter, of polished wood and platforms, with blue cloth upon its floor, and blue silk seats beside one platform. To this platform of seats was I led, and the aged male whom I had seen with the Crystals rose from a seat and bowed to Galiose. Beside his seat, upon the platform, stood a pile of leather and cloth, and now I was able to see strokes of black upon the leather. But briefly did I glance at this, for to my disappointment, the armed males remained without the room, closing the door firmly so that it would not swing. Neither Crystals nor weapons were then within reach, therefore was the time to pass uselessly.

"Jalav, this is Phanisar," said Galiose, gesturing toward the aged male. "You have, I believe, already met, though far less formally."

"Indeed," nodded he called Phanisar, a wry sharpness to his gaze. His hand showed itself to be wrapped about with white cloth, and gingerly did he hold the hand. "Jalav and I have indeed met," said he, "yet was my acquaintanceship closer with her teeth. I trust the incident shall not be repeated?"

The males laughed somewhat at the comment, and Ceralt shook me by the neck. "I shall see to her behavior," said he, "and I do, most sincerely, sympathize. Her teeth have almost the sharpness of her tongue."

"Perhaps we may lessen her sharpness," said Galiose. "Let us seat ourselves, and Phanisar may inform our war leader here of the true nature of the Crystals."

All took seat upon the blue silk, and he called Phanisar placed his hand upon the pile of leather and cloth. "This, Jalav," said he, "is a writing of the Early Times, a belonging of those who had for themselves the Lost Knowledge, for they were able to speak with the gods themselves. Within this writing is there spoken of the comm, and the Crystals of power as well."

So sincere did Phanisar seem, that I said naught of the foolishness he spouted. All knew that lore was handed from mother to daughter and therefore never lost, and all knew as well that leather and cloth had naught of a tongue with which to speak. Addled with age was this male Phanisar, an object upon which a warrior was to look with pity.

Phanisar smiled and said, "The comm, Jalav, is a device which may be used to speak with the gods, to ask of them the questions which men may not answer. Many and many a kalod ago, long before the time of my father, and his father, and his father's father, perhaps as much as three hundred kalod, the crystals were taken from the comm, so that men might no longer speak with the gods. The crystals hold within themselves a power which the device does use to reach the gods, a power without which the device is useless. For some mysterious reason is the power within the crystals painful to females, therefore were the crystals taken by females, and hidden away from the sight of men."

"The Crystals are the belonging of Mida," said I, "sent to her Midanna to be kept against the time she again wishes them. Males have naught to do with them."

"Males have much to do with them," corrected Phanisar with a smile. "It is the destiny of men to speak with the gods, and soon shall our destiny be fulfilled. Two of the crystals lie within our grasp, and it shall be only a matter of time before the third lies here, as well. We may not use the device save with the third crystal in place, for we would not cause undue pain to our women. Tell me, girl, what feelings did the device cause within you when Vistren set it working? The High Seat has told me of your presence at that time, and also of your appearance."

Again I felt the touch of agony, the stabbing of the fiery blades about me, the depth of darkness without end. A small shudder took me at the memory; however I merely replied, "The pain was great and difficult to bear, far beyond any other given by males. Wise was Mida for having taken the Crystals from them, and it is my hope that such may again be accomplished."

"We regret your pain, lovely Jalav," said Galiose quite softly as Ceralt's arm circled me, "yet must the Crystals remain with men. Closely guarded shall they be from this time onward, for we have no wish to see them again taken by females."

Quite sober and regretful did Galiose appear, yet unmoving as well. Unarmed, the Midanna would not again possess the Crystals, therefore must they, in some manner, rearm themselves. The problem was one to be thought upon; however Phanisar drew my attention to him once more.

"Tell me, wench," said he, "how quickly the pain left once the device no longer operated. Did the pain linger for hind, disappear in a moment, come and go, remain as it was? Were there other effects upon you or the others? Speak of all that you recall."

I knew not why that would interest the male, but I shrugged and replied, "The pain eased at the going of the darkness, yet were its echoes felt for many hind. In feyd were we again as we had been, save for the new lives which were lost."

"New lives?" frowned this Phanisar, and a stir passed among the other males. "Some of your wenches had been with child?"

"Some few," I nodded, "but I was unable to return them to our own lands. All lost the quickened seed within them, a great loss to the clan of the Hosta."

Phanisar gazed sadly upon me in silence, yet did Telion's hand come gently to my arm. "Which of your wenches were with child?" he asked with difficulty. "Have I—met any of them?"

"Most are known to Telion," said I, gazing in puzzlement at his pain-filled eyes. "Most took his seed in the Hosta use tent, and others made full use of the hunters of Ceralt. Fayan lost the seed of Nidisar, and Larid lost that which she carried. Others were—"

Abruptly were my words cut short, for Telion raised himself quickly from his seat and left the room, his red-gold head bowed as he walked. The other males followed his departure in silence, sadness full in their eyes, yet had I no understanding of the actions of any of them. How may the loss of new lives to the Hosta touch the males of the city of Ranistard? Much confusion did I find in the matter, and further still, for Ceralt turned to gaze upon me.

"And Jalav?" said he, a quietness to his tone. "Was there naught within Jalav to be lost?"

"Jalav is war leader," I explained, not knowing why his hand was on mine. "A war leader may not have life within her, therefore does she chew the leaves of the dabla bush. No life was there to be lost by Jalav."

Ceralt frowned, then Phanisar nodded. "The dabla bush," said Phanisar thoughfully. "I have heard of such a use for it, and my records do contain notes upon a counteragent. Fear not, my boy, the matter may be properly seen to."

Ceralt greeted these words with pleasure, though I was still confused. I knew not the meaning of "counteragent," and I knew no reason for Ceralt's pleasure; his light eyes gazed happily upon me, his large hand tight upon my fingers. Small time was there for such considerations, however, for Phanisar turned to me once more.

"See here, young Jalav," said he, his hand moving upon the pile of leather and cloth, and easily did it open to show further strokes of black, though smaller. "These writings do speak of the Crystals of power and where two were sent, yet the place of the third remains unknown. Were naught save two sent to the Midanna?"

"Two only are known to me," said I, gazing upon the small, black strokes. The hand of Phanisar turned the cloth quite slowly, and truly did I wonder upon the reason for placing so large a number of strokes upon a cloth. That the strokes spoke was foolishness, fit only for the mind of age-addled males, yet did I continue to wonder. The cloth was slowly turned, showing line upon line of strokes, and then the signs appeared without warning. The first I saw of it was a line of hands, some alone, sone with a second hand, though all were hands and all seemingly moving. No true recognition came to me till I stared upon the first hand to the left, a hand which showed the thumb between the second and third fingers, palm out, moving from left to right. That was obviously the word "the," in the silent speech of the Midanna, yet for what reason would it be put upon the cloth? Further did I seek, to the second sign below the first, and then did I see two hands, that to the left higher than the other, each in a fist save with the smallest finger, which was held erect. The hand to the left stood pointing upward, that to the right pointed right, clearly showing the word, "last." To each further sign did I go, and the message was brought quickly to me. "The last of the Crystals may be found within the Palace of the High Seat of the city of Bellinard, buried deep below the ground, fully fifty paces from the first, then left twenty paces farther. There may it be found within, yet not, we pray, by men."

The message seemed strange, so strange that I had not noticed the cessation of the movement of Phanisar, yet when I raised my eyes from the signs, well I knew that Phanisar had watched me closely, therefore did I ask, "And what meaning have these signs upon the cloth? Do they not speak as well?"

"In no tongue known to me," replied Phanisar with a shake of his head, his eyes still upon me. "I thought perhaps the signs might speak to another, therefore did I show them to you. For a moment, it seemed as though you read them."

"Perhaps their meaning is known to Mida," I suggested with a smile. "As the Crystals are hers, their locations must also be known to her."

Galiose began to speak, but was quickly silenced by the hand of Phanisar. Phanisar smiled and firmly withdrew the leather and cloth. "Of course the wench knows naught of the signs within," said he with satisfaction. "We must seek elsewhere for the answer, Blessed One."

"As you say, Phanisar," replied Galiose with some puzzlement. "Have you further questions for the wench?" At the aged male's head-shake, Galiose rose from his seat. "Perhaps, lovely Jalav," said he, "you now understand why we hold the Crystals. The Crystals belong to men, and once were they stolen by females. Not again shall that occur. She is once more placed in your keeping, Ceralt. Should she again be found within these walls without permission, it shall go hard with her. I shall inform you when I wish her to address the others."

Ceralt nodded without comment, rose from his seat, pulled me from mine, and hastily departed, my wrist held firmly within his hand. To the level of the entrance did we descend, and thence to the open beyond the dwelling. The light shone grayly about us as we walked, the wind quite chill in its presence. A shiver reached me because of the wind, and again I longed for the warmth of the lands of the Hosta. Ceralt turned to place his arm about me with a hearty grin.

"I see a wench shivers with the coming cold," said he. "Soon shall the winter descend upon us, to make this fey seem warm, and then shall the breasts of foolish wenches freeze in the points the cold causes. Yet Jalav shall not be forced to give over her bit of cloth till *she* wishes it. A man enjoys the sight of points."

Most miserably did I see that Ceralt spoke the truth, for indeed had the chill reached out to touch me. Should the cold grow greater still, the Hosta would not be seen, for which of them would shun clan colors for comfort? Too slowly did we walk toward Ceralt's dwelling, yet the hunter seemed unhurried in his pace, his arm about me holding me to his stride. The thought came that he walked so with a purpose, though the nature of the purpose was not clear. Surely Ceralt knew a Hosta would not forsake clan colors of herself, and Jalav was yet Hosta.

At last we entered the dwelling of Ceralt, and most welcome was its warmth. I stood upon the entrance cloth, of a brown and green like the forests, thinking to return to the room which was mine so that I might consider what I had learned, yet Ceralt looked upon me again with a frown.

"You appear unreasonably thin, wench," said he in disapproval. "What was given you to eat in the Palace of the High Seat?"

"Naught was given me," I answered, thinking instead, of the Palace in Bellinard. Where, below ground, did the Crystal lie hidden, and how might the Hosta claim it as their own? Were we able to escape the city of Ranistard, enter Bellinard, find the remaining Crystal, and return it to our own land, surely would the other clans of the Midanna return with us to once again free the other Crystals. Yet would it be necessary to make very sure that Ceralt was not harmed during the attack, for I would see him live as safely as might be. He was a strange male, this hunter, and strange were the feelings he produced within me.

"You were given nothing?" Ceralt repeated in outrage. "Does the High Seat think to save his coppers? I shall speak to him of this, Sigurr take me if I fail to do so!" Then he turned to me sternly. "Jalav," said he, his hands upon my arms, "you shall this moment request the sharing of my food, else shall I be greatly angered! Do you wish to see me angered?"

So sternly did he look upon me, yet was there a faint worry in his eyes as well. Unbidden, a smile came to my lips, and my hand touched his covering. "Jalav does not wish to see Ceralt angered," said I quite softly. "Therefore does she request the sharing of his provender."

"Beautifully done," laughed Ceralt gently, pulling me to him so that he might hold me. "I must continue with your lessons, for I would see you civilized as quickly as may be. The process shall not be overly painful."

"I am to be given further pain?" said I, raising my eyes to look up toward his. "Ceralt is displeased with Jalav?"

"No, no," said Ceralt quickly, his arms full tight about me. "I merely meant the remark as humor. There shall be no further pain given you."

"Ceralt finds humor in pain?" I asked, my cheek against his covering. Strange indeed were the ways of males.

Ceralt sighed, then chuckled a bit. "No, my Jalav," said he, stroking my hair. "There is little humor in pain, and I shall not attempt such foolishness again. Come, Inala shall fetch our meal for us."

Wordlessly did I go with Ceralt to the room of red silk, where the female Inala was bidden to fetch food. She nodded in obedience to Ceralt's order, then paused as she was about to depart. "Master," said she, in innocence, "shall I fetch a pitcher of renth as well?"

Ceralt winced at the mention of renth, and quickly shook his head. "Not yet am I able to face further renth," said he. "Still do I feel the touch of it in my head, therefore shall I drink only water."

"As Master wishes," Inala murmured, then she turned to me. "Does Mistress alone wish a flagon, then?"

"I would be pleased at the taste of some renth," said I, and then saw the female's amusement at the look Ceralt gave me.

Wide-eyed was the hunter, and disbelieving, yet then he nodded as though touched by a thought.

"Of course," said he in satisfaction. "Jalav could not have drunk as much of the renth as Telion and I, therefore did it have less effect on her."

"Oh, no, Master," said the female, her amusement again masked behind innocence. "The Mistress had as much renth as the Master, yet was she entirely untouched by it. Never before have I seen the like of it!"

Ceralt frowned and dismissed the female, then he slid low within his seat, his eyes unhappily upon me. Many times did he shake his head, as though to deny some thought which had come to him, yet did the thought persist in its return, for he continued to stare and shake his head. The meal proved to be a silent one, and each time Inala refilled my pot of renth, Ceralt closed his eyes and muttered to himself.

With the meal done, Ceralt had the platform cleared so that he might fetch a large piece of stiffened cloth and a stick of charcoal, much as the female Lodda had had. I felt quite pleased that my hunger was gone, therefore I refrained from laughter when Ceralt made strokes with the charcoal, and then informed me that the strokes said the name, Jalav. Jalav sat beside a foolish Ceralt, not upon a stiffened bit of cloth, therefore how were the strokes to be termed Jalav? As Ceralt formed other strokes, called "letters" by him, I thought again upon the problem of the Crystal. That Hosta must depart from Ranistard was clear, yet how was that to be accomplished? Long did I think upon the matter, and truly angered was Ceralt that I had failed to heed him, as he learned upon speaking to me of the strokes. Naught had I heard of the foolishness of the strokes, and Ceralt sent me from him, saying that I would know the foolishness, else I would know a punishment. His anger saddened me quite a bit, and in silence did I bathe in the large pot filled by Inala, for soon would I find the need to leave Ceralt again. Though it was not my wish to leave the hunter with anger, all my efforts seemed to accomplish this undesired end. Perhaps that was due to the displeasure of Mida, and therefore was I unable to change the matter. I knew not, yet did it trouble me.

Darkness had come when my hair was dried and combed at last, and Ceralt called me to another meal. His anger at the foolishness of the strokes was still upon him, and I began to feel a great annoyance. I cared nothing for strokes and letters, and had little patience for the matter. I raised my renth to the male each time I drank, and pleased was I to see annoyance at such action displace the anger of the strokes. By meal's end the hunter glared upon my smile, and abruptly did he rise to stand quite straight.

"As darkness is upon us, my wench," said he, "I feel it best that we retire. The new light shall see you again with your letters, and I shall see that you learn them."

"Jalav has learned many things," said I, and also rose to my feet. "Jalav knows the ways of the hadat, and the lenga, and the falth, the song of the lellin, the flight of the wrettan, the temper of the gando. Jalav knows the means by which to feed herself, to see to her safety in the forests, to search out water. Jalav knows the bending of a bow, the casting of a spear, the flashing of a sword. May the strokes you speak of compare with the knowledge already held by Jalav?"

"The—'strokes' contain all such things and more beside," said Ceralt with a smile, "Does Jalav know the manner in which metal may be found, the way that stone must be placed to form a building which will stand, the proper season for the ground to take a seed, the manner in which men's words may be sent to one another by mirrors? These things do the—strokes—contain, and these things may you also learn, should you first learn your letters."

"Jalav has little need of such," I informed him firmly. "Think you the Hosta be city folk, to wish metal, buildings and seedlings?"

"The Hosta now are indeed city wenches," laughed Ceralt, and his arm came to me. "They must learn the things their men know of, else shall their men be displeased with them. Come you now, for the time of darkness passes too swiftly."

Firmly Ceralt led me to the level above, yet was I not to return to the room which had been mine. Another room did we enter, one larger than the first, one of many shades of brown, both light and dark, upon the silks and floor cloth. Some white was there too, among the browns, and brightly did it stand in the glow of the fire. Up to the platform called bed did Ceralt lead me, and firmly did he point to it.

"This is what a civilized wench sleeps upon in the city," said he, "and this is what my wench shall learn to use. Remove your bit of cloth, and the lesson shall begin."

I looked upon the height of the platform, and then shook my head. "Jalav shall sleep upon the cloth by the fire," said I, also pointing with my finger. "Sooner would I sleep upon gando-back than upon yon platform."

"Unfortunately," said Ceralt with a grin as he removed his covering, "my house lacks a gando, therefore must it be upon the platform—ah, Sigurr take it! Upon the *bed*! It is called a bed, Jalav."

"I care naught for what it may be called," said I, my arms folded upon my chest. "Jalav shall not use it."

"Jalav shall," said Ceralt, and he stepped to me and raised me in his arms. Full hard did I struggle so as not to be placed upon the platform, yet did Ceralt place me there, and himself as well, his arms about me preventing an escape. My clan covering yielded to his greater strength in turn, and then was I merely held as Ceralt sighed and closed his eyes. Great dislike did I have for the platform, yet was I uncomfortably aware of the hunter's nearness, the great chest against which I lay, the male heat and smell of the body of him. Slightly did I move in the tight circle of his arms, then raised my head a bit.

"Jalav is captive to the hunter Ceralt," said I, and his eyes opened somewhat. "Is Ceralt not to use her?"

The hunter smiled faintly, and his lips touched my forehead. "Ceralt has considered it," he murmured, his hand amove upon me. "Has Jalav any wish of it?"

"Jalav has not the strength to halt the will of a male," said I, rather unsteadily. The hand of Ceralt moved about me, and truly did I wish the chance to take him.

"Then, should Jalav have some interest," murmured Ceralt, his leg as well upon me, "she must speak of it to Ceralt."

In misery did I attempt to remain still, yet that was impossible. The feelings fired by Ceralt in me turned me weak with the need for him. "Jalav—Jalav—has some interest in her use by Ceralt," I muttered faintly, and the hunter laughed gently.

"I feel it would do well for Jalav," said he, "were she to request her use by Ceralt. I seem to recall another who was made to ask for use, and most fitting would the same from Jalav be."

I groaned then, and struggled again to free myself, yet was freedom not to be mine, nor escape from the nearness of the male. My need could not be denied, and therefore was I forced to say, quite faintly, "Jalav—Jalav asks that she be used by Ceralt."

"Let us not be quite so formal," Ceralt grinned. "Who asks to be used by whom?"

Desperately, I threw myself about, then cried, "I ask to be used, Ceralt! In the name of Mida do I ask to be used!"

"And so you shall be, Jalav mine!" Ceralt laughed, yet no mockery was there in his laugh. Quickly did he take me then, and many times did I cry out at his use, for truly did Mida move him well.

19.

A plague of strokes —and a further search

The new light brought the beginnings of much difficulty. Truly angered was Ceralt when he awoke to find that I slept upon the cloth before the fire. No sleep had come to me upon the platform, for thought of its height had kept my eyes wide till Ceralt had slept. Silently had I moved from his side and warmth to the fire, and there had slept well and easily. The reason for taking sleep upon a platform was beyond me, and further so with the floor cloth to be had by city folk. Should they not wish leather to sleep upon, as was proper, the cloth was there for use in its stead. Ceralt would not consider that, and gave his word that next I would be bound upon the platform, should I again attempt to leave it in the darkness. No word did I address to the matter, for already had I spoken, and Ceralt took a fresh covering, of a blue like the skies, and we both descended for a meal.

When we had fed, again was I plagued with strokes and the learning of them. No meaning could I find within the charcoal marks, and quickly fled my temper with Ceralt's speaking of them, yet Ceralt refused to fall to anger. Again and again did he repeat the strokes and their callings, insisting that I, too, take charcoal in hand and attempt their forming. My attempts seemed the scratchings of a lellin upon the dirt, of no likeness at all to those of Ceralt, yet did Ceralt nod and smile most happily, as though something had been accomplished. For hind, then, I moved the charcoal about quite aimlessly, to Ceralt's vast enjoyment, then did we feed once more. Immediately following our meal, Ceralt found the need to leave the dwelling, and firmly did he insist that I continue with the charcoal, yet no sooner was he gone than I abandoned useless waste of time, and considered the means by which my warriors and I might leave the city.

Ceralt returned in darkness, and once more did we go to the platform within his room. Most completely did the hunter see to the needs of both of us, yet was he not asleep when I rose to leave the platform. Quickly was I seized and held, and then was the hated collar placed about my throat and chained to the metal of the platform. Wildly, I struggled to remove it, yet was naught accomplished save the movement of a cover of cloth, which Ceralt had placed upon us. Ceralt rescued the cloth from loss, then was I taken in his arms for the matter of sleep. Little sleep did I find through the darkness, and Ceralt wakened before the new light, used me well once again, and then departed, the collar in place as it had been. The entire fey did I spend upon the platform, for Ceralt had taken a party of hunters to the forests, and most miserably did I note the passage of the light. Inala brought something to feed upon, and also brought the stiffened cloth and the charcoal. All did I cast from me in anger, and full fury was I filled with upon the return of Ceralt. The hunter cared little for my temper, placed himself beside me once again, and then used me despite my struggles. By deep fury was I held, yet sleep found me rather quickly.

The new light brought release, though no satisfaction. Ceralt vowed most solemnly that should I again attempt to leave the platform in darkness, two feyd would I pass chained so. I refused to speak on it, for already had I spoken my word upon the matter. No platform would Jalav pass the darkness upon, not if she could choose otherwise. Only just had we completed our meal, when two armed males in leather and metal were brought before us by Inala. They had come to inform Ceralt that the female Jalav was required by the High Seat, therefore did we all leave the dwelling and walk toward that of Galiose, before which many males and warriors were beginning to gather. Though the light was bright, the air was cool, yet did each of my warriors, like myself, appear in clan colors. Not easily were clan colors taken from Hosta.

Galiose waited before the entrance to his dwelling, therefore did we mount the steps to approach him. Easily might it

be seen that the High Seat was displeased, and Ceralt walked
quite near to me as the attention of Galiose centered upon
my arrival. Galiose stepped forward to meet me.

"Now!" said he quite briskly, placing his hand upon my
shoulder. "When all of your wenches have gathered, Jalav,
you shall order them to cease this—this—activity of the
darkness, and immediately! I shall not have dark-roving females in Ranistard!"

"Jalav may say naught," said I with a shrug. "The Hosta
are no longer hers."

The anger deepened upon the features of Galiose, and his
hand left my shoulder at the reminder of my previously
stated position. "You refuse to address them?" he demanded,
his anger quite cold.

"Have I not said so?" I asked most reasonably. "Is Galiose
now prepared to face me with sword?"

The male stared at me for a moment, then he turned angrily to another who stood beside him. "When the wenches
have gathered," he snapped to the second male, "I, myself,
shall address them!" Then he walked from all to stand alone,
his gaze lost among those who continued to arrive.

Ceralt, beside me, uttered a small sound of surprise, and I
turned to see that he, too, gazed upon my warriors, yet was
there little to be seen among them to cause surprise. One
group of perhaps two hands of warriors stood somewhat
apart, and happily engaged themselves in a game of stone
casting. The game was one for young warriors-to-be, ones
who had not yet learned the full way of weapons, and my
warriors, having had their weapons taken from them, used
the game to keep hand and eye well honed. They each held
large stones in both hands, and circled warily, watching in all
directions, for one must cast as well as evade during the
game. To be hit meant loss of game, and each might choose
her target as she would. Those who succeeded in scoring hits
while remaining untouched themselves formed a later, smaller
set, to produce the winner of all. Once had I seen two excellent warriors facing one another, each well skilled in meeting
her mark, each as fleet of movement as a nilno on the run,
and then did the game take on a true beauty, a dedication to
the glory of all Midanna. As I watched, Gimin, who played
as well as one might, cast her stone and threw herself to the
left, thereby evading a stone cast at her. Her stone landed
well and truly, striking a tall, light-haired warrior upon the

forehead, and the warrior fell senseless to the ground, as yet unknowing that her place in the game had been lost. Three others were quickly struck as well, the game proceeding slowly as was to be expected when played by warriors of skill, yet were there suddenly males among them, seizing the stones left to the players and angrily casting them aside, then roughly pulling my warriors away to stand beside them as they spoke more angrily yet. Those warriors who lay upon the ground were anxiously tended to by other males, who seemed quite beside themselves at the condition of the fallen. Most annoyed were the others at their game having been disrupted, and well was I able to appreciate their view, yet Ceralt nodded in approval of the disruption, and then folded his arms.

"Well halted," he muttered. "The foolish wenches would all be senseless, were it to be allowed to continue. It is easily seen that all the Hosta require those with wits to guide them."

"The Hosta require only their freedom and weapons," said I. "Had their weapons not been taken, little need would there have been for indulgence in a child's game."

"A child's game!" exclaimed Ceralt. "You cannot mean that children are permitted so dangerous an activity?"

I gazed with puzzlement upon him, for his meaning was unclear. "Children are not *permitted* such activities," I informed him slowly. "The Hosta young are taught such games, preparing them for the battles of adulthood. How else are warriors to be made?"

Quite long and soberly did Ceralt gaze upon me without speaking. "The making of warriors," he muttered faintly. "Praise be to the Serene Oneness that such is no longer to be done."

Frowning, I was about to pursue such an odd statement, yet Galiose chose then to approach, grasp my arm, and roughly lead me to the edge of the set of steps. Nearly all of my warriors stood before us with the males who had taken them, and many eyes watched the actions of the High Seat, and listened for the words he would address to them. Galiose stared about at warrior and male alike, and then his head raised slightly as his hand still grasped my arm.

"Heed my words!" said he in a voice which carried easily to all. "The city of Ranistard has welcomed the presence of Hosta wenches, yet have these selfsame wenches returned the

welcome with ungrateful and shameful rovings in the
darkness! The activities which the Hosta have indulged in
shall cease, and cease immediately, else shall their leader,
Jalav here, be punished for their actions! Should you not wish
to see this wench hung by the wrists in the city's center and
beaten, pass the darkness in peace with those men who have
claimed you! I, Galiose, High Seat of Ranistard, have spoken,
and shall not speak again upon the matter!"

An angry mutter arose from my warriors, and a growl
grew as resentment against such reference to a war leader
fired my warriors' blood. The males among them attempted
to silence them, but they were unwilling to be silenced.
Movement was there, here and there among the throng, and
Galiose frowned mightily at such reaction to his words. Foolish, indeed, was the High Seat of Ranistard—thought he that
Hosta warriors would be pleased to hear of proposed pain to
be given their war leader? No more than a moment did I
stand in such silent consideration of the throng, then I, too,
raised my voice.

"The Hosta have ever been free to act as they would!" said
I above my warriors' growls. "Let it continue to be so as long
as they live!"

Cries of, "Jalav!" and "War leader!" came in salute from
my warriors, in concert with their laughter, and the fingers of
Galiose tightened about my arm.

"Bravely spoken," said he for my ears alone, and his dark
eyes showed hard and grudging respect. "Yet, should the matter come to it, wench, the lash shall be given unstintingly.
Best you hope that it may be received with equal bravery."

Briefly, I shrugged as I met his gaze. "Should Mida wish it
so," said I, "it shall be so. Jalav lives in accordance with the
will of Mida."

"And I in accordance with the will of the Serene Oneness,"
said Galiose, and his hand left my arm. "Perhaps they shall,
at some future time, move us both in concert." Then his eyes
left me, to touch Ceralt and Telion, and one or two others.
"Return your wenches to your homes," said Galiose to them,
"and then attend me in my study with your full force. Plans
have been made, and I would have you know of them."

The males nodded in obedience to Galiose, and soon were
my warriors and I separated once more, with no opportunity
for speech among us. Most anxious had I been to speak of
my thoughts upon leaving Ranistard, yet were none allowed

to approach me, though Larid and Gimin and Fayan wished
to do so. All were taken firmly away by the males who stood
beside them, and I saw with amusement that Fayan still refused to acknowledge the presence of Nidisar. Quite irate did
Nidisar appear to be at such a condition, yet, despite the fact
that Fayan limped somewhat, as though in pain, she was
Hosta warrior enough to discount that and continue as she
would. Most pleased was I with the warrior Fayan, and
pleased, too, was I to learn that the dwelling of Telion lay
closest to that of Ceralt. Larid was taken there as I was led
by Ceralt to his own entrance, and once inside, Ceralt
laughed at the evidence of the chill upon me, then left once
more, saying he would return as soon as might be, and I was
to remain within the dwelling. Most happily did I remain
within, for I wished to think further about leaving Ranistard,
and also to speculate upon the plans which Galiose had spoken of. Did the males concern themselves with that which
would interest the Hosta? That they sought the third Crystal,
I well knew, yet were they prepared to act in an attempt to
reach it? Slowly, I mounted the steps which led to Ceralt's
room, and thoughtfully I stretched myself upon the cloth before the fire. The hind passed in silent contemplation of the
future, only once disturbed by the arrival of Inala with something to feed upon. I fed as silently as I had lain, and then
returned to my thoughts alone.

I knew naught of Ceralt's arrival till the hunter's arms
circled me and pulled me to him, and so eager was he for the
use of Jalav, he took me there, upon the cloth before the fire.
Most surprising were these actions, yet Ceralt refused to
speak of it. His need well seen to, we descended to the room
of red silk, partook of the meal set before us by Inala, then
returned once more to the room. Firmly was I lifted to the
platform, and small chance had I to descend again, for the
darkness was filled with Ceralt's need, which seemed to be
immense. No understanding had I of why, yet was I used to
satisfaction and beyond, without halt, till the new light was
little more than a hin away, then was I held to the broad
chest of Ceralt, as the hunter knotted his fingers within my
hair. My face was raised by the pull upon my hair, and the
hunter pressed his lips to mine with great heat, then he
chuckled.

"The memories of this darkness must remain strong within
me," said he quite softly, his face no more than a finger from

mine. "I shall not again have the use of my wench till my return, which may be quite some time."

"Where does Ceralt go?" asked I, knowing the question must be asked, yet nearly lost in the nearness of the hunter. So strong was the heat within him, such pleasure was he able to give!

"I ride with others in search of the third Crystal of power," Ceralt replied in a murmur, his lips upon my face. "We have heard of a place where it might be found, and shall make our way there as quickly as may be. My hunters shall provision the party as it goes, and aid as best we may upon our arrival there."

Speaking presented great difficulty, for my hands stroked the strong back of him as his hands held me to him by the hair, yet was I able to say, "I shall accompany Ceralt upon his journey, therefore shall he find no lack of Jalav. To whence do we ride?"

Again Ceralt chuckled, and his head moved in negation. "Jalav does not ride," said he with amusement. "Jalav shall remain within the house of Ceralt, there to practice the reading and writing of her letters, and there to greet him properly upon his return. Truly great shall my need be then, therefore I give you warning now: rest well in my absence, wench, for little rest shall you find upon my return."

"I care little for letters and rest," said I quite firmly. "Already have I decided to accompany you. To whence do we ride?"

"You, my girl, do not!" said Ceralt with equal firmness, his face a shadow in the dark. Again he pressed his lips to mine with strength, then were his hands gone from my hair, and to my fury was the collar again clapped about my throat! Little sense was there in struggle, yet struggle I did as the Mida-forsaken male laughed at my outrage, then pulled me to him once more. A final memory he took unto himself, then he arose and clothed himself while I lay, angry, upon the platform.

"You shall remain as you are till our party has gone," said he, smug in his satisfaction. "I shall leave the key to the collar with others, though you well deserve to be left upon the bed till my return. Galiose has given me his word that no lash shall be taken to you till I am able to see what may be done with your stubbornness, yet his patience grows exceedingly thin. Behave yourself in my absence, Jalav, else shall I find the need to add to the hidings you have already received." He paused and approached me slowly, then his hand touched my cheek. "Better a hundred hidings, my girl," said he, "than one taste of the lash. Never again shall you be beaten while I live." Again he hesitated, then his hands raised to the leather which held my life sign about his neck, and quickly he removed the life sign and slipped it again about my own neck, in its accustomed place. I was speechless at such an action, yet Ceralt left it so, gave his lips to me a final time, then hurriedly left the room.

The silence of the darkness sat heavily upon me as I lay there, the metal of the collar tight about my throat, the strong male smell of Ceralt still upon me, my hand clasped firmly about my life sign. The chain of the collar did not allow a sitting position, so short was it, therefore did I lie upon the platform as I had been, my eyes upon the swing of the door by which Ceralt had departed. Again had I my life sign about my neck, my soul again secure, and thus did I know that Mida once again smiled upon her warrior. Yet was I disturbed that Ceralt had returned it then, as he prepared to ride in search of the Crystal, for surely did such action mean he thought it possible he would not return. Great pain was there in the thought of the loss of him, and he had even refused to speak of where he rode! Quickly must I find myself and my warriors free, so that I might ride to his aid. Blessed be Mida that she had already revealed to me the location of the Crystal!

Many hind passed before my release, so many hind that I fell asleep where I lay upon the platform. At last I awakened to the presence of Inala beside the platform, and with a smile she showed the small bit of metal upon her hand.

"The key was brought but moments ago," she informed me as she reached toward the collar. "You are now allowed the freedom of the house, yet are you forbidden to leave it."

"None save Mida may forbid the actions of a Hosta," said I, pleased as the collar opened and fell from me. Briefly, I rubbed my throat, then rose to find and don my clan covering.

"There are Guardsmen here to see to your obedience," said Inala softly. The female stood quietly in the white of her covering, and deeply concerned did her dark eyes appear. "Mistress shall find the need to obey," said she, "for the Guardsmen have been instructed by the High Seat."

"Galiose does well in adding to my annoyance," I mut-

tered. "Much pleasure would I find in facing him with sword.
What number of males has he sent?"

"There are three," said Inala with a frown. "Surely,
Mistress will not attempt to. . . ."

"All shall be seen to," said I with a gesture of my hand,
which silenced her. "Let us now look upon these emissaries
of the High Seat."

Without further speech, Inala proceeded to the lower level,
I in her wake, and there we found the three males, each in
leather and metal, each armed with sword and dagger, and
each with a grin upon his large, broad face. Larger were
these males than any I had ever seen, larger, even, than Telion, Ceralt, or Galiose. Full amused were they that I saw
weapons before me, yet was unable to make them mine. With
dignity and lack of concern I passed these males, and allowed
Inala to lead me to the room of red silk, where awaited my
provender. The males entered as I seated myself, and
watched silently as I partook of the foods and drink, yet
when their eyes were upon my pot of renth, I sipped but
slowly with the thought that had come to me. The thought
seemed an excellent one, therefore did I call to Inala and
hold high the pot of renth when she appeared.

"I would have this drink brewed before I partake of it further," said I to her. "Do you know the manner of doing so?"

At her indication of ignorance, I explained the proper
manner of brewing, then ordered her to brew an amount sufficient for the balance of the fey. At these final words a light
began to gleam within her dark eyes, and most hastily did she
withdraw to do my bidding. The males watched her departure
with smiles of approval for her grace, yet they remained
within the room as I fed quite slowly, awaiting the brewing
of the renth.

Some reckid later, the female returned, a large pot held
carefully before her, the strong aroma of brewed renth arising from it. Not as pleasing as daru was the aroma of renth.
yet the males fastened their eyes to the pot, and watched
carefully as my drinking pot was filled therefrom. I sipped at
the brewed renth with satisfaction, and then smacked my lips
most heartily.

"Excellent," said I to a smiling Inala, who stood beside me
with the pot. "It still has not the body of daru, yet has brewing done much to improve it."

"I have prepared much of it, Mistress," Inala said, again in innocence. "Your slave hopes that there shall not be too much."

"It shall be seen to," I assured her, taking a further, much pleasing, sip of the renth, and the males glanced upon one another in indecision. The largest of the males, he in the center, drew the back of his hand across seemingly dry lips, and then he stepped forward.

"Fetch three more flagons, slave," said he to Inala, his eyes upon the pot she held. "My men and I shall sample that creation, and perhaps we shall find it acceptable."

"Brewed renth is not for males," said I, and again sipped from my pot. "Best you bid the slave fetch unbrewed renth, and leave the other for warriors such as I."

"The cheek of the she!" growled another of the males, and all stood forward to frown. "Leave the other for warriors such as she indeed!"

"The wench begs to be taught a lesson," said the third, quite coldly, his light eyes hard upon me. "A shame we have been forbidden to touch her."

"Yet, naught was said of what she might be made to drink," mused the first. "A lesson would be taught, I think, should the wench be made to match us cup for cup."

"Aye!" laughed the others in full agreement, and so it was decided. The males, seated all about me, tasted of the brewed renth and found it most pleasing, and then was I forced, by dire threats, to drink as did they, one for one, many pots of the renth. The hind passed with the drinking of the renth, and though the light had been high when first I had begun to feed, full darkness had nearly descended when the last of the males dropped his head and his pot of renth together, with a thud, to the platform top. The others slept quite soundly, loud noises emergent from their opened mouths, their bodies sprawled upon the seats about me. Somewhat dizzy did I also feel, for brewed renth was not like unbrewed renth, but I was able to take my feet and stand.

"Mistress, are you in difficulty?" Inala asked quite anxiously from beside me as I shook my head to rid it of the mists. Much renth had the males withstood, and unsteady was I upon my feet.

"The air without the dwelling shall clear my head," said I to the female, and then I turned to the first of the males, silently asking the aid of Mida as I removed the weapons from about him. I turned from placing the weapons upon myself to find the female Inala busily engaged with another of the males, his dagger already upon the platform, his swordbelt nearly in her possession. I smiled at the eagerness of her assistance, then turned to the third of the males, and when all of the weapons had been removed, Inala and I faced one another again.

"Jalav thanks the female Inala for her assistance," said I with sincerity. "Perhaps we shall one fey meet again in the sight of Mida."

"You shall leave the city," said Inala, her eyes large and somewhat tragic. "I beg you, Mistress, take me with you!"

"We shall go as warriors," said I, with a small headshake and smile. "Inala does not know the way of warriors, nor would she find the pace to her liking. Remain here, city female, for Mida has not blessed you with soul nor life sign to guard it."

"Here, I be slave!" said she most forcefully, and then she took a step forward. "I need not ask of your love for the collar, mighty Jalav, for I have seen your fury with my own eyes! Take me no farther than without the gates, and then abandon me if you must! Sooner would I die in the forests in freedom, than live longer as slave!"

Her hand reached toward me beseechingly. Truly did Inala wish for freedom, and this was I able to understand, yet was there another thing which puzzled me.

"Should it be true that death is your preference to slavery," said I, "how is it that you have not sought it sooner?"

"But I have," said Inala quite bitterly. "By the former High Seat was I declared slave, for the terrible crime of having no family here in Ranistard, nor a male relative of any sort to speak for me. Most earnestly did I seek death then, attempting attack upon all who approached me, yet was I given, in its stead, many strokes of the lash, for a female slave is too useful to destroy. When I persisted in my search for destruction, the former High Seat grew exceedingly wroth, and ordained that I was to be given to his Guard for three feyd as punishment. The memory of those three feyd shall ever be with me, and not again have I had the courage to disobey."

Her voice had dropped quite low, and pained. Fully taken with the renth must I have been, for my hand touched her shoulder as she stood, head down, before me. "Without the gates shall you find yourself," I said, only then aware of the decision I had made. "May Mida guard you from then on."

Her head raised, and her eyes shone with happiness. "I thank you," said she quite simply, a twisted smile upon her lips. "I shall thank you for eternity!"

"No thanks need yet be given," said I with a grin, "for we still stand within the city. Let us see if Mida smiles upon our venture."

We gathered up the weapons then, and carefully departed the dwelling, Inala close behind me in my track. Much noise did the city female make in moving; however, there were none about to hear her. Not far was the dwelling of Telion, and I looked within a lighted window to see Larid, two armed males within the room as well. Larid saw me as I moved quickly aside, and she smiled with pleasure briefly. Leaving Inala without the dwelling with the excess weapons, I silently entered the dwelling and moved to the door behind which were Larid and the males. I placed myself with dagger in hand beside the door, then made the smallest of sounds. No notice did the males take, therefore did I find the need to repeat the sound, albeit louder, and then I was finally able to draw one to me. Through the doorway he came, sword in hand, back toward me, and the hilt of my dagger cracked his head quite nicely. As he crumpled to the cloth at my feet, I was quite sure that never again would he scorn the wearing of his head protection. Quickly, then, I entered the room, only to find the second male sprawling like the first, and Larid grinning with a length of firewood in her hand. I, too, grinned at the sight, and Larid stepped forward toward me.

"Most pleased was I to see you, Jalav," said she, and then she rid herself of the firewood. "These males kept me prisoned here, while that misbegotten Telion rode off Mida knows where! Ceralt, I take it, accompanied him?"

"Most assuredly," I nodded my agreement, "yet do I know their destination as well. They ride in search of the third Crystal of Mida—which we must reach before them."

"I had forgotten the existence of a third Crystal." Larid frowned, and most pleased was I to see that she, too, wore her life sign once again.

"We must gather others and leave the city quickly," I said, moving toward the fallen male. "Let us take their weapons and bind them, for they do not sleep as soundly as those in Ceralt's dwelling."

With a nod Larid aided me, and soon were we ready to depart the dwelling. Most surprised was Larid at Inala's presence, yet was she unquestioning of her war leader, as was proper. We continued on through the darkness, and in two hind there were five of us upon the roof of a dwelling close by the city gates. Fayan we had found in the dwelling of Nidisar, guarded by two unarmed males, therefore we were unable to add to our stock of weapons. Gimin and Binat were two of those prowling in the darkness, seeking males, and eagerly did they join our set. The others also wished to join us, but that was contrary to my thinking. Long would be the journey to Bellinard, and it would be best if none there knew of our presence. Unarmed Hosta would be easily taken captive, and our presence would be known to all should we obtain arms for our set in Bellinard. But a single hand of Hosta must do to obey the will of Mida.

Upon the roof of the dwelling, we concealed ourselves from those who moved below, then we used the knotted leather we had taken to scale the walls. Some difficulty was there in raising Inala to the sharpened metal atop the wall, yet was it, and her lowering, at last accomplished, and we stood without the city of Ranistard, armed and in possession of climbing leather. Most rapidly, then, we moved off to the south, for in such a direction did Bellinard lie. Inala hesitated briefly, then trotted in our track, attempting our pace, her slight form shivering from the chill. I silently wished her well, though I was unable to offer further aid. Mida had given her warriors her word, and this time it would be obeyed.

20.

A second visit
—and a final call

Pale light shone down upon the city of Bellinard, and once again I looked at it from a distance. Those at the gates moved slowly forward; however there were considerably fewer than had been there when first I had looked upon it. I watched their movement with grim pleasure, for soon the darkness would come, the gates would close, and the Hosta would enter to claim the Crystal.

Many hind had we been upon the trail, but we were little the worse for the traveling. To my great surprise, Inala was still among us, for she had proven tenacious beyond expectation. The balance of the first darkness had been most difficult for her, for we had slept upon the ground in the forest, with none of the comforts of the city folk. Exhaustion had claimed her quickly, though the chill of the air was sufficient to waken her many times, leaving her shuddering till the weariness took her yet again. My warriors and I had stood watches through the darkness, and when the light came, we prepared ourselves for our travels. Meat was quickly hunted for, and with some small difficulty was the track of the lenga found. Lacking bow and spear, the lenga must be trapped, yet were their pelts needed for their warmth. Within three feyd were the needed pelts obtained, and all slept in comfort through the darkness. Inala found the taste of uncooked meat unpleasant, but forced herself to partake of it, for no fires would the Hosta build. Early upon the fifth fey, we passed a range of low hills to the east, and grazing upon these hills was a set of wild kand. Binat and Gimin took the climbing leather to snare one of the set, and then taught the captive to hold a rider. With one kan were a hand of others easily caught, and soon were we mounted upon the trail. Again, Inala found some difficulty, but was quick to learn whatever was necessary. My warriors, at first amused by her presence, at last approved fully of the city female. Inala lacked the abilities of the Hosta, yet she was willing to attempt whatever must be done, and all with dignity. That is all any might ask of another.

Gimin approached my position, where I stood and gazed upon the city, and her eyes, too, studied the walls. "All is prepared, Jalav," she said. "We need only await the darkness."

I nodded my head at these words, finding no wish to speak. Within the walls of Bellinard lay the Crystal we sought, yet through all of our journey, we had been unable to find sign of the males who preceded us. The thought had come that they traveled elsewhere, unaware of the true location of the Crystal, and that disturbed me greatly. When the Crystal rested in Hosta hands, I would send it on and ride in search of the hunter Ceralt, asking Mida to protect him till I, myself, was able to do so. The Hosta home tents would be empty indeed without the male I hungered for.

With Gimin beside me, I mounted my kan and withdrew to where the others waited, seeing Inala busily preparing the nilno we had obtained for her to feed upon. The city female would see to our kand till our return, and great was our fortune that she had accompanied us, for she had aided me in determining the true location of the Crystal. The message had read, "The last of the Crystals may be found within the Palace of the High Seat of the city of Bellinard, buried deep below the ground, fully fifty paces from the first, then left twenty paces farther. There may it be found within, yet not, we pray, by men." That the place referred to was the dungeons of the Palace, all agreed, still, the balance of it puzzled us till Inala quietly asked if perhaps the first referred to the first of the doors of metal. Slowly we all agreed to this, and then we each of us, save Gimin, recalled the doors of metal within which we had been placed. Behind such a door, then, lay the Crystal, and we must see that it was recovered. Inala would take the kand and the nilno and await us by the caves she had been shown, and should we fail to return by the time she no longer had fodder, she was free to take the kand and do with them as she would. Not pleased was Inala at this thought, yet she was aware of the dangers the Hosta faced, and therefore remained silent.

At the arrival of full darkness, before the appearance of the Entry to Mida's Realm, we took our leave of Inala, and silently made our way to the walls of Bellinard. All moved easily and well, yet was Larid as concerned for Telion as I for Ceralt, and Fayan, though silent, also seemed preoccupied. Gimin and Binat, displeased with the males who had claimed them, cared naught for their lack of presence, and were eager to return to Hosta lands. All were in possession of their life signs, and therefore did the thought of battle disturb us not at all. Mida's task would be seen to, and then would we go our separate ways.

Quickly we scaled the wall and then descended and easily found our way to the Palace of the High Seat. Few were the males who moved about, and those, in leather and metal, were as unhearing and unseeing as all city males. About the Palace of the High Seat did we move, mindful of those who guarded the dwelling, seeking an entrance which might be used for my purpose. A small entrance did we find, guarded only by two, and this entrance was the one I desired. With stealth we approached the males, and then were our swords at their faces. Beyond a first, abortive attempt to reach their weapons, they remained motionless, till we forced them within the entrance they had guarded. Once within a small doored area, no part of the main Palace, the coverings of leather and metal were stripped from the males, and I stood coldly before them.

"One of you," said I to them, "shall accompany us where we would go. The other shall remain here, a dagger to his throat, his life to be lost as well as the first's, should we be betrayed. Is this clear?"

The males glanced at one another, finding no amusement in their predicament, and then they nodded without speaking. I knew not why they looked shocked; perhaps they had memory of the first of our visits. If so, well and good. Belief in the certainty of their deaths would aid in our effort.

To the first of the males did I return his covering and weapons, the second being well bound upon the floor, the dagger of Binat at his throat. The second looked pleadingly at the first, and the first nodded in weariness, indicating that he would not attempt betrayal. Little note did I take of this indication, for city males are not to be trusted to stand by their word, yet the male did as he was bidden. Larid, Fayan, and I removed our swordbelts, our daggers fast in our fists, and we three preceded the male, our arms behind us as though bound, and so did we present ourselves to the males who stood before the door to the depths, as prisoners being conducted within. Gimin followed to the door of this area, awaiting without for sign of disturbance, yet was the matter easily seen to. The males before the door to the depths fell quickly to our blades, and he who conducted us found the deed done before a sound might be uttered by him. Rapidly, then, did Gimin join us, and the bodies were placed within shadow before we descended.

Gimin and Larid I sent ahead, Larid once more armed, for the large metal door must be approached quite openly. When Fayan and the male and I reached the depths ourselves, my two warriors crouched below the opening in the metal, unseen by those who stood within. The sound of our descent brought the attention I had expected, and Fayan and I walked before the male, as though bound, making no attempt to mask the illness brought by the stink of the dungeons. The males within, seeing only a male with two captives, opened the door, and but two reckid later lay upon the stones in pools of their own blood. Larid and Gimin cleaned their swords, and all entered the door, then we slid the bar of metal behind us.

Gimin I left by the door to guard the remaining male, and Larid, Fayan and I took a torch to seek the Crystal. Fully fifty paces did we walk as bidden, the stench unbelievably strong in our nostrils, the stones slimy and cold beneath our feet, and we were then faced with dilemma. Two areas to the left were presented us, the second being fifty paces from the first of the metal cell doors, and nothing was there to do save search the both. The first area to the left, twenty paces down, showed an empty cell and nothing else. No Crystal was there within it, therefore we proceeded to the second of our choices; however, the opening of the door showed the cell inhabited. Chained to the wall, cringing from the light of the torch, sat what once had been a male. A gibbering sound came from the bloated skin and bones of him, and difficult was it to see how he remained alive. No hair was there upon him, nor a covering, yet covered was he with indications of the teeth of scarm. But half of his feet and hands had he, and too, what might be seen of his face showed the feeding of the scarm as well. Larid gagged at the heightened stench and turned away to empty herself; the proper course of action was clear to me. As quickly as I might, I ended the misery of the wretch, and little was the blood which flowed from him. The needful seen to, we began to look about, and most grim were my feelings toward the High Seat of Bellinard. No honest death did he propose for those who offended him, and much would I have enjoyed the return of his actions in kind. The fattened male was unfit for any save the chains he decreed for others.

Nearly did our search end in vain, for the Crystal was not to be seen within the confines of the cell. Again and again, I pondered where it might be placed, and then my eyes fell upon the flow of water through the stone of the wall. Where the water struck the floor, a cavity had been formed, and within the cavity, the water seemed much cloudier than that of the first cell. Quickly, I moved to the cavity, and within the water did my fingers touch what we had sought. I drew it forth, fearing it had been harmed by so long a submersion in water, but it did not show a single flaw. The Crystal, unharmed, was then in our possession, and I placed it within the small sack hung about my neck for the purpose, and gratefully did we leave the cell to the dead.

Most relieved was Gimin by our return, and once again, we ascended to the air which might be breathed without effort. The male in our midst was silent and fearful, for his weapons had once again been taken, and well he knew his usefulness was at an end, yet are Hosta not without a sense of gratitude. The male had served truly and well, therefore was he merely returned to where the other lay, and bound as was the other, both being gagged against sound which they might wish to make. Binat seemed pleased with something, which gave me to believe that she had used the male she guarded in our absence, but that was unimportant. We took ourselves from the dwelling with care, and joined the silence and shadows of the darkness. We passed through the city unseen and unheard, and at last stood upon the ground without the gates of Bellinard, our freedom intact, the last of the Crystals within our hands. High was our elation as we made for the caves where Inala waited, and much was the laughter we shared when once away from the walls of the city. Larid, as well pleased as were we all, still seemed a bit pale from the visit to the cell, yet when I spoke to her of it, she only grinned. Again was she with child, she informed me, and that was the reason for her illness. At such tidings were we all much pleased, for well might her illness indicate the child would be female. Another Hosta in the making was ever a cause for joy, and happily did we at last approach the caves.

The caves lay above the level of the ground, and were reached by a narrow trail which led between the stand of rock. By habit did we ascend the trail with caution, yet was the caution insufficient for our safety. In the darkness there was lack of all sound and sign, and quite silently did the nets fall upon us from above. Wildly and furiously, we struggled to reach our weapons, yet the males were upon us before that might be accomplished. With the speed of prior thought were our weapons taken, and then were we dragged within the caves themselves. Torches flared all about us then, and before our eyes stood Galiose and Telion, and Ceralt, and Nidisar, and others of the males of Ranistard. Inala lay bound and gagged in a corner, misery clear in her eyes, and Galiose laughed quite heartily and stepped forward.

"What lovely fish we have netted." He grinned, examining us where we stood in the grip of males. "Is there, perhaps, other treasure to be found in out nets?"

The males about me removed the net, and then was the Crystal taken from me, the leather of the sack in which it lay cut from about my neck. Galiose peered within the sack, assured himself of the presence of the Crystal, and then wrapped the leather of the sack about his hand.

"Excellently done." He nodded in approval, indicating that the remaining nets were to be removed. "Quite sure was I that you would have small difficulty acquiring possession of the Crystal, did you but think it was about to fall to us. You all shall be rewarded for your efforts in behalf of your city, and we shall all return there with the coming of the new light. You may now rest and feed yourselves."

With great satisfaction he turned away, and I found that the illness of the depths had returned to me. No sign of the males' travel had we found before us, for the males had traveled in our track, not before us. Naught had they known of the location of the Crystal, simply had they stood aside and allowed the witless Hosta to fetch it for them. Deep disgust did I feel at myself, for I had been gulled as easily as a child, and not soon would the shame thus given me again be taken away.

"I am much relieved to see you unhurt," came a soft voice, and I raised my eyes to see Ceralt before me. The hunter grinned with great pleasure and placed his arms about me, yet his lips upon mine found no response. Although deep had been my concern for his safety, he had used me to gain possession of the Crystal for Galiose, telling me of his journey merely to send me to Bellinard. Of small worth are city males, and again had the lesson been taught me. Without a word, I pushed from him, and walked to where Inala lay bound, tears streaming from her eyes. Shame seemed to be upon her, as though she were true Hosta warrior, though the matter was beyond any effort of hers. Nothing could she have done in the presence of so many, and this I explained when I had released her. She and I and my warriors sat together in silence, taking no note of the presence of the males, refusing them the least of glances. Well betrayed had the Hosta been by the males who had claimed them, and nothing further might any save Mida do upon the matter.

Rapid was our return to the city of Ranistard, for Galiose wished to place the third Crystal with the others. Bound upon their kand were the Hosta, and Inala as well, for we had attempted escape the first fey upon the trail. Each of us had chosen a direction in which to ride, thinking that some, at least, would win free, yet the numbers of the males had destroyed such hope. Each of us was pursued and quickly caught, and then returned to the line of march. The leather was placed angrily upon my wrists by Ceralt, and I cared naught for his anger. No word nor look did I address to him, though many times he attempted to speak with me, and Larid, too, did much the same with Telion. Fayan alone merely did as she had done with Nidisar, and Nidisar seemed somewhat pleased that Ceralt and Telion too found themselves ignored.

The darkness I passed at Ceralt's side, his lenga pelt and mine placed close together, yet he found little response to his touches and caresses, and soon he ceased all attempts at either. The two hunters, Ceralt and Nidisar, and the warrior Telion, rode together through the light, the leads to our kand in their hands, misery upon their faces. All had been shown the Hosta opinion of them, and none found the opinion attractive.

Galiose caused a stir among us, for the High Seat looked upon Inala and found her pleasing. The first darkness, he carried her to his sleeping pelt, yet the small city female refused the order to please him. The metal collar still about her neck, she held her head high and denied the needs of the High Seat, much to the annoyance of Galiose. Firmly he attempted the use of her without her will, and the forests rang with the sound of his shout when her teeth sank deep in his shoulder. In full disgust, he thrust her from him, and her look of satisfaction caused him irritation. For two feyd he spent the light in contemplation of her, and upon the coming of darkness upon the second, he threw her to his shoulder and strode off into the trees, saying that none might follow. No lenga pelt did he fetch with him, yet he did not return before the coming of the new light. Much quieter did Inala seem upon their return, and wary was her gaze when she looked upon the High Seat. The next darkness was the same thing done, and the next, and not till the fourth fey was I able to learn what had occurred. The High Seat had not again attempted use of her, yet had he, each darkness, taken her covering and placed himself beside her. When the chill of the air had caused her to shudder where she lay, he had taken her in his arms and had merely held her. Yet the last darkness, so she said, he had made no attempt to place his warmth about her, but had waited till the chill had driven her to him. Soon, she knew, the nearness of him would begin to reach her, and she knew not what to do. Small council or comfort was I able to give, for strong was my memory of Ceralt before his betrayal, and deep was my hurt and need, never to be eased. I knew when Inala had been able to refuse Galiose no longer, and deeper did my misery grow.

The sight of Ranistard was welcome to all, yet Telion felt the most relief at its presence. Four feyd earlier, Larid had grown ill upon the trail, and thereafter had found herself unable to feed. Neither raw meat nor cooked could she retain, and each of the hunters searched most earnestly for something she might be fed. Roast lellin seemed the sole thing which she was able to feed upon, and little enough of that tempted her. Telion freed her wrists and held her before him upon his kan, his face pale and drawn with concern, his arms desperately about her. Larid lay herself upon his chest, her eyes closed, her breathing uneven, and well did I know that pain was hers, though she gave no other sign of it. I rode upon my kan with deep felt misery, for the punishment for failure should have been mine, not Larid's. Oh, Mida! Will we never find success and approval in your eyes?

Once within Ranistard, Larid was taken to the dwelling of Galiose, and Fayan and I, again unbound, with Ceralt and Nidisar, were told we might accompany her. Inala rode close beside Galiose, at his bidding, and was not permitted to return to the dwelling of Ceralt. She had been ordered to remain with Galiose, and much fear had she that the High Seat would name her slave to him, for she had discovered deep feelings for the large, dark male. As free woman did she wish to serve him, not as slave, for, as she had said, her love was enslavement enough. Gimin and Binat had been met at the gates of the city by those males they had ridden from, and grim indeed were the looks upon the faces of the males. Two of the warriors of Galiose were they, yet had they seemed barely male to my warriors, who had scorned the softness of their ways. Now it seemed that their softness would be no more, for my warriors were pulled from their kand by the hair, and taken off by the males in such a manner. The males had spoken of much leather awaiting runaway wenches, and my warriors had not seemed at all pleased. By the sides of the males had they stumbled along, and we rode past them to the High Seat's dwelling.

Within the dwelling did Telion carry Larid, and Fayan, Nidisar, Ceralt, and I were led by a slave to a room of wide seats and small platforms, and told that we might await word of Larid there. The males took their places upon the silk of the seats, and Fayan and I seated ourselves upon the cloth by the room's fire. The cloth was a blue like the skies, and I recalled the words of Telion of the covering which he had wished Larid to don, and then I covered my eyes with my hand. In but a matter of reckid, Telion entered the room as well, saying that Phanisar had forbidden his presence, and he seated himself to one side of the room, desolation etched upon his features, tragedy deep within his eyes. None spoke with him of the pain we shared; when renth was brought, all partook of it.

More than two hind passed in the waiting, and often did my eyes move to Ceralt where he sat, a pot of renth clasped miserably within his fist. Over and again I found the need to remind myself that the darkhaired, light-eyed hunter had betrayed me, and over and again did the pain of such a memory twist me deep inside. Greatly did I long for the gentle touch of the male, the knowledge of his presence beside me in my misery, the feeling that he cared for more than just the use of me, yet never were these things to be had again, for truly had I been betrayed by him. Unbidden did the thought bring weakling tears to my eyes, and was I unable to stem the flow; down my cheeks they streamed as the hunter suddenly looked at my face. Shamed, I turned away again, not wishing my weakness to be seen by him, yet with a muffled cry he jumped to his feet and started toward me. Only two steps had he taken, when the appearance of Phanisar at the door caused all to halt what they had been about and rise quickly to their feet. No word did any of the males speak, and I, too, found great reluctance to voice a query, therefore was the matter left to Fayan.

"Does Larid live?" she asked quietly, a calmness to her voice which I did not share.

"Of a certainty, she lives," responded Phanisar pleasantly, and he entered farther within the room. "It was merely a matter of too great an exertion, for the loss of the previous child weakened her somewhat. With rest and comfort, she shall soon be up and about."

"Praise be to the Serene Oneness!" Telion choked out, and then he finished his renth in a swallow. Great relief flooded his features, until a moment later a frown appeared. "What meant you," said he to Phanisar, "when you spoke of the *previous* child?"

"Surely you must know," responded Phanisar with a chuckle. "The wench is again with child, and confidently assures me that the child is yours."

"Mine," breathed Telion, and then he raised his voice and shouted, "Mine! The child is mine!" An insane laughter roared from him, and then he raced from the room, unmindful of the stares of others. Some confusion did I feel over the exchange of the males, for surely they knew that the child was Larid's, and not Telion's, as they had insisted. Any but an infant or a dolt is aware that a male cannot bear a child.

Phanisar had come to stand by the fire between Fayan and myself, and now he looked about himself most comfortably. "Perhaps," said he to the rest of us, "you would care to see the device of the Crystals. It is now readied for use, although

I wish to await the departure of the female Larid before it is activated. In but a hin or two, small men once again speak with the gods."

Fayan and I exchanged looks of distaste, yet was it possible that Mida beckoned with the invitation, therefore did we nod our agreement. The males, too, indicated their interest, therefore Fayan and I began to walk toward the door.

"A moment," called Phanisar from where he yet stood by the fire, and Fayan and I turned to see that he held our pots of renth. "Good renth should not be abandoned," said he with a smile. "You may finish your flagons, should the deed not be beyond you."

Again Fayan and I exchanged glances, then with a shrug returned to where the male stood. My pot contained a mere half of the renth it was able to hold, therefore I swallowed it quickly, seeing that Fayan did as I did. No reaction to the renth did Fayan show, yet mine seemed to have soured in the pot. Most bitter was the taste of it, and my face obviously showed this, for Phanisar laughed heartily,

"I see the renth is not to your liking," said he quite smoothly. "My apologies, wench, and I shall not suggest a like action again. Shall we now retire to the comm room?"

Somewhat suspicious of Phanisar did I find myself, yet I knew not where my suspicions should lie. I thought upon it as we walked to the room of the device, but nothing occurred to me. Ceralt looked quite closely upon me, though he had not again attempted to approach me. Such action should have pleased me, yet was I unsure of the presence of pleasure. Of many things did I find myself unsure, and I did not care for the feel of it.

Within the room of the device stood many armed males, among them Galiose. The High Seat appeared in great spirits, and most pleasantly did he approach us. "I was pleased to learn of the well-being of the red-haired female," he said as he neared. "Inala, too, shall be pleased to learn of it, for my woman has much liking for the wench."

"Do you refer to the slave-woman Inala?" Ceralt murmured, an odd look upon his face.

"A slave no more," Galiose laughed in reply, "for she has proven herself free. She informed me quite soberly that sooner would she face death than slavery, therefore what choice had I but to free her?"

"What choice, indeed." Ceralt laughed in agreement, and

he, too, seemed pleased with Inala's freedom. Strange were these males, to first enslave a woman, and then rejoice at her having been freed.

"In a fey or two," continued Galiose, "we shall have further cause for merrymaking. A rider reached me but moments ago, saying that the party fetching the Silla wenches shall soon be here. My men wait most eagerly for them, for I hear they are a toothsome lot."

Ceralt and Nidisar chuckled with Galiose, while Fayan and I looked at each other in distress. Completely had we forgotten the coming of the Silla, and a way must be found to arm our Hosta before their arrival. Most pleased would we be to face Silla with sword, yet first must the sword be found to be used.

Phanisar had gone to look more closely upon the device, and easily was it to be seen that the golden air now carried the third of the Crystals as well. I did not care for the look of the device, yet Phanisar gestured Fayan and myself the closer. With reluctance did we approach him, and the male pointed to a projection upon the side of the device.

"See you here," said he to us, indicating the projection. "The writings speak of this as an 'operator testing outlet,' yet have I been able to make sense of such gibberish. It is a manner by which one may know if she who uses the device is fit. Vistren, in his insanity, did not realize that only a female may speak through the device, else we may assume that he would have taken care to see that so many females did not die. Each female in Ranistard have I tried here, saving the two now before me, and those who accompanied them, and I have found none save three who may, in dire need, be used. A light shines brightly at the touch of her who is ideal, yet naught have I gotten from the others save a feeble light. Perhaps one of you shall be the proper user, eh? Step closer, singly, and place a finger upon the knob."

This time Fayan and I did not look upon one another, for neither of us cared to touch the device of pain. Clearly did I recall the first time I had attempted the touch of it, and not again would I attempt so foolish a thing. Even had I known that the Crystals would be mine in the touching of the device, still would I have hesitated, for with so many males about, escape with the Crystals would have been impossible.

"Come, come," urged Phanisar with a trace of impatience.

"There is nothing to fear, and each of the others have already accomplished it. Are you two less than they?"

The accusation stung my pride, for a war leader is always first into danger. As my warriors had already gone before me, naught was there to do save act as they. Feeling great reluctance yet showing none of it, I stepped the closer and placed my finger upon the projection, braced against the pain I expected, yet no pain did I feel at the contact. Only a faint tingling ran through me, and a light showed upon the device above the projection.

"Better than the others," Phanisar murmured, studying the light, "yet still below the required strength. Let us try the second now."

Fayan approached as I stepped to the side, and bolstered by my example, she touched the projection quite easily. Immediately did the light grow bright, and a cry of elation came from Phanisar.

"A true sender!" he shouted, his hand pounding upon the platform of the device. "See here, Blessed One, we have our sender!"

Galiose hurried forward, and other males as well, and much time did they spend in explanation of their wishes. Fayan was to use the device at their direction, said they, and her fondest desire would be hers for the asking. Fayan quickly came to understand that the device might not be easily used without her, and she turned thoughtfully to Galiose.

"Am I to understand that I might be forced to the use of the device," said she, "yet my full cooperation would be much the better?"

"Aye," nodded Galiose, "and also it would be much the wiser. You may make any request of me, within reason, and I shall see it done."

"Might the Hosta be released from Ranistard?" she asked at once, but the firm headshake of Galiose negated the thought. "Very well," said she, accepting the decision. "My cooperation is yours, should you agree to my alternate terms."

"Which are?" prompted Galiose, suspiciously.

"I wish the gift of a slave," Fayan announced quite calmly. "A slave of my own choosing." Slowly, her eyes moved till they rested upon Nidisar, and the eyes of everyone about also moved to the male. Not a sound was uttered in the room, and Nidisar's eyes widened and moved anxiously about.

"That is foolishness!" Nidisar protested with hollow laugh. "I am a hunter and a free man, not a slave to be given as gift!"

No reply did any make to this, and greater did Nidisar's agitation grow. His hand moved upon his face, and Phanisar stepped the closer to him.

"Think, my boy," said Phanisar earnestly, "of the service which would be performed by you for Ranistard! We shall speak with the gods themselves, and your sacrifice shall be remembered forever! Is such a thing not worthy of your effort?"

Nidisar gazed about weakly, stuttering, "B-but—bu-but—" however the matter was already decided. Galiose, with a shrug of resignation, gestured to two of his males, and a collar of metal was fetched and placed about Nidisar's throat. Most miserable did the collared Nidisar seem, and I approached him with the intention of adding to his misery.

"It seems, Nidisar," said I quite blandly, "that the spear has now been cast again. Should a slave be erect upon his feet as though he were free?"

"He should not," came Fayan's voice from beside me, before an angered Nidisar might reply. "On your knees, slave," Fayan ordered, "and remain there till otherwise bidden!"

Nidisar, nearly livid with rage, stood quite straight, therefore two of Galiose's males approached and forced him to his knees. Most amused did they seem to be at the plight of the hunter, and Fayan and I, too, laughed.

"Much the better," I nodded at the kneeling Nidisar, seeing the strong satisfaction upon the face of Fayan. "Think you, Fayan, he requires a leash, that he might not forget himself and wander off?"

"An excellent thought." Fayan grinned. "I shall see to it quickly, for I would not have my slave wander off. There are many things one might find to occupy a slave."

Upon hearing her words, Nidisar closed his eyes as though in pain, for it was clear to all that Fayan meant to show her displeasure with him quite forcefully. Some small sympathy did I feel for the hunter, for I knew the strength of Fayan, yet had Nidisar well earned the punishment he was now to receive. With a grin, I left Fayan with her gift, and moved once more toward the platform of the device.

"Soon all shall be prepared," said Phanisar to Galiose and Ceralt. "I now await word that the female Larid has been removed from the Palace. The operation of the comm should not be overly painful for the others, yet she, in her weakened condition, need not be made to suffer."

Most pleased was I to learn that the device would cause but little pain, and then was I struck in the stomach with the twist of my insides. Without volition I bent forward with the pain, and surely did I think the device had been activated.

"Jalav!" shouted Ceralt, and in a flash was he by my side, his arms about me in support. The ache eased so that I might straighten, yet was I still touched by it. Ceralt looked anxiously toward Phanisar, and the tall, aged male shook his head.

"It is only the action of the counteragent," he said to Ceralt. "The dabla bush held her childless, and now must its grip be loosened. The cramps shall pass in a matter of feyd, and then shall she be as other wenches, able to bear your seed. I placed the counteragent in her renth, and now the time is past when she might void herself of it."

Most relieved did Ceralt seem, and his light eyes looked upon me with pleasure as his arm tightened about me, while I remained confused. "I do not understand," I said to Phanisar, bringing the aged male's eyes to me once more. "I am not able to bear a child!"

"You soon shall be," he replied with a grin. "The counteragent shall see to that."

"That may not be!" I insisted, my head shaking in negation. "Jalav is war leader, and no war leader may have life within her!"

"That is also easily seen to," grinned Ceralt, his arm yet about me. "Jalav shall no longer be war leader, therefore is the difficulty overcome. Life there shall be within you, my girl, placed there right quickly by me."

Ceralt and Phanisar laughed with each other as males are wont to do, and the words of the males angered me greatly, for Jalav was not slave to be ordered about and done contrary to her will. In some manner had the leaf of the dabla bush been overcome, yet had I seen dabla bushes growing there in the city of Ranistard. When the Silla arrived to battle the Hosta, the war leader Jalav would be well prepared!

Ceralt insisted that I take seat till the pain left me; however I had been seated but a moment when a slave entered to say that Larid was well away from the dwelling. All then eagerly pressed toward the platform of the device, therefore did

I, too, rise once more so that I might join them. Whatever was to occur would not occur without Jalav.

Fayan had been seated beside the platform of the device, and now the male Phanisar placed a band of sorts about her brow. The band led, by a very thin length of metal, to the device itself, and naught else touched the warrior Fayan, though the band seemed sufficient. Fayan sat unmoving and expressionless, yet I knew that the matter cost her dearly in courage. Phanisar touched briefly about the device, and then I, too, found the need to call upon courage. A deep, sharpened tingling touched all parts of me, and a darkness, the darkness of the Crystals, descended once more. Completed, now, was this darkness, and deeper, if possible, than the instance previous, a darkness unending in its distance, of a height and a width incomprehensible. The darkened Crystals in their golden air beckoned to me, pulled at me, toward where surely my soul would be forever enmeshed. My right hand clutched my life sign, my left hand grasped at the covering of Ceralt, and then was the strength of his arm about me, holding me from the dreaded dark.

"Now, wench," said Phanisar softly to Fayan, "there is a thing you must say till a response is elicited. Say the word, 'calling,' then repeat the word, slowly and clearly, till I bid you to cease."

"Calling," said Fayan, without inflection, and indeed she repeated the word, over and again, her eyes full closed, the inner part of her seemingly afloat in the golden air beside the Crystals. Most distant did Fayan appear to be, and distantly did the echo of her call resound.

Two hands of reckid passed to naught, and still did Fayan speak the word. How long a wait was to be faced, none knew, and then, of a sudden, from the golden air, came a voice, and the word was, "answering."

A brief stir moved all about, and the air that had been that of eld, became charged with hope, and fear and awe. Galiose stood triumphant in his place, and Phanisar seemed to glimpse the making of his fondest dream. His hand moved toward the shoulder of Fayan, though he halted short of contact, and his voice, quite hoarse, reached forward instead.

"We do send our fondest greetings, lady," said he, for truly had the voice been that of a female. "We seek the ears of the gods, and would speak with your masters if we may."

"My masters?" the female voice echoed. "What station are

you calling from? And why does your speech sound so strange?"

Confusion touched the features of Phanisar, and he stumbled. "Truly do I beg your pardon, lady, yet do I lack understanding of your words. What might be a station?"

"I don't know what's going on here," the female voice muttered angrily, "but I'll sure as sending find out! I'll have a fix on your comm in just—about—now!" A silence surrounded the female voice, and then it returned, at first awed, and then filled with joy. "You're way out in sector V!" the voice exclaimed. "We haven't heard from anyone there since the rebellion! Then your power crystals were saved! Hell and damnation, won't Mida be pleased!"

"Mida!" I cried most happily, and the males looked toward one another in deepest shock. Mida reigned where the male gods dwelt, and all happenings came at her bidding!

"We know naught of any rebellion!" Phanisar blurted, his eyes wild. "The crystals had been taken from us by females and now have we recovered them so that we might once again reach the gods! I know naught of what you speak!"

"You poor boonies," the voice commiserated with true sadness. "Out of touch for all this time, and probably regressed, too. Maybe if I tell you what happened, it'll help you to understand.

"About two hundred and fifty standard years ago, all comm stations, like the one you're calling from now, were controlled by men. Oh, sure, only women could be senders, but what they sent was at the direction of men. Then Mida came along, and decided that enough was enough, so a call went out to all stations to hide the power crystals until men came around to our way of thinking. It took a long time—you men are so stubborn—but to keep the Union from falling apart, the men finally gave in. Mida took over running things, and now women do the calling and the directing—and a good job we've done, too! The Union is stronger than ever, and we have a fully trained group that will hop over there and help you get your planet straightened out again. I've got a good, solid fix on the booster station built into the satellite of your planet, and we'll come as soon as we can. With our women around to run things, you'll be civilized in no time."

The shock held each of the males in a grip unbreakable, therefore was I free to step forward and say, "Yet you spoke of Mida. Mida is with you?"

"No, honey," laughed the voice, "it would be more accurate to say that I was with Mida. All of us are with Mida—members in good standing, too. Mida does it all, and its name comes from the job of sending. You'll be learning it soon enough, but it can't really hurt to tell you—Mida stands for 'Minds In Dark Adventure.' It started out as a club for senders, and ended up running the Union. But just you wait. As soon as we get there, you'll have a chance to learn everything we know. You'll love being civilized—all of you."

Again there was silence, most agonizingly from myself as well, yet Ceralt stepped forward to stand beside me. "Civilized," he said in a musing tone. "We are to be civilized." And then he laughed and laughed till the tears came down.